Chroma

Book 2

Imogen's Journey

B FLEETWOOD

Imogen's Journey is dedicated to the memory of
Barbara Baggaley, a real-life 'Shani'
(Shani means wonderful)

PROLOGUE

The prisoner walked slowly through the wooded glade, his head bent, his shoulders slumped. He discarded his robes and footwear on the rough grass beside a moss-covered mound in the centre of a small clearing. As the warm breeze caressed his bare flesh, he paused to listen to the distant voice of a lone songbird. He slowly raised the back of his hand to his nose to breathe deeply of his essence. He sat on the edge of the organic altar. A barely perceptible shudder rippled across his body. Raising his eyes briefly to the sky, he shook his head sadly before lifting his legs and lying down on the spongy surface. A look of grim resignation was set on his lined face. Relatively young for one of his race, he looked much older than his close-to-eighty years.

The tension in his muscles was clear as he let out a deep sigh, almost a groan, and crossed his arms over his chest. His hands were tight fists. He lifted his chin and the setting lights of the two suns shone upon his once handsome features. He closed his eyes to feel their dying warmth on his lids.

The representatives from the five key councils, clad in the traditional gold-edged robes of black, moved as one to circle the naked man. A female stepped forward. She held a pen-like object and spoke his name. Reciting the words from an internal script, she began, "Guilty. You have been found guilty of the crime of High Treason. This is the verdict of the Holan Inquisition, now empowered to pass judgment by the Sanctus High Court. The Inquisition proved you wilfully assisted the known defector, Nuru Zuberi, in his escape from justice and colluded with his brother, Sefu Zuberi and other subversives in their illegal development of a prohibited technology. Furthermore, you were found to be complicit in the forbidden contact with the primitive race, deliberately concealing your activities from the Supreme Council. Accorded a position of privilege, you wilfully betrayed the trust once placed in you. Your pre-meditated treachery has endangered our people and exposed us to contamination potentially catastrophic to the Holan race."

The official paused and held the pen aloft before continuing.

"In accordance with the Sanctus Laws you were offered a choice of punishment, erasure or termination. You have chosen termination and today you forfeit your citizenship and your life."

The only visible sign of response from the condemned man, who remained completely still, was a small teardrop welling in the corner of one eye.

"May you be at peace as we commit your being to Ra and return your body to the elements."

Each member nodded affirmation, repeating the words 'the peace of Ra' in unison. The pen was then placed against the carotid artery on the side of his neck and in one press, activated.

It was almost instantaneous. His body momentarily trembled as his eyes sprang open, fixing into a glassy wild stare before fogging over. The teardrop spilled and rolled down his cheek as his chest fell for the last time. An eerie silence, devoid of any natural sounds, filled the air.

The robed witnesses bowed their heads and after a few minutes began their echoed lament, in broken harmonies:

"From dust we are born,
to dust we are laid;
this life relinquished,
the penalty paid."

The chant reached a crescendo before petering out. The five then filed past the dead man, each touching a hand briefly to his head.

Dusk fell. The moss bed below the lifeless figure rippled and began to rise around his form. He was gradually subsumed into the mossy cradle to become part of the undergrowth. A layer of lichen was all to remain atop the fauna, glistening in the starlight.

NEW YORK

"*H*appy birthday!" Chrissie squealed from the small screen on Imogen's phone. "I am so jealous! New York on your seventeenth birthday, you lucky thing! And we're stuck here in the chilly UK!"

Imogen smiled back at her friends. She was sitting in Sefu Zuberi's air-conditioned apartment in a light sleeveless dress, the sun streaming through the windows. Chrissie was in a jacket huddled next to her tall companion, the English evening sky darkening behind them. Richard's head was just visible leaning against Chrissie's with an affectionate closeness. Without being able to observe her Chroma, Imogen could see how happy Chrissie was - positively oozing warmth and contentment.

"Wish we were there with you," moaned Chrissie, quickly adding, "how's your mum doing?"

"Thanks Chrissie. Mum's doing okay." Imogen was careful to keep her smile wide as another part of her mind focussed on her mother's health. This morning they had walked through Central Park in the sweltering heat, her mother clutching her arm just a fraction too tightly, jumping at any sudden sounds and recoiling from anyone who passed by too close. Physically she was gaining strength every day; mentally there was a long way to go.

Sefu, the eldest Zuberi brother, had suspended the therapy sessions. He had left the apartment before Imogen had arrived with Adam and Araz, so the illusion there were only two Zuberi brothers was maintained. It was decided Araz should believe his assumption that Adam was the infamous Sefu, elder brother to Nuru. He might suspect they were twins, but he could not know they were in fact triplets. The secret of the third brother was not even known amongst their supporters on Holis.

Imogen knew Sefu's treatment had helped to reduce her mother's panic attacks, but she was concerned her memory appeared increasingly muddled and she was also permanently anxious and fearful. Elizabeth Reiner no longer spoke of Imogen's father and Imogen was unable to ask her anything about her past or her home planet, worried it could trigger a bad reaction. The long years of waiting for her mother to wake up from her coma, desperate for her companionship and to find out more about her identity, had culminated in bitter disappointment and yet more worry.

Imogen thought fretfully about her father and Leo, both captured. *Are they alive? Well, I will soon find out.* Tomorrow she would be setting off into the unknown. The thoughts flew around her head as her stomach churned, whilst she maintained an outward calm and responded to her friends as if she had no worries.

"She is slowly recovering, but it will take time. How are things there?"

Chrissie beamed as she gave a summary of the last few weeks at college. "The Reef was furious she hadn't been informed about you going to America with your mum," she giggled. "She practically burst a blood vessel when I mentioned it." Chrissie then mimicked the voice of the plump college tutor, "Why was I not told? After all I have done for the ungrateful girl – disgraceful!"

Imogen grinned as Chrissie chattered on.

"Danny's been looking after your cat. Seems he's better with animals than people! He got loads of scratches at first, but he says Sadiki has finally settled down. Hey, he even allows Danny to stroke him now and then. Oh yes - he told me to tell you - your drawing for the art exam got a special commendation, you clever thing."

"Really?" Imogen said with surprise. It seemed like a lifetime since she had layered and blended pastel colours into a paradise-style landscape of snow-capped mountains, green valleys and cascading waterfalls running into a crystal-clear river. Back then she had allowed her imagination to visualise a place of peace and escape from all her worries and questions. To think she had been so blissfully unaware of why she was so different. *I should have worked it out sooner.*

"They've put the picture up in the college entrance and some national artist saw it and said you were - get this - a unique talent! And a local newspaper wants to interview you as well, so fame awaits you when you come home!"

Imogen shuddered. *Fame? The last thing I want! And home? Just where exactly is home?*

The events and revelations of the last four weeks suddenly slammed into her mind and she realised with a deep sadness she would never be able to tell Chrissie anything about what she had discovered. *How could I tell her I was born forty years before her and then shot forward in time? Imagine her face if I told her I am actually from a different planet - oh and for some unknown reason, I'm wanted dead by my own people!*

She fingered the symbols of the pendant hanging around her neck, picturing the five matching marks hidden on her body denoting she was the first ever Penta-Crypt. She still had no idea what it all meant.

Chrissie, unaware of Imogen's inner turmoil, continued chatting in her bubbly manner. "Oh, and Gen, no one's seen anything of Araz since you left. He's just, well, vanished. Maybe he's not got any reason to come into college with you gone?" Chrissie gave Imogen a conspiratorial wink as Richard gave an impatient snort.

"Wonder where he's got to?" smiled Imogen innocently, glad to turn her thoughts to her new companion. She glanced across the apartment to where Araz and Adam were deep in quiet conversation over a laptop. Araz, his face set in studious concentration, sensed she was looking his way and briefly looked back to her. A surge of gold-edged scarlet erupting in his Chroma as their eyes fleetingly met.

She gave him a stern 'go back to your studies' look but could not stop her own chromatic flutter of rich tones betraying the growing intensity of her feelings towards him.

"Well I don't think we've seen the last of him," continued Chrissie. "Reckon he's got to show up when you get back." Richard frowned briefly at Chrissie who nudged him affectionately until the frown melted away and he lightly kissed her forehead.

"So, when will you be coming back?" asked Chrissie. "Have to plan some sort of birthday celebration and, before you object, just a few of us."

*Good question. Although it's not so much **when** I come back, but **if** I come back.*

"I'm not sure. I may be out here for the summer. They're moving Mum to a new style rehabilitation place, but it's in the middle of nowhere and there's no phone reception or Internet, so I won't be able to call or text for a while." This was the line agreed with Araz and Adam for when she left for Holis. It seemed the most plausible reason for not being able to contact her friends without causing concern.

"What! No way! I hate being stuck without a phone," Chrissie complained. "Well, try to find your way to civilisation if you can. Climb a hill or something! Call me anytime. It doesn't matter about the time difference!"

Imogen nodded whilst inwardly groaning at the irony of the remarks. *According to Araz, I'm supposed to be heading for the ultimate civilisation, and Chrissie - if only you knew - the time difference isn't a mere five hours, it's twenty light years.* A sinking feeling ran parallel with her thoughts.

"I'll do my best," she answered, externally cheerful.

"Take care Gen and have a great birthday. See you soon." Chrissie blew a kiss and they waved before disconnecting.

Imogen murmured, "hope so" as she switched off, subconsciously rubbing her fingers across the groove of the scar tissue on the back of her right hand. She knew she should return to the intense discussion on the other side of the room where Araz and Adam were planning their travel for the next day, but paused to look out of the high apartment window. Below people moved in all directions, many going in and out of the Central Park opposite.

What if I can't ever get back?

She had grown to love the city in the two weeks she had been there. She walked the streets and park whenever she found an opportunity, escaping for a few hours by herself on most days. The intense training, in addition to caring for her mother, had not only taken up most of her time, it had been overwhelming in every sense and she needed a break to analyse all she had learnt and soothe her troubled thoughts.

Everything outside looked so familiar, so normal. Lovers clasped hands as they walked in the sunshine, children ran with balloons, families laughed and chattered on the sidewalks as joggers ran through the park and hot drivers grew irritated with the traffic queues, blaring the horns of their bright yellow taxis. It felt like home and despite the descriptions Adam and Araz had given her, she could not picture her so-called 'real home' at all.

It sounded bizarre, two suns in the sky, one red. Wouldn't the effect be to dramatically change the colour of everything? It was all so alien. How did people live? What did they eat? Would she still be able to see Chroma? Requests for information had not given her any clear answers. Araz would use terms like 'beautiful' and 'peaceful', as Adam countered with words like 'oppressive' and 'dangerous'.

She had been assured once she arrived on Holis, she would be able to access all the information she needed from the libraries of Data Encounters available to all citizens. Until then she would have to trust in whatever Adam and Araz had told her and hope Araz would protect her and ensure her safe passage.

She crossed the room with a sigh and listened to Adam's instructions to Araz. For her benefit they spoke in formal Holan whenever they were together. She had a basic grasp of her native tongue, thanks to Eshe's early tuition in her infancy, but this had grown exponentially since being forced to speak it constantly. With her powers of recall and the ability to replicate pronunciations, she had fast become proficient and almost fluent. Some terms still baffled her, so when Adam had delighted in her assimilation of new information, saying she was no 'Zeroid', she had just guessed at its meaning. She anticipated a lot more guesswork would be needed when she finally arrived on Holis.

"Araz, it is vital you go ahead of Imogen, every step of the way. Understand, until you have infiltrated The Hub to input her DNA, she will not be recognised. She will be unable to access anything - transport, food, accommodation..."

"The Hub?" Imogen quelled the rising sense of foreboding she experienced every time they spoke of this alien environment.

Araz responded with an authoritative pride, "It's the centre of everything: government, administration and genetic operations. The DNA reservoir held in The Hub is the most sophisticated and comprehensive storage facility ever conceived - a reserve of all life. It holds the chromosomal makeup of every species to have ever lived on Holis or Ankh. This is where the hereditary codes for all inhabitants are placed in the network, normally done at birth unless, of course, they have been unlawfully bred." Araz broke eye contact with Imogen as his colours flared a strange mix of purple with shades of bronze and red.

Annoyance, frustration, and fear; he's worried about the reception I will get. What was it he said? I need to be legitimised? Imogen bit her lip.

"So, we just need to get your DNA into the system," he mumbled awkwardly.

And if they have my DNA, they will surely discover I'm a super freak. What then?

Imogen started to squash the grey flurry of worry surfacing in her Chroma as she huddled her shoulders and absentmindedly pushed her hands together, squeezing her fingertips tight. A sudden vision burst into her thoughts stopping her in her tracks. She was somewhere else. Loud alarm bells rang. She was running. Her heart was racing. She was being chased! Sprinting through strangely lit corridors, she rushed through an open door and dived into a concealed opening in the far wall. Dashing headlong into a dark and narrow rock-lined passage, she flew down steps. The deafening sound of gushing water grew in her head, louder and louder until it hammered every sense. The passage ended in a cave opening. She was trapped! Huge torrents of water coursed down rock funnels above and around her before crashing down to an abyss below. Aware only of the soaking clouds of spray, the thunderous noise, and the flashing of the arrow on her pendant, her scream was drowned as Repros burst into the space. Faceless, they bore down upon her, the visors of their helmets reflecting the racing waters around. The only escape was to plummet down into the pounding water. She clambered onto the low wall, poising herself to jump. Her heart thumped… She pulled her hands apart and the scene was gone as swiftly as it had appeared.

Imogen stifled a gasp and forced her heart to slow. *What the hell? Where did that come from? A premonition? A waking nightmare? It seemed so real.* The place was unknown to her. *Was it Holis?* She glanced at Araz. *Will he be able to protect me from those things?*

Araz looked quizzically at her brief, but explosive, chromatic response. Assuming it was triggered by his reference to the DNA sample he said soothingly, "It will take but a few seconds. A volt of your flesh is all we require."

"Volt?"

"Nothing to do with electricity!" he quipped but his smile rapidly faded when he saw how pale Imogen had turned. "Are you okay?"

When she didn't reply he continued, "The volt is just a microscopic sample of your cells. It won't hurt." He gently touched her arm. "Once absorbed, you will be free to go anywhere - well anywhere unrestricted," he added cryptically.

Imogen clamped her mouth shut and nodded slowly. Araz's attempts at either reassurance or intimacy could not erase the hallucinatory images she had just experienced. *I'm okay - whatever it was, it's gone! I need to rise above it.*

Adam, puzzled by Imogen's flash of alarm, thought better of asking her what caused it. He coughed awkwardly and took charge of the conversation. "So, The Hub is the centre of genetic studies and one of the largest complexes located in the capital city of Holis." His voice reverted to his now-familiar lecturing tone. "And this is called?" Adam raised an eyebrow encouragingly to her as his bright, yellow colours prompted her answer.

"Karnak," Imogen said mechanically.

"Yes, home of our Supreme Council. And the leader's official title is?"

"Her Greatness, Kekara."

"And the Viziers of the five councils?"

"Odion, Vizier of Stability, Merit, Vizier of Enlightenment, Ubaid - Vision, Jabari – Well-Being, and Shani, Vizier of Sanctity," Imogen replied woodenly as she recited, verbatim, from one of Adam's frequent lessons. At least this was calming her and pushing the strange vision to the deeper recesses of her mind.

There's no point dwelling on it - it was just an intrusive thought. Probably triggered by apprehension. I need to focus on all this Holis stuff. She took a deep breath and forced herself to engage with Adam.

"Unfortunately, we have no Data Encounters available to show you what each Vizier looks like, but you will have this information once you get to Holis. Now explain what you have learnt of each sector. Let's start with Sanctity."

"Sanctity? Seems a weird name for the council of genetics?"

"It is also grossly inaccurate," responded Adam. "Many of their practices masquerade as being sacred and essential, but this is far from the truth…"

"Well, that is a matter of opinion," Araz interrupted angrily. "It is this council who safeguard our entire race. 'Sanctity' stands for the immense value we place on all Holan life."

"That's what you are supposed to think," Adam snapped.

Ignoring Adam, Araz continued, looking only at Imogen. "It is unlike anything you have on Earth. Here, most humans are devalued, cast aside, and downtrodden. This is truly a 'rat race'. Not on Holis! There life is sacrosanct and no one is worthless."

"Providing they haven't been falsely bred?" Imogen challenged.

Araz glared at her.

Whenever they spoke like this they always ended up in opposition. He held an unwavering conviction in the ethos and superiority of his race; she questioned everything.

"Look, let's not start this again," she began regretfully.

"Just remember," began Araz, his voice bitter, "you have no experience of Holis, only what you have been told." Imogen observed a slight sneer towards Adam, implying he had been more than biased in his accounts. "There are many things you do not understand and…"

"And many things you do not realise, young man!" interjected Adam, his voice frosty.

Their chromatic responses said more than their words as they looked fiercely at each other. Imogen could see their combative auras surge. Adam's anger and disdain blazed in hot reds; Araz's self-righteousness and arrogance spiked black and gold shards.

"We don't have time for this," Imogen whispered, absentmindedly massaging the scar on her hand. Araz broke eye contact with Adam before nodding his head in agreement as he calmed.

"You are right, Imogen," he conceded. "Anyway, two of your names are wrong. The Viziers of Sanctity and Well-Being are no longer in post. Shani retired a long way back and Jabari was recently replaced. I am unsure who took over from them."

Adam blinked at this new information and briefly put his hand to his mouth. Imogen saw he was smothering his sharp yellows colours of questioning and deep swirls of grey worry. *He wanted to ask more. Shani and Jabari? Were they on our side? I will remember those names.* In another part of her mind, it struck Imogen she had already resolved which side she was on.

No one spoke for a few minutes until Adam, regaining his composure, turned back to Imogen to quiz her again. "So, each Vizier oversees affairs for their area of government and each has a place on the Supreme Council. All their decisions must be approved by this ruling body and should a major decision be required, the entire populace vote in the forum known as?" he prompted.

"The Sanctus High Court where everyone who has 'come of age' has a vote," Imogen answered irritably.

Before Adam could pose another question, she put her hand up to silence him. "Look…" she quickly stopped herself calling him Adam, instead saying, "Look, Sefu, there's no need to keep testing me. You forget I have the same power of recall as you…" she tailed off as an image of Leo jumped into her head, saying the same words to her. As Adam pushed his hands through his hair and looked slightly embarrassed, Imogen was suddenly struck by the likeness in mannerisms of father and son. In an effort to push the thoughts of her own father to one side, she revisited her questions about Leo. Why did Adam appear to dislike his son so much? Was it true Leo was falsely bred, like her? And was he even alive after his beating and capture? With Araz always present, she had been unable to discuss this openly with Adam.

"My apologies Imogen," said Adam with a bow of the head. "I should know I do not need to keep going over old information, but it is vital you appear to be a normal Holan, so no one will give you a second glance."

Imogen resisted the temptation to retort she had already succeeded in looking like a normal human for years when this was far from the truth. *But I'm not a normal Holan either, am I?* All the unwanted thoughts rose forcefully again, and she glanced to the window, her brow furrowed, touching the outline of her pendant inside her dress.

"I need to go out," she announced, standing abruptly.

"May I come with you?" asked Araz, a faint tinge of navy hurt bordering his colours in expectation of the usual refusal.

Imogen had been true to her promise in Paris, she needed time and a degree of distance from him, to cope with all the new information. Araz and she rarely spent time together alone (Adam was almost always with them) but this had not stopped him growing ever closer to her. When they were not arguing, he was attentive and affectionate and she found herself longing to be alone with him, despite any misgivings. When he spoke with confidence about her being 'legitimised' by the Supreme Council so they would then be free to be together, she stopped herself hoping this might be the case. Her life had been completely flipped in a matter of weeks and she needed to steel herself against further surprises and disappointments. *Better to stick to reality not fantasy.*

"Okay, yes!" said Imogen suddenly and decisively. "But only if we drop all talk about Holis."

Adam went to object. "But Imogen, my dear, you leave in less than twelve hours."

"No Sefu," interjected Araz. "Imogen is right. This is her last night here and she deserves a break. Besides, it is her birthday. Her coming of age should be celebrated."

Adam shrugged and despite surges of purple annoyance, he nodded reluctant agreement, urging them to be careful.

After a brief exchange with her mother in the other room, Imogen returned and indicated for Araz to follow her. Leaving the apartment and walking into the heat of the late afternoon, Imogen determined to drink in her surroundings and imprint them in her mind. Today could be her last day on Earth. Holis would be so different, alien and unknown. *I may never see home again,* she thought and in doing so realised it was this world she thought of as her home.

As if he could read her mind, Araz put his arm around her shoulder and risked a brief reassuring kiss to the side of her head.

Steering her through Central Park, they walked in companionable silence until they reached the busy streets leading towards the Rockefeller Centre, where Araz grinned and pointed to the top of the skyscraper.

"I booked us in for dinner," smiled Araz. "I was hoping... well, I knew you would let me accompany you."

"You did, did you?" *That's not what your Chroma said!*

Smothering a slight flush in his colours he added, "Okay, I hoped you would agree. We can celebrate your birthday in style and then watch the sunset over the city from a place called the rainbow room. It seemed, somehow, appropriate."

Imogen, avoiding his fingertips, squeezed his hand in a gesture of thankful acceptance.

During the delicious meal, high on the sixty-fifth floor, Araz, at Imogen's behest, talked about his family. He spoke fondly of three key people who had influenced his early life. His father, who had been responsible for the transport links between the main cities, and what appeared to be two mothers (Imogen did not question him on this). One was both a farmer and botanist who travelled a lot, the other was a sort of teacher and a member of something called the Ethics Board. *Probably part of the Council of Sanctity - better not go there again.* Avoiding any questions prompting long technical explanations of life on Holis or a defensive reply, Imogen ventured to ask if his surname, Vikram, belonged to his father.

Araz instantly shook his head. "The convention of naming a child after the father's line does not exist on Holis. Why should it? Unlike here, all men and women are completely equal." He explained the 'family' name was determined by a test which established the balance of physical similarities and personality lines.

Imogen tensed. This was the first time he had mentioned anything to do with the five lines. She cloaked her colours so he could not detect her unease.

"Vikram was my birth mother's name," continued Araz enthusiastically. "She and I do look and think alike! But I could easily have taken my nursing mother's name, if her features or crypts had been more dominant. Or my father's, for that matter."

Araz explained this without any sense having two mothers was out of the ordinary, so Imogen just accepted it, making a mental note to find out more at a later date. *If I get a chance!*

"So, what's your family name?" asked Araz. "You are so physically like your mother, I would say it is Omorose?"

Imogen frowned. "I don't know. I mean, no one has ever told me I have any name other than Reiner."

Araz looked askance and rubbed his forehead before his Chroma flashed a bolt of cobalt blue. "They couldn't have done the tests! Of course, being born on Earth, they haven't established which are your dominant crypts, not that it matters much anymore..." he began.

"Shhh! No more Holan talk," interrupted Imogen, who quickly squashed her rising shades of alarm and turned the topic of conversation away from the dangerous ground of personality types.

At least it confirms he doesn't know I'm a Penta-Crypt. She knew she should be relieved but instead felt it was yet another barrier between them.

Their conversation petered out as they looked out to the view over the New York skyline. The numerous skyscrapers glinted with the light of the setting sun and they exchanged frequent glances as they watched the lights of the city slowly twinkle into being as darkness fell.

"If you think this view is good, wait until you see the view from Karnack Observation Tower... Sorry – no talk of Holis. I will stop! But the tower view is second to none."

She regarded him, no longer checking the chemical attraction surging each time he was close. His absolute belief in the goodness of his race and the righteousness of his commanders, despite misgivings about the Supreme Council, was still visible, but now the sharp gold edged blacks of superiority and certainty in his Chroma appeared softer and less clearly defined.

A waiter delivered two glasses of champagne to the table.

"I am told this is the convention here," explained Araz. "To drink champagne at a coming of age?"

"It certainly is!" she smiled, and quietly added when the waiter had left, "and we can overlook the fact it is a year early – in fact three years early here!"

As they chinked glasses, Imogen's face dropped as she mumbled, "After all, I may not get back for my eighteenth, let alone my twenty-first."

Araz leaned across to her and whispered into her ear, "Don't worry. I will keep you safe. Wait and see."

Let's hope he's right. There will be no turning back in a few hours

16

THE ORIGINAL CHRONICLES OF HOLIS - AN INTRODUCTION

WARNING: Be advised this DE contains the original, unabridged and unadulterated Chronicles of Holis, as written by my erstwhile colleague, Tanastra Thut. His account, accurate and unbiased, has since been altered to exclude information now considered harmful by our current leaders. The sections removed from later editions are clearly marked so you can see what is no longer considered to be 'educational'. Be warned, those found in possession of these original chronicles will be deemed subversive. It is therefore vital you keep this DE hidden. May the blessings of Ra be upon you.

Barbara.

$\mathcal{G}$ oodness – I am humbled! What an honour I have been accorded, to write the official chronicles of Holis, our incredible home. I am told every Holan, young and old, will use these and should anything happen to our people (a dreadful thought indeed), they will remain a universal record for all future races to behold.

I must caution you, my pride in Holis knows no bounds! It has become the absolute blueprint of how a civilisation can achieve peace, harmony and total fulfilment. ~~However, this has not always been so. Holis has had a dark and troubled past. Our ancestors destroyed our original home and made terrible decisions. Decisions taking us to the brink of extinction. The perfection we have since achieved was a state hard fought and hard won and, in these journals, I will endeavour to relay how this came about.~~

But I race ahead, for I must introduce myself. Tanastra Thut at your service. I realise many of you may have heard of my name in connection with various engineering projects, but I have always yearned to write. I love history and I am delighted to share my passion for our Holan past with you, your parents, your children and all who show an interest.

As your age and status are unknown to me, I will assume your knowledge is minimal and will deliberately write as if you know nothing! My sincere apologies if this is not to your liking, but please humour me and perhaps you will enjoy my rendition, even if you are already aware of the facts.

So where to begin? As an introduction, let me briefly summarise the physical attributes of Holis. It is one of the twin moons orbiting the dead planetary mass of Sheut. The other moon, Ankh, was in fact our place of origin.

They say Holis, Ankh and Sheut were once a single interstellar mass - all co-joined - before the catastrophic events of trillions of years ago when they exploded and separated into the three distinct bodies seen today. It is a good enough theory and would explain why Holis and Ankh have so many similarities. As smaller satellites, these moons became habitable environments whereas the planet Sheut has no atmosphere, water, or any of the necessary ingredients for life. To all intents and purposes, it is just a large lump of rock, useful only for its gravitational anchoring keeping us from flying off into space!

Now, the twin moons, Holis and Ankh, lie on the exact opposite sides of Sheut. One is completely hidden from the other as they orbit in identical trajectories. They are in perfect balance, a phenomenon not found anywhere else in either our galaxy or our neighbouring galaxies. Ankh was, of course, the former home of our ancestors and for thousands of years the existence of Holis was only guessed at and not confirmed until space travel came briefly into fashion. A lucky discovery indeed! When Ankh was finally rendered uninhabitable ~~by the corruption and stupidity of those in power~~, Holis was the natural location for our new home.

As the fifth planet from the main sun – Ka – Sheut lies in the outermost segment of our planetary group and both Sheut and its moons are also lit by the red light of Ib, a dying star close to our solar system, but outside the gravitational pull of Ka.

So, the light on Holis comes from two suns, the white and life-giving light of Ka and the cyclical red light of Ib. Again, a most extraordinary phenomenon. Now I appreciate you do not want an astrology lesson but be assured, the physical characteristics of our globe is most relevant to our history. You see Holis does not turn on its axis, unlike Ankh. This renders half of Holis uninhabitable as the same aspect always points towards Sheut, like many other moons in the universe. Holis therefore, has a dark side and a light side.

~~This is also true in many other ways; dark and light have littered our history. To understand the Holan race, you must know although Holis has been our home for the last ten thousand years, it is only considered a temporary home. Holis has more oceans and less landmass than Ankh, less habitable terrain and it cannot support all the diverse lifeforms once thriving on Ankh. With so little space, the population of Holis has had to be restricted and tightly controlled. It is indeed unfortunate, but the lack of freedom is accepted as a necessary restriction as we bide out time, waiting to return to our true home.~~

We ~~also~~ wish to see the original species of Ankh reincarnated. You see, most of the larger animals that dwelt on Ankh no longer live and breathe. They are held in genetic reserves - frozen in time. We are the custodians of these creatures and duty bound to protect them, but there just isn't the space for them to live in this world.

~~Whilst Ankh continues to be restored - a process already taking thousands of years - and made ready for re-population, the inhabitants of Holis have a desperate will to return there. Once it is made safe, we can move back and reintegrate our lost animal kingdom. It will be then that we will have achieved the goal of our race and our people will finally be home and free.~~

~~I end this introduction with our race's lament: a song handed down from generation to generation for thousands of years. This expresses the overriding desire of the Holan people, to move back to our original home:~~

> ~~The ages pass as we await~~
> ~~Return to a home so far.~~
> ~~We thirst for pastures, near forgot~~
> ~~We await your sign, Oh Ra.~~
> ~~Restore to us our homeland~~
> ~~From limits, set us free.~~
> ~~Make your face to shine on Ankh once more,~~
> ~~And hear our heartfelt plea.~~

THE JUMP

*I*n the hour before sunrise, Imogen, Araz and Adam entered the secret door of St Patrick's. She and Araz wore black bodysuits made from a strange material she had not seen before. Outside, skyscrapers dwarfed the cathedral but inside, the vast vaulted ceiling - barely visible in the pre-dawn light - encompassed an enormous space.

Imogen had visited the week before to familiarise herself with the layout. Although much larger than the Oratory Church in Birmingham, there were similarities that struck her. Marble steps led to the altar area, ornate cream columns rose tall and high as the first glimmers of the morning sun caught the stained-glass windows, dimly illuminating the sanctuary. Adam ushered them to central steps leading down to a dark crypt, his Multi-Com turned to torch.

They walked down a long corridor lined with brick and cement walls, past a lower chapel until they reached a recess with a small altar and cross set into the brickwork.

"What is this place?" asked Araz.

"Underground vaults and tombs," replied Adam.

"Tombs? Who's buried here" asked Imogen, already on edge.

"Mainly archbishops and a man who was born a slave."

"Slavery! Completely barbaric!" Araz sneered.

Ignoring Araz, Adam spoke to Imogen. "He won his freedom in New York over one hundred and sixty years ago; became respected by all, despite being born into slavery and oppression. Anyway, we could not risk placing the marker up in the main cathedral space. The building attracts many visitors. Even down here, there are frequent tours."

Throwing a backpack over his shoulders, Araz gave Adam a stiff nod of the head. He was ready.

"All set Imogen?" asked Adam, tentatively opening his arms towards her.

She did not hesitate and rushed to give him a heartfelt hug.

"I would prefer to send you separately," he began, "but we will not debate this again."

"No, we will not!" Araz's tone was unyielding. He had been the one to insist they must arrive on Holis together, arguing should the Resistance members fail to meet them or worse should government forces intercept them, he could protect Imogen.

Imogen swallowed hard. Adam had told her everything was arranged but had also hinted they may not get a good reception. He had warned messages between Earth and Holis were problematic. His voice replayed in her mind: 'Radio communication is not possible; information would be twenty years out of date by the time it reached its destination! We therefore use the Tractus for regular messages. A form of Data Encounter, heavily encoded and impregnated with a known DNA sample, is sent to and from the hidden markers on the two worlds.' He had added, to her revulsion, this was a vast improvement on using small tame animals - the only option before the DE with genetic coding was devised. 'So, messages are not instantaneous,' he had warned. 'They have to be picked up at the marker on each planet and communicated to others before a response can be returned in the same manner. As you can see, this all takes time and if the marker is unmanned, it could be days before a message is received.'

Adam had not told her the precise contents of the delayed response to his proposal, detailing the plan to jump Imogen and Araz into the heart of the subversive underworld. He had been deliberately vague and had not let her read the full reply:

'Fellow allies, your communication is acknowledged and it is hoped we can comply with your request but the situation here is grave. Our numbers fall by the day. Last week there was a hurried and unjust trial resulting, I am sorry to say, in the termination of a key resistance member. We all mourn his loss. Another awaits trial and we are constantly being watched. Concerns have arisen to there being a traitor in our midst. There is division amongst us as to the advisability of your mission. Although a few are calling it foolhardy, saying you are exposing us to further danger, I personally welcome your arrival and hope it will trigger much needed change in the empire. I will endeavour to do all I can to help. Safe crossing and may the protection of Ra be upon you. Barbara.'

Adam had no way of finding out who had been terminated, but the thought it could be Kasmut or Tarik had made him sick to his heart. He felt helpless, crushed by both fear and regret. He could not allow Imogen to set off with additional anxieties, so he had vowed not to tell her, explaining his concerns were purely for her safety.

Imogen's skills at reading Chroma had enabled her to surmise from Adam's reactions, he was hiding something. *So like his son.* She had therefore not questioned him further. She had to go on, even if they could be jumping straight into the enemy's clutches.

Thank goodness Araz insisted we must jump together. Imogen recalled his argument with Adam with a flutter in her heart. "I must remind you, Sefu," he had said, "we have proved it is safe to jump together, having already done so." Araz's colours, hot with the memory of Imogen saving his life, had blazed with such an intensity of love for her, Adam could not but fail to read it. Her protector's determination was clear and there would be no arguing with him; they would jump together or not at all.

As Imogen asked Adam to take care of her mother, she was surprised to see tears well into his eyes.

"I wish we had had more time to prepare you against the perils..." he started before thinking better of it and continuing, "Imogen, if you find Tarik – Leo. Tell him... tell him, I am thinking of him. And when you return, make sure you use the London marker. This one is too exposed. If you are in any danger, then, then..." Adam faltered as he opened a hand in despair. Imogen instantly squeezed his open palm and he brushed his fingertips against hers. The unspoken message: 'find Barbara', came clearly and forcibly through the link, along with a warning: 'Do not share this name with Araz'.

"Don't worry. I intend to return with both my father and Leo," she soothed, with more optimism than she felt. Giving Adam the tiniest nod of understanding, she stepped back to take Araz's hand, careful to place her thumb and fingertips safely away from his so a cognitive link was not possible. Her skin prickled and clammed, this time not connected with touching Araz, but to her deep-seated fears of using the Tractus. *Please, please don't go wrong.*

Araz gave the back of her hand a reassuring squeeze as Adam looked to the pulsing marker, concealed above the small altar. Once activated, Imogen silently counted, quelling the urge to be sick. There was a momentary glow of red light reflected in Adam's sombre face, then the airless blackness hit her.

TWENTY YEARS EARLIER

The eight-year-old boy looked at his mother in alarm. He had never seen her so distressed. In fact, he had never seen her cry. Her normally clear blue eyes were red and wet as she hugged him into her arms before pushing him violently away. He could not make sense of what she was saying to him. Why did he have to go? Why was his life in danger? What had he done wrong?

His normally serene and calm mother now seemed incapable of answering any of his questions, urging him to leave via their secret passage. Where would he go? He wanted to stay with her and this was clearly no game. The fear and raw panic in her voice moved him to stumble backward towards the concealed entrance, not taking his eyes off her.

Crouching down with his hands behind his back, he felt for the membrane opening on the wall. Once located, he touched the tissue causing the entrance to open like an interleaved shutter on a camera. The far door of his mother's room suddenly opened and, as he looked on in horror, two tall stocky figures, helmeted and clad in black, marched in followed by... by her! The Supreme Leader herself.

He trembled from head to toe, staring at the woman rather than the huge bodyguards towering over her. He should have known it would mean trouble when she had caught him just a few days ago. He had watched her uncover a secret compartment in the wall of her rooms and open it with some sort of key hanging from a chain around her neck. She had turned to see him, fury written all over her face.

Wrenching his arm, she had asked him questions he could not answer. She had forced him to transmit a picture of his mother using the cognitive link. He had seen, from the self-satisfied look on her face, this would spell disaster. If only he had had the courage to warn his mother, but then she would know he had strayed to a chamber strictly out of bounds. He had, naively, hoped life would go on as normal. Now he was filled with regret.

As 'Her Greatness' looked across the room towards him, he glanced at his mother's terrified face and hesitated. She urged him on with her eyes and as the guards advanced, he quickly turned away, ducked and rolled through the aperture, which instantly closed and sealed behind him. He would not have long. Whilst only he or his mother's touch could activate it, they could easily press her hand to the film to force it open. With his head down, the boy ran as fast as his legs would carry him.

The passageway, his mother had told him, had been constructed by the father he had never met. His mother said he must never talk of him; she would be all the father and mother he ever needed. Even so, it was his father he must thank for the secret corridor made long ago, in the days when he and his mother had been young and in love. It had enabled the boy to meet with her frequently.

Raised by several 'grandparents', all sworn to secrecy, he was able to visit his mum daily and often spend the night with her, laughing and talking together into the early hours.

The corridor spiralled up and down, under and around the dwellings of the government complex. Where it dipped and rose, rough steps were carved into the rock. The boy was sure of his footing, having used the route for years, and did not risk activating the lights as he sped along.

The sound of rushing water told him he was near the end as he leapt down the final flight into a cave of natural rock, water cascading into the narrow causeways around him before thundering over a waterfall into the depths of the distant caverns below. The boy had played hide and seek here for many years. He knew where to hide and hurriedly squeezed into a crevasse in the rock just before the guards stumbled into the dead end.

Grunting from the effort of the chase, they peered over the waterway looking for signs of the escapee, waving their torches. Once they had passed his hiding place, the boy quickly sprang free and canyoned himself over a lip of rock and into the freezing cold water, which swept him over the fall. The guards cried out in frustration as he disappeared.

Arms crossed and breath held, the lad dropped, allowing his torpedoed shape to be carried along the smooth rock waterway with the icy torrent. With a grin on his face, his adrenalin-fuelled body felt the familiar rush of exhilaration as he sped down the chain of channels. As the strait widened and other waterways joined his, the water swelled to deeper rapids and the velocity increased. Eyes wide with excitement, he timed his moment exactly, to hook his arm around a protruding rock, swing his legs onto a submerged ledge and haul himself out, as he had done countless times before. He then eased himself into a higher pool. Here the water was warm, heated with natural geothermal power. Catching his breath and allowing the warmth to tingle back into his chilled muscles, he shook his soaking blond curls out of his eyes and stepped out to stand on the precipice over a gulley. Warm jets of air streamed upward from the magna chambers deep below the ground, flowing around his open arms and body and drying him off in a matter of minutes.

After dipping his hand in the pool to damp down his now crazy hair, he headed up the incline towards the exit, only metres from his home. The elation of having made his escape soon shrank as his mood dropped. His mother was in danger and it was his fault. What should he do?

A glance across the stream coursing alongside his neighbourhood below, told him something was amiss. His grandmother and a team of others were usually on the riverbank, nursing babies and toddlers. There was no sign of them - adults or infants.

Reaching the dome-shaped structure of his home, he crept around the side to peer in. He could not see anyone through the transparent walls. The place was usually abuzz with noise and activity. Then he spotted it. The red skateboard his grandmother had made for him was outside the door and, significantly, upside down - the signal for danger. He must go! What had she said? 'Do not attempt to enter the house – get to Barbara – use the cave entrance I showed you at the bottom of the mountain pass.' So, after years of her oft-repeated warning, the day had finally arrived and he must go in search of this unknown Barbara.

Creeping to the entrance, he hurriedly grabbed the skateboard and dashed away, launching it as he ran. He jumped onto the narrow length of wood and careered down the paths of his village, leaping boulders and streams, speeding across meadows and dodging trees. He cut through a forest and when it became too dense, he picked up his board and walked. Following the route imprinted on his mind long ago, he continued until he reached the low rock entrance of a concealed cavern at the bottom of a sheer mountain face.

Pressing his fingertips into a recess, the rock face cracked open and the boy squeezed his way in. As the rock slid back into place, a vine-like strap encircled his body, securing him in place. The magnetic levitation tube in which he was standing then catapulted him several miles into the centre of the mountain. Had he not been so apprehensive, he would have enjoyed the thrill of its speed and the sense of adventure. As it was, his brow was beading with perspiration and his breath had quickened to rapid pants.

When the capsule eventually came to a gentle stop, his harness slackened and the door slid open. He had arrived at the headquarters of the underground movement and found himself staring at the back of a female technician, dressed in a dark bodysuit, and bent over a chamber pulsing with an eerie light. As she stood and turned to face him, her shock of ginger hair and kindly eyes sent a bolt of recognition through him.

"Barbara?" he asked tentatively, suddenly feeling reassured.

"Now, let me see, you must be Tarik?" The boy nodded, eyes widening as her voice confirmed who she really was. Her image was everywhere, her voice the gentle one of reassurance used in national broadcasts, although she was normally dressed in traditional council robes.

"Ah, you recognise me? Well, young Tarik, you need to make a solemn pact not to share my identity with anyone else. My life depends upon it." Tarik nodded, in awe.

She held up her hand and indicated for him to do the same. They connected - her fingertips to his. She transmitted the words to him, he dutifully repeated them via his nervous system: 'The codename - Barbara - and her secret identity, I will not share with anyone. I make this oath in the presence of Ra and will hold true to this promise until released from the obligation.'

Smiling at the child, she broke the connection and stepped to one side. Tarik looked beyond her to find a tall man standing in the shadows of a far rock pillar.

"Tarik, it is time for you to meet someone."

Barbara steered him gently towards the dark-haired man. With furrowed brows and arms firmly folded, the man did not move or take his eyes off the boy.

'Tarik, this is your father. He is going to take you to a place of safety. There is no time now, but he will explain everything to you once you are there.'

Tarik's stomach knotted and he stared at the man. His 'father' just stared back - face unreadable.

The silence was broken when a flash of light lit up the rock walls and a kitten suddenly appeared in the centre of the space, cowering on the floor. Tarik jumped back, amazed to see the animal materialise from nowhere. Blinking in disbelief, he watched the man march over to the now squealing kitten, remove a black ovoid shape attached to its collar and push the small cat to one side with his foot, as it hissed and tried to scratch him. Tarik recognised the object as one of those new Data Encounters. The man put his fingertips into the indentations of the device and his eyes glazed over as he connected to it.

Barbara waited with baited breath; the boy looked on in confusion.

After a few moments, the man released the DE. "We're good to go," he announced, throwing a bag to Tarik and indicating for him to put it on his back as he drew Barbara close to speak privately to her.

The kitten started to mew piteously, so Tarik reached down to pick it up. It's mewling switched to a purr as the striped creature snuggled gratefully into his hand. With the adults engaged in an earnest whispered exchange, Tarik, his heart in his mouth, gently placed the kitten into his bag and swung it over his shoulders, just before the man strode over to him.

'Tarik, be brave,' Barbara urged as she raised her hand to activate the marker.

'Where you are going, it is… it is different. But you will be safe. May the blessings of Ra go with you.'

Before he could recoil, the man forcefully grabbed his arm and in a flash of light, the world turned black and airless.

THE CHRONICLES OF HOLIS – ANKH

WARNING: The following chapter from The Chronicles of Holis has been removed in its entirety in subsequent editions. Be warned: those found in possession of these original chronicles will be deemed subversive. Keep this DE hidden.

Barbara.

*A*nkh was a most beautiful place, a turning globe of blue seas, green valleys, high mountains and verdant land masses. It once teemed with life. The nearest planetary equivalent is, surprisingly, in another sector of our own galaxy – a mere twenty light years away – and which we now know as Earth. Earth is a lot younger than Ankh, but our original home once resembled this splendid blue planet, until our ancestors destroyed it. Sadly, this was the consequence of thousands upon thousands of years of war, pollution, the plundering of the planet's resources and the use of the deadliest of weapons. Once the soil and seas were poisoned and the atmosphere was thick with toxic clouds, the light of Ka was blotted out and the air rendered so noxious, it was barely breathable. All life on the surface of Ankh then died. A tragedy!

Had it not been for the foresight of a group of scientists, who predicted total destruction and formulated a plan of action to relocate to Holis, our race would have been annihilated. It is thanks to them we now have a habitable, if small, home on Holis. And, although only supposed to be a temporary measure, it seems it will be many more years before we can return to Ankh. How we all long for that day!

Back then, Holis needed a boost of breathable gases, in order to make the atmosphere conducive to life and cut down on the overpowering red light of Ib. So, the largest and most amazing engineering project, aptly named the 'Elysian Scheme', was undertaken. Organic energy, using the marvellous element, InvertIon – mined from the volcanic depths of Ankh – was generated in the mountain regions of the North. This gave the planet a network of highly sophisticated, renewable energy. The by-products of this awesome process were a continuous supply of pure water, which formed the Southern Sea and reservoirs in the flooded valleys of the Northern mountain range, and Oxygen, released into the air for respiration. It also gave us the other gases necessary to enrich the stratosphere, give protection from harmful rays and increase the intensity of Ka's white light, resulting in a stable weather system.

Overall, it took nearly five hundred years from start to finish, to make Holis a viable environment, but goodness, our history would have ended had they not succeeded in this life-giving project. These early pioneers were the true visionaries of Holis and they created a wonderful home for our people.

Tavats - some called them space arks - were used to secretly ship everything from Ankh: building materials, supplies like InvertIon, insects, plants and the genetic crypts of all life forms once living on the land and in the seas.

In the final days before the catastrophe reached its climax, the terrified population descended into anarchy. Panic set in. No one noticed the activity on a remote island where the final shipments were being stealthily loaded. The cargo? Those chosen citizens who would bring the Elysian Scheme to fruition, so life could start afresh on Holis.

Numbering a mere three thousand, they came from every sector of the planet. The finest minds of Ankh, plus their families. They remained on-board the Tavats orbiting Holis until their new home was complete. Over the years new generations were born on these ships and instilled with the desire to create a faultless society, one eventually able to restore Ankh to its former glory. From these brave folk, came the making of Holis and Holankind. Thanks be to Ra!

ARRIVAL

$\mathcal{T}$he first gasp of air filled her with relief. Imogen tried to stand but her legs were too wobbly and her stomach was churning, threatening to overwhelm her with rising nausea. A band of pain shot through her head. *Ouch! Well, at least I'm alive!*

She breathed a little easier, swiftly going through the internal drills to check her mental faculties and banishing the headache before gradually slowing her heart rate and forcing her anxiety to a manageable level. *My memories seem okay. No fog – thank goodness! So, is this Holis? And have I been shot to the future or is it still the present?*

Pitch black with no background noises, she had no clue as to where she was. To her relief and with a sense of 'Deja-vu', she could still see the Infrared glow of Araz, who was slumped beside her on the cold floor. She hesitantly touched the surface. *Feels like rock – maybe this is a cave? I should have asked Adam precisely where we would wind up,* she admonished herself, thinking, in hindsight, there were probably a lot more things she should have asked.

Araz groaned as she fumbled for his backpack to feel for the Multi-Com. Finding what she needed and switching it to torch, Imogen slowly got to her feet and looked around the small rock-lined room. It was like the World War Two concrete bunkers on Earth with four flat walls, but instead of an armoured door there was an archway opening on the far wall. Scanning the area, the beam of light caught the reflection of a small black globe, nestled in a high cavity hacked into the wall. *Must be the marker.*

Araz gave a deep, raw moan.

What on Earth is wrong with him? Or should that be, 'what on Holis'?

Araz had come to and was beginning to gag, his arms flaying around wildly as he urged Imogen to get something called Baladi. Realising he meant the nourishment cubes he had packed before they left, she reached into the bag and swiftly unwrapped two. She pushed one into his mouth and another into hers. The power-packed nutrients flooded her body and she was rapidly refreshed. They each drank a full carton of juice from their stores and Araz began to recuperate, although Imogen noted his skin had paled to an ashen tone, tinged green.

"Those jumps don't get any better. In fact, that was the worst to date," he groaned. "How do you manage to recover so quickly?"

Imogen shrugged her shoulders and helped him to his feet, thinking acerbically to herself: *Maybe you have to be stuck in a Tractus wormhole for forty years to pick up fast!*

"So, where are we?" she asked.

"I don't recognise this place! Could be anywhere on Holis, or Earth for that matter," he said looking around the space. "Looks like your subversive friends are not here to greet us," he added caustically.

"Shhh! Someone's coming"

A set of heavy footsteps resounded down an adjoining passageway.

Imogen cut the torch and they drew closer to each other, hearts thumping, as a beam of light lit up the archway.

The light turned the corner and shone directly into their eyes, dazzling them. Imogen tentatively put both her hands up high, remembering Adam had said it was a universally accepted form of surrender. The light slowly lowered and in front of them was a tall and strapping young woman with a closely cropped head of spikey hair and a tattoo of an open eye, high on one cheekbone. She was dressed in a black bodysuit, similar to theirs but ripped at the knees, thighs and around the arms. Marks looking like old bloodstains were visible on the exposed flesh, but there was no sign of any injuries, which must have healed.

She advanced on Imogen and Araz, moving her torch up and down as she looked them over. Imogen was relieved to see the woman looked humanoid, although another part of her mind smiled at what Leo might have said: *'what did you expect? Green Martians and bug-eyed monsters?'*

Standing disconcertingly close, the burly female grabbed one of Imogen's hands, splayed out her fingers and held her own free hand above, demanding loudly, "Last face!"

Araz took a step forward and went to push the hand away, but Imogen shook her head at him and then pressed her hand to the woman's - fingertip to fingertip - so they could connect.

Imogen transmitted an image of Adam with the name 'Zuberi', as Adam had instructed her in their brief secret session. She also 'told' the woman her companion was called Araz and implied he had been born on Earth. She was deliberately ambiguous but communicated he had already visited Holis and his DNA was registered in The Hub, giving him open access. Adam had said she must shield the fact Araz was a government agent; his presence in the heart of the underground would not be tolerated and could jeopardise their mission.

The woman locked eyes with Imogen before nodding and releasing her hand. Imogen had received, in return, confirmation she was in the same time frame as when she had left Earth. Along with the woman's name. Unknown to the sender, she had also received a garbled set of thoughts in Holan. She could not make out all the words, which translated to broken English, but she got the gist of what 'Em' was thinking and had to repress a grin. No one could know she was able to receive a person's inner thoughts as well as the ones they deliberately sent, Adam had been clear about this. *'Don't tell them you can read Chroma either'*, he had cautioned.

Em motioned them over to the archway and spoke quietly into an opal coloured sphere which she then placed on the floor where they had been sitting. She activated the marker and in a flash of white light, the globe disappeared. Turning on her heels she stomped out of the room.

"What was that all about?" asked Araz in an irritated tone.

"Guess she's sending a message to say we've arrived safely," answered Imogen.

"You know what I meant!" Araz demanded and held his hand up splaying his fingers wide with a questioning tilt of the head.

"Oh, that! Just checking who we are," shrugged Imogen, making to set off after Em.

Araz grabbed her arm, a little too forcefully, saying, "Well, it might have been helpful to have been told about this procedure. Who is she anyway? And what else did she say?"

"Name's Em. That's all I know," Imogen lied, relieved in the knowledge Araz could not see the violet flashes in her Chroma, which, like his colours, were not visible.

She freed her arm and followed 'Em - line of Lateef'. The name was comfortingly familiar; this fierce looking woman must be related to the breakaway scientist who had developed the Tractus. Imogen remembered the report from the Chronicles: Firas Lateef had been slaughtered by Repros and it was clear Em knew this and now wanted revenge.

"You," she remarked to Araz, over her shoulder as she walked through the arch, "would probably class her as a subversive." *I won't tell you she now classes you as a Falsebred, like me. Would you be furious! And you probably won't want to know she doesn't like the look of you, or, for some reason, she thinks I'm a 'lovely specimen'!* Imogen had deliberately not responded to Em's fingertip question: 'Brooding hunk - your bonded one?' Instead, she had feigned a lack of understanding at the Holan terms.

"There's no 'probably' about it," he grumbled, catching up with Imogen to advance down the corridor together, towards a far glow of red light. "Be careful, I don't like the look of her! What? Why the smile?" asked Araz, reaching to touch her lips.

Imogen avoided his hand, shook her head and hurriedly mumbled something about smiling with relief - glad they had arrived safely. Her quick assessment of their escort, Em, had given her a renewed strength. The woman was fiercely pro-subversive, hated the rule of Kekara, and her responses were not tainted with any 'Araz-style' inbuilt prejudice against Falsebreds. *Definitely on my side,* she thought gratefully.

As they picked up speed Imogen was aware of her muscles feeling heavy and needing more effort to propel her now leaden legs forward. Adam had said this was to be expected; gravity was slightly stronger on Holis than on Earth. He had also said she would soon get used to it.

Warm and humid air entered the cool rock space as they got closer to the exit. Em stood at the edge of the opening, silhouetted by the strange red light now flooding into the tunnel. She indicated the way out, bowing slightly and saying in a sarcastic tone, "Welcome! This Holis!"

The red light was blinding. Imogen and Araz both put their hands up to screen their eyes as they stepped outside.

Imogen blinked in the dazzling light and peered around. They had emerged in the middle of a moss-covered clump of rocks in what looked like a rainforest. But everything was wrong. The plants, trees, groundcover, even the small flying insects similar to bees and butterflies, were blackened and dark. Imogen quickly realised she could not distinguish detail and most of the shapes were charcoal and blurry.

It's the red light! It changes how everything looks. How the hell am I going to see anything properly, let alone Chroma? Why did Adam tell me it would be fine?

As panic began to rise within, her head started to pound and she quelled the urge to be sick. From the corner of her eye she could see Araz, in strange negative colours, blinking rapidly and leaning against the outer rock wall. *It's the same for him.*

Suddenly, without warning, she felt a film drop down over her eyes. The effect was immediate. The red light instantaneously disappeared. The leaves and plants switched to normal shades of green, the sky to blue, the butterflies and bees now bright yellow, with multiple coloured details in their wings.

Imogen put her hands to her eyes. *What just happened?* She appeared to have an inner eyelid. Dumbfounded, she stared all around her. The verdant surroundings were crystal clear and beautiful. A canopy of leaves, vines, exotic flowers and branches hung above and around her. Grasshoppers chirped, birds sang, a small green tree frog jumped from a large leaf next to her. She could easily be in the Amazon rainforest on Earth. Taking it all in, she noticed a large lake or sea, visible in a gap between the far trees, sparkling in the light of two suns. Imogen looked away from the far reflections in the water and up to the sky. There they were! Framed by the foliage - the two suns of Holis! A small regular white sun, so like the one seen from Earth; next to it, or so it seemed, a large glowering red orb, shimmering bright.

Her heart missed a beat and she swallowed hard as the reality sank in. *Incredible! I'm here, on Holis. Twelve trillion miles from Earth!*

Em, watching her reaction, nodded appreciatively. "Quick! Very quick! Primitive upbringing not disable Tarsus filter." To Imogen's ears, her accent sounded, bizarrely, Russian.

Of course! The inner lid - it's a filter! Filtering the red light.

Imogen just nodded, sheepishly opening and closing her outer lid until she was sure the inner film was staying firmly in place.

Marvelling at the inbuilt filter, which must have been with her from birth, she realised Em had spoken again.

"…Faulty?"

Imogen employed a memory scan to retrieve the words from her subconscious. She had missed Em saying something like, 'your Earth friend taking bit longer. Maybe lids faulty?' *Did she say they could possibly create some lenses for him?* Imogen hadn't quite taken it in, her new eyelids proving a huge distraction.

"Sorry, what did you say about the red sun, Ib?"

Em repeated her words. "If lids don't drop, will have to wait for change in light to see clearly. Not much help like this,' she added disparagingly.

Imogen followed her gaze. Araz was beginning to look anxious, his eyes widening and bulging with an intense concentration, as if to force the hidden lids into being. After a few minutes she observed them dropping. She had to replay the moment in her head, slowing it down to see the nearly transparent layer of cells neatly glide into place from under the outer eyelids. *Amazing!*

Araz was instantly relieved and rubbed his eyes before taking in the lush backdrop and then looking over to her. "You can see already?" he asked, slightly incredulous.

Imogen crossed her arms and glowered at him "Yes. And surprise! It would appear I have an inner lid." Her voice was full of accusation.

He shrugged his shoulders in response.

"Well, it might have been helpful to have been told about it," she echoed his words.

"They work, that's all that matters," he responded without apology.

"Just as well," she glared at him, suddenly aware she could still not see his colours, despite the red light now being filtered out.

When Em started to speak, Imogen looked to her, *I can't see hers either.* Her heart sank. It confirmed her worst fear; her one advantage, the ability to read Chroma, would be useless here.

"So, you not know Tarsus filter?"

Imogen shook her head.

"It reactive. As red light in atmosphere change, filters adjust," offered Em in explanation. "It dependent on time of month. Ib now at brightest but when Ka is at full sun, Holis flooded with white light. Then filter, it thins, until nearly transparent. After this, lid lifts for few days. You get used to it," she said matter-of-factly.

So, will I be able to see Chroma when my inner lids lift?

Araz marched over to Em and demanded to know precisely where they were.

Her reaction was to push her face up to his, causing him to recoil slightly. "Steady, hot lips," responded Em, pursing hers at him, as he leaned further away.

Hot lips! Imogen put her hand up to her mouth to stifle a giggle as she watched Araz recoil from Em's wicked wink and puckered lips.

The teasing tone swiftly transformed to one of challenge. Em moved even closer towards him and practically spat out the next words into his face. "Remember this. Have no idea who are you! Risk everything to greet you. Had lucky escape to get here," Em indicated her ripped bodysuit with a hand, keeping her eyes fixed on his all the time. "So, guess? You must earn trust. My recommendation? Back off demands."

Araz glared back at her but stayed quiet.

Em turned to Imogen. "I take you nearest village. Is at edge of Southern Sea. Is safe there - can train before going Karnak. Your timing - is good. Is Festival of..." Imogen thought the word translated to 'Lotus' - *Maybe the Festival of Flowers?* Em added, "All work suspended next three days."

Em then strode over to a low rock and reached behind it to retrieve what looked like a few rolls of material in soft stone colours. Passing one each to Imogen and Araz, she stripped off her bodysuit, showing no sign of being self-conscious and revealing several other bright tattoos dotted around her muscular body (Imogen easily identified the stars, circles and arrow from her pendant).

Araz averted his eyes and turned his back on them as he started to change.

Imogen tried not to stare at Em's naked form, although part of her mind was relieved to see she looked completely normal. Adam's words jumped into her head: *'Human / Holan - it is all the same — all advanced life forms have the same basic make up'*. Instead she concentrated on how skilfully Em's hands worked, draping the strange fabric around her body and manipulating the material with pinches and folds until it was shaped into a tight jumpsuit. Adam had said the textiles on Holis were organic in origin and adapted to the wearer. She recalled him saying they would keep the wearer cool, warm, or dry, depending on the weather conditions. He had tried to explain how they could be worn, but his description did not do justice to the process.

Imogen quickly pulled her length of cloth around herself like a towel and wriggled awkwardly out of her bodysuit beneath it.

She watched Em squeeze a small, slightly darker, circular area on her cuff. The material responded by turning a bright shimmering green, the colour of the huge green leaves around her.

Imogen's eyes widened with wonder. Em blended into the foliage perfectly, camouflaged as part of the jungle. *Like a chameleon!*

"Is called Flecto," Em explained, turning full circle. "When activated, colour of immediate surroundings reflected, changing as fauna and flora change."

Glancing to Araz, she saw he had styled his piece of Flecto into a sharply cut tunic, a little like those worn by Roman gladiators. It remained the colour of stone and he kept his back firmly to the women, as if waiting to be told he could turn around.

"Want hand?" asked Em, an amused look on her face.

Imogen nodded gratefully. She had no idea how to manoeuvre the cloth and observed Em carefully as she grabbed the edges of the fabric. At first, Em worked slowly demonstrating each move, but she soon sped up as she crossed, stretched, squeezed and folded the malleable textile around Imogen's body. When she doubled the cloth, or crushed it between her fingers, the substance glued itself together seamlessly. When she gently tore at it, the Flecto separated and re-joined anew beneath her fingers. It was fascinating. Moulding the fabric this way and that, Em soon fashioned footwear and a long flowing dress, nipped in at the waist, with loose long sleeves and a daring low-cut crisscross over her chest.

"Shows off locket," Em winked, touching Imogen's pendant with a degree of reverence. "Perhaps wiser keep hidden?"

Although astonished at her elegant medieval-style dress, Imogen couldn't help but frown at the plunging neckline and instinctively went to hitch it up. To her relief, the material lifted and re-formed into a higher line, obedient to her touch. She experimented with a few folds until it soon looked like part of the design. The locket was now hidden from view.

"Also good - your choice," Em said, unperturbed, adding, "So, press circle at end of sleeve, will change from neutral colours."

Imogen nodded appreciatively. Not only had Em created this stylish gown, she had skilfully engineered the Flecto so the small organic 'switch' was positioned right by her wrist. Imogen squeezed it with her good hand and watched the entire garment flood with leafy colours. She twirled to see the effect of the cloth taking on the hue of grass, bark and even the butterfly shades as it billowed out in a full circle. Wherever it glanced it changed to the colours around, looking almost fluid as she moved. *Would Chrissie like this!* As her thoughts turned to her friends and family, her immediate concerns crashed forcibly back into her mind and she stopped abruptly.

"I need to find my father, Kasmut Akil. And Leo, I mean Tarik – they were taken prisoner some weeks ago."

Araz swung around and she briefly caught the look of surprise and admiration in his face when he took in her outfit, but all her troubles were now bombarding her mind.

"Prisoners - they held in capital, Karnak," responded Em. "If still alive."

Imogen bit her lip.

"Kasmut Akil? Your father? Know name. Not know what happened with him. Will make enquiries. As for name Tarik, this known in capital. Population advised - is accused of being Falsebred. Falsebred and exposing Holan race to contamination from primitives. Trial scheduled few days after festival. Personally, think no hope for him," Em said sadly, with a shake of her head.

Imogen rubbed the scar on her hand. *At least he's still alive.*

Em pointed at the scar. "May want hide this too," she added, her brows knitted. "Must know, Holans not have scars?" She stared at Imogen awaiting an explanation but Imogen just lowered her head and after an awkward silence, Em merely shrugged her shoulders, mumbling something like, "please self".

Tearing a narrow strip of material from the hem of Imogen's dress and teasing the torn edge to stretch and repair itself, Em wound the swatch into a decorative shape and secured it around Imogen's hand, covering the disfigurement.

"Is easier hide body art," Em said with a smile. She touched a corner of her 'eye' tattoo which promptly faded and disappeared.

Imogen barely noticed. She was suddenly pensive. Her scar was just one of the many peculiarities marking her as different to her own kind. *I must try to help Leo, although I've no idea how. These people will give me the same labels. Falsebred, contaminated and heaven knows what else. What chance will I have? Only my dad will know what to do.* "Please find out where my father is," she implored Em, tears springing to her eyes. "He came here as an envoy. I have to find him."

"I will be helping you," announced Araz, taking Imogen's arm and giving Em a sideways glare.

Em merely sneered at him as she turned to set off for the village.

Imogen nodded gratefully at Araz. The intense love and devotion shining from his eyes did not need any chromatic confirmation. She touched her fingers to her mouth and then to his lips in silent thanks as they followed Em.

If only I was completely sure of him. He may want to protect me, but is he still on the side of the enemy? Without my dad, I have no other option but to trust him - for now. Quelling her fears, she resolved to focus on her surroundings and take in everything about this new world, imprinting it all deep within. Everything held a fascination for her and observing it lifted her spirits. *Besides, no one on Earth can help me now.*

THE CHRONICLES OF HOLIS: THE MAKING OF HOLANKIND

WARNING: In the following chronicle, deletions and new additions have been made to the original version. Deletions and additions are clearly marked. Be warned: those found in possession of these original chronicles will be deemed subversive. Keep this DE hidden.

Barbara.

The Elysian project, to develop the Holis biosphere was a wonder to behold. Everyone played their part in bringing it to fruition. Once the globe achieved full capability and could support life with clean air, a stable weather system, a global water supply and planetary power generation, our people left the Tavats and colonised the new world. They had to adapt in all sorts of ways. For instance, the night time temperatures on Holis are far more extreme than on Ankh, dropping to sub-zero and colder. Elysian One had to ensure all plant life would be able to resist this extreme cold and sensitive crops with no defence could be grown under protective covers that sealed during the dark hours. Shelter would be required for every Holan as they would not be able to withstand the freezing cold of night without special attire.

Every preparation had been made. Extensive organic dwelling places had been created along with an underground transport link. The government headquarters were constructed – a most magnificent edifice – known as The Hub and holding all records of universal life in sophisticated genetic banks.

The biggest difference between Holis and Ankh was that of useable terrain. The dark side would not support life and the light side had only a relatively small portion of habitable land (the Southern hemisphere was intolerably hot and the only landmasses were mainly desert).

Holans would have to live in a reduced space and this inevitably led to restrictions. The population had to be carefully controlled. Every possible measure had to be taken to ensure Holis did not succumb to the fate of Ankh. Only those ready to adhere to the strict rules and charter had been selected for entry to this new race.

It was a tough adjustment for a people used to being free but it is also thanks to the discipline of constraint we have been able to refine and perfect our physical forms. Genetic enhancements were painstakingly made, so we now live for longer, diseases and disabilities have been eradicated and our bodies self-heal until we reach a ripe old age.

These marvellous adaptations have been achieved as a result of biding our time until we return to our true home. Holans, as a race, do not rush things. Why should we? We have plenty of time! Every project and advancement, small and large, is researched, deliberated and the process repeated over and over, until the value of any new development is incontrovertible. Only then can it go ahead.

The consequence of all these improvements and careful controls, was, ~~as many would say,~~ the achievement of perfection: a peaceful healthy nation ~~striving to repair our former home. This was the case for the first thousand years or so — after all, the fear of a repetition of what happened on Ankh kept everyone united by a common bond.~~

~~Holan nature, however, eventually came into play as rules were relaxed and memories of Ankh faded. There came a newfound freedom, promoting diverse ideas and differing philosophies. With this, sadly, came argument and unrest. Dictators rose from the midst of dissension; hatred, prejudice, civil unrest and war followed. The history of Holis took a very sorry turn. Once the extreme despots, the worst of which was Anubis, a most evil tyrant who turned our home into a deathly underworld, were finally defeated (after a terrible two hundred year conflict). Holans were forced to think again. How could we guarantee extremism would not scupper our hard won, peaceful world, whilst allowing diversity and freedom?~~

~~The solution was inspired.~~ Genetic breakthroughs allowed us to predict personality types: five basic lines. Each line had traits suited to different walks of life. So, a person with strong creative and artistic skills would be unlikely to enjoy a repetitive or mundane task as their mainstay. Conversely, a person with a need for precision and order would no doubt prefer tasks with a finite outcome. This is, of course, purely an illustration. In reality personalities are far more complex. But the research showed, deep down, one line was consistently more dominant than the others and this gave a reliable indication of how a person would develop in life. With this knowledge, occupations could be allocated to suit the character and disposition of each person, according to their overriding characteristics.

~~The principle is simple. People who are well occupied, valued and fulfilled, do not feel the need to cause unrest. So, the possibility of frustrated individuals whose anger could grow into a force for evil would, quite simply, be eliminated. Prescriptive, some may say, but it proved to work!~~

There were a few Holans who turned out to hold multiple personality lines in equal quotas: The Bi-Crypts, Tri-Crypts and rare Tetra-Crypts (only two of our race are known to have this mix, including our new, young leader, Kekara). With such an advantage, these protégés were nurtured to attain the highest positions in our society. They had the ability to empathise with differing viewpoints and appeared to possess a capacity for analysis, vision and fair judgement far superior to those with a single dominant line. It was found these few multi-crypts were best suited to research, visionary developments and leadership.

Strangely enough, no one was ever born with all five of the lines in equal measure. Oh yes, our geneticists tried to engineer this, but every attempt failed. The perfect balance of all the lines – the existence of a Penta-Crypt – ~~did not appear~~ was not found to be possible. ~~Finding the illusive 'Sanctus Cryptus', as it was reverently known, became an obsession for many long years. Such a one would, surely, make a great and wise ruler?~~

~~As I write, it has been decided to abandon this research. It is said to have caused a distraction from other worthy projects and had the effect of making single dominant lines feel inferior. It seems a shame, but understandable, given the circumstances. Perhaps this research should have continued? I do, like all Holans, trust the decision of our Supreme Council, in ending the mission. It did, after all, consist of the finest minds and they put the vote to the Sanctus High Court which agreed with them. Democracy at its best! Even so, I wonder what would have happened should they have been successful?~~

~~But I digress!~~ In a further innovation, each person's personality line, or mix if they held more than one in balance, was made outwardly visible from birth. A mark, the symbol of the relevant line or lines, can be found on the body in simulated light conditions. Those with the line of Ra have a solid circle on the side of the neck; Iris, a clear circle by the eye; Hathor show a clear star on the chest; Nut will have a solid star on the hand, and Amon, an arrow on the underside of the foot. Once it is known which lines are predominant, upbringing is adapted to suit the personality of each Holan, so they use their gifts and talents for the good of all, and in return, they feel fulfilled and content. The consequence of this amazing piece of genetic categorisation has been an unprecedented period of peace and wellbeing.

We ~~may not have had a 'Sanctus Cryptus' to lead the way, but~~ we have ~~trusted in~~ depended on the authority of our leaders, chosen by personality from birth and trained for governance since childhood. ~~This is how we have succeeded in avoiding despots and dictators for the last thousand years~~. We can be assured our leaders have the best interests of our race in their hearts, just like those visionaries who set up Holis in the first place. ~~Never again will an Anubis lead our race, of that we can be assured.~~

LEO

*L*eo paced the floor of the small gardens of his enclosure and reviewed the events of the last few weeks. Barely conscious when the Repros had thrown him to the floor after his forced jump back to Holis, he had woken intermittently from his pain-filled sleep to hear Kasmut's voice insisting his injuries be attended to.

Kasmut had stayed by his side as practitioners repaired his broken nose and arm, his split spleen and other wounds. Once the breaks had been re-joined, he had healed in no time. The severe wounds were now, thankfully, a blurred memory.

Since being patched up, Leo had seen nothing of Kasmut and assumed he was being held in separate quarters. There was no information about Imogen and he could only hope she was safe on Earth. She must hate me, he thought despondently. It was his fault Imogen had returned to the church in Birmingham. He had had no idea they would send in Repros to attack and as a result of his actions, she could be captured or worse. Weighed down with guilt he could not bear to think about it.

The gateway opened in the soft hedging on the perimeter of the garden and a Repro stepped through, standing aside to admit a member of the Supreme Council. The small gowned figure, with pointed beard, strode across to Leo.

"Ubaid," Leo gave an awkward bow of respect whilst throwing an anxious look to the Repro..

"Tarik, you are looking recovered. I am glad."

"Where is Kasmut?"

"I am unable to give you any information about Kasmut. He has been... well, let's just say he has been uncooperative, which was not a good move on his part. Now, we need to speak."

"Sure, nothing I like better than a cosy chat! But first you need to tell me if my mother is safe," answered Leo, sitting down defiantly on a mossy seat.

"Your mother? Yes – she is safe. Would you like to see her?'

"Is this a trick?"

"A trick? No! I keep the promises I make, Tarik." Ubaid paused and sat down next to him. Keeping his voice low, he stared into Leo's eyes. "The thing is, Tarik, you do not appear to have kept yours?"

Leo feigned surprise and shrugged his shoulders as if to say he didn't know what Ubaid was talking about. He went to rub his ear but found the usual small swelling to the side of his lobe had gone. Leo rubbed harder and, with a perplexed expression on his face, looked at Ubaid enquiringly.

"Ah yes, the implant below your ear! We have removed it and taken the data from it. Tell me Tarik, or perhaps I should call you Leo, as they do on Earth? Why did you not return the illegal offspring, this Imogen, to us? Your orders were to terminate her should you fail in this mission. You do not appear to have done this either? You haven't grown fond of this subversive-born Falsebred, have you?"

Leo nervously flicked his fringe out of his eyes. "She escaped. The Repros had us both, but she managed to outrun them. That's all there is to it." He looked defiantly at the beady-eyed councillor.

"I see. And your impromptu jump back to Earth after your initial capture? Was this to carry out our orders? Or bring her to us? Or, perhaps it was to save her? Hmmm?"

Leo stared down at his feet and offered no explanation.

"Well, no matter. We have another agent taking care of the girl. But I have another question to which I must have an answer, Leo. We have examined the implant data and there is a rather bizarre inconsistency. It would appear that you have not aged as you should?

Our tests show you should be near your twenty-ninth year, yet you are still only nineteen, or thereabouts."

Again, Leo shrugged his shoulders. "Maybe all those unchecked radio waves on Earth interfered with the aging process?"

"Unlikely," Ubaid answered, leaning closer to Leo and stroking his beard. "And you see, here's a strange phenomenon. The implant appears to be blank for a full ten-year gap. One minute it is recording your moves in the Earth year of 2006, the next it is 2016. Ten years gone in an instant. Perhaps you would like to explain?"

"Well, I would if I could," Leo replied, adding, "Guess they must have frozen me for a while – bit like a fish finger! Oh wait, you don't know what that is…"

"Don't play games with me, Leo," hissed Ubaid as he got to his feet. "Your conversation with this Imogen was also recorded and we know she skipped forty full Earth years. It's the Tractus, is it not? The Tractus is capable of vaulting a person forward in time? This can be the only explanation. Well?"

Leo remained silent.

"I would suggest you cooperate Tarik. Or…"

"Or what?"

"Well, let's just say, it may not be good for your mother."

Leo jumped angrily to his feet. "Is that so? How do I even know if she's alive?"

Ubaid paused for a moment and then signalled for the gateway to be opened.

"Surprise!" he said as two cloaked figures entered, standing either side of a pale blonde-haired older woman. His mother, Sekhet, stared ahead with a vacant look in her eyes. She looked years older than when he had last seen her and Leo rushed to her, opening his arms to embrace her. Sekhet gave him a puzzled look as he advanced and when he reached her she jerked back, a look of confusion on her face.

"Tarik? Is that you? Is it really you?" Before he could reassure her, she slumped to the ground with a sob, wringing her hands crying, "No – it can't be – my Tarik was just a young boy. This is a trick. Where is my son?"

"It's me – I'm here," Leo tried to still her hands, to no avail. He turned to Ubaid angrily. "What have you done to her?"

"I think you should be more worried about what we could do to her," retorted Ubaid.

"Has she been erased?"

"Erased? No, nothing so permanent. Yet!" threatened Ubaid. "You see, Tarik, we had to ensure she didn't talk. A little implant to restrict careless words and prevent any mention of your leaving Holis with your father." Leo looked miserably at his mother, who had curled into a ball on the ground and was whimpering sporadically.

Ubaid continued, "It has the unfortunate side effect of inducing paranoia and despair, but it was a necessary measure to deter her from contacting the subversive movement, in which your father appears to be a major player. I can only say it pains me to see her like this Tarik, but her restoration is entirely in your hands. We must know everything about the subversive bases and the capabilities of the Tractus. You, of course, have a choice: to keep quiet and seal your mother's fate, or to enlighten me. What will it be?"

Leo bent to his mother and tenderly stroked her hair until she finally calmed. He helped her up, gently sitting her on a grassy mound. She glazed over, hugging herself, and Leo turned angrily to Ubaid.

"I can't tell you much. Why? Well, I don't know much! My father didn't exactly confide in me; I barely saw him. And you're right, I skipped ten years in an instant, but I have no idea why or how this was achieved. If it was your precious Tractus, then for all I know it was a freak accident." Leo felt reassuringly secure in the knowledge that even if Ubaid were able to read them, his chromatic flashes of violet untruths were invisible in the current red light of Ib.

"So, I wake up one day and find I've missed ten years, which is kinda why I have no idea where all the other Earth bases are, or what the Tractus can do. Look, I have done as you asked. I led your thugs to Kasmut Akil, didn't I? You have him now. He can give you the answers you require, although without a guarantee for his daughter's safety, you will have little chance of getting these from him. Now please, leave my mother be!"

Ubaid paused and pressed his lips together with his finger and thumb before responding, "You're right, Tarik. Quite right. Kasmut's daughter? Yes, she is the key. You have given me a splendid idea. Thank you. You have no idea how helpful you have been."

Leo looked confused as Ubaid turned away and snapped his fingers for Sekhet to be escorted out of the garden. Turning to Leo one last time, he said, "Oh yes, I should have told you, Tarik. You are to face trial in the Sanctus High Court. I'm afraid you are accused of being a Falsebred and putting the Holan race at risk of contamination from the barbaric people of Earth."

Leo paled.

"Afraid it must have slipped my mind. Still, you have several days to prepare a defence, if you have one. Of course, if you mention anything about your mother's captivity it would not go well for her. I thought it only fair to warn you."

With that, Ubaid turned on his heels and left Leo to fret over his situation.

THE CHRONICLES OF HOLIS - THE LOTUS FESTIVAL

WARNING: those found in possession of these original chronicles will be deemed subversive. It is therefore vital you keep this DE hidden. May the blessings of Ra be upon you.

Barbara.

*T*he festival of the lotus flower happens every third lunar month. A wonderful event, it lasts three days and nights. I can tell you, after three full months of continuous labour and toil, it is a most welcome break. Work stops and everyone celebrates with dancing, feasting, leisurely pastimes, love-bonding and relaxation.

So why the lotus? Well, apart from its outstanding beauty and medicinal properties, it requires great patience and loving care to cultivate this flower in the extreme climates of Holis. It was not a native plant to our world. Just like us! It therefore represents all that is carefully transplanted and nurtured; the symbol of the Holan population. We use the four festivals punctuating our year to celebrate our people, our good fortune and the love of Ra.

~~A quick word about the spiritual beliefs of Holans — there is no formalised religion. Not since the reign of Anubis, one of the most terrible dictators of our history. Although now over five thousand years ago, his persecution of those holding religious beliefs is still remembered with horror. He ostracised those with artistic flare, victimised those with liberal views and wiped out entire segments of the population, just because he didn't agree with them. Barbaric, if ever a word could be applied.~~

~~A long and bloody war ensued and when Anubis was finally overthrown, a universal declaration of the one true spiritual being, Ra, was adopted by the entire race. We all believe in the same power of good; acknowledge our talents and good fortune come from this deity and we are here to serve the purpose of Ra.~~

~~So, we all believe it is the rectitude of Ra permeating the universe and the choice of all lifeforms is to either ignore their creator or tap into this amazing force of goodness. It is not an easily explained or tangible phenomenon, but more a spiritual dimension. Our primeval ancestors worshipped the sun, Ka and whilst it is true this burning star gives us the physical light needed for our very existence, it is without consciousness and utterly unworthy of reverence. We now all accept Ra created the universe and gives us spiritual light, essential for giving our lives truth and meaning.~~

~~A part of our spiritual health~~, the four festivals of the Lotus provide a positive and necessary holiday from the hard work needed to sustain Holis. On the Southern Sea, people fish, in the capital there is dancing and feasting in the central gardens. In recent years, some have even taken to skiing on the high slopes of the North ~~(a pastime introduced from listening to the early sporting broadcasts from the radios of Earth. Of course, this was from the days when we were permitted to tap into the communications from this primitive place. But, as directed, we are no longer at liberty to watch the streams of endless noise from this fledgling planet. The Supreme Council deemed the fascination with Earth to be not only a huge distraction, but an~~

unhealthy influence. To be fair, the reports of constant wars and want did have a most depressing effect on our kind.)

It is also interesting to note the festivals coincide with the quarterly waning of the light of Ib, as the orbit of Holis reaches its furthest distance from this red sun. It is said it is possible to discern the auras of our feelings and emotions at these times of year — to see our Chroma. But as the red light is only reduced for a few days at a time, this is generally considered a questionable talent.

SOUTHERN SEA

*T*he small sea settlement of Qus was a few miles away on foot. The tropical canopy gradually gave way to a rocky stream which they followed down to the edge of the Southern Sea. The walk was therapeutic for Imogen. Not only did her muscles begin to feel normal, her dress kept her cool in the steamy temperature and she calmed as she took in the picturesque environment, full of exotic plants and small creatures. She kept glancing up at the suns in the sky to remind herself she was on another planet.

Araz fell in step with her, eagerly glancing at her face to see her reactions. He nodded proudly each time she gave a smile at the new wonders around her. His concerns about the reception he would get from his commanders were pushed to the back of his mind as he reached to hold Imogen's hand or arm at every possible opportunity. He assisted her over rocks and boulders and mentally thanked their prickly escort for the ridiculously inappropriate clothing she had created for Imogen. He was determined to protect Imogen. There was something extraordinary about her. He could not define it, but she had triggered something deep within him he could not deny. She had saved his life twice, when she could easily have let him die, and despite her ridiculous challenges to his firmly held beliefs, he had realised - at the point when she had nearly died - she must be his soulmate. Until that moment he had dismissed talk of instant bonding as rubbish. But now, now he had a new purpose in life. He would not let her answer for crimes committed by her subversive family and those who had kept her hidden on Earth. She was innocent, of that he was sure. She just needed to be convinced of the impeccable logic of the Holan regime and experience the astonishing wonder of their peaceful lifestyle.

"Em's accent is different to yours?" Imogen ventured to ask as they walked. Em was far ahead and out of earshot.

"She was raised in a… another part of Holis. They have a different dialect."

Imogen thought she could detect a reaction close to a sneer in his reply but did not pursue it further. She decided to stay focussed on her remarkable surroundings as they headed for the village.

Beautiful! The word kept going around and round in Imogen's head as they wandered into Qus. The dwellings along the tree line of the shore looked, at first sight, as if they had grown out of the ground. Canopies of tropical long-leaved trees wound together, the boughs forming the living walls and roofs of numerous dome shaped habitations. The branches and roots growing from the base of the trees and bushes were plaited together, forming wooden boardwalks across the sands before stretching out into the sea as floating piers.

"It takes years," Araz explained proudly as Imogen bent to examine them. "The pathways are living structures we have coaxed into position. We use this method to 'grow' buildings, paths and bridges. The oldest living bridge is in Karnak. Trees, thousands of years old, form the crossing over the main alpine lake. It is stunning."

"The technique is also used on Earth by some remote tribes," Imogen added, remembering a documentary she had seen.

"I doubt there is anything on Earth like this!" Araz sneered.

"Well there's a surprise," she responded sarcastically. "That you doubt anything good could be produced by us primitives!" *Where does he get off!*

"Us?" Araz stared at her incredulously. "You are not one of them!" he spat.

Imogen pursed her lips and turned away. *I'm not one of you either - am I? Just where do I fit in?*

She decided to ignore him and instead marvelled at the beauty of the village. A world without concrete, steel or tarmac; it was extraordinary.

"Where is everyone?" she started to ask when a wave of people, dressed in an array of bright colours, surged out of the largest domed structure and headed towards the sea.

Araz, Em and Imogen watched as hundreds of villagers passed them, laughing and talking loudly. Many gave a nod of the head by way of greeting, whilst others waved and smiled their way. As instructed, Imogen gave no outward sign she was completely new to the activities. Automatically cloaking her colours, even if they could not be seen, no one paid her any untoward attention and she realised her apprehension was unfounded. Feeling more relaxed, she concentrated on observing 'her kind' from a safe distance.

It was not immediately obvious from their outfits who were men and who were women. Skirts, shorts, tunics, trousers and gowns appeared to be worn arbitrarily and were fashioned differently on each person. Shaped into stylish and flamboyant garments, the Flecto lit up with the colours of the sand, sea, palm trees and sky as they moved. This, with the volume of happy chatter, intermingled with excited shouts, gave the mood a bright and distinct carnival feel.

Some of the adults and youths launched small boats into the water from the end of the floating walkways. They rowed the vessels out a short distance from the shore and began beating their paddles into the sea. Imogen watched in fascination as large shoals of silvery fish were gradually herded into the shallow waters. Children ran and played in the water, catching the fish and placing them into reed baskets until they were full to overflowing. It was a team effort involving every age group.

Imogen noted the differences between the Holan people before her and the inhabitants of Earth. Numerous shades of skin colour were apparent, no single one predominant, and whilst no one here could be classed as stick-thin or obese, there were all shapes and sizes. Hair was worn in a variety of styles, from bald to long and flowing, to pinned back and cropped. No one appeared to have any visible infirmities and the elderly people in the group, only evident by their lined faces and silvery hair, seemed almost as sprightly as the youngsters.

The smallest of the children threw off their garments to swim naked amongst the fish, squealing with delight. Imogen was alarmed to see some infants, barely walking, were teetering their way into the gentle lapping water, unsupervised. Startled, Imogen instinctively went to rush forward to protect a grinning baby who had crawled head first into the ocean. Em stopped her with a laugh. "Look!"

A wave washed over the tiny boy and Imogen held her breath. To her amazement, he merely re-surfaced, turned on his back and began splashing and making swimming movements. An older child spotted him and stooped to gather him up into his arms. The lad, who only looked five or six years, put the baby on his hip before setting off in the water to catch more fish.

"Good job his brother was there," exclaimed Imogen in relief.

"Probably not brother," Em replied. "Few families have more than one childrens."

Before Imogen could ask more, Araz intervened.

"Each infant has someone ascribed to look after them, to teach them skills like swimming. The carers change each day. One day the responsibility is given to another child but often it is the job of an elder or a parent. Everyone plays a part in upbringing."

"Aren't they worried about creeps?"

"This is not like Earth," was Araz's insulted response. "There are no creeps on Holis!"

"Matter of opinions!" retorted Em, as she turned to Imogen. "I like this word – creep!" Em's remark was accompanied with a piercing look directed at Araz, who glared back.

The boats came back into shore and the fish-filled baskets were passed to those on the sands. One was thrust into Imogen's arms and she followed Em and Araz's lead as they took the catch to a large cart outside a palm-covered arena. Most of the fish were then packed up into wicker boxes, whilst some were prepared for cooking.

The whole community joined in, including Araz, whilst Em went to sort out their sleeping quarters. Imogen soon picked up what was required and the villagers chatted happily to each other as they worked. Imogen processed the conversations around her, her comprehension improving by the minute. She would just smile back when asked a question, rather than risking saying the wrong thing. Araz covered up for her and if an answer was demanded, he implied Imogen was merely shy. This was respected and the locals made nothing of it.

With the fish prepared and packed, a call was put out for anyone who could play a lute, to come forward. To Imogen's surprise, Araz took one of the instruments – a form of a guitar - and began to play with several others as a young boy started to sing.

Em reappeared and settled on the warm sands with Imogen and the others. They listened to the melodies, one after another. The locals swayed in time with the rhythms.

"Is all old songs," Em commented. "Not have new composers in years."

"Why?"

"No artistic Holans anymore," Em shrugged.

She means those born with the dominant line of Iris. Tanastra said it was being phased out. Why?

Imogen studied Araz. He had closed his eyes as he played. Unable to observe his Chroma, it was still obvious how the music affected him. *He's clearly got a strong artistic side, so perhaps Iris is his dominant line?*

Araz seemed to lose himself in the tunes as he had at Chrissie's party barely a month ago. She thought back to how her life had changed since that fateful day. *I was blissfully unaware of why I was so different. Would I want to rewind, and go back?* She deliberated as the melodious notes permeated the air. *No! I need to find out where I belong.*

An elderly woman stood and requested a song. The crowd gave a low murmur of disapproval and most of the musicians looked awkwardly at each other, putting down their lutes and shaking their heads. Araz, however, glanced over at Imogen to see her admiring gaze. He nodded and began to play a melancholy tune.

The woman started to sing. Her voice was so clear and soft, it reminded Imogen of a choirboy she had once heard. The words were full of sorrow and soon echoed by other voices gradually joining in. More took up the song as it was repeated. Many added harmonies, some hauntingly discordant. The lament reverberated around the seated crowd. The sentiment resonated in the depths of her mind, as the lyrics struck a chord with her sense of not knowing where she belonged.

"The ages pass, as we await, return to a home so far.

We thirst for pastures, near forgot, we await your sign, oh Ra.

Restore to us our homeland, from limits, set us free.

Make your face to shine on Ankh once more and hear our heartfelt plea."

When the song finally stopped there was a marked silence. The only sound, the gentle lapping of waves.

Imogen self-consciously wiped a tear from her eye and looked around to find many were doing the same, although a number looked troubled and awkward. *Why should this song have such an effect?* Her inability to see their chromatic responses added to her bewilderment.

The reverie was broken when a loud gong sounded. The citizens of Qus all rose to their feet and surged towards the arena. Imogen was swept up in the crowds as they headed to the palm covered space. It was filled with seats, sculpted in hardened sand and arranged in groups. These, in turn, were placed all the way round a centrally raised stage.

Teams of people were serving meals from several clay ovens at the periphery of the area. The crowds spread out to be served. Imogen was surprised to see small children involved in the process but remembered Adam telling her everyone took turns with all general tasks. Appetising aromas filled the air and Imogen realised her stomach was rumbling.

She turned to look for Em or Araz, suddenly aware they had become separated, when a small girl grabbed her hand and pulled her across to the furthest most serving point, with fewer people. She tried to resist, but the girl was insistent.

"Come - try my friend's kushari – it's the best!"

Not wanting to cause a scene, Imogen complied. The child almost ran with her, grabbing the hand of an older looking man as they passed him. He willingly let the girl lead, joining in the near run and smiling broadly at Imogen as they jogged. Although disconcerted to find complete strangers engaging with her, Imogen could not fail but warm to the open and friendly community. She realised here she was accepted without question and she began to feel safe.

When they got to the large steaming cooking pot, the girl pushed them both forward, giggling as she called to a wide-eyed boy, who could be no more than six, and who had to stand on a raised step to reach into the container.

"Aly – come – these people want to eat your kushari!"

Imogen watched as the older man picked what looked like a large leaf, from the top of an adjacent bushy structure. To her surprise, he moulded it into a deep bowl shape and gave it to Aly, who spooned a mix of fragrant smelling rice, vegetables and pulses into the dish. The boy then nodded eagerly to Imogen and indicated the next 'leaf'. She went to touch it when her hand was suddenly grasped and pushed back against her side. Her stomach temporarily lurched, but it was with relief she realised the hand belonged to Em. Smiling widely to those around her, Em's eyes communicated a sharp warning to Imogen as she stood in front of her and removed the leaf herself. She shaped it as the man had done and handed it to the boy to be filled.

"Tasty," she told the boy after trying a small morsel with her fingers. "Is good!" Aly beamed proudly as Em steered Imogen away to a quiet seat further round the arena.

Em's expression changed instantly, once she was sure no one was observing them. "Not touch salver!"

Imogen looked blank.

"Leaf for food, is 'Salver'. Is only released if crypts known. Your what-you-call? Ah yes! Your 'DNA'. Is not yet in hub. So, is dangerous. Must give more care!"

Imogen blinked as Em handed her the plate of food. She hesitated.

"Take! Is safe. Is released. Only problem for you if touch when on plant. My crypts logged. Now eat!"

Imogen sheepishly took the bowl and watched how others were eating. She followed suit and dipped her fingers into the rice mix, gingerly trying a small amount. It was light and delicately flavoured. Hunger pangs meant she was soon eating quickly, listening to Em as she explained a few other 'do's and don'ts' of communal dining.

Araz, who had been searching the arena for them, sprang across to their seats. Anxiety, close to anger, was written all over his face.

"Where did you go?" He looked at the remnants of her meal. "Tell me, you didn't get the food yourself?"

Em responded first. "Manage fine. No thanks you!" she glared back at him.

"You were supposed to stay with me," he hissed at Imogen.

"Sorry," she mumbled. "I guess I let my guard down."

"Is good expression," Em mused. "Must keep guard up for words and movements. More so in Karnak. Is dangerous place."

Araz went to say something in response, but checked himself and, seeing Imogen had cleared her plate, bid her stay still while he got more food. After eating a salver of freshly cooked fish and finishing with an exotic fruit dish, made with something close to pineapple, they all sat watching the villagers. Toddlers ran around collecting the 'plates', returning them to a central container, and boys and girls danced on the stage.

Eventually, a black-cloaked figure took to the platform, shooing the children back to their places.

"Is announcement," whispered Em. "Perhaps hear more of friends?"

Imogen pricked up her ears.

The official began by thanking everyone for their work since the last festival. She congratulated them on the unusually large catch of fish, explaining most would be sent to Karnak for the people of the capital to share. As she continued Imogen was relieved to find deciphering the Holan language was becoming second nature to her, but the next words made her heart sink.

"Fellow citizens, you will recall from the last festival, Her Greatness, Kekara, informed us of the Tractus Project, a proposed instantaneous transport system allowing us to jump back and forth to Ankh."

I thought it was a secret?

Imogen glanced at Araz. He also looked surprised to hear the Tractus being named but said nothing.

If only I could see his colours.

The audience around them rippled with excited comments, such as, 'Imagine, a direct link to Ankh!', 'Amazing concept!' and 'Wondrous'.

When the response died down, the official continued, "You will also recall, it was decided to restrict the development of the Tractus, its use being potentially hazardous to all life." Imogen caught words like 'understandable' and 'perilous' being voiced, as she gave an involuntary shudder at the thought of being catapulted forward in time.

"The Tractus project was one of the most complex to be undertaken since the Elysian Scheme. It had been the vision of the great Tanastra Thut, whom we still mourn after his sudden death some seventy years ago." The arena rang with heartfelt reactions, such as 'horrific tragedy' and 'terrible loss'.

Imogen could not fail but see the reverence in which Tanastra had been held. None of them knew he had feigned his death and escaped to Earth. *Or that he had only died a few weeks ago, to save me!* Memories of his sacrifice for her flooded into her mind as the official continued.

"The project was then entrusted to our most eminent scientists as work continued to complete this incredible device and test it under the most rigorous safety measures. Citizens, I am afraid it is my sorry duty to inform you of a heinous crime. A foolish youth, whose name we now know to be Tarik Zuberi, has illegally used the prototype.

Furthermore, he used it to make contact with the far-off planet of Earth."

There were shocked murmurs throughout the arena as the words 'Earth' and 'Zuberi' were repeated with horror. Imogen looked at Araz whose expression was unreadable.

They're blaming Leo! No mention of my mum or dad. Why?

"As you know, the Sanctus High Court has declared the primitives of Earth to be a self-gratifying and dangerous race. These humans wield power, technology and weaponry without caution or consideration. Communication, let alone contact with these primal beings has, quite rightly, been forbidden. The Supreme Council ruled these savages must never find out about Holis. We have cloaked our presence in the galaxy so even their most sophisticated astronomical techniques cannot detect our home. It is therefore with a heavy heart, I must tell you the actions of this irresponsible man, also thought to be a Falsebred..." The official deliberately paused, to allow a disapproving murmur to swell, before raising her hand for quiet.

"This Falsebred has endangered us all. It is feared the barbaric people of Earth now have a means of jumping to our home and threatening our very existence."

Cries of 'No!' could be heard as many stood up shouting protests. A small boy started to cry. The official put her hands up in the air and called for calm.

Imogen felt at such a disadvantage. *If only I could see her Chroma! I might see if she believes this pack of lies.*

"It is the wholehearted desire of the Supreme Council to protect the Holan race and to this end measures will be put into place to ensure no primitive will ever put a foot on Holis ground. It is imperative we now guard our cities and villages. For this purpose, a number of constructs have been engineered for your protection. They will watch for any signs of an invasion."

Em swore under her breath, "Vlag!"

Imogen turned to her and mouthed 'Repros?'

Em nodded a disgusted affirmation. Imogen swallowed hard.

"These guardians will arrive in this area at the close of the Lotus festival. Your normal lives will not change, however you must all be vigilant. If you observe any unusual or suspect behaviour, this must be reported to the authorities. As for the Falsebred, his trial will take place in four days' time. How should we respond to those who imperil our lives? Should one person be allowed to jeopardise the good of the entire race? I remind you, particularly those who have recently come of age, you are directed to vote at the Sanctus High Court to decide on Tarik Zuberi's fate. You all know your responsibilities." The crowd mumbled affirmation.

So much for a fair trial! Imogen would have clenched both fists had her scar not prevented her right hand from doing so.

"Her Greatness, Kekara, wishes to reassure you, this must not cause undue alarm. The festival period is a time for rest and celebration. We will not allow the barbarism of Earthkind to destroy our peace and wellbeing. May the blessings of Ra be upon you."

The crowd repeated the blessing in noticeably subdued voices and started to disperse as the sky began to darken. Imogen got up to follow Em and Araz to the dwellings on the shoreline and spoke in a low whisper to Em.

"What will they do to him, if he is found guilty?" She rubbed subconsciously at the cloth covering the scar on her hand as they walked.

"Is choice, termination or erasure."

Some choice! "Can we do anything?"

Em shrugged her shoulders and Araz turned his head away to avoid eye contact with her.

"Is good for this Tarik. Good trial not in Sanctus High Court. This better than secret court. Here only small few have power to pass sentence. Is rumoured they terminated two of our peoples in recent weeks. No one know for sure. Is classified."

Imogen shivered; the meal she had just eaten was beginning to feel like lead in her stomach.

"She didn't mention my dad? You don't think he's..." She could not finish the sentence. When no one spoke, Imogen came to a standstill and started to hug herself. *What if he's been executed?* Her sense of helplessness threatened to swamp her, but she steadfastly refused to succumb to despair. *He has to be alive! I have to try and find him and help Leo. But where the hell do I start?*

Araz also stopped, took her arm gently and put a finger to his lips before touching it to her mouth. "Come," he urged quietly.

Following in Em's footsteps, they walked in silence, Imogen forcing herself to remain calm. The locals talked in downcast tones as groups peeled off to enter different domes.

Araz stopped at the edge of the sea to point to the 'sunset'.

Imogen took a double take. The outline of a large black globe advanced over the sky, gradually eclipsing the light of Ka. As the dark planet moved, the light dulled to a glowing corona around the edges of the spherical body, before disappearing. Only the red glow of Ib remained and the temperature suddenly dropped.

"We call it 'Atma', the 'small death' or darkening of the sky," Araz murmured.

It was like nothing on Earth. Imogen blinked. *This is so alien.* The stars sprang into view. A thought struck her. Even if she could discern the direction of Earth, she would be looking at the planet of twenty years ago, the time it took for the light to reach Holis. *Twenty years ago, I was lost in time.* She shuddered. Her sense of safety began to subside.

Em grabbed Imogen's arm, as much as a gesture of reassurance as to hurry her along. "Cannot survive outside at night-time. Is too cold. Come." She led them to a far dome entrance, the one with the least number of people.

The space inside was warm and lit by what looked like starlight. Despite her worries, Imogen marvelled at the clever lighting. Em explained the effect was from the glow generated by the planet's organic power source, similar to Earth's electricity.

They crossed the mossy floor which led to a labyrinth of separate chambers. Imogen looked around and could see all the walls and floors were formed by trees, rising to several levels. The trunks branched out into steps and walkways reaching up to openings carved into rock, the corridors beyond lined with leaves.

It's like a magical treehouse!

The Holans, some with children and babies, all stopped at different points of the living walls. Imogen watched, fascinated, as they pressed their hands to the centre of each access area. The 'door' area of the wall opened like the eye of a chameleon, as the material quivered, liquified and separated. Half moved up as the other half moved down, revealing the chambers within. Once the families had gone inside, the door appeared to re-grow back in place.

"Phase-Seal," Em said in a low voice. "Door is part-plant. Has phases of liquid and solid. Will open or seal room. Not touch, crypt-activated. Okay?"

Imogen nodded briefly, keeping her hands close to her body.

They climbed up the steps to a higher level and Em indicated one of the entrances. Araz pressed his hand against the Phase-Seal which 'melted' at his touch. Indicating for Imogen to go in, he turned to block Em's way. She hesitated before determinedly pushing past him. Araz glared at her back as she addressed Imogen and, unseen by him, held up her open hand close to her body, her fingers splayed.

She wants to tell me something by fingertip.

"Worry - is bad. Sleep while can. I leave now. How you say: 'meeting you was good', on Earth?"

Imogen smiled, "We shake hands!" She and Em then gave, what looked like, a clumsy handshake, but this allowed them a glancing touch of fingertips.

'DE in bed – your eyes only,' came the cognitive message, with a background of thoughts about her attraction to Imogen, which would normally have triggered a deep blush had Imogen not quelled all responses. Araz must not know they had communicated.

Em left without a backward glance. Araz closed the entrance, sighed loudly and crossed to Imogen. He stood in front of her, his eyes searching hers.

She realised, with relief, he had not seen the exchange and the reason for his look was one of longing. Her misgivings and worries spiked, her predicament was overwhelming. But despite this, she knew she wanted nothing more than to be in his arms. She needed comfort, reassurance and, as she saw in that moment, his love.

As if he read her mind, Araz first held her shoulders then pulled her close to him. Holding her firmly, he tilted back her head, murmuring the words, "At last we are alone, my light." The words ignited her entire being and he leaned closer until their lips touched. Gentle at first, the kiss grew in intensity as each mouth hungrily sought the other. Stress drained away and Imogen felt her heart flame as powerful surges coursed through her frame. Time seemed to stand still as they remained locked in a passionate embrace, his hands lightly tracing her body contours, her fingers running through his hair. Imogen breathed in his aroma and tingled at every point of contact. She let her colours of desire soar and flutter freely, appreciative she had finally found one advantage to Chroma being invisible.

For those precious moments nothing else seemed important. Albeit briefly, she felt more alive than she had ever done before. In his arms she was safe. *If only it was like this all the time.* She eventually broke the kiss, lowered her head, moved her hands to his shoulders and pulled back, smiling self-consciously.

"Come, see our rooms." Araz's voice, deep with longing, sent a further shudder through her body. He lightly kissed the side of her neck and then took her hand.

He walked her around the chambers carved into the rock. Imogen forced herself to concentrate on the rooms, happy to have Araz's strong hand firmly locked into hers.

The quarters were festooned in flowers and foliage, which grew to form both carpet and wall coverings. The bedrooms had one wall without vegetation, and, like the doors, it was made of a shimmering liquid texture. *These are where the transmissions from Karnak are shown,* she remembered from another tutorial with Adam. The rooms were far more beautiful than he had described. The vision wall, now showing the sparkling night sky outside, complete with shimmers of light and in holographic detail, looked amazingly similar to the Northern Lights on Earth. It gave the impression the room was in the open air and a much larger space. This, with the lush greenery, made her feel as if she had been transported to a fairy-tale land. She was puzzled there did not seem to be beds, but the floor was springier in the centre of the room, so Imogen assumed this was for sleep.

Where is the DE Em told me about?

The bathroom, thankfully, had a separate entrance and was similar to those on Earth with a raised sort of rock pedestal, covered in soft lichen. It was linked to a water source branching off into a natural basin made from a huge rubbery leaf. No shower or bath, but Adam had told her these were communal facilities. She guessed they were elsewhere on the site, unless they bathed in the Southern Sea.

"You should get some sleep," Araz murmured close to her ear, making her squirm inside. "I will sleep in the other room, unless…" the unspoken question hung in the air and Imogen gave a small shake of her head as she reached up to kiss him briefly on the cheek.

"I need the bathroom. And I need my bed, wherever it is!"

"Your bed is here," Araz touched a glowing leaf she had not noticed before, and part of the floor slowly sprang up into a hollowed-out mound, bath-shaped.

"It is something like a hammock on Earth, only far superior."

"Well, it would be!" Imogen rolled her eyes to heaven.

Araz pursed his lips but could not hide the start of a smile behind his eyes. "You will see. Oh yes, our escort insisted this room was yours. She fashioned you some night attire over there." Araz sneered towards the light Flecto bodysuit, draped over the side.

"I will bid you good night. Tomorrow we must prepare for Karnak." He brushed her lips with his fingers and left.

Imogen, close to calling him back, gave a sigh and shiver and forced her mind back to more pressing matters.

Returning from the bathroom, Imogen searched the light bodysuit Em had made. Enfolded inside a hidden pocket was the Data Encounter.

She sank into the bed which, to her delight, gently massaged her tired body with subtle, undulating movements. She closed her eyes and connected to the device.

The opening warning from 'Barbara' was stark. The chronicles were the original ones, full of information the Supreme Council now deemed subversive. She must not be caught with them.

The young voice of Tanastra, Father Jonathan, from seventy years earlier - now so familiar from the chronicles he had left her on Earth - flowed into her mind. His tone was one of optimism and pride as the history and background of the Holan race was laid out before her. This world had appeared, to all intents and purposes, perfect. Solutions to every problem had been developed and every person was valued.

What changed to make everything go so wrong?

Imogen concentrated on the information as the hours passed. *The explanation must be hidden in the deletions.* She trawled her memory for everything she had learnt so far, trying to fit the pieces of the puzzle together. However, try as she could, she couldn't make the connections and the answers eluded her.

Dwelling on the events of the last weeks, Imogen's mind was besieged with images, her childhood nightmare, her mother's awakening only to be paralysed with anxiety, the discovery of the five hidden marks on her body, the brutality of the Repros, Father Jonathan dying in front of her and her father and Leo's capture. Silent tears welled up and ran, unbidden, down her face. *I must uncover the truth,* she vowed. *No more secrets.* She replaced the DE in the pocket of her bodysuit, but despite her exhaustion and the caress of the responsive bed, sleep was a long time coming.

NAOMI

Some weeks earlier, two new recruits to the Supreme Council were being given a tour of the restricted areas of the government complex as part of their induction. Walking through the labyrinth of underground tunnels, hewn from rock, they were each accompanied by an established councillor. The fresh-faced Horus, who looked much younger than seventeen and highly nervous, was with the burly, bald Vizier of Stability, Odion. Naomi, the same age as Horus, but contrastingly serene in manner, was with Merit, an elegant lady of later years and the Vizier of Enlightenment.

Horus stood to attention almost the entire time, giving a formal nod of his head to Odion each time he was questioned. Naomi got the distinct impression Horus was terrified of Odion and, whilst she could easily understand why (Odion treated everyone, apart from Kekara, with disdain), she refused to be intimidated by one such as him. He was not even a Bi-Crypt. At least her sponsor, Merit, was a Tri-Crypt like herself and the female Vizier spoke to her as an equal and with respect.

"This next area," explained Odion stiffly, activating a closed door in the underground corridor, "is the research facility of our defence division. Do not touch anything. You will see our technicians are protected by masks and skin barriers."

Naomi stared at the team of workers, all clad in over-garments, their faces covered by transparent masks. She and Horus were handed similar outfits to seal over their own.

"What's wrong with them?" Naomi whispered to Horus. "Their eyes are glazed and they're not talking at all."

"Zeroids!" responded Horus, glancing anxiously back to Odion, to check he had not been heard. "They've all been erased!"

Naomi looked again at the nearest workers. She had wondered what happened to those who chose this form of punishment instead of termination. Their faces were blank, eyes soulless, and they appeared to do things by rote. If it were not for the fact they were flesh and blood, they could have been automatons. She shuddered inwardly, thinking it would be better to be terminated than to be rendered a shell, blindly following orders with no ability to remember anything other than the task in hand.

Once they were all in the protective clothing, the tour continued.

Merit began the commentary, "The development of toxins to break down our body's defence cells, was recently authorised as a direct result of the threat from Earth."

Naomi raised an eyebrow but Merit did not elaborate. Naomi was puzzled. Having specialised in Earth studies, she knew there was no evidence humans had discovered their segment of the galaxy, let alone Holis. She resolved to find out more when she spoke to her mentor later in the day.

Merit continued, "We have blended a toxin, 'Expirite', the strength of which is such that the tiniest amount will be lethal to both primitives and, of course, Holans. We have no natural defence against this poison. The antidote is prepared at the same time," she indicated an adjoining laboratory.

"Will it work on humans too?" asked Naomi.

Odion bristled as Horus visibly tensed at the audacity of the question.

"An antidote for the barbaric race of Earth?" Odion poured contempt into his words.

Naomi turned to look only at Merit, studiously ignoring Odion, who sported an expression of infuriation.

"I doubt it," answered Merit, her amusement at Odion's fury apparent in a slight upturn of her mouth. "The antidote is devised to trigger additional curative stem cells in our bodies. Once it has been administered, there will be a lifelong immunity to Expirite. The primitives of Earth have an inferior genetic make-up, so for them there would be no cure."

Naomi nodded understanding although she wanted to find out more. The quantity of poison being produced was enormous considering only a small dose was needed to kill. Her questions would have to wait.

She and Horus were given a Data Encounter each. Once connected they swiftly assimilated the technical information and formulae of the poison and the cure. Discarding their outer garments, they left the research facility and followed the Viziers deep underground.

Odion stopped at the rock face at the end of the passage. He removed a chain from around his neck and took the arrow shaped pendant hanging in the centre.

Naomi recognised it as the official chain of office. Each Vizier had their own chain, adorned with one of the five symbols representing their council.

Odion pressed the tip of the arrow into a small indent in the wall. It sparked as the electro-chemical key was activated. A split in the centre of the rock face appeared before dividing and melting open to admit them.

The air was cool and their eyes had to adjust to the semi-dark. A vast cavernous room, it was lined with blocks of long casket shaped containers, standing upright along the walls. They were stacked high, and all connected to an organic energy supply, linking each one to the next.

Looking closer, Naomi saw the caskets contained the constructs. These had, hitherto, only been seen in the restricted areas in the central hub. She took in a sharp intake of breath as the scale of the operation became apparent. There were so many of them! All seemingly asleep in the dim red light of the facility. Only a handful of

Holans had seen these Repros close up, their existence being a secret outside of the Supreme Council until recently. Acutely aware this was privileged information and the rest of the Holan race knew little of the project, she was anxious to find out more.

Seeking permission from Merit, Naomi crossed to stare at the nearest figure. Tall, thickset and indescribably ugly, its eyes were closed and it appeared to breathe, albeit very slowly. It reminded her of something she had seen in her studies of Earth.

Odion explained the 'Repros' were held in a state of suspended animation. A glance around the massive space told her there were close to thirty thousand. This must be the best-kept secret ever, she thought, intrigued as to their composition.

"They look organic, not robotic," Naomi observed, reaching up to touch the squashed face. The texture felt rubbery but was smothered in large pores and was slightly clammy. It was more like flesh than the natural latex used in the industrial androids constructed for menial tasks. It made her shiver inside. Her memory banks retrieved the name 'Neanderthal' and she could see the similarity between the beings, although the demeanour of the human ancestors was short and stooped, not tall and upright like these specimens.

"How was this achieved?" she asked.

"You are not authorised to access that information," sneered Odion, a self-satisfied look on his face.

"Only the Viziers and Her Greatness are privy to the finer details of this project," added Merit, slightly apologetic. "However, you may like to see them in action?"

Before Naomi could nod agreement, Odion gave a flick of his arrow pendant and the Repro in front of her opened its eyes. Slightly sunken and blood red, the eyes stared wildly at her as it lurched clumsily forward, its hands ready to grab her by the throat. Naomi reacted quickly and side-stepped out of the way, heart thudding in her chest.

Merit glared at Odion and took out her own pendant – a solid circle - and quickly pressed the centre. The Repro instantly stopped dead and closed its eyes.

"It's huge!" exclaimed Horus. His eyes were wide in fright. The creature in front of them was immobile but Horus was careful to keep his distance from it.

Naomi nodded appreciation to Merit as the Repro was sent backwards into its casket.

Merit took up the explanation, "Each Repro has an implant behind its ear. This enables us to control where they go, what they do and what they say. They will also respond to your orders when you are made full council members in a few weeks' time."

Naomi, feeling intuitively uneasy, was unsure she wanted anything to do with these creatures.

"Let me demonstrate," Merit said, with the emphasis on 'me'. Moving her hand over the perimeter of her locket, she activated four Repros further down the room. They stepped out into the central space, each taking up a large weapon like a sword. They proceeded to fight in pairs, the blades clashing, sending sparks flying. The forces used were enormous, more than capable of slicing a person in two, but the Repros were skilled enough to duck and dive to avoid injury. Loud grunts and cries of effort rang out, echoed by the stone walls. After twenty minutes of ferocious fighting, the Repros began to slow, one suddenly dropped to its knees, screaming. A large cut was carved into its leg. Looking on in horror, Naomi was sure she saw blood. Odion stopped the duels, technicians appeared to tend to the injured Repro, and a screen dropped down preventing them from seeing more.

"As you can see, they are most effective," Odion's sneering comment appeared to contain a warning and Naomi swallowed hard.

Lethal, she thought with a shudder, knowing she would not want to face such an adversary. Another part of her mind was baffled as to why mechanical constructs should tire, or bleed. These were not androids.

"How are they powered?" she asked.

"They are fed by the organic connections in each casket and the slow release nutriments means they can go for days without a recharge. They have been controlled... I mean, engineered, to look and act like carbon-based lifeforms." Merit added, looking away.

This doesn't add up, thought Naomi, who persisted with her questioning. "Why are their eyes so red?"

"They do not have a Tarsus filter. Their eyes have evolved to see the world better by the light of Ib..." started Merit.

"Evolved?"

"You ask too many questions!" spat Odion, angrily.

Naomi felt deeply uncomfortable and began to suspect there was a lot more to these Repros than they were being told. Yet more to ask her mentor later.

"How do they see in white light?" she found herself blurting out, to the annoyance of Odion.

"Helmets," Merit explained. "They act as a reverse Tarsus filter. They are helmeted when the light of Ka is at its strongest and can see quite adequately with these. In fact, they have been successfully tested in the light on Earth."

"Really?" Naomi asked in amazement. "They've been sent to Earth? So, the rumours about the Tractus are true?"

Odion went to say something, but Merit got there first.

"She can know, Odion. The Council have started to advise the entire populace about the status of the project. Besides, Naomi will be invaluable in the Tractus research, given her specialism in Earth studies."

Odion grunted in clear disagreement.

"So, to conclude our tour," Merit began, putting a stop to further comments. "The Supreme Council have been forced to take measures to protect Holis. With the threat of a possible invasion from Earth and given our long-standing policy not to possess automatic weaponry, a defence plan had to be drawn up. The use of Repros and poison should, hopefully, not be necessary, but at least we are ready to defend ourselves."

Later, Naomi spoke to her mentor in private. Despite having seen him on a frequent basis throughout her childhood, she still did not feel fully relaxed in his presence. Some indefinable barrier prevented her from being completely open with him.

After listening to her report of her induction, he would give no further information on the Expirite or the Repro projects. All he would do was confirm the Repros had been tested on Earth.

"I should like to visit Earth," Naomi mused, adding, "if it is allowed. I have studied it for so long, I am now curious to see these primitive people."

"Only a handful of our agents have been to the planet," was his response. "The risks are huge, and some have not returned. It is a dangerous place. However, there may be opportunities in the future, for the right person."

As Naomi began to give an excited response, her mentor stopped her.

"Naomi, I need you for an assignment. It is top-secret and it could involve you using your Earth knowledge."

"What assignment?"

"We have a prisoner. Very obstinate. He is withholding key information about the Tractus project. I am sure you could help us ascertain the facts. You will need a full briefing."

"Of course," Naomi responded, both delighted to be considered suitable for a secret mission and intrigued as to what it could involve.

"Come to my quarters in the morning, and we will speak further. Thank you, Naomi. I am sure you will be a most valued member of our Supreme Council."

"You're welcome," was her response, "and thank you, Ubaid."

THE CHRONICLES OF HOLIS - A DAY IN THE LIFE OF A HOLAN.

WARNING: Deletions and additions have been made to the following chapter of these chronicles. These are clearly marked. Remember, those found in possession of these original chronicles will be deemed subversive, it is therefore vital you keep this DE hidden. May the blessings of Ra be upon you.

Barbara.

*I*t occurs to me the pattern of our regular everyday lives may be something of a mystery to those of you who have not experienced it. So, please allow me to give you a picture of how it all works.

The first point to make is there is no such thing as regular! Our lives are not dominated by the same humdrum repetition of events, day in, day out. No, we prize variety and new experiences! Regardless of personality line, each Holan needs to have an awareness of how our planet functions and how to sustain our existence.

From infancy, children are shown the mechanics of our power generation, how water is purified, the production of food and so forth. This is not according to age, but to how quickly a child will assimilate new information. Once ready, they will be given hands-on experience in every single area of Holan life. This is intermingled with theoretical and practical lessons in astrology, cooking, physics, swimming, biology… in fact, you name it and it will be included! There is no such entity as a central school – far too prescriptive! Teaching is 'in the field' and tailored entirely to the individual. Each Holan child is a polymath; that is, they are educated in numerous subjects and specialisms. This allows each individual to develop their innate talents in a way both beneficial to Holan society and also satisfying their needs for growth and development. They are taught drills and self-discipline to ensure they remain in the best physical and mental health.

By the time they have come of age, every Holan knows how to: set bones, cook meals, construct homes, cultivate plants, mathematically model simple engineering projects (such as our underground transport system) and understand basic genetic precision techniques. They will have numerous proficiencies. Most importantly, each will know they have the capacity to learn any new skill – they merely need to access the data in our amazing libraries to assimilate the necessary knowledge and training.

So, how does it work? Who will tend to the land, assist in research projects, deliver new babies, repair our buildings? Upon waking, we each connect with the central Hub computers, usually from the libraries – although I am told the new Data Encounters will be available on an individual basis for this purpose in the very near future. The tasks and experiences for the day ahead, generated by our powerful organic computers in Karnak, are laid out for all to see, and we ~~choose~~ are allocated which ~~we would like~~ to do.

One day I may be showing youngsters how to plait the roots of trees to grow walkways or demonstrating how we culture the organic Flecto material we use for clothing. Another day, I may join a team to excavate a new tunnel for our transport system or create additional geo-thermal bathing centres. I could be advising on astrological phenomena – a deep-seated love of mine - or I could be harvesting peppers or cooking a meal for our local community.

~~Last week I led a research session to share ideas on how to develop an instantaneous transporter system – one capable of folding space itself and safely landing a person in a completely different part of the universe! I was so inspired by this project I intend to continue with this research once these chronicles are complete. Imagine being able to jump to and from Ankh! The work we could do to speed up the cleaning of our true home. A longing we all share.~~

The reward for taking part in every aspect of our planetary lives is everything you could ever need in life: shelter, sustenance, companionship (for the majority, a bonding of love), interest, security, a sense of well-being and fulfilment. None of these are dependent on who you are or where you were born. Equality underpins our society. There is no ownership or monetary system, as used to exist on Ankh. Why should there be? This only leads to greed and corruption. We are all entitled to the fruits of our combined efforts.

If people achieve a high status in our society, it is because they deserve it. Pioneers in research and innovation, those serving on the Supreme Council, those who help improve our lifestyles, these are the Holans who are, quite rightly, accorded honour and distinction.

Of course, Holans have a long lifespan. In fact, this improves almost daily with the marvellous advances in our genetic resilience. The Holan life does not need to be rushed, and whilst underpinned with complex upbringing and training, it is, essentially, a simple life. We love the open air and have few forms of mechanised transport, preferring to use our feet!

Technological devices like robots, are used only for mundane, monotonous or dangerous tasks, or where absolutely essential. Yes, it is possible to use communicators to talk to others and never leave our dwellings, but we prefer to be out and about and converse face-to-face.

Holans do not have many, if any, possessions. No one owns land or buildings or any part of our globe. All resources are Ra-given;

they are communal and shared by all <u>citizens</u>. We are the custodians of our world and everything in it. This sense is engraved on each of our hearts from the outset.

~~You must wonder, are there ever any problems with this system of upbringing? Of course, every now and again there may be the odd little one who needs a different approach. One could say, the wonder of us all being individuals. These rare children are often the most artistic of our race — though not always — they can be more temperamental or challenging than their peers. However, with sensitive nurturing, their progression can be adjusted to suit their needs. The benefit of adapting the programmes can be huge. I can think of one such unusual youngster who initiated the development of the new Data Encounters. Marvellous devices! She had great artistic flare requiring channelling in the right direction.~~

In conclusion, our race has adapted a fool proof system of refining our basic nature and nurturing accordingly. A blueprint indeed for all Ra-kind. The basis for peace and happiness. Long may it continue!

END OF FESTIVITIES

*I*t was time to set off for Karnak. Imogen took a last look around her sleeping quarters which had become home for the last three days. She would miss this place of refuge and safety. Her forced stop in Qus had allowed her to absorb information about her planet and learn how Holans went about their daily tasks. For that she was grateful, but her anxieties had increased with no further word about Leo and no news of her dad.

She had spent her time either joining in the festivities, or, whenever possible, studying in the incredible coral library. This submerged dome, accessed by a tunnel leading deep under the sea, was like being in a massive goldfish bowl, with the fish on the outside. Delicate coral structures encased the gigantic air bubble of the facility. Shoals of fish and brightly coloured sea creatures threaded in and out of the pink-hued network encasing the library. She imagined Leo's reaction. *He would probably say: 'SeaWorld, eat your heart out!'*

Imogen had connected to as many of the Data Encounter devices as she could. Araz had released the DEs from their casings, which were crypt-activated like the salvers for food, and surreptitiously passed them to Imogen. He had checked the DEs were not DNA-triggered, so Imogen could use them. He would then sit back and study her as she assimilated the records, answering any questions she had. The other Holans took little notice of the pair. They assumed this was their way of bonding and many smiled knowingly when they observed them in companionable silence or earnest conversation.

Each day Imogen had risen early to walk alone along the shoreline and watch the light of 'Ka' rise from behind the dead planet of Sheut. This daily 'declipse', known as De-Atma on Holis, did not fail to amaze her and, along with the presence of the second sun in the sky, remind her how far away she was from Earth.

By the third morning, Imogen had thought the red sun of Ib appeared slightly smaller, the difference almost imperceptible. She was also aware of subtle changes in her inner eyelids and guessed this meant the red light was waning. She hoped the white light would soon dominate, causing her Tarsus filters to lift. *I need to be able to see the Chroma of these people. It could make all the difference.*

Bathing in the communal spa for the last time, Imogen had a heavy heart. She felt secure here. She looked around fondly at the local people swimming and washing in the hot springs. Like most adults, she wore her Flecto attire from the previous day, which covered her locket and the scar on her hand. She washed both her body and the garment with soft soaping sands, before diving under waterfalls of fresh warm water. The drying area was a walkway of natural jet streams, blowing hot air from underground. The Holans stood and talked as their gowns billowed out around them; children laughed and dodged around the adults as they dried off.

Now adept at manipulating the Flecto, Imogen had fashioned herself a loose bodysuit from the material. Following what others did, she did not activate the reflection switch. This was no longer festival season and the populace wore their plainer styled robes in staid, stone shades.

Those assigned to grooming tasks, cut, combed, and styled hair, encouraging little ones to assist. One of the stylists persuaded Imogen to sit as he entwined thin ribbons of Flecto into her hair, pinning it up into a soft swirl of plaited tresses at the back of her head. Araz looked approvingly at the new style. She smiled to herself as she recalled him touching his lips to the bare flesh beneath her ear, and his murmured word: 'Beautiful!'

Imogen reflected on her ambivalent feelings for her enigmatic admirer. Somewhat overwhelmed by his attention, there was still a small part of her unable to allow herself to completely trust him. Was he still the enemy? His work for the Supreme Council remained a mystery to her. *How could he stay loyal to this corrupt regime?* One minute he was infuriatingly judgmental, pompous and arrogant; the next he was protective, kind and loving. She recalled their conversation from the day before:

"What do you think of Holis?"

"Well, on the surface, it appears to be a very peaceful place."

"But you must agree - our world has everything Earth does not. People here are happy and fulfilled. No one goes hungry and everyone is valued."

"Yes, well you would say that!"

"Can you not see? It's obvious - Holan society is as close to perfection as you could get!"

"Perfection! Yes, so bloody perfect no one knows about the disappearance of my dad, people can be tried for being born without permission and one of your five lines is being phased out under your nose! Perfect indeed! Why the hell are you so blinkered?"

"Wait a minute, I have been to Earth. I have witnessed the barbarism; the ignorance of the human race. Do you think that's better? We have rules and laws to protect us from becoming dysfunctional like the people of the primitive planet. And anyway, what do you mean about a line being phased out? If you are referring to Iris, they are just a rarer personality type."

"And you believe that? At what point do you question what is going on?"

"You read too much into everything."

"And you only see things in black and white."

He had stormed off, but returned a short time later, taking her hand and kissing her scar. It was the closest she would ever get to an apology from him. The one thing she could not deny was he triggered within her a deep desire she could barely control. *I must tread carefully. After all, how well do I really know him?*

The community had all shared a meal before starting their workday. Imogen had listened to the happy chatter around the tables. For years her daily morning routine had been to check on her sleeping mother, communicating by touch with little response and having no one to confide in other than her grandfather, who turned out to be her real father. Here the contrast of living amongst a caring community was proving a refreshing change.

With a pang of guilt at the thought of her mother far away and now under the care of the Zuberi brothers, Imogen had bid farewell to a couple of small children over the breakfast. Aly and his friend had consistently sought her out since their encounter in the food area on her first day. They seemed to instinctively know she was new to their way of life and so rushed to release the salvers for her food and open doors for her. They had seen Em and Araz help her in this way and had automatically and trustingly done likewise, without knowing she must not access these herself. The children delighted in showing Imogen how things worked with a freshness and clarity beyond the capabilities of Araz. They were so confident and bright; their enthusiasm was infectious and she would miss them.

"Tell us all about Karnak when you return," Aly had pleaded. Tousling his hair, she had explained she may not be back in Qus again. Her studies had made it clear Holans prized honesty and never lied to children. This included what on Earth would be termed as white lies. Truthfulness here was a matter of honour and ingrained into each generation from the word go.

It made Imogen wonder further about why segments of the history of Holis had been deleted from the original Chronicles. Even a chapter about the myths and legends of Holis. *Why?* In the library, Araz had selected the current Chronicles of Holis for her, but she had felt unable to discuss the differences with him. Em had made it clear he was not to know she had the full and illegal version. All she could do was ponder why certain facts and notions were now considered to be subversive by a race which valued candour so highly. *What are they trying to hide?*

Without Araz's knowledge, she had searched every DE for information about her parents and the other scientists who had escaped to Earth but apart from Tanastra Thut who was revered by all, she could only find reports about one Zuberi brother, Nuru. He had been publicly decried as a subversive. There was no mention of a second brother or Firas, Eshe, her mother or her father. *Why would they label Nuru Zuberi a subversive, but not the others?*

Araz interrupted her thoughts as he called from the open doorway and Imogen took a deep breath. It was time to go. As she turned, a disembodied female voice spoke. It came from the vision wall.

"Good day!"

The scene of gentle lapping waves outside switched to a view of a food arena which, she guessed, must be in Karnak. It was filled with residents wearing bright Flecto outfits. Imogen stopped to watch and listen, amazed when the multi-dimensional figures spilled into the room. She could feel the breeze, smell the food on their plates. She could almost touch them. Araz stood next to her, watching the broadcast.

"The Lotus Festival is now at an end. Our Greatness sends her thanks to the people of Qus for the magnificent catch of fish and sincerely hopes you have all enjoyed a well-deserved break." Accompanying the words were countless happy faces enjoying their meal from the day before.

The crowds dissolved and reformed into a sea of faces. They all looked to the elevated figure of a middle-aged, elegant woman, dressed in a black flowing gown. Cheered by the multitude, the female smiled and nodded graciously as the eager onlookers reached to touch her hand or arm. The commentator proudly announced, "Today we honour our talented Vizier of Sanctity, the eminent Merit. Her genetic research on ageing has resulted in genome modifications predicted to extend the average life-span of our race. This has now increased to over two hundred and fifty years." Imogen glanced at Araz as the narrator gave more technical details of the innovations.

"Two hundred and fifty years? Who wants to live that long?"

"You forget, we remain healthy and active for practically all our lifetime. It is not like reaching old-age on Earth." The sneer in Araz's voice was clear.

Imogen thought of Eshe before she died. *Was she as old as two hundred? She had looked so wizened. Or did she age quicker because she was on Earth?*

The view then changed to a quiet garden area and homed in on a blond curly-haired figure. He was sitting on a mossy seat, chewing his lip and wringing his hands.

Imogen gave a gasp. *Leo!* He looked like he was next to her and her hand automatically fluttered up to touch him. She was relieved to see his broken arm and nose appeared to be healed, but her heart lurched to see the looks of deep worry etched on his face. He was clearly unaware he was being filmed as he put his head in his hands and rocked back and forth. *Leo – I'm here!* She willed her unspoken words to be transmitted to him.

The commentary continued, "All citizens are advised the trial of the Falsebred, Tarik Zuberi, will take place tomorrow." The image now switched to the empty trial area - a vast, square indoor arena with tiered seating for thousands. The central floor was raised and in contrast to the angular lines of the stone walls, it was circular. The pattern carved into the white marble was instantly recognisable.

The symbols of my pendant!

The stars, circles, and the arrow gleamed, the outline of each picked out in precious stones. *This must be the Sanctus High Court. It looks ancient.*

The announcer reminded viewers of their duty to take part in the proceedings, even if they were unable to get to the capital. Work would finish early across the globe and adults living outside Karnak would need to go to their local library facility, to watch and listen to the evidence. It was as Adam had told her; everyone who had come of age would take part by voting on the verdict.

What chance does Leo have?

The picture pulled back, retracting through the doorway and, as if the camera was attached to a drone, rose. The slanting stone walls of the building shrank, and the view panned out, prompting a slightly giddy feeling in Imogen, until it was framed from a vantage point high in the sky. A sharp point crowned the colossal edifice, the full exterior now completely in view.

Imogen gasped again. *It's a pyramid!* She knew there must be some connection with the ancient Egyptians, but this was a surprise. She glanced at Araz.

"It's the oldest building on Holis," explained Araz, proudly.

"It's Egyptian!" she exclaimed. "How did…"

Araz stopped her by raising a hand. "It's Holan. What you have seen on Earth, is the result of our ancestors visiting the planet over five thousand years ago."

Imogen reeled. *Incredible!*

With a wave of his hand towards the pyramid, Araz seemingly pushed the image back into the screen and muted the sound. He sat down with his back to the vision wall. Imogen joined him, eager to know more.

"The voyage from Holis, was thought to have taken hundreds upon hundreds of years. The ships, however, lost contact and never returned."

Imogen gave him her full attention. *This is mind blowing! My kind came to Earth thousands of years ago.*

"It was only when the first radio broadcasts started arriving from Earth, around seventy years ago, we discovered the mission had succeeded. The same news reports also made it clear they had broken all the laws regarding primitive races. Instead of quietly observing the beings of the planet, they had lived with them and exerted a great deal of influence on them. They were, quite rightly, condemned for their interference."

"Visitors from outer space! No wonder there're so many Earth myths and legends about this," Imogen mused. "Do they still use spaceships?"

Araz went quiet for a minute, deep in thought. "Holans now only use conventional space travel to get to Ankh, for the ongoing 'Elysian Two' project - to make it habitable. Our people swore they would never again make contact with an embryonic race. It is considered unethical to meddle in their development or history. It was also decreed we must hide our existence from barbaric races, for our own protection."

Barbaric, subversive – how I hate these labels, Imogen thought with irritation. But she was beginning to understand why there was such a negative reaction to her parents and their group of scientists living amongst humans. Imogen dwelt on Tanastra's secret jump to Earth. *I suppose it was the perfect hiding place. And, back then, no one knew he had got the Tractus to work.*

Araz gave a sigh before concluding, "This is one of the reasons there has been such an outcry at the Tractus project being misused. Although, I am unsure why they are blaming Tarik Zuberi."

"It's not Leo's fault! We have to help him..." started Imogen.

"Come, we need to go!" Araz said, refusing to be drawn into a discussion.

Imogen couldn't say for sure, but she had caught an imperceptible flash of grey as a feint aura. *Grey - the colour of worry.* It was the first sign her chromatic sight was beginning to return.

Araz stood and led her out of the room, deactivating the screen and sealing the door behind.

They had missed the final news item on the vision wall, which had played silently behind them as they had talked. The introduction of the two new members of the Supreme Council, Horus and Naomi, being cheered by an excited crowd of onlookers at the official ceremony. They had smiled and waved, enjoying the accolade, as they were given their official council robes ahead of the trial the next day.

Em met the pair at the transport hub, a little way down the coast and located inside a natural rock cavern. Imogen thought Em looked anxious as she hurried them down the wide stone steps of the brightly lit, hewn-out channel leading deep underground. Hundreds of others were heading the same way.

"Is everything ok?" asked Imogen.

"Friend – one of us – is caught earlier. Crypts no longer logged. He forget - tried use Phase-Seal door at Hub. Taken Karnak prison."

"I'm sorry," Imogen responded as they got half way down.

Em pulled Imogen closer to her so she could shut Araz out of the conversation. "This Araz," Em hissed, "is agent. Works for Supreme Council. Is danger…"

"I know."

"You know this?" Em look appalled.

"He's with us, for now…"

Their conversation was cut short when a loud command came from below and abruptly forced the crowds to stop. Everyone spread out to either side of the stairwell. Em quickly sidled her way into the group next to them, until she was hidden at the back. The sound of feet marching resonated throughout the shaft and Imogen's stomach folded. She knew that sound. She had heard it in the abandoned underground station in London.

Before she could speak, a squad of fifty or so helmeted Repros stomped up through the centre of the stairway. The ones at the front looked left and right, scanning the travellers as they ascended. Coming closer with each step, Imogen grabbed Araz's arm tightly. He gave her a piercing look, urging her to stay still. Her heart thumped.

The Repros at the front of the regiment came level with them and suddenly stopped. Those behind also came to a halt.

Imogen wanted to scream but remained motionless.

The Repro leading the squad took a step forward and scanned both she and Araz. It lifted its visor and stared directly at Araz with blood red eyes. It then turned to Imogen, who forced herself to look calmly back, as Araz had. Her legs felt as if they were going to buckle.

These things tried to kill us on Earth. Stay calm.

After a few seconds, the Repro raised its hand and Imogen winced, but instead of striking out, the creature closed the visor and touched its head in a form of salute. It turned and continued to march up the steps, the whole company following suit as they passed them by.

Imogen breathed again. "What just happened?"

"Formal acknowledgment," Araz replied, through gritted teeth. "This means they now know I'm back on Holis," he added, careful to check Em had not reappeared. Worry was etched on his face.

"What do you mean?"

"They have visual recognition programming. My face is registered as a government agent. Let's hope they are too stupid to report this back to my commanders, who still think I am on Earth. I need more time before I report in."

Em interrupted any further talk, pushing forward from her hiding place and grabbing Imogen to pull her away from Araz.

"Is not safe! Repros in Karnak. Vlaggers!"

"Em, I have to go. I must help Leo and try to reach my dad."

Em paused but then gave a nod of understanding. She took Imogen's hand, in a show of giving a handshake, her glancing touch saying: 'Keep guards up. Not trust this Araz. Is creep.'

Imogen 'saw' Em was planning to head straight for Barbara. *Presumably the Barbara who wrote the warnings in the original chronicles.* She had to discuss some issue to do with the new council members, but the link was so brief, her thoughts did not explain what this was.

"Take care Em, and thank you," Imogen said with heartfelt gratitude.

At the platform entrance, Em gave Araz a last glare before disappearing back up the steps.

Imogen brought Adam's explanation of the planet's transport system to the forefront of her mind. Powered by magnetic levitation, the Velo-City train travelled deep under the surface of Holis. It consisted of a continuous chain of large compartments running inside the vacuum of an airless tunnel, allowing it to reach fantastic speeds. It did not stop, but remained on a continuous loop, linking up every town and city. At each station, passengers embarked by entering an interlinking shuttle. This picked up speed, eventually pulling alongside the Velo-City when the pace of both trains matched. The two then briefly docked together, enabling passengers to transfer to the high-speed cabins. To disembark, they did the same in reverse.

Imogen nervously stepped onto the slow-moving shuttle behind Araz, only vaguely aware it was gradually getting faster as they walked. Her apprehension had been heightened after the encounter with the Repros and she needed to suppress her fears. *They didn't stop us! So far, so good.*

The Holans all moved in the same direction, along the smooth walkway of the transfer tube. Some strolled and some jogged. All nodded polite greetings as they passed by. Imogen kept pace with Araz at a fast walk. She was aware of a slight mechanical buzz growing louder when the shuttle eventually came alongside the main train. They crossed over and the buzz ceased the minute they were inside.

Imogen had thought the transport might be reminiscent of the London underground, but it was nothing like it. In fact, it was hard to believe she was on a moving vehicle. For a start the 'vision' walls were filled with images of the Holan seas and sky, which gave the illusion of being outside in light airy spaces. Secondly, there was no sensation of motion.

"The internal construction of the compartments has been upgraded to produce a counterbalancing movement to the outer shell, something like a gyroscope," Araz had explained. "So, as the main train travels at speeds of over two thousand kilometres an hour, passengers are unaware of the motion and move around freely. My father was responsible for some of the engineering," he added proudly.

Imogen took it all in, following Araz through several linked cabins until they came across an empty seated area.

She knew the journey would take a few hours, despite the high speeds, so she settled in a seat next to Araz, determined to go through the plan of how they would get to The Hub and the protocols expected there.

The time passed quickly. Araz sounded confident and decisive about where they were going. They would input Imogen's DNA as a priority, so she could access everything. This would be vital if they got separated, although he assured her this was not going to happen. He also had a few ideas about the whereabouts of Leo. He had seen where pre-trial prisoners were held.

"What about my father?"

"He could be there too, if…" Araz trailed off and although he didn't use the words: 'if he's still alive', she knew they were going through his mind.

Seeing her troubled expression, Araz took Imogen by the hand. He glanced his fingertips against hers, sending the message, "You'll be fine. I am with you."

Unknown to him, Imogen also read his concealed thoughts with a sinking feeling in her stomach. *He's as worried as me! He is sure the Repros will report he is here and he has no idea how his commanders will react.* Even if it was no surprise he was so apprehensive, she cursed her ability to cognitively read his state of mind. It did nothing to reassure her or allay her fears. Her awareness of a blur of chromatic greys emanating from her outwardly confident companion, was the only positive news. It confirmed her earlier sense; her Tarsus filters were thinning.

CHRONICLES OF HOLIS – THE MYTHS AND LEGENDS OF HOLIS

Warning: This chronicle has been deleted in its entirety. Anyone found in possession of these original chronicles will be deemed subversive.

Barbara

*S*o, I interrupt these Chronicles for a different sort of history and something of a favourite topic of mine – myths, rumours and legends! I think it is true to say every race has them. Often there is either a basis of truth or a glimmer of authenticity, but usually this is somewhat tenuous. They do, however, make wonderful stories for firing the imagination. So, I crave your indulgence to give you my top five:

  1. Legend: The space travellers of our early race gave rise to the population of Earth. Yes, the primitives! We are supposed to imagine they are our close relatives and they

are, in fact, descended from us! What a quaint idea! Our ancestors postulated it was not possible for any other life to exist on other planets. They believed the people of Ankh were the only 'humanoids' in the entire universe! Of course, it was soon realised this is as ludicrous as saying the globe of Ankh is flat! Preposterous! The legend talked of a group of our primordial kind stumbling on some kind of wormhole in space and disappearing, some few millions of years ago. The legend had it, two of these beings reproduced and gave rise to the entire human race on Earth. Wonderful! And of course, Ankhkind were but simple beings when this legend began and loved a good story. We must, however, thank this folklore for introducing the idea of 'instantaneous' space travel. From legends come ideas, from these ideas come initiatives and progress. As I have mentioned elsewhere in these chronicles, it is hoped such a phenomenal transport device will eventually become a reality.

2. Rumour: Ankh was destroyed in its entirety. This was a prevalent rumour on Holis during the awful reign of Anubis, but I can honestly say there is not a grain of truth to this. The evil regime under this dreadful dictator put out this lie to subdue its enemies. Our race has always had an overriding need to return to Ankh, to release the treasured species we have painstakingly stored. If we could not return, there was no purpose to our lives; the Elysian Project was all for nothing. The only reason Holans were prepared to accept the restrictions imposed here, was the belief they would one day return to Ankh, even if it was not within their lifetime. It was, and is, our key objective. We frequently sing a lament about this core desire of our people, but I now realise, I have told you of this elsewhere! So, was Ankh destroyed? Of course not! The rumour was a deliberate ploy to drive our people to despair. Ankh was poisoned and damaged, but not beyond repair. The Elysian

Two project will see it is eventually restored and then the Holan race will become the new Ankhkind. What a wonderful day that will be!

3. Myth: There was an indigenous species on the moon we now call Holis before we arrived, and this native genus was annihilated when we took it over. An interesting, if dark, proposition. We have found no evidence Holis could sustain any life other than simple organisms and basic plant life before we invigorated the planet and boosted the oxygen in the atmosphere to enable sophisticated lifeforms to live here. Until Holis was made viable, a task taking three hundred years, it was impossible to live on the surface. The former cloud coverings of mildly toxic gases - since eliminated – blocked most of Ka's life-giving light. The light predominating on the surface was the red light of Ib. Anything living on the surface would not have been able to see in this red light, not without the sophisticated Tarsus filters genetically developed for the Holan people. It is therefore highly unlikely this myth is true. It is just a fanciful train of thought, popular once the horrors of the reign of Anubis were over, when people told all sorts of tales to implicate Anubis and his supporters in even more dreadful acts. We may be a superior race of beings, but we are all agreed, this does not give us the right to eliminate other species.

4. Rumour: InvertIon is so depleted we will run out of this precious element soon. Sadly, there may be more truth to this than had been credited. We are quite dependent on InvertIon for our power source. It is such an amazingly flexible element it may make the difference to being able to develop an instantaneous travel device – one capable of bending space and time. InvertIon was mined from the deep magma pockets on Ankh. Our Holan ancestors took the precaution of mining enough of this material for a good number of millennia, but it is said Ankh has next to no

reserves of this element and to date it has not been found elsewhere in the universe. We will have to find another power source for our future energy - a long-term project will be required. There is, of course, a certain inevitability to this problem. We are long-lived beings, so can expect to outlive some of our key resources.

5. Myth: The existence of a Sanctus Cryptus will save Holankind. This is one of our more recent myths and a result of the genetic search for a Penta-Crypt. Many years were spent testing combinations of the reproductive cells of Tri-Crypts and Bi-Crypts. We succeeded in producing a couple of Tetra-Crypts – you may know our Supreme Leader, Kekara, is one - but it was decided to abandon the search. After all, it was taking valuable time and resources from other more pressing projects, such as Elysian Two. I, however, am inclined to agree with the few Vatics left on Holis (those who have prophetic abilities to see into the future) who say one day a Penta-Crypt will be born into our race. However, whether they will have the capability to lead our people to full maturity, is purely a matter of conjecture.

So, there you have it! These form the foundation of the folklore capable of dominating unoccupied minds from time to time. Can fairy tales become reality? Perhaps. Can truth be found in the most unlikely myths? It's possible. One thing is for sure, we all need to keep an open mind as to what counts as truth.

KARNAK

*A*raz and Imogen disembarked with hundreds of other passengers via the linking shuttle when it gracefully slowed to walking pace. They surfaced from the subterranean station into a blast of icy air. Imogen felt the Flecto clothing tighten against her body as it bristled into a thicker, furry texture, perfect for keeping out the cold. She stroked the material with a renewed admiration. Araz steered her to one side where everyone seemed to be stopping and adjusting their attire.

"This is the north of Holis," explained Araz. "Much more like the North of your UK on Earth for weather, although the comparison stops there."

He reached for the material at the cuff of her bodysuit and his own garment where he proceeded to tear a small piece of Flecto from each edge. He then swiftly and expertly stretched the fabric into long lengths, fashioning two scarves. He teased the cuffs of their sleeves to reform around their wrists, ensuring Imogen's cuff was long enough to cover her scar, before wrapping the scarves around Imogen's neck and his own.

"This is the Karnak way of dressing," he explained as he activated the switches, so both scarves took on the shiny reflections of everything around them.

Imogen watched the other passengers making similar alterations to their clothing. Some had created hats, others cravats, belts, sashes or gloves from the small pieces of Flecto. All then switched them to 'reflect' once the accessories were in place. The result was each person sported a swatch of apparel 'moving' with the mirrored colours of their surrounds, brightening the otherwise plain outfits. Imogen again marvelled at the amazingly adaptable material. She allowed Araz to lead her into the open where she took her first glimpses of Karnak.

They had emerged from the base of a large foothill into a green valley, surrounded by snow-topped mountains. The green slopes were filled with gently swaying trees above meadows full of wild flowers.

Imogen's mouth dropped open and her heart skipped a beat. *I know this place!* Several waterfalls cascaded from the heights above, pooling into channels joining a fast-moving, azure river and running through the centre of the valley. Bridges crisscrossed over the river, their structures organic, like those on the Southern Sea. It was stunningly beautiful and chillingly familiar. It dawned on her why she knew the landscape so well and she gave a gasp, putting her hand up to her mouth. *This is my picture!*

'What's the matter?" asked Araz anxiously.

"I painted this - in my Art exam."

"How could you? You've never been here?" Araz looked confused.

"I don't know, I made it up, or thought I had... I don't understand." *How did I know what this looked like?*

Araz paused and Imogen knew she was not mistaken when she saw the flash of cobalt blue, the colour of inspiration, in his Chroma.

"Your parents probably sent you images of this valley when you were small, using the cognitive link. This was their home, after all." Araz sparked gold confidence and certainty as he dismissed the coincidence and led her forward along the riverside path.

Yes, that might explain it. Strange, I have no memory of them doing this.

Imogen allowed Araz to lead her along the winding river walk as it opened into the lip of a large alpine lake. Many others were heading in the same direction. Turning with the bank of the lake, a vast glassy mountain rose into view. The highest of all the mountains in the natural range in which it stood, it reminded Imogen of a gigantically exploded version of the London Shard. *It could also be a modern-day pyramid, only on a fantastic scale.*

The gleaming surface reflected the clouds of the sky above, the two suns and the neighbouring snowy peaks. Imogen wondered if glass, like the Earth variety, had been used to achieve the effect. The slanting façade rose so high its top was hidden in the clouds.

"Ice!" Araz pronounced, as if he could read her thoughts. "Ice and a form of organic crystal to keep it solid were used to form this incredible construction. The Karnak observation tower is perched on the top, but it's just above the cloud level." Araz paused to look proudly at the great structure, delighted to see Imogen's appreciative nod.

"You're looking at The Hub. Stay close."

Just before the lake widened, they reached the famous Karnak bridge. It was made from intertwining trunks from several enormous trees stretching high on either side, forming a tower at each end. The boughs and branches looped down from these supporting towers, crossing, linking and meeting in the middle. The graceful curve of these limbs connected to the locked roots of a suspended walkway, via hanging vines between the two. The bridge was wide enough to hold fifty or sixty people abreast.

It's like a naturally grown Golden Gate bridge. Beautiful! Imogen stopped to admire the living bridge, only broken from her reverie when Araz nudged her, indicating a few Holans who had turned to look quizzically at her.

Close your mouth and act normal she told herself. She hastily cloaked her amazement and set off with Araz, projecting a guise that everything around her was nothing out of the ordinary.

They crossed together, slowing in the throng of people who funnelled across the structure. The Hub was now in front of them, dwarfing everything in sight.

Gradually thinning out, the large group of Holans mounted the slope. Imogen and Araz staying at the core until they reach a wide grassed area outside the massive headquarters. It was swarming with people going to and from their work and activities. This was much busier than Qus. Noting the bustle around her, Imogen thought the furry bodysuits, worn by almost all the locals, could almost pass as animal skins if it were not for a small bright reflection of sky flashing from differing parts of their outfits.

They reached the centre of the piazza and Imogen stopped in her tracks and gasped. Bang in the middle, high on a plinth, stood a life-sized, crystal statue of Tanastra Thut. *Father Jonathan! He looks so young!* Staring up at the sparkling figure, she was disconcerted to see his face turn in her direction as he looked down at her and smiled. Her heart skipped a beat to see the familiar kindly eyes look into hers. She wanted to reach out and touch him. A tear sprang to her eye.

All the pedestrians gave the effigy a nod of respect or waved in passing. Tanastra appeared to smile at everyone and Imogen guessed it was some sort of hologram. *You look so real and alive. How I wish I could speak to you.*

A young man stopped at the statue beside them and explained to the small child in his care, "Here he is! Tanastra Thut. The most honoured scientist and historian of Holis. He was exceptional in every way. He was also one of the few to have died whilst working on a restricted research project." The child gave a serious nod and waved at the figure, thrilled when the wave was returned.

Araz gave Imogen a knowing look and Imogen realised she could see his sepia tones of sorrow and sage greens of admiration and respect. She touched her eye to wipe away the tear, and this confirmed to her - her inner lids had lifted.

"Are you going to tell your commanders he's one of the so-called subversives and escaped to Earth, all those years ago?" she asked quietly.

When Araz replied there was no point in doing so, given the great man was now dead, she was reassured to see his quartz colours shining clearly. *The colour of truth.* Glancing at the other citizens of Karnak she could discern their Chromatic auras too. *Thank heavens! My sight is back!*

"This way," urged Araz, a troubled look on his face accompanied by shadowy shades surfacing is his Chroma.

Walking towards The Hub, Imogen sensed a kerfuffle ahead. The calm tones emanating from the citizens closest to the edifice began to pulse mauve flickers of alarm. The anxiety spread outward in a ripple effect. She strained to see what was causing them to react in this manner.

A shiver went down her spine and Imogen grabbed Araz's arm to pull him back. Something was amiss.

Before he could question her, a troop of Repros trudged heavily into view. They towered over those around them. The Holans stepped back in trepidation and watched in silence as the Repros spread out and took up guard at close intervals around The Hub base. Many drew in to look at the new sentries; they were curious, having only seen distant images on the daily news. All were unnerved to find the so-called protection force, close up, looked disquietingly threatening.

The Repros stood too with fists clenched, ready to spring into action. Their helmet-clad heads swivelled menacingly as they stared intently around. A small child broke free from a group near the entrance and went to touch the leg of the closest figure. It instantly snarled a warning at the youngster who recoiled in shock before being whisked away by a startled carer.

Wary, the Holan people tentatively approached the entrance, giving the fearsome constructs a wide berth. At the doorway they were stopped and checked before being allowed to enter. A nervous queue started to form outside the main lobby.

"What are we going to do?" asked Imogen, eyes darting from one Repro to another.

"We have to get inside. Remember, they didn't stop us before," reasoned Araz.

They joined the line, their expressions determined. Imogen stilled her heart rate and dulled her colours to cloak her apprehension.

She nearly fainted with relief when they passed through the entrance unimpeded, barely noticing the repeated salute from the Repros at the front.

Thank goodness!

Araz gave her a smug smile, the spikes of black authority and the golds of renewed confidence rising in his Chroma. "Told you it would be fine. This way."

So why the underlying grey swirls of worry?

The lobby of The Hub was strangely similar to a luxurious hotel on Earth. Big open spaces led to numerous doors and stairways, although the floors and walls looked like polished ice. Thankfully they were not slippery and Imogen could see a web of pale lichen clung to the surface of the floor allowing the thick Flecto footwear to grip and walk safely. She looked at the vast walls. At first, she thought it was artwork hanging there, but soon realised these were liquid screens. The vistas changed, one by one, as scenes of the valley outside switched to waterfalls, lakes and a skyline panorama showing puffs of cloud nestling under the rugged tips of mountaintops, the red and white suns shimmering in the sky.

"The view from the top of the tower," Araz glowed with pride. "Come, we need to get to the Sanctity headquarters, where the genetic reserves are held."

The air was warmer inside The Hub, and their Flecto outfits responded automatically, changing from velvety fur to a linen feel, to suit the higher temperature. Imogen copied Araz and removed her scarf, placing it around her waist, like a belt.

Araz walked her over to the far wall and a row of five doors. Above each was a different, three-dimensional symbol: solid circle, clear circle, solid star, clear star, and an arrow.

The symbols of my locket. Ra, Iris, Nut, Hathor and Amon.

"The ancient symbols over each of these elevator doors denote the five personality lines of our race. One symbol for each of the five councils. Adam told you about the five lines?"

Imogen gave a slight nod, looking above the doors to avoid looking at Araz's eyes. *He has no idea I hold all five in equal measure.*

"This one denotes Sanctity." Araz put his hand to the Phase-Seal door under the symbol of a turning solid star.

Adam had already told her which symbol represented which council. She looked at each in turn repeating his lesson in her head, *Ra: solid circle and Council of Enlightenment. Nut: Solid star and Sanctity. Hathor: clear star and Well-Being, Amon: the arrow and Stability. And Mum's line: Iris, the clear circle, representing the Council of Vision. It's also one of my lines - the line Tanastra said is being phased out.* Imogen swallowed hard and gave a small nod, not trusting herself to speak.

As the solid star symbol lit up, the door beneath it melted open at Araz's touch. They stepped into the tubular capsule, the door closed and they were whisked upward hundreds of floors, with little sensation of motion. The super-speed lift delivered them to a wide landing, high in The Hub. They had risen several thousand feet, the ground and valleys visible below through the 'ice' windows.

A further Phase-Seal entrance took them into the Council of Sanctity. Imogen had expected it to look like a laboratory or a hospital, like those on Earth. In fact, it looked more like a vast art gallery with helix shaped sculptures suspended, seemingly, in mid-air. A number of people were going in and out of various doorways and did not make eye contact with Imogen or Araz as they walked around the open space. When it was clear no one was about to pounce on them, Araz indicated for Imogen to follow him to a far exit, activating the door opening when he got there.

"Don't touch anything." Araz warned, unnecessarily.

The interior of this next area was more like an office. A few hammock-type seats hung at the end of the room and several Holans moved around the space holding thin pen devices. They appeared to be scanning data from the displays on the numerous refrigerated units lining every part of the remaining walls. Hundreds of thousands of units. *This must be the genetic store Adam spoke about.*

The technicians gave Araz and Imogen a friendly nod as they passed. They did not seem to think anything was out of the ordinary. Adam had told her as long as they could gain access, no one would suspect any subterfuge as the Phase-Seals only allowed authorised personnel into the area.

"The volt of flesh is normally taken at birth, so we need to go to the new-born area."

"And you're confident no one will stop us?"

"If we were going to be stopped, it would have happened already." Araz's colours no longer held any sign of apprehension - he was swathed in the bold gold and black shades of confidence and authority.

I wish I shared his conviction.

Marching towards an opening at the far end of the room, they stopped when a group of three Holans emerged from the adjoining space, laughing and cheering. One held a small baby, soothing its cries. They attracted the attention of those closest to the doorway who all crossed to congratulate the adults, each saying something to the child as they touched the infant's forehead, before returning to their checks.

Imogen could not distinguish what was said but could see these were amicable encounters.

"Come – this is protocol," Araz indicated for Imogen to follow him and strode over to the group to greet them.

"Welcome to your little one," he said in a respectful tone. The three adults smiled and nodded. Araz looked at the baby and touched it on the brow, adding, "The blessing of Ra be with you."

The three looked expectantly at Imogen who saw Araz give the slightest of nods, directing her to do the same. She followed suit, blessing the baby with the same words used by Araz and touching its tiny head. Their response was bewildering. All three clasped her hand in turn, thanking her and calling her 'Quora' as they bowed their heads. She had no idea what it meant but found herself blushing. As they left, they kept turning back frequently to look at her, as if they had met some sort of celebrity.

What's going on?

Araz looked disconcerted, his colours flaring yellow flashes of questioning, but he dulled these when he turned to Imogen.

"What does it mean?" she asked, nervously. "Quora?"

"It is a sign of respect. Usually accorded to those in high office," his brows knitted together.

"Maybe they have mistaken me for someone else?"

"Maybe." The burst of violet in Araz's Chroma made it abundantly clear he did not buy this explanation.

"Well, how else would you explain it?"

When he didn't reply, Imogen persisted, "Araz, why do they recognise me?"

"You look like your mother. She was a renowned scientist. That will be it."

Imogen glared at Araz. His Chroma made it evident this was an outright lie, plus there had been no mention of her mother in any of the DEs in the underwater library.

Araz, worried they were drawing attention to themselves, took her hand and pressed his fingertips to hers, transferring what he thought was a message of reassurance: 'Don't worry. Whatever the reason, I will protect you.'

When his hidden thoughts leaked across the link, they did nothing to allay her fears. Araz's train of logic was plain to see. In her mind's eye, he 'paced the floor' and spoke these words to himself:

'If Imogen's image has been circulated then our arrival on Holis has been reported to the Supreme Council. How did we miss it? Unless, unless it was broadcast whilst we were travelling to Karnak? So, why is she now held in such high regard? Of course! This is a cunning ploy to locate her! The bulletin probably said she was to receive some kind of award or accolade - bound to bring her much unwanted attention. It's just the sort of scheme Ubaid would devise. All the more reason to meet with him as soon as possible...'

Imogen's hand recoiled from his. She looked anxiously around the room to see if anyone else was looking at her.

Who informed the Supreme Council? The Repros? She realised she wouldn't be able to go unnoticed if everyone knew her face. *What will they do to me if they catch me?* It was all she could do to stop herself shaking.

"Come, we must input your crypts - quickly." Araz demanded, oblivious to inadvertently sharing his theory.

They entered the room from where the group had emerged (Imogen thought the space looked much more like a scientific laboratory on Earth, with its benches, stools and computer-style equipment) and finding they were alone, Araz led Imogen to a tall plinth at the centre of the space. Floating above the stand, with no visible means of suspension, was a large silvery sphere. It appeared to be liquid but held its own shape reminding Imogen of a viscous fluid a little like mercury. The surface rippled slightly as they approached.

"The Lineator," declared Araz, indicating for Imogen to place her hand on the outside of the shining orb.

"Is this where the sample is taken?"

"No, this is the first process. A liquid-crystal scan. It determines your pedigree." He saw the hesitancy on her face.

"It won't hurt, and you can see if you are, indeed, an Omorose," he reasoned, unsure why she was holding back.

Imogen kept her hands close to her side and bit her lip. *This will show my dominant personality lines – he will see I am a Penta-Crypt.*

"Is there a problem?"

"You said we need to be quick. Surely, we can skip this and go straight to where we enter my DNA? We need to find my father and Leo." She pleaded with her hands and looked wildly around to see where the main input area might be.

Araz gave her a hard stare. Yellow spikes of questioning blazed in his Chroma.

"This takes less than a second!" He impatiently grabbed her arm and pushed her open palm onto the surface of the Lineator.

Imogen, with no time to resist, gave a small cry of surprise and angrily pulled her hand away. It was too late, the skin of the mercurial-type orb shimmered and glowed as, simultaneously, an Ultra-Violet type of light flooded the space. Imogen saw the glow of a solid circle below Araz's ear. *Ra! His dominant line.* She instinctively touched the matching mark on her neck, and then hurriedly moved her hand to the side of her eye, in attempt to hide the clear circle of Iris. This only succeeded in drawing Araz's attention to both marks. Flustered, she realised the solid star of Nut was now also visible on her raised hand and she froze to the spot.

Araz was confused at Imogen's reaction. He looked at the three separate symbols glowing on Imogen's face, neck and hand before the UV light switched off, his mouth opening slightly. He slowly turned to look at the sphere to see the results.

Imogen held her breath. She couldn't look. Instead, she watched Araz's face intently.

He gazed at the exterior of the Lineator. Symbols and letters 'swam' in a random manner before settling in a formation proud of the surface around the central line. The letters R-A-I-N-H were embossed on the fluid, along with all five symbols. The circles, stars and arrow all moved mystically around the globe, above and below the letters.

"Not Omorose or Akil then," Araz started to say. "R-A-I-N-H - Rainh? This is not a known line." His brow furrowed in concentration, sifting through his memory for any matches.

Imogen gulped and glanced at the device. *Is that why my surname's Reiner?*

"Let's go," she urged pulling his arm.

"Wait!" Araz stopped and stared at the undulating symbols. They now floated from the extremities of the orb to the centre, before converging under the letters. All five merged into a molten and perfect replica of her pendant. Imogen gawped at the display, unable to speak.

"Your dominant line is... What? All? All five? But that means..." he looked up at her, incredulous. "It means you're a..."

"A Penta-Crypt," finished Imogen, casting her eyes down.

"You knew?" asked Araz, almost in a whisper.

"It's no big deal," she looked around, concerned others may enter the area alerted by the test. "We need to go."

"No big deal?" Araz's eyes pierced hers. "And just when were you planning on telling me this?" he hissed. His Chroma swirled with dark clouds of anger, betrayal and disbelief, lightning flashes of 'why?' and 'how?' completing his now thunderous aura.

Two technicians appeared at the doorway, anxiety written on their faces.

"Who just used the Lineator?" They crossed to look at the orb, but it had already cleared of the results and was, again, a shimmering ball of dense liquid.

"Quality control," answered Araz, sounding official, calm and confident in contrast to his enraged colours. "Just had to make a few checks. Nothing to worry about."

Quick thinking!

Imogen hastily projected self-assured, authoritative shades to match Araz's commanding air and although the technicians did not look convinced, they wavered uncertainly, giving Imogen a respectful nod as one mumbled "Quora".

The hesitation allowed Araz to smartly steer Imogen towards the doorway and out into the vast genetic storage room. Here, more workers had assembled, and all stopped to stare as they passed through the space heading back out towards the lifts.

The landing was, thankfully, devoid of any other people. Araz punched the Phase-Seal lift door angrily. It slid open and they entered, standing face to face. Araz was fuming, his face full of accusation.

"You should have told me!"

"You shouldn't have forced my hand!"

Araz, without any apology, retorted, "Don't you see? This changes everything! It's rare enough you hold the line of Iris! But a Penta-Crypt! It's not supposed to be possible. They were told to stop looking for the so-called 'Sanctus Cryptus' eons ago. Have you any idea what this means? No wonder they tried to hide you on Earth. What were they thinking? They had no right! What will my commanders say? What will they do? If you'd been honest with me, I would not have made you take the test. They will be on to us now. Plus, we failed to enter your crypts. You still can't access anything by yourself. Once Odion finds out about this, there will be serious repercussions..." Araz continued, unaware he was ranting, whipping up waves of churning shades in his Chroma.

Imogen detached herself from the storm of his words and, as if entering the eye of a hurricane, felt a calm descend on her as she looked up to her own blue-quartz colours of logic and lucidity. She realised she could not care less how this changed things for Araz. It changed nothing for her. She only had one priority, to find her father, now more than ever. She stopped Araz in mid-sentence.

"Stop! For crying out loud, stop!"

Araz blinked, his mouth opening to speak again, but no words emerging.

"Look, I'm sorry you feel so aggrieved. As for not telling you, I only found out myself a few weeks ago. And you know what? I don't care if you classify me as a Penta-Crypt, a Falsebred, a Subversive, Barbaric or any of those labels you seem to love so much. I am only interested in one thing. I need to find my father and Leo and I need to find them now!"

Araz looked stunned. He shook his head as if to clear it and Imogen was relieved to see a green-blue calm starting to spread across his colours as his anger began to subside.

"All I ask, is that you help me to find them," she spoke quietly. "What you do after is up to you."

Araz was about to answer when the elevator door opened onto a now deserted lobby. He glanced around the space. He had never seen it so quiet. Something was wrong. Imogen sensed this too and they stepped gingerly into the vestibule, scanning left and right.

Breathing a little easier, Araz led Imogen towards the exit.

"Perhaps everyone has gone home early – it is the trial tomorrow," he rationalised. "In fact, it may be a good idea to search for your father when the trial is underway."

"But I need to help Leo too." Imogen started as she picked up speed to keep up with Araz.

"You cannot risk going anywhere near the Sanctus High Court."

They were nearly at the entry doors.

Suddenly, right ahead, an inner sheet of ice crystallised over the doorways sealing them inside. Araz stopped in his tracks and began to back away, reaching for Imogen's arm. A deafening klaxon began to sound continuously. Imogen put her hands to her ears. It was the same noise she had heard in her vision in New York. Her heart began to race.

Part of a far wall appeared to 'melt' and six Repros burst into the space.

"Run!" Araz shouted above the alarm. He stood his ground.

Imogen backed away in the direction of the lifts, unable to tear her eyes away. Her heart was pounding. Then she saw the glint of metal.

Knives, they have knives!

Three Repros sprang forward and grabbed Araz by the shoulders and arms. After a brief struggle, he was immobilised. He looked wildly at Imogen, his eyes willing her to go.

Three Repros advanced towards her. She did not hesitate. Heart in her mouth, she ran the last few yards to the furthest capsule (glimpsing the lit up holographic arrow above) and pressed her hand against the Phase-Seal. It opened instantly at her touch. She jumped in and to her relief, it sealed shut seconds before the Repros reached it. The sound of the alarm stopped, leaving a buzz in her ears, and the lift descended deep into the bowels of The Hub.

Her mind was racing. *They have him! At least they didn't use their blades. Thank heavens the door opened at my touch? Perhaps it is not crypt activated?* She tried to calm herself but with little success. She felt alone and trapped. *Will they be waiting for me when this thing stops?*

With only a vague awareness the capsule was being plunged down a vast distance, she finally came to a halt. Imogen tensed. The door slid away before her. She could have wept with relief to see nothing but an empty stone corridor ahead. Her way was clear and she half-ran, half-walked down the passage, grateful no one appeared to be in pursuit.

Imogen walked apace. Attempting to calm herself, she trawled her memory banks for relevant information. *Think logically. Where will they take Araz? Probably to his commanders. Will I be able to find Dad or Leo by myself? Think! Where did Araz say pre-trial prisoners are held? Where am I now? The arrow, Amon, the symbol for the Council of Stability. Adam said the Stability Council is responsible for defence. Who was the Vizier? Got it! Odion. What did Araz mean by 'once Odion finds out, there will be repercussions'?* An image from the library DEs of the large, bald Vizier sprang into her mind. He had looked formidable, even in the photograph. She put more and more distance behind her, remaining alert for any sounds indicating she was being followed.

The passageway narrowed and took a downward turn. Imogen followed it until she came to a fork. She quickly opted for one of the routes, hoping it would be the safest way. She had only gone a few steps when the lights went out, plunging her into darkness.

She let out a small scream of surprise, automatically reaching for the wall. *Don't panic! I need my torch.* Leaning on the stone surface, she fumbled for the Multi-Com hidden deep in the folds of her bodysuit. Abruptly, the supporting wall receded without warning. Her stomach lurched and she half-fell, half-stumbled through the gap, suddenly blinded by the light blazoning from within. Awkwardly regaining her balance, she shielded her eyes. A silhouetted figure rushed at her and before she could react, she was seized. A hand clamped over her mouth as a strong arm forced her inside.

The gap in the wall closed. A voice whispered in her ear, "Imogen. We've been expecting you."

LEO

Leo's stomach was in knots. As the day had dawned, he knew this was it; the day of the trial. He had been escorted from the secluded prison gardens in Karnak to the basement of the Sanctus High Court via an underground passage, where he had been left in a small anteroom. A youngster had briefly appeared with a salver of food, which he had timidly thrust into Leo's hand before turning on his heels to exit.

Leo had little appetite and went to place the salver on the floor. In doing so, he noticed there was something stuck to the underside. Lifting it high, he realised it was a black flat ovoid. His heart leapt as he detached it from the salver. He leaned against the door, so he would be alerted if anyone tried to come in and ran his fingers around the edge. It sprang into the regular, egg-shaped Data Encounter and he immediately placed his thumb and fingertips into the indentations to connect. His mind flooded with a holographic image of Barbara, who smiled reassuringly and spoke in clear, strong tones.

"Tarik, I am sorry we meet again in such grim circumstances. We are working on a plan to free you, but I must be truthful, your situation is precarious. It had been our hope Kasmut would speak for you at the trial, but we have had no word of his whereabouts. When our Resistance movement was discovered and found to be actively supporting the so-called subversive scientists, a new court was created. A secret court with the power to pass sentence on those deemed a threat to Holis. It consists of five representatives from the main Councils and is known as the Holan Inquisition."

Leo shook his head. Once this would have triggered a humorous response, but the gravity of Barbara's words quashed anything other than an unsettling sense of foreboding. He concentrated hard on her words.

"Tarik, this will be hard for you, but I am duty bound to tell you. It is our belief Kasmut was questioned and tried by the Inquisition in the last few weeks. I am sorry to say it is our understanding he was sentenced to death."

Leo pushed his free hand through his curly hair, pulling at the roots. He felt himself welling up as she continued.

"Furthermore, we have reason to believe this sentence has been carried out."

Leo gripped the DE tightly and slid slowly to the ground as his knees buckled.

"One of our number was surveying the termination site. She witnessed a tall thin prisoner, a male with grey hair, being led out by the Inquisitors..." The image changed to a shaky, distant video of a robed person being escorted away by Repros. Leo caught his breath and reeled at the enormity of watching the figure walking calmly towards his own execution. He felt his heart chill. It was so typical of Kasmut, to accept his fate with such grace. His blood then ran cold as Imogen's face appeared in his mind. This was her dad!

"...She was too far away to be able to clearly identify him and she did not see the termination, but when they returned, he was not with them. The evidence points to the condemned man being Kasmut Akil. I am very sorry to bring you this dreadful news. May the peace and blessings of Ra go with him."

Leo released the DE as he put his head in his hands and rocked to and fro. Tears coursed down his face. Kasmut had been like a father to him. When Leo had had no one, abandoned to Earth aged only eight and far away from everything he had ever known, this gentle man had shown Leo kindness and given him a home. He had taken care of him, despite being inconsolably bereft of his wife and daughter, who had been missing for years since being involved in the accident with the Tractus contraption.

Leo thought of the last time he had seen Kasmut, just a few weeks ago. Then Kasmut had insisted Leo's wounds were treated before he spoke to their captors. Wracked with guilt, Leo tore at his hair. How had he repaid this loyal protector? His own part in Kasmut's capture hit him with tremendous force. Remorse overwhelmed him.

It was his fault! Leo felt sick to the stomach. The cumulative effect of his actions struck him to the core. He was the one who had insisted on returning to Holis a few years after his arrival on Earth. Yes, he had only been aged eleven, but it was still his doing. He had been caught by the enemy and blackmailed by the vile councillor, Ubaid. If he hadn't cooperated, what would they have done to his mother who had already been incarcerated for over three years? He had had no choice. He had agreed to do anything to save her. Anything! And they were watching. They had put an implant in his head. One false move and his mother would be killed.

As Leo recalled all his actions, he realised it was no good. No matter how hard he tried to justify his conduct, he knew he had betrayed those who had trusted and protected him. There had been a time when he would have been loyal to Kasmut, regardless of any threats. But then he had risked his life for this man, who had vaulted him forward in time for ten whole years as some sort of crazy backup plan to rescue his family. He had expected thanks and praise, but on his return Kasmut had been distant, changed. Leo had been distraught. He had sacrificed ten years for the man and was gutted to find it counted for nothing. He now knew he should not have let his anger take hold. He had succumbed to petulance and had wanted to retaliate. He had led the enemy to Kasmut's door. He had disabled the deflectors at the care home. He had collaborated with those on the Supreme Council. He had even told Ubaid about Imogen; an Earth-born Falsebred. Ubaid had been seized with interest, but Leo had decided it didn't matter. She was a distant figure who had been lost in the Tractus for years. When he finally met Imogen, it was too late. How was he to know she would survive, or she would be so smart, so beautiful, so vulnerable? He had no idea the chain of events he had unwittingly put into place would have such repercussions.

The weight of responsibility was crushing. He could not bear to think of Imogen finding out her father was dead and worse, it was his fault. He had failed her. She would be devastated; devastated and angry. He would have no hope of her now.

Leo reflected miserably on his predicament, thinking he deserved to die. His tears of anguish turned to those of self-loathing.

As he reached the depths of despair, an image of Imogen's shining face and radiant colours burst into his mind. This is how she had looked when her mother had woken from her coma. The vision seemed to be smiling at him, telling him to snap out of it, to focus on what was needed and to think clearly.

Out of the blue it dawned on him he could still make amends. He could still stop any harm coming to her. Someone needed to protect Imogen in Kasmut's stead and if she forgave him - No! even if she did not - he would play his part. He was about to go on trial with little hope of defending himself. His life was forfeit. He had nothing to lose.

Feeling a little less wretched, Leo recovered himself sufficiently to reconnect with Barbara's recording. The rescue plan she outlined was at best sketchy. It presumed he would be found guilty and banked on his choosing termination and there being a gap between the trial and the execution. He hardly cared. With a steely determination he pressed the DE with his little finger, switching it to 'record'. He whispered a brief response before flattening the device and hiding it back under the salver.

Well, he thought to himself, if I am going down it won't be without a fight. I owe Kasmut and Imogen that much.

ARAZ

$\mathcal{A}$ t the top of the Karnak Tower, in the clouds above The Hub, Araz was admitted to the enclosed Observation Deck. He had spent a sleepless night in the agent's quarters of The Hub. There he had been scanned and probed for any signs of contamination; the usual routine when an agent arrived back from Earth. Following the medical examinations, he had been confined to quarters, unable to communicate with anyone. He had not been able to eat and had barely slept, fretting over his situation and worrying about Imogen – where was she and where had she spent the night?

The Repros had escorted him to this, the highest point of The Hub and when he stepped into the glass walled area, itself perched on top of the glass pyramid, he held his breath to see which member of the Supreme Council would be here to greet him.

Slightly relieved to see the small pale figure of Ubaid rather than the burly form of Odion, Araz waited in silence. He had always respected this commander. Ubaid's actions had always been underpinned with reason and logic, as opposed to Odion's which appeared driven by volatile emotions.

Ubaid was looking out of the glass walls at the magnificent view of the mountain ranges and valleys. He had his back to Araz and stayed in this position when he finally spoke. "Tell me Araz, at what point were you going to tell us you had returned? Hmm?"

When Araz didn't respond, he turned to face him. "Come now, it is not a hard question."

"I must ask you a question first." Araz replied, boldly.

"Fire away!"

"Why were the Repros on Earth ordered to kill me?"

Ubaid twiddled with his pointed beard as he responded, "You are asking the wrong question. You should be asking, who ordered the Repros to kill you? I can add, it was not me. We had an agreement, did we not?"

"Did you know they used poisonous blades?"

"I believe the poison was being tested."

"Tested? But surely not authorised for use on Holans? The toxins are lethal."

"So I believe. Look, Araz, I don't wish to be a bore, but I really have no time for this. The trial of the Falsebred is due to start. I need information from you and I need it quickly."

"What information?"

"What happened to the girl? The one born on Earth? Did she live?"

Araz hesitated. This must be a trick question. They knew Imogen was in The Hub. Didn't they? "What do you mean?"

Ubaid paused before standing and slowly pacing around Araz as he responded, "How disappointing. You used to have an intuitive mind. Perhaps contact with the primitives has dulled your senses?" He stopped in front of Araz and leant in close, looking up at his face, the spittle from his words flying upward. Araz resisted the urge to wipe his chin and swallowed hard.

"Let me give you a quick recap: You report you have located the base of the subversives, you do not report you have located the girl. You advise us to hold back, you do not advise us you have captured the girl. Then a surprising twist! Repros witness the girl saving you from their knives. What expression did they use? Ah yes, 'vanished into thin air'. So, what can possibly have been used to 'vanish' two people into thin air? Let me hazard a guess. A Tractus link? Using what can only be a moveable marker - yes? By the way, you should know this interests me far more than your inexplicable actions. And then where did you go? Of course, you were seen at our underground portal where you outran our forces and assisted the girl in her escape..."

Araz interrupted, "They were trying to kill me!"

"Yes, that would be a good reason to do your own thing. And when I think about it, quite clever of you to stick with the girl and keep her in your sights."

Araz could only guess where this was going and looked stoically ahead.

"Now, we come to the strange part of this account. You were next seen at the subversive marker with three of the escaped scientists, Kasmut Akil and the Zuberi brothers. You sent several damaged Repros back, all requiring delicate repairs I might add, and then you had the gall to negotiate with the remaining Repro. It cannot be denied, we have accessed the information on its implant. You allowed it to return to Holis with Kasmut and Tarik Zuberi, but you stayed put. How interesting. Perhaps you did not know the girl was struck with a poisoned blade? Maybe you stayed to ensure she was eliminated? After all, these were your orders if you could not capture her."

"It was complicated," was all Araz would say.

"I am sure. So, I need to know."

"Know what?"

"Let me spell this out for you. I need to know, the girl - is she or is she not dead?"

Araz floundered. Was this a trap? He suddenly realised his Tarsus filters must have dropped, as he could discern the haze of Ubaid's Chroma. It was not as clear in Holan light as Earth light and, whilst he was no expert, he could see the bright yellow flashes of questioning were underpinned with an ice blue logic. No dark colours of subterfuge or deception. Ubaid genuinely did not know if Imogen was alive!

Araz struggled to give a response that would satisfy. Imogen's ability to conceal her colours jumped into his head. It changed how others perceived her, even if they did not read Chroma. Perhaps he could do the same? She had given him an idea of how she achieved this, when they were in New York. He could try her concealment drill.

He focussed his thoughts on something he knew to be true – the scientific formula for the Velo-City's speed in the vacuum tunnels – then detached the words he spoke from his thinking. In his mind, he was imparting the truth of a mathematical principle, rendering his Chroma to honest quartz shades as his answer was delivered - in somewhat clipped sentences - without deliberation.

"I assume she is dead. I did not wait to see. I made my escape whilst the Zuberi brothers were distracted. I travelled to London. To our marker. I then jumped to Holis. I had no idea if I was wanted dead, the reason I did not come directly here."

Ubaid stood back and slowly stroked his beard. "Plausible… yes, that is plausible. I detect you are telling me the truth."

Araz continued to crunch numbers in his head, not allowing himself to chromatically disclose his self-satisfaction in knowing the cloaking was working.

"And the reason you were 'testing' the Lineator in the Council of Sanctity?"

"I wanted to ensure my crypts remained logged and I was still considered a full citizen of Holis." Araz's dark eyes challenged Ubaid to counter this and after a brief pause Ubaid returned to the window.

"Well, that clears that up then!"

Araz inwardly breathed a sigh of relief. He needed to work out what was going on. It suddenly struck him this was all connected to Imogen being a Penta-Crypt. He had never understood why Ubaid had wanted Imogen captured in the first place. But if he had originally wanted her returned as the first ever 'Sanctus Cryptus', why should he now seem to want her dead? And why did other Holans recognise Imogen? Araz could not fathom it out. This was a new game and he did not know the rules. He was determined to remain quiet in the hope it would buy Imogen valuable time.

"So, we are still left with a rather awkward situation on Earth. The Zuberi brothers remain at liberty and more importantly, the Tractus technology remains encoded there, out of our reach. None of our Holan scientists have been able to decipher the intricate workings of the marker devices. I suspect Nuru Zuberi encrypted the Holan marker he engineered before he escaped. Most clever. And we need to know what further developments have been made since the project was stolen all those years ago."

Araz said nothing.

"You see, Araz, it is vital we take control of this equipment. Elysian Two depends upon it. The Holan race depends upon it."

When Araz remained silent, Ubaid turned to the window and looked up to the sky. "I will confide in you, Araz. I have sent an emissary to negotiate with the Earth scientists. This operation has yet to be approved by our Supreme Council, who do not meet for a few more days, but it is time to stop this silly quarrel and to put the Tractus project back on track."

Ubaid turned back to face Araz. "And this is where I will need your help."

Araz nodded stiffly.

"Whether or not this mission is a success, I will need you to jump to Earth. You will either assist the emissary in retrieving the Tractus or eliminate those standing in the way. Whatever happens, it is crucial you return with the Tractus device intact, with all its coding and any new innovations."

Araz clenched his teeth and gave the slightest nod. His mind was in turmoil. He needed to find Imogen above all things.

"You can, of course have a few days off - I need to await the emissary's report. Before then, there is one more duty you must undertake."

Araz remained still.

"The trial of Tarik Zuberi is due to take place shortly. And Araz, I will need you to testify how he misused the Tractus and made inappropriate contact with the primitive race. You will not be required to say much, just to answer in a way where blame can be apportioned to this Falsebred."

Araz looked askance. "You want me to lie?"

"Lie? Such a strong word. I want you to agree with the statements of the prosecutor. I am sure you can manage that, can't you?"

Araz dare not refuse. Ubaid had him cornered.

"Can I ask, why is all the blame being placed on Tarik Zuberi? It was the other subversives who jumped to Earth first. Surely, they are the ones to be held to account. Is Kasmut Akil not to be tried?"

"Ah! An impossibility. You see, a trial must have an accused. We only have Tarik," shrugged Ubaid.

"And Kasmut?"

"I'm afraid you do not have clearance for that information. Let's just say, he is beyond needing a trial."

Araz did not flinch outwardly, but his heart sank. He knew what this must mean. He had not thought they would terminate this man, not without a fair hearing. Did this not go against all the Sanctus laws underpinning their society? A further thought stuck him, Imogen would be bereft at the news.

Ubaid continued, oblivious to Araz's internal dismay.

"Tarik Zuberi is the only one to face condemnation, for now. His father, Nuru Zuberi, has already been condemned. There is no point naming the other subversives. By your own report, Firas and Eshe are dead and Rashida incapacitated. This leaves only Sefu Zuberi hiding somewhere with his brother on Earth. We know Sefu was the lead scientist on the Tractus after the death of Firas and we know Sefu will hold invaluable information. So, at my behest, the Supreme Council took the decision not to publicly name Sefu Zuberi. You see, young Araz, sometimes it is better not to alienate your enemies. They may come in useful one day. The details of the Tractus project remain far more important than the individuals who developed it. Talking of which, I need to know more of this moveable marker; a most interesting innovation. Come, accompany me to the trial."

Araz had no option but to follow Ubaid out of the Observation Deck. He was churning inside. He was not sure what was going on and only hoped Imogen was safe and would be able to find her way out of The Hub to their fall-back rendezvous point near the Karnak station. Aside from worry, he felt sick with guilt. He had sworn to protect Imogen but had failed miserably. He needed to think things through. His initial plan to discuss Imogen's future with Ubaid had gone awry.

Did Ubaid really believe Imogen had died at the hands of the Repros. Did he know she was a Penta-Crypt? Frantically trying to devise a plan of action, he resolved to find Imogen first, deciding he could probably slip out of the trial once he had given his testimony.

Travelling the thousands of floors down to ground level, Ubaid was disappointed to find Araz knew no technical details of the portable markers.

As they left The Hub to walk to the High Court, Ubaid turned to Araz. "Tell me, Araz, what was your impression of the people of Earth?"

"Much as we had anticipated," Araz replied without having to cloak his colours. "At best, blinkered and self-obsessed; at worst, barbaric."

"Pity, I was rather hoping it was all an exaggeration. Ah well, no matter. That will make things a lot easier."

Araz had no idea what Ubaid meant, but his head was so full of concerns for Imogen, his focus was completely on how to find her and fathom out a way to legitimise her Holan status.

THE CHRONICLES OF HOLIS - THE SANCTUS LAWS

WARNING: In the following chronicle there have been deletions and additions to the original version. Please take note of the underlined additions. Those found in possession of these original chronicles will be deemed subversive. It is therefore vital you keep this DE hidden. May the blessings of Ra be upon you.

Barbara.

So, dear reader, I now come to the Sanctus Laws; the founding philosophy for our entire race. These wonderful laws protect each and every Holan Citizen. These ~~six~~ <u>seven</u> simple but fundamental rules, drawn up after the terrible reign of Anubis, underpin our peaceful society. Without these, there would be no unity and our race could be at risk of disintegrating into warring factions.

THE SANCTUS LAWS:
1) Every Holan <u>Citizen</u> is born free and equal.
2) The life of every Holan <u>Citizen</u> is sacrosanct.
3) Every Holan <u>Citizen</u> has the right to be clothed, fed, sheltered, educated, nurtured, valued and loved.
4) Every Holan <u>Citizen</u> has the right to freedom of thought and freedom of expression.
5) Every Holan <u>Citizen</u> has the right to be free of illness, disability, or mental defects.
6) Every Holan <u>Citizen</u> has an intrinsic responsibility to the Holan race; to contribute to the development, well-being and prosperity of Holan society.
7) <u>Every Holan Citizen will safeguard the genetic purity of the Holan race. Contact with alien races is expressly forbidden.</u>

So, there we have it! Simple, but essential laws, they make up the charter of Holan rights giving us a lasting peace for centuries.

Warning: The following Rules of Holan Citizenship have all been added as 'sub-laws'– these did NOT form part of the original Sanctus Laws.
Barbara.

<u>HOLAN CITIZENSHIP</u>
<u>PRE-BIRTH:</u>
1. <u>The Ethics Board of the Council of Sanctity will screen all prospective parents to ensure suitability, both genetically and socially, for parenthood.</u>
2. <u>All new life will be approved and screened by the Ethics Board to ensure each Citizen is born free of any defects (physical, mental or personality disorders).</u>
3. <u>Only one child per family unit will be permitted unless there are exceptional circumstances. (Twins and multiple births are expressly forbidden.)</u>

4. If anyone is born who does not satisfy the above rules, they will be deemed to be Falsely Bred.

AT BIRTH:

1. The dominant personality lines of every Holan child will be identified at birth. These will determine suitability for future occupations and placements, for the good of both individual and society.
2. The crypts of each Holan child will be logged at birth, enabling them to access food, shelter, education, training and occupation.
3. Each Holan child will be nurtured to reach their full potential and play a full part in Holan Society.

ADULTHOOD:

1. If any Holan Citizen threatens, endangers, or subverts the peace of Holis, they will be brought before the Sanctus High Court to be tried by their peers.
2. Every Holan Citizen has the right to a fair trial.
3. The Sanctus High Court, or any other body authorised by The Supreme Council, may confer or remove Citizenship.
4. If Citizenship is removed, there will be no entitlement to anything on the surface of Holis. The life of a Holan without citizenship will, therefore, be forfeit and they will be given a choice of Erasure or Termination.

FALSEBREDS

1. Falsebreds will not be deemed full Citizens of Holis unless they are legitimised by the Sanctus High Court.
2. If a Falsebred is not legitimised, they will not be entitled to Holan Citizenship. Their life will be forfeit and they will be given a choice of Erasure or Termination.

Of course, you cannot have laws without structures to regulate them. So, who upholds our Sanctus Laws? It is our Sanctus High Court, the ultimate decision-making body; a forum of justice and democracy.

Here, every Holan Citizen, who has come of age, ~~is entitled to~~ must vote in this court. The majority verdict will decide the outcome of any issue put before the court. I have to say, in the history of this court there have been few close votes. They are almost all unanimous, such is the accord within our race. ~~The vote to stop the search for a Sanctus Cryptus was probably the closest result every recorded. It was passed by the narrowest of margins.~~ This rule is accepted as a fundamental principle of our democracy, after all, everyone ~~can~~ must vote.

The Sanctus High Court is held in one of the oldest buildings on Holis, in the capital city of Karnak. A replica of an ancient Ankh construction, the central trial area is a raised circular marble stage. The five symbols of our ~~five personality lines~~ five Sub-Councils are beautifully depicted in precious stones, inset in this marble dais. Depending on the light, the symbols appear to revolve below the surface, forming the solid sphere of Ra or the clear orb of Iris, alternating with the solid star of Nut and the clear star of Hathor. The arrow of Amon protrudes from the top of the outermost circle and it points to the Chair of Justice, where our Supreme Leader presides over the Sanctus High Court hearings.

I can tell you, it brings a lump to my throat to see this magnificent and awe-inspiring home of justice; the forum ensuring our peace for so long.

The everyday running of Holis is overseen by the Supreme Council and the five Sub-Councils, so the Sanctus High Court only meets when there is a matter of national importance. It could be the determination of key policies, ~~such as the Elysian Two Project,~~ or a trial for those who break the Sanctus Laws_or to consider the legitimisation of those who have been Falsely Bred.

The Supreme Council members are the guardians of our nation, ensuring smooth and effective government. It acts on behalf of the Sanctus High Court ~~but ultimately, it is the Sanctus High Court which holds absolute power. If there is an immensely important decision to be made, such as: a change of Holan policy, or a matter~~

concerning the defence of Holis, the Sanctus High Court will have the final say.

The Supreme Council consists of the Supreme Leader, the five Viziers of the Sub-Councils and other representatives, all chosen for their flair and innate abilities to hold public office. They are chosen and trained from a young age – many from birth! Quite rightly, these public servants are held in the highest regard and are some of the most honoured members of Holan society.

The Supreme Council cannot, of course, do everything! The day-to-day management of Holis, is therefore overseen by the five Sub-Councils: Enlightenment, Sanctity, Stability, Well-Being and Vision. These are further divided into appropriate organisational groupings such as the Ethics Board, Agriculture Board, or Transport Board for example. So, there is a pyramid structure to the organisation of our government, similar to the physical structure of our High Court.

As I have said before, a blueprint for democracy, unity and peace.

Of course, there will always be those who do not wish to conform to the rules. Thankfully only a handful of rebels have emerged over the last millennia. If they cannot make any useful contribution to our society and refuse to engage with our laws, they will have few options. They would perish without the food, shelter, energy, transport - well, just about everything - which is all provided freely and abundantly. Communal ownership is based on one premise, everyone will play their part. Those who refuse (as I have said, very few to date) can make no useful contribution to Holan society.

So, what to do with these miscreants? In the past, they have been allowed to remove themselves to remote locations, such as the dark side of Holis, or the Tavats which still travel from Holis to Ankh as part of the Elysian Two project. They live as recluses on a subsistence diet with little or no change to their daily lives. They are not allowed to produce children or have a say in the democratic decision making. Why should they? Contempt for the Sanctus laws should not be rewarded! These laws are there to safeguard all, and the repercussions from an act of subversion could not only be wide-reaching, but catastrophic ~~as we have seen from the reign of Anubis~~.

The penalty for breaking the Sanctus Laws is to forfeit Holan Citizenship. It is punishable by death.

THE TRIAL

*E*very seat was taken inside the Sanctus High Court pyramid, apart from the first row of raised gold and black benches to all four sides of the arena. A solitary stool stood on the central raised circular plinth of marble symbols. A hush came upon the crowd as the council members processed in from the entrance tunnel. They were dressed in the traditional gold edged, black Flecto robes and all took up their positions in front of the reserved seats as they awaited their leader. Several musicians struck up the familiar tune on a variety of stringed instruments. The entire audience rose and Her Greatness, Kekara, entered, her golden gown sparkling in the lights of the dramatic setting. At a nod of her head the crowd began to sing, the words of the anthem ringing out from the stone walls as everyone took up the song:

'Wholeness and unity,
Ra-given rule,
Fortified future,
Decided by all,
Justice and sanctity,
Decreed for our race,
Peace and democracy,
Resolved in this place.'

When the sacred song had ended, Kekara nodded graciously to the cheering crowd before taking her seat above the arrow symbol of the marble plinth in the Chair of Justice.

Everyone then sat, silent and expectant, as the lights dimmed and spotlights flooded the central area.

Two elderly Holans, dressed in sand-coloured robes, led Leo to the stool. There he sat flicking a blond curl of his fringe out of his eyes as he turned full circle on the rotating stool to take in the filled courtroom surrounding him. He could only make out the silhouettes of the onlookers as he blinked in the glaring light. The spotlights were dazzling and prevented him seeing any face other than the Supreme Leader, who sat within the illuminated area staring straight at him. He gave a small gulp as he recalled her interrogation of him when he was just a small boy. This had set off a whole chain of events resulting in his mother's arrest. How could he have been so foolish? Although he instinctively wanted to cringe from her presence, he determined he would not be intimidated. Not now. He fixed his stool to face Kekara, head on, and stared back into her impenetrable eyes.

"The Sanctus High Court is now in session," came an official voice.

The tall, heavily-built figure of Odion entered the centrally lit space, the spotlights reflecting off his bald head. He addressed the crowd, his voice filling the court, "Your Greatness, people of Holis. I will now read the charges."

He walked a slow, full circle around the stool before turning to face Leo as he began, "The prisoner, formerly known as Tarik Kemet, has been missing since he was aged eight of our years; his whereabouts, until now, unknown. Since his discovery, a volt of his crypts was taken for re-testing, and the Lineator was employed. This has confirmed the accused is not, in fact, a 'Kemet'. Furthermore, it has been proven his lineage was deliberately falsified at birth."

There was a low, disapproving murmur from the audience before Odion continued, "Our tests show his conception and birth were not authorised by The Ethics Board of the Sanctity Council and that he is, without question, a Falsebred!"

Odion held up a small black ovoid and indicated for those assembled to connect to the DEs available in each seat. The incontrovertible evidence of Leo's genetic lineage, his birth parents and his dominant line of Amon, was laid out for all to see.

"Citizens of Holis,' continued Odion, enjoying the drama of the moment. "As you have seen, it has been ascertained the prisoner is of the Zuberi bloodline. He is the son of Nuru Zuberi – the scientist who subverted the development of a new and potentially hazardous technology."

Leo looked from Odion to Kekara, his brows furrowed. Kekara appeared to all who observed her, to be weighing up the evidence with a meditative look, but her eyes and her Chroma betrayed her malevolent delight with Odion's wording.

Odion continued, "The prisoner's biological father was a trusted member of the restricted Tractus project, which, as you now know, had been expected to give us an instantaneous means of transport to Ankh. Nuru Zuberi betrayed the trust placed in him and conspired with the prisoner, Tarik Zuberi, to hijack the prototype and travel to the fledgling planet, Earth."

There was more tutting from those gathered and a few voices called out: 'No!' and 'Disgraceful!' as they shook their heads.

"I must tell you, it was not only Nuru Zuberi who set this disastrous chain of events into being. Another is also responsible for this travesty. I hereby call to account the mother of the prisoner, the former and once trusted member of the Supreme Council, Sekhet Kemet."

Leo swung round on his stool as the diminutive figure of his fearful mother was led into the central space. Leo gave her a weak smile as she was steered to stand next to him. She did not respond; her eyes were glazed over.

Odion addressed the blonde-haired woman as she blinked in the bright light, "Sekhet Kemet, former member of the Supreme Council, did you or did you not willingly conspire with Nuru Zuberi to conceive and birth an unauthorised child? The prisoner before us?"

Sekhet spoke in a barely audible whisper, "I did."

"And did you or did you not conspire to hide this fact from the authorities, presenting the Falsebred as your legitimate son?"

"I did."

"Have you anything to say for yourself?"

"I… I wanted my own child. I… loved him… I…"

"This has no relevance!" spat Odion.

"Let her speak!" Leo shouted, getting to his feet and taking his mother's shoulders. She looked into his eyes and began weeping as she stammered out the rest of her statement.

"I loved him. Nuru Zuberi – I loved him! I was put in charge of him when he was imprisoned. I thought he loved me. All I wanted was to have his child, but his words of love were a lie! He could not wait to make his escape. He left me. But at least I had my little boy. And then they took him away… they took my Tarik away from me!" Sekhet broke down in uncontrollable tears, slumping into Leo's arms, seemingly unaware her son was the one holding her. Leo was horrified. The implant they had used on his mother had rendered her a jabbering wreck.

Odion snapped his fingers and Sekhet was removed from Leo's arms. He was pushed back on his stool, fighting back tears of anger as she was escorted out.

"The first charge, that Tarik Zuberi is a Falsebred has been corroborated," announced Odion. "The High Court would now normally consider whether Tarik Zuberi should be legitimised and therefore granted citizenship of Holis, however there are other charges. Namely that the Falsebred made unauthorised contact with the primitive race, contact expressly forbidden by decree of the Sanctus High Court. And that he colluded with an enemy of the state. If found guilty, he will forfeit any right to become a Holan citizen. I now call the witness, Araz Vikram, a special agent of the Supreme Council."

Leo looked up in surprise. Araz had been in the church with Imogen? How did he get back, and where was Imogen?

Araz was admitted from the tunnel. He marched directly onto the centrally lit area and stood in front of Odion, recalling Odion's words of menace just minutes before the trial began: 'So, you eluded the Repros on Earth? I know you deliberately disregarded your orders. Think yourself lucky Ubaid has saved you. As far as I am concerned, you are a traitor! Now, play your part or you will be tried as such.' Araz was under no illusion Odion had meant every word. His position was perilous.

Odion now addressed his statements to all four corners of the courtroom, concealing his fury with Araz.

"Araz Vikram, you were sent to Earth to recover the Falsebred were you not?"

Araz answered truthfully, "Yes," knowing those assembled presumed Odion was referring to Tarik Zuberi, not Imogen.

"Can you confirm the prisoner had made contact with the primitives and risked exposing the Holan race to discovery by these primal beings?"

Araz looked at Odion, askance. He could not agree without qualifying the statement. "If you are referring to the fact the prisoner was residing amongst the natives of Earth and, by his very presence, there was an inevitable possibility his Holan background and link would be discovered, thus exposing our race, then yes."

Odion looked at Araz furiously but kept his voice calm as he addressed the court again, "We now come to the final charge of illegal contact with alien beings. Araz Vikram, was there any evidence the prisoner had inappropriate relations with any of the primitive race?"

Araz, knowing he was expected to answer 'yes', looked directly at Leo. He disliked Leo intensely, thinking him to be a fool and a rival for Imogen's affections, however he could not bring himself to lie. Instead, he answered, "I did not witness any first hand, but that is not to say inappropriate liaisons were not made."

The inference to Leo was all too clear – he was referring to an imaginary liaison with Imogen. Leo shook his head and gave a derisory laugh. "In my dreams!"

"Silence! The prisoner will remain quiet until it is his turn to speak!" spluttered Odion before continuing.

"Finally, I ask our trusted agent, did the prisoner collude with the known subversive, Nuru Zuberi, in stealing the technology of the Tractus from the Holan race, thereby perverting the course of its development?"

Araz frowned. He had not witnessed first-hand who had 'stolen' the project from Holis, but his commanders did not know about Tanastra Thut. The man had paid the ultimate price. He resolved he would not tarnish his memory. Araz knew he could not mention the other scientists involved, not after his exchange with Ubaid. So instead he answered, "The prisoner is a fool. I do not know his capabilities."

"I did not ask you about his capabilities. I asked if he colluded with Nuru Zuberi?" Odion grunted through clenched teeth.

"I surmise this to be the case," was all Araz would say.

Although Odion glared angrily at Araz, those in the courtroom took Araz's statement to confirm Leo's guilt and loud calls of condemnation circulated the High Court, rising in volume until Odion called for quiet.

Odion then turned to Leo.

"Tarik Zuberi – stand! Have you anything to say in your defence?

Leo stood and shrugged his shoulders, "What's the point? I've got as much chance of proving my innocence as bringing a dead parrot back to life!" He folded his arms and glared at Araz and Odion.

"Your Greatness, the accused has declined the right to speak in his defence, so this therefore concludes the case against Tarik Zuberi," Odion bowed obsequiously to Kekara.

The leader gave a gracious nod of her head and addressed the courtroom, "All citizens, present both here and across our lands, are now required to vote on the verdict." There was a ripple of movement as everyone connected with their DEs again.

The Supreme Leader waited a few moments, connected to her device for the result and rose, slowly walking the outline of the circles on the marble floor. "People of Holis, you will know our Sanctus laws attest to every Holan life being sacred. Every citizen is sanctioned, nurtured and given full life. In return for this freedom, each Holan has a fundamental responsibility to our society. That is, to abide by the laws and statutes of the land, to ensure the protection of our long and hard-won peace and to play a full part in the evolving of our race." Kekara then turned to Leo.

"Tarik Zuberi, you stand accused of being a Falsebred, subverting the direction of an essential research project and making contact, which is forbidden, with the race of primitives on Earth thus breaking the Sanctus laws of Holis. The populace has now voted on the verdict. The decision was unanimous. You have not been legitimised. You have been found guilty. Guilty as charged."

The courtroom erupted with shouts of approval. Kekara put her hand in the air for quiet. "Has the condemned anything further to say?"

Leo rose to his full height and spoke, "Yes." He then 'flicked open' an imaginary communicator and, as if speaking into it, called, "Beam me up, Scottie. I'm in a hot spot!"

A small number of those assembled gave a chuckle at the strange response, and Kekara glared at Leo. "The Vizier of Stability will now ask your choice in the manner of sentence. Bring the lights up so you may see your peers; those who have decided your fate."

Kekara returned to her seat and the spot lights dimmed as the main court lights came on.

Odion began, "Tarik Zuberi, you have been found guilty. In accordance with the Sanctus Laws of Holis, you..."

Leo did not hear the rest of the statement, he had slowly turned to take in the faces of the thousands of Holans gathered in the pyramid, and then he saw her! There! In the front row - staring right back at him! Imogen!

His heart skipped a beat and he blinked. The words, what? And how? dashed across his thoughts before he hurriedly composed himself. He knew he must not give her away. He quickly attempted to communicate with her using his Chroma - a cream circle with a black outline - their code for staying silent. Her Chroma did not respond. Yellow veins of curiosity mingling with green calms were evident, but there was no sign of recognition in either her colours or her body language. In fact, she was glancing at the people either side of her, to check if Leo had intentionally gaped at her.

Leo stared in barely concealed horror - what have they done to her?

Araz followed Leo's stare and hurriedly stifled a gasp when he saw Imogen's face. She did not seem to be under guard. How did she get here? He must not give her away and as for the stupid Falsebred, he must be stopped before he could say anything.

Araz marched up to Leo, standing directly between Imogen and Leo's line of sight.

"The Vizier of Stability has given you a choice?"

Leo re-focussed on Araz's eyes, which pierced his own with the unspoken demand, 'Do not look at her!' Araz's colours swam with dark vivid flashes of alarm. Leo knew Araz had seen Imogen too. Confused as to whether Araz was helping or hampering the situation, Leo decided to play along. After all, Imogen's very presence meant Araz had not eliminated her. On the contrary, he seemed to be trying to hide her.

"Choice?" Leo mumbled.

"Erasure or termination?" Araz repeated Odion's words.

"What?"

"You heard!" sneered Odion.

"Erasure or termination? Now let me see…" Leo, recovered himself and, his mouth breaking into a forced grin, finished, "Er… no, actually I'll go for freedom!"

"What?" growled Odion.

"I'm just pulling your leg!" laughed Leo, hoping to draw away any unwanted attention towards Imogen. "I do so love having a choice! So, let me think… Yes, that's it! I choose termination!" Leo said with a flourish. A few more chuckles were heard.

"You do not appear to understand the gravity of your situation," Kekara said icily, casting her eyes over the spectators and instantly silencing those who had dared to laugh. She searched the crowds to find out which person the prisoner and the agent had noticed. Who had prompted such a strange and diversionary display? Her eyes settled briefly on the face they had seen. She resolved to investigate this further.

Rising from her seat, the assembled followed. Silence fell and the Supreme Leader pronounced sentence, "Tarik Zuberi – you have chosen termination. Your sentence will be carried out tomorrow."

Odion closed the session and Leo was led away, not daring to look back to Imogen. Kekara then left, followed by Odion.

Araz and the other council members filed out with the rest of the audience through the stone tunnel.

Araz drew to one side of the passageway and lay in wait for Imogen, heart racing. He was sure Kekara had spotted her. He must get to her first.

As soon as she stepped out of the courtroom, he jumped next to her, hissing a warning as, walking alongside, he matched her pace. "You have been seen!"

"What?"

"What were you thinking? To put yourself in such a position of exposure?"

"I beg your pardon?"

Half way down the tunnel Araz suddenly pushed her into a doorway, activating the Phase-Seal with one hand and manhandling her into an inner stone corridor with the other, before sealing the door.

"What? What are you doing?" she said angrily, pulling away from his arm.

"It's another route out. Look, I'm sorry I didn't protect you and I am incredibly relieved you are okay, but to go to the Sanctus High Court! You risk everything!"

"I have no idea what you are talking about Araz Vikram, special agent. And you had better let me go right now!" was her only response. Her eyes showed no recognition of him, just genuine astonishment and annoyance. Her voice was, somehow, different. He looked to her Chroma. Normally there was an undercurrent of grey worry or quartz analysis, but the dominant colour appeared to be copper indignation, a shade he had rarely, if ever, seen in Imogen's aura.

Then it dawned on Araz. They must have caught her and used an implant to control her. Ubaid had known she was alive all along!

Now Ubaid would know he had lied and he would be deemed a traitor by both commanders. He quickly resolved he must seek help from other quarters and knowing Imogen would not go willingly whilst under the influence of the implant, he only had one option.

He put a hand into the folds of his outfit as he opened his other palm in supplication. "Sorry! I'm sorry. Please forgive me."

Before she could answer, his hidden hand found the pen and he swiftly pushed it against her neck, pressed the button and caught her as she slumped, unconscious, into his arms.

Gently lifting her, he moved quickly down the passage, one he had used often during his training. Breathing hard with the effort, he slipped out of a side exit, half a mile away to make his way to his father's living quarters at the edge of Karnak.

In the organic, domed structure, there was a spare room Araz had often used. Luckily, the populace was slowly making its way back from the High Court and no one saw him enter.

He was relieved to find his old room unoccupied and he placed Imogen on the bed as he caught his breath and sat beside her. He gently moved his fingertips over her neck and checked behind her ears for the tell-tale sign of an implant but could find none. Where had they embedded it, if not here? As she started to stir, he took one of her hands, stroking it lovingly. Then alarm struck him. He grabbed her other hand and turned it over before releasing it to her side. His mind raced, and he leapt to his feet in dismay.

No scar! There was no scar! This could only mean one thing. The person before him was not Imogen!

IMOGEN

*T*he day before the trial, Imogen had been on the point of screaming when she had been hauled into the secret passageway below The Hub. But as her eyes adjusted to the bright light and she saw who was there, she knew instantly she was safe. Next to a red-haired older woman, the one who had spoken in her ear, was the familiar cropped-haired figure of Em.

Imogen let out a sigh of relief.

"Is good surprise?" Em winked, smiling wickedly.

"You gave me the fright of my life!" answered Imogen, slowing her heart rate. *Thank goodness! Now I can get help finding my dad and Leo.* "How did you know I was here?"

"Chronicle DE – is tracer inside," stated Em, simply. "Araz too has tracer – he not know! So much for clever agent! I observe this Araz – one minute on surveillance, is with you - then sudden, he left! Should have guessed. Not trust this creep. So, made plan and track you down here."

"I am so glad you did! Although Araz didn't exactly leave me." Imogen felt a stab of anguish when she thought of Araz's capture. He had been so cross she had not told him she was a Penta-Crypt. She hoped he was safe, but her mind was full of questions. *Why did he have to force me to use the Lineator? Will he tell anyone? What will his commanders say when they realise he has helped me? Will his life be in danger?*

"Is good you entered crypts in Hub?"

"No – no, I didn't," Imogen began, wondering how she managed to open the Phase-Seal lift door with her hand.

Em was about to question her further when the red-haired woman interrupted.

"We must make haste." She indicated for Em and Imogen to follow her down the narrow passageway until they emerged in what looked like a dead end. Em touched a small indentation in the stone wall and it melted to reveal a large elevator capsule inside. Moving horizontally for several miles and then rising numerous floors, they finally emerged into a circular stone room, sculpted into the rock.

"Is headquarters – adjacent mountain to Hub. Is safe."

Em led Imogen to an area filled with organically powered computers, like those she had seen in the Qus undersea library. She looked around. There was a suspension chamber in the middle of the room. It contained a familiar pulsing black globe.

"Is that…?"

"Yes, is secret marker. To jump to Earth. Council not know of this." Em confirmed.

Imogen felt a tug on her heart. To escape back to Earth was a real temptation. She could almost touch the activation switch. *So close - what I would give to go back home!* Thoughts of seeing her mother again started to intrude, but she put the brakes on these. *No, I must remain here until I free Dad and Leo.*

At the behest of the other woman, Imogen sat at a bench.

"Imogen, I am Shani," she spoke quickly and quietly. "I was once the Vizier of Sanctity."

Shani? Yes, Adam was visibly upset when Araz said Shani was no longer in post. What was the other name? Got it - Jabari!

Shani continued, "I have, to all intents and purposes, retired from public office in order to undertake a research project on the dark side of Holis. In reality, I am directing the Resistance here. My codename is 'Barbara' but my true identity must not be revealed to the enemy. I have managed to stay undercover for many years."

I thought I knew her voice. She's the one who gave the warnings in the original Chronicles of Holis.

"Codename is my idea," Em said proudly. "Is for Barbarians - the barbaric peoples of Earth!"

"They're not all barbaric," protested Imogen.

"Is what you call?" Em clicked her fingers repeatedly until the word came to her, "Ironic!"

"Hilarious!" Imogen rolled her eyes to heaven, then turned back to Shani. "Do you know where they are holding my father and Leo?"

"Tarik, the one you call Leo, his trial is taking place tomorrow. He will be moved to the High Court and we hope to make contact with him. We have managed to devise a rescue plan, but this relies on him being taken to the place of termination on the following day for sentence to be carried out. There we can intercept him, away from the city guards."

"Termination? You think he will be found guilty?"

"We know he will," was the grim answer.

Imogen's stomach folded. *Poor Leo!*

Em continued, "Good news is, Shani send secret message to this Tarik, so he find out plan. He must choose termination, not erasure. Is always next day. Then we be there – in waiting for him - yes?"

Imogen nodded as optimistically as she could. *What if he's executed before then?* She could not bear to think of Leo being killed.

Imogen turned back to Shani. "And my father?"

Swirls of sepia shades engulfed Shani's colours. Her eyes lowered for a moment and with a sigh she went to reply, but Imogen saw the answer all too clearly in Shani's chromatic tones of sorrow, pity and regret.

With tears welling behind her eyes, Imogen held up a shaking open hand to stop the woman speaking. She could barely catch her breath as she cried out, "No! Don't tell me he is dead! No! I won't hear it. He's alive, I know he is alive, I have to believe my father is alive." Blood thumped around Imogen's head and her heart seemed to erupt, misery and grief exploding from within. She turned to run, anywhere, but Em's strong hands grabbed her shoulders, stopping her and easing her down to the stone floor where the molten tears of bitter despair flowed down her cheeks. Guttural sounds she barely heard vented from her chest and she beat her fists against Em's arms until she was utterly exhausted and spent.

Eventually Shani spoke. "This is so hard for you Imogen. Yet there is still a small, very small chance your father escaped death, but we have found no trace of him and there were sightings of a man sent to his execution… I feel it would be wrong to give you false hope. We have also lost trace of the former Vizier of Well Being, Jabari. He was under arrest for months and we fear he may also have been terminated." Shani's eyes misted as her colours flared gold edged reds. Her Chroma spoke volumes. Imogen could see Shani was in love with Jabari.

Shani took a deep breath and her colours took on soothing shades. "Imogen tell me of your mother, Rashida. Is she safe?"

Imogen breathed deeply to stop any fresh tears. *Mum! So far away. What will this news do to you?* Knowing her mother would be inconsolable, discovering her life's love had been slaughtered, it was all she could do to keep a check on her emotions and stammer out a reply, "My mother was in a coma for ten years. She only awoke a few weeks ago and is now recovering with the help of those who are left on Earth."

Shani nodded and gave Imogen's shoulder a light squeeze of comfort before helping her to her feet.

"Your mother was an incredible scientist. One of the rare Tri-Crypts. It is thanks to her we have Data Encounters everywhere. I am sure she is in safe hands and will make a full recovery. Now it is time to eat and rest."

Imogen did not feel like eating, the food tasted like cardboard in her mouth, but she forced down a little before being led to a small room with a hammock-style bed.

"Here, drink this," Em said kindly, offering her a salver-style 'cup' of warm liquid. "It help you rest."

Imogen drank gratefully and as she transferred to the soft bed, she instantly fell into a deep and dreamless sleep.

The next morning Imogen woke with a heavy heart. Em and Shani treated her with kindness and care, but she felt numb from the shock of her father's death. She ate and drank mechanically and Shani had to coax her to make eye contact to converse with her.

"Imogen, I need to run some tests on your DNA. We have been unable to do research into the effects of travelling by Tractus on the Holan cells. There are still safety concerns we need to investigate. Do I have your permission to do a full body scan and take a volt of flesh?"

Imogen merely nodded compliance; she did not care what they did. All she could see were the faces of her father, Tanastra and Eshe, all incredible scientists, all now dead. They had died protecting the blueprints and prototype of the Tractus. It was their life work and now they were gone. *What was the point of it all? And if they find out I'm a Penta-Crypt, so what? What can it matter now?*

Shani patted Imogen's shoulder before holding a small clear globe above Imogen's head and releasing it in the air. It lit up, hovered and then spiralled around Imogen's body, going from her head to toe, before returning to Shani's hand. She then took Imogen's palm and, with a passing glance, stroked the open hand with the same device. Imogen was only aware of a slight tingling, a little like a small shock of static electricity, but she didn't react.

Other tests took up most of the morning, but Imogen was not within her body. Her mind was deep in the recesses of loss and despair.

Em and Shani talked in low whispers, clearly worried about Imogen's disposition.

"Imogen, we need to turn to more pressing matters. There is something we must show you." Shani walked to the far wall and touched the screen which sprang into life.

"We have had an interesting development - it could help us rescue Tarik. This may come as a surprise to you, Imogen, but I want you to watch the broadcast from yesterday morning."

Imogen's thoughts were far away, torment and desolation for her parents clouding her mind. Her focus on the news bulletin was negligible until Em made a sweeping hand movement towards the faces of the two new councillors. Shani slowed the speed of the multi-dimensional clip and Imogen homed in on the image of the female councillor. She shot up in surprise, mouth open, as her finger pointed reflexively to the person in front of her.

What? No! It can't be!

There before her – it was her! Her body, her face! Large as life and identical in every way! This duplicate had her hair pinned up in a similar style, she smiled in the same way and she seemed to have the same mannerisms. The holographic Imogen tousled the hair of a small child who came to touch her arm, as the real Imogen watched.

It could be me! Imogen reeled, although she could see this other version of her had an air of confidence she had always lacked. *What the hell? Is she a twin? Some kind of Doppelgänger?*

"Who is that?" she managed to ask, unable to peel her eyes from the slow motion moves of her double. "What's going on?"

"You have sibling, yes?" Em saw Imogen shake her head, mesmerised by her double. "This one name, is Naomi, is new member of Supreme Council. Just come of age, like you. Maybe your cells duplicated in womb?"

Imogen shook her head. *She's the same age, yet I was born over forty years earlier. If she was my twin, she would be fifty-seven!*

Imogen looked at Shani. "I was born on Earth – just me - how could they have placed a twin on Holis? Could this Naomi be an android?"

Shani froze the broadcast on Naomi's smiling face and sat down, indicating for Imogen to join her. "No, not an android. Imogen. I believe… I believe she must be your clone."

Imogen replayed the words in her head. *Clone? How can she be? It doesn't make sense.* "You can't clone a person without their DNA. How did they get mine?"

"I have been trying to figure that out." Shani responded. "The only person to have returned to Holis since your birth, was Tarik. He was only eleven, but he may have been given a fragment of your crypts to give to one of our number to enter in The Hub, in case you came here. I can't think how else you could have been duplicated."

Is that how I was able to open the Phase-Seal door of the elevator?

"My dad would know…" Imogen started, before a fresh realisation of his loss swamped her train of thought.

"And Tarik," added Em. "This Tarik also know. We ask, if rescue work."

If it works? It must work. They can't kill Leo as well as my dad… will I really never see him again? Her grief threatened to overwhelm her again.

"Imogen, we need you to stay focussed," said Shani kindly, placing an arm around her shoulders.

Imogen bit her lip, dragging her mind above her crushing wretchedness and fiercely brushing away the tears spilling, afresh, down her cheeks.

Shani continued, "My specialism was genetic modelling. I trained under Eshe – I think you knew her on Earth?"

Imogen nodded, not trusting herself to speak.

"Eshe was a marvellous teacher. Some say she was a Vatic - someone who could see into the future. I don't know about that, but she was aware of the techniques for molecular cloning and maybe she knew it would happen one day. However, no one was allowed to experiment with this. The Board of Ethics, quite rightly, banned such a practice. They have since also prohibited multiple births, so there is no concept of twins on Holis. For this to have been possible," Shani nodded at the frozen Naomi. "Someone must have broken the rules."

Imogen sharpened her focus to deliberate on this new information. *I have a clone! Who did this? And why?* Her need to rise above her overpowering sorrow forced her to concentrate on this conundrum. *No wonder everyone stared at me when we entered The Hub. When they called me 'Quora', they thought I was her. Even the guards saluted me! And I thought that was for Araz!* Another powerful thought slammed into her mind. *This Naomi must be a Penta-Crypt, like me! Of course! That's why she is on the Supreme Council. Is this the reason I was cloned? If so, someone must have known? Leo? Does Shani know? No one has mentioned the Sanctus Cryptus.*

Shani interrupted Imogen's meditations, "Imogen, to get to Tarik we can use this to our advantage. We will need you to act as if you are Naomi. As a member of the Supreme Council she has authorised access to areas we do not. You will be able to free him from his imprisonment once the trial is over."

"If it means rescuing Leo, I will do anything."

Before Shani could say more, Em gave a loud cough. "Is one problem with this plan."

Imogen and Shani both looked at Em who flicked her head towards the motionless newsreel.

"Is already one Naomi. So, need remove her for this plan to work."

"Yes, we can't both be in the same place."

"Now that may be a more complicated problem," mused Shani, getting up to walk around the stone room. "I can't see how this can be done without alerting the authorities to our scheme. We may just need to chance it."

"Chance it?"

"Take a risk you will not both end up in the same place at the same time. I think you call it 'needing a lucky break' on Earth?"

Her father's face jumped into Imogen's mind, as he spoke his old adage: *'You know what I say about luck – you make your own luck in this world'*, and a sob escaped her mouth as she gave a slight dip of her head, indicating she was willing to take this risk.

"Come, is time for trial." Em switched the screen to the Sanctus High Court, ready for the live broadcast as Imogen brought her emotions under control.

I will rescue Leo. They will not kill him too.

NAOMI

*N*aomi began to wake. Where was she? Random images started to seep into her thoughts, a man's harrowed face, the one haunting her dreams since the encounter set up by Ubaid. She had looked at him through a glass partition. Ubaid had forbidden her to say anything. When the elderly prisoner had seen her, he had leapt to his feet pressing his hands against the window as tears flowed down his cheeks. She had wanted to reach out and touch the glass to connect with his hands - she did not know why - but she had, dutifully, remained motionless before being ushered from the room. The meeting had left her feeling deeply uncomfortable and his face of abject sorrow had stayed with her.

Then the image mutated into first one, then thousands of Repros. All wielding knives and snarling. She seemed to look on from above – as if out of her body - as they encircled and advanced closer to a second helpless and terrified figure of herself below. Naomi swept the vision to one side, attempting to take heed as troubling theories bombarded her thoughts. What are these Repros? Brutal. Savage. She strongly suspected there was some deep subterfuge connected to their development.

Her conscious mind stirred further and another face glimmered - the curly-haired Falsebred on trial. He had seemed unaware of the seriousness of the charges and had looked straight at her as if he knew her. She sensed he had been trying to communicate with her.

Fully roused, Naomi shook the mirages and the drowsy feeling from her head as her mind cleared and she slowly opened her eyes. There he was, the agent from the court, Araz Vikram, pacing the floor with a troubled expression on his face. Naomi sat herself up and waited in silence. How did she get here? The memory slammed into her mind accompanied by a growing outrage. He had waited for her and forced her into a hidden passage, speaking to her as if he knew her. She had not been able to make sense of his words. Now they were in a dwelling place. Where? Karnak? He must have anaesthetised her as she had no recollection of how she had got here. Her immediate response was to feel fury. How dare this agent abduct a member of the Supreme Council? But the anger was also accompanied by curiosity. Why has he seized me? Plus, another odd emotion, one she had not experienced before, attraction. He had stroked her hand so lovingly as she stirred, it had sent a flicker of electricity through her nervous system.

Finally noticing she was awake, Araz stopped pacing. "Who are you?" His eyes flashed some unspoken accusation.

"I think I am entitled to ask the same question," she replied, before adding, "Who did you think I was?"

"I mistook you for someone else," Araz said dismissively.

"Who?"

"I cannot explain, but I need to know your status."

"You should know my 'status', retorted Naomi. How did he have the audacity to question her? She kept tight-lipped for a few minutes, but the way he wrung his hands together made her realise he was genuinely in turmoil, so she relented, answering, "I am one of the new members of the Supreme Council. Do you not recognise the robes?" Naomi held out her Flecto robe of black and gold. "Do you not watch the daily broadcasts?" The derision in her voice was clear.

"Yes, No! I... I have been away for some time..." started Araz.

"Where?"

Araz stared at her long and hard before giving a truthful answer, "Earth."

Naomi got to her feet, an eager expression on her face. "Of course. Your mission was to Earth. Only a few agents have been allowed to explore the primitive planet. I am hoping to go there too - I specialised in Earth studies over the last few years."

Araz did not seem to hear what she said as he paced the floor again.

"So, why did you capture me?"

"Capture? I meant to rescue... look, it was a mistake. I apologise. As I said, I thought you were someone else."

"You knew the Falsebred on trial, didn't you? Tarik Zuberi. I could tell you had met before. You were both staring at me. Why?"

"I knew of him, but I have not associated with him." His words were filled with contempt. "Look, I don't have time for this. What did you say your name was?"

"I didn't! But as you're one of the few who doesn't seem to know, I may as well tell you. It's Naomi."

"Naomi," Araz repeated quietly.

"Am I free to go? If this was a mistake?" she asked.

"Yes... No! That is, I need your help."

"Why on Holis would I help you?"

Araz glared at her but, appearing to control his response despite his clenched fists, he began, "I have a pressing problem I need to discuss with you."

It seemed to Naomi, Araz was trying to make this sound more like a request than a demand, but he wasn't quite able to curb the haughty edge to his voice.

"Do you normally sedate and kidnap people to get a conversation?" she asked in an icy tone.

Araz lurched backward staring wildly at her. These were the exact same words Imogen had used when he had abducted her on Earth.

"Are you okay?" Naomi edged her way over to the door as she spoke, wondering what was wrong with the guy.

Araz shook his head as if to dislodge a thought from inside. He seemed to decide on something and quickly advanced on Naomi, took her arm and sat her back on the side of the bed.

A small shudder coursed around her body as she flushed and found herself complying. Her mind raced with questions: What is going on? Why does he have this effect on me? But she told herself to stay calm and quash any outward reaction.

"I have no intention of hurting you, but I require your help to rescue someone who is lost in The Hub."

"Why would I help you? You'd better know, if this is an act of subversion I will not cooperate."

"Look, I am on your side. I have worked for the Supreme Council for the last two years, searching Earth for those who stole the Tractus project, investigating the reports of illegal Falsebreds. I have been fighting the subversive movement since I became an agent. However, there have been some new developments and… All I can say is this is a lot more complicated than you think."

"Try me!" Naomi folded her arms and fixed a determined expression on her face.

Araz nodded slowly. "Okay. I have a theory about this – about you."

Naomi looked sceptical but remained silent as Araz continued.

"This may sound bizarre, but I need you to listen to the full explanation. If you think the same way as Imog… I mean, if you analyse everything I tell you, you can come to your own conclusions. Then it's up to you if you assist me."

Naomi nodded, intrigued by this enigmatic stranger. His rich voice and musky scent had a weirdly unnerving effect on her. He was not unattractive, but she determined to keep her emotions in check and hear him out. After all, thanks to the waning light of Ib, she could see his quartz colours of honesty and his Chroma would instantly show if he was lying.

NEW YORK

*I*n the flat above Central Park, the three, almost identical Zuberi brothers were in each other's company for the first time in over a decade. Nuru could barely wipe the smile off his face. He had been longing for this day. Reunited with Sefu and Amsu, his past annoyances and irritations began to melt away.

"Finally, we are altogether!" beamed Nuru. "Sefu and Amsu..."

Adam interrupted, "I prefer the name, Adam, brother. Whilst I was on Holis, everyone called me Nuru thinking I was you. Here on Earth, I have grown accustomed to Adam."

"Adam it is. So, what has changed to allow us to work together?"

Sefu replied and spoke in serious tones, "Many things have changed. Most significantly, we have just had an update from Holis." Sefu looked up as the door opened and Rashida entered, crossing to join them. More youthful than her peers, a result of being catapulted forward in time by thirty years, she exuded a sense of calm and rationality.

Sefu felt a surge of pride at the transformation he had worked on this woman. Once broken and on the point of being permanently deranged, he had used sophisticated therapies to ease her troubled mind and nurse her back to a healthy mental state. It had been at the cost of some memory loss, but the recollections causing distress were nothing but a distraction from clear logical thinking. He congratulated himself on a job well done.

"Imogen?" asked Rashida. "Is she safe?"

"Rashida, your daughter is alive, but as to whether she is safe, I'm afraid we have scant information."

Rashida nodded. What would once have prompted blind panic, was now received with a minimal trace of concern. "Who sent the communication?"

Sefu hesitated before replying, "An emissary from Holis. He has jumped to Earth using the enemy marker in London. He made contact from there and he is hoping to broker a peace between us and the Supreme Council."

"Who is he? One of our supporters?"

"I cannot say," Sefu gave an apologetic wave of his hand. "His mission has not been made public on Hollis. In fact, Kekara may not know of it yet. However, with many of our people in danger, I feel we have no option but to trust this source, for now." He shot a glance at his brothers who both gave an imperceptible nod of understanding at the unspoken communication. He did not want them to question him further in front of Rashida.

Rashida missed this. She had closed her eyes momentarily whilst taking a deep breath and putting her hands in her lap. She calmly looked to Sefu for him to continue.

The therapy drills were working well, thought Sefu as he began, "At least we have had some intelligence from this emissary and it would seem Imogen has reached Karnak. She has spoken to one of the Viziers, however the situation is not straightforward."

"And Tarik?" asked Adam, anxiety and guilt colouring his question.

"Tarik has been held prisoner since his capture. He is to be tried as a Falsebred."

Adam swallowed. He had never bonded with his son. He had been furious when he discovered Sekhet had stolen his crypts. She had bypassed the Board of Ethics and without his knowledge she had authorised, birthed and then raised up their child. She had even made genetic modifications to ensure the boy's features looked more like his blonde-haired mother, disguising the Zuberi characteristics. She had had no right! However, he knew he should not have blamed Tarik. He should not have taken his annoyance out on the lad. Now his son's life was in danger and he may have lost the chance to try to be the father he should have always been. He sighed as he listened to the rest of Sefu's report.

"Tarik is also accused of subverting the Tractus project. And for some reason, the rest of us, other than Nuru, have not been publicly named."

Nuru laughed. "Notorious – that's me! Even if they are no doubt referring to you Adam, as you spent thirty years there as Nuru. What did you do to get such a bad reputation for the Zuberi name?"

Adam took this as a rhetorical question, but Rashida turned to him and asked, "What did you do? I don't recall what happened."

"I stayed on Holis, Rashida. When you all came to Earth, I covered up your absences and reported the Tractus project was not going well."

"You lied?"

Adam paused. Rashida had once known all this, but since her time-vault, coma and Sefu's treatment, she had lost many key facts. He patiently explained, "Not so much lies, more like being economical with the truth! But given the Supreme Council was rife with deceit, I felt no qualms. Anyway, I was finally discovered along with our Tractus link - even though it took nearly ten full years - and I was arrested. I had to broker my freedom by seeming to cooperate with those who held me."

"You gave them the Tractus technology?" Rashida's voice was full of accusation.

"Not exactly. I was forced to give them the means to set up their own link from Karnak to Earth. Our original marker, the one linking to the Birmingham church, was now under constant watch by the Council of Stability. However, I did not divulge the intricacies of the markers' construction. They were so desperate for their own device they took it 'blind'. I also persuaded one of the councillors to put her trust in me." Adam coloured at his memory of using Sekhet and pouring on the charm. Little had he known it would result in Tarik's birth.

"And we all know what that means!" Nuru nudged his brother with his elbow.

Rashida gave Adam a disdainful look as he shook his head sorrowfully. He continued, "So, I ended up furnishing them with a marker, sited in The Hub. One linking to the Earth marker they had set up in the London underground after the attack in 1966. This remains the only enemy marker on Earth. I encrypted the workings, so they could not be interrogated without rendering the marker unusable."

"And how did you escape?"

"The council eventually placed their trust in me. I gave an eloquent account of how you had all abandoned me, so they thought I had returned my allegiance to them. As I gained more freedom, I secretly summoned support for our cause and set up new markers on Holis for the underground movement. One is sited close to the Karnak Hub, another near the Southern Sea and a third on the dark side of Holis. These locations remain hidden, but added to our new Earth markers we now have many escape routes in order to flee from those seeking to find us. They only have one way in and out, as the Birmingham marker is unusable, so it is vital they do not discover our other markers or the fact we now have portable markers allowing for jumps from any location."

Rashida pressed her hand to her forehead as if trying to remember something.

"Sefu, you said Imogen was going to find her father?"

"Yes."

"She will do it, I am sure. Then Kasmut will ensure Tarik is freed and Imogen is unharmed. He has kept us safe all these years."

Sefu, unable to concur, merely smiled as if he agreed.

Nuru spoke with some urgency, "If we are going to have any chance of exposing the corruption in the Supreme Council, we must prepare to confront them. Yes, they hold some of our people, but we hold the specifications of the Tractus design. Our original research must be resumed and at speed. This information is our most powerful weapon."

Sefu responded, "I agree, especially as the latest information suggests the Supreme Council is now willing to negotiate. The proposal is basically this, in exchange for the Tractus design they will grant everyone their freedom. Everyone apart from Nuru, who has been publicly condemned and will therefore need to stand trial"

Adam shrugged his shoulders as Sefu added, "But it has been indicated Nuru will be reprieved, providing we cooperate."

The brothers looked to each other, highly suspicious of this, but no one spoke for fear of prompting a train of thought capable of upsetting Rashida's finely balanced psyche.

"I have been thinking of the time vault capability of the Tractus," was Rashida's response, as she stared distantly at a clock on the wall. "And I think I know why this happened."

Adam and Nuru looked surprised at Rashida's statement but Sefu felt this was final proof - Rashida's clear thinking and sharp mind had returned.

Sefu concluded, "This is a good idea – to find out how and why this occurred and, more importantly, if we can replicate it. Aside from the Tractus blueprints, we have another huge advantage. The update makes it quite clear, the Supreme Council believe you are no longer operational Rashida, and they still only think there are two of us brothers! That being the case, I propose we all go to the United Kingdom. The rendezvous will be our original marker in Birmingham. Nuru and Adam can meet this ambassador and start the negotiations with Holis. They can also ensure our new sites and markers are protected. In the meantime, Rashida and I will attempt to mathematically model how the Tractus can be altered to a Tempus and leap a person forward in time. We must ensure this capability is never discovered by an untrustworthy regime."

The four stood and shook hands in agreement.

After hasty preparations, they closed down the New York apartment and used the portable marker to jump to their London marker in the UK. They then travelled to Birmingham and set their plans into action.

IMOGEN

$\mathcal{S}$ hani insisted they all eat as they waited for the trial to start on the vision wall. The refreshment held little appeal for Imogen, but it served to restore her and she felt a renewed determination to do her utmost to free Leo. She boxed away her thoughts about her parents, burying them deep. She needed to keep her focus on the task in hand.

The vision wall sprang into life with an official broadcast. The scene showed the Repros, poised for action, outside The Karnak Hub. A disembodied voice announced, "The Supreme Council wishes to reassure the citizens of Holis with regard to the protection constructs. They have been placed in every town and city and are perfectly safe. Rumours of a child being fatally wounded near the Southern Sea have been grossly exaggerated. The youngster had been warned not to approach the guards, as have you all, but unfortunately chose to ignore this directive. It is hoped the boy will eventually make a full recovery. In the meantime, the Principal of the Repro project had this to say..."

What did they do? Imogen shuddered, the face of little Aly springing to mind. *I hope he's safe.*

A huge ruddy face, sporting a large bushy beard and moustache running into each other, appeared in front of them. His hair looked frizzy and wild (he reminded Imogen of Rasputin) as he looked straight into the camera. He spoke apace and Imogen had to concentrate hard on the audio track to make out what he was saying, the mass of facial hair making it difficult to see his lips move.

"Is safe. These Repros – can assure you. Is safe. But must not be touched."

His accent is the same as Em's.

"Reproduction life forms - is on alert. Is ready to stop primitives and protect Holis. Must not provoke as may be misinterpreted. Please take heed. Not touch constructs. Thank you."

The image changed to the High Court pyramid as music played in the background.

"He has the same accent as you Em."

"Yes, from same place. Is feature of those from Tavats," Em said matter-of-factly.

Tavats, isn't that the name of the space ships mentioned in the original chronicles?

Before Imogen could ask more, the display changed to the inside of the High Court. The Supreme Leader entered and everyone burst into song. Imogen bristled at the words, justice and democracy. *Let's see if there is any justice here.*

When the anthem had finished the lights dimmed and Leo was brought into the arena. Imogen sat upright as she watched.

The trial made for grim viewing. Imogen, initially relieved to see Araz safe, could not believe he spoke for the prosecutors. She was infuriated with him, regardless of a small question in her mind, *what if he had no choice?* Yes, she knew he had never openly committed to the underground cause, but this had not stopped her hoping he was now wavering in his support of the Supreme Council.

Surely, he owes my family and friends some loyalty? Standing in the courtroom, giving bogus evidence, Araz looked every bit the loyal lackey to his commanders. Even if she did not know his reasons for being there, she felt disillusioned and betrayed by him. She wanted to shout at the three-dimensional figure before her, *how could you do this?*

The proceedings were short and utterly one-sided. Imogen's heart grew even heavier when Kekara announced the verdict. *No!* Even if it was a foregone conclusion, Imogen was appalled. She watched Leo's response intensely and saw the moment when Leo appeared to see something, or someone, off screen. If only she could discern his chromatic shades on the broadcast. Araz then stepped into his line of vision. *What's he doing?* Annoyingly, the camera only centred on the raised marble plinth and not the audience, but Imogen guessed the reaction had been caused by the presence of her clone. *They must think she is me!*

Imogen found herself desperate to catch sight of this Naomi. The more she thought about the situation, the angrier she became. *How dare they! How dare anyone engineer a duplicate of me.* It was wrong in every sense and she already felt hatred towards this imposter in her skin. *Well, we will see how she likes it – having someone imitate them!* A small voice inside said, *I don't suppose she had any choice in the matter,* but Imogen chose to quash it. Her mounting anger was proving a powerful tool to overwhelm her sense of loss for her father and she felt invigorated with a courage she had previously lacked.

No one spoke when the trial ended and the monitor blacked out. Imogen stewed over her situation as Em and Shani communicated with other supporters using Multi-Coms.

Shani suddenly stood up, the communicator still in her hand. "They are not waiting until the morning. We have had word a group of Repros are about to be dispatched to take Tarik to the place of execution. We need to move now."

Launching into action, Em quickly busied herself with Imogen's outfit as Shani handed Imogen a Data Encounter.

Imogen connected to the DE without a word. She quickly absorbed the maps and layout of The Hub and the prisoner's area, committing them to memory. Now she could navigate the secret passages and walkways to get Leo to the escape route.

Shani gave the briefing, "Imogen, once at the prison you must maintain an air of confidence. You must believe you are the newest member of the Supreme Council. Act as Quora Naomi. Gracefully acknowledge those recognising you, do not be drawn into conversation. Stay aloof. We will deliver you close to the secure unit where Tarik is being held. The Phase-Seals should all open to your touch. The Repros will follow the commands of the Viziers but they are also programmed to respond to your orders, providing they do not counteract their original instructions. So, you may tell them to halt or wait, but you cannot dismiss them."

Imogen briefly nodded, her mind burning with a sense of indignation. *I will show Araz and these self-righteous people what loyalty means!*

"There! Is good, yes?" Em had doctored Imogen's Flecto garments to create a gold-edged black robe, the cuff covering her scar.

When Imogen didn't answer, Em murmured a sarcastic, "You're welcome!"

Imogen did not hear her. She was psyching herself up for the task in hand. She instinctively pressed her fingertips together but immediately pulled them apart. A snapshot of the disturbing vision of being chased by Repros down the stone passage leading to the waterfall, had briefly buzzed her head. *No! Not even those vile creatures will deter me now. I will do whatever is necessary to save Leo. He will not suffer the same fate as my dad.* Using her anger and outrage to swat the apparition, she forced herself to concentrate on Shani's instructions.

"Repros are used to chaperone prisoners to the termination area. Here the council representatives take over. We must get to Tarik before he is handed over by the guard. You will hopefully get to his cell before they arrive and smuggle him out using the secret passageways. However, if the Repros are already there, you need to fall in step with them when he leaves the prison, as if you were meant to be part of the escort. They will not question you as they will believe you to be Naomi. When you get to the edge of the Karnak woods tell the Repros to stop and wait. Engage Tarik in conversation and slowly walk him towards the East stream. As soon as you are near the stream edge we will grab Tarik and conceal him in the foliage. (We have warned him of this, although he does not know you will be involved and he also thinks it will be tomorrow, so he may be worried we are not coming.) You will then run back to the Repros saying Tarik has escaped and order them to catch the prisoner, pointing for them to go in the opposite direction. Once they have set off, you will backtrack to join us. Okay?"

Imogen blinked. There were so many things that could go wrong with this simplistic plan she couldn't begin to list them, but what else could they do? There was no time. She nodded compliance and with no small amount of trepidation, they all set off to deliver her to the Karnak prison.

LEO

*L*eo spoke to Ubaid after the trial. He begged to see his mother and for her implant to be neutralised for the meeting. A little astonished Ubaid complied, Leo met with her a few hours after he got back to his locked quarters. Relieved to find her restored and in control of her emotions, they sat leaning into each other as she expressed her regrets.

"Tarik, I am so sorry. I feared they would end your life when they discovered I had unlawfully birthed you. I did not want to send you away, but it seemed like the only solution. It must have been dreadful living amongst the primitive people?"

"Dreadful? No! Different. In fact, I got quite used to the place. It began to feel like home, almost. Apart from missing you and my grandparents."

Sekhet tenderly kissed his hand. "Ubaid told me they have commuted your sentence to serve on the dark side of Holis for a short duration and then you will be set free. Such wonderful news." Tears of joy began to run down her cheeks.

Leo nodded. This is what he had insisted Ubaid told his mother. She must not know his death sentence stood. He choked back a tear to see her colours shining with relief and unconditional love. He could only hope Barbara's escape plan would work. Then he would find Imogen and set her and his mother free. He would never again be blackmailed by Ubaid.

"When do you leave?"

"Tomorrow." Leo swallowed hard. What if the plan didn't work? He needed some distraction from his fate, so asked, "My father - tell me about him. Why was I falsely bred?"

"Nuru Zuberi! Such a brave and handsome man. I knew he was one of the subversives, but I loved him, that's all you need to know. He was trapped here, I knew he was unhappy. He had some sort of special bond with his brother, couldn't bear to be without him. I know he only pretended to be fond of me in order to plan his escape, but I loved him all the same. I wanted to retain a part of him forever. I confess, I did engineer your birth and I didn't tell him. I know this was wrong. I wanted you so badly, I overrode the database in The Hub and authorised your birth, naming someone else as the genetic father. I should be sorry, I know, but I cannot regret this. You were the best thing that ever happened to me."

Leo, with a flash of understanding of his father's reluctance to engage with him, embraced his mother, praying it would not be for the last time.

The door suddenly opened. The shadowy figures of the Repro guards were visible outside. He sprang to his feet. Something was wrong. The sentence was supposed to be carried out tomorrow. Vlaggers! How would he escape now?

Glancing down at his mother's alarmed face, he bent down and whispered in her ear, "It's ok. I will be ok". He kissed her tenderly on the cheek, saying, "Until we meet again."

NAOMI

*N*aomi paced the floor. Araz sat on the bed, pressing his closed fist against his mouth.

"So, let me get this straight. You're saying I have an identical twin?"

Araz nodded. He had talked for half an hour as Naomi had listened. It was now her turn to speak.

"It doesn't make sense. I mean, apart from twins being forbidden, this other person was born on Earth. Amongst primitives! That's like, ridiculous. Anyway, if what you are telling me is true - that I had a surrogate mother - then who are my genetic parents?"

"Rashida Omorose and Kasmut Akil."

"The subversive scientists who have not yet been publicly condemned?"

"The very same."

"This is getting worse by the minute! But my line is the line of Thut. I was raised by relatives of the great Tanastra Thut – I thought two of them were my parents."

Araz stayed silent as Naomi processed all the new information.

"Who else knows about this?"

"I don't know."

"What is she called? My twin?"

"Imogen."

"Well, where is this Imogen?"

"I don't know. We got separated in The Hub. I need to find her. And maybe you need to find her too."

"Look, I can see you have a number of concerns but how do I know if I can trust you? You say Imogen's father – my true father – was taken prisoner and she has come to Holis in the hope of rescuing him, but he has since been executed?"

Naomi stopped suddenly, going white. "No! I… I saw him. I didn't know who he was. No wonder I felt some sort of connection to him I couldn't explain. I didn't speak to him, but now I know why he was so distraught." Pain flashed into Naomi's eyes as the full horror of the situation hit her. "He must have thought I was Imogen! Ubaid should have told me – he used me." Naomi clenched her fists in frustration. "This did not go through the Sanctus High Court. How could they terminate someone without a trial? For the love of Ra! He must have been… He was - he was my real father!"

Araz stared as Naomi wrung her hands together. She appeared to force the deep colours of hurt under a rising quartz logic and he acknowledged to himself, the parallels between Imogen and Naomi were more than just those of physical appearance.

"And you say Ubaid knew about Imogen's existence?"

Araz merely nodded.

"And they wanted her dead?"

Araz kept silent.

"But she is still alive and Ubaid doesn't know this?"

Araz gave a brief affirmation with his eyes.

"Does Ubaid know Imogen is identical to me?"

"I'm not sure," was the wooden reply.

"Do you realise what this means?" Without waiting for a reply, Naomi voiced her fears, "My whole life has been a lie! My parents are not my real parents. I was engineered… why? For what purpose? Who did this?"

Araz stood. "There's more. You may want to sit down."

"More?"

"Please," Araz indicated for her to sit on the edge of the bed. "I only found out yesterday, but Imogen is in fact a Penta-Crypt."

"What?"

"She holds all five lines in equal measure including that of Iris."

"I know what a Penta-Crypt is! But, but that means she is the Sanctus Cryptus! It's not possible. She must be the first ever..." Naomi's words trailed away, as the full realisation hit her with a bolt of cobalt blue reverberating around her Chroma.

"The second," Araz said gently.

"No! I... I am a Tri-Crypt... Unless... They couldn't have lied about that, could they?"

Araz recognised Imogen's chromatic tones of grey worry now racing around Naomi's colours. He felt almost as disconcerted as Naomi. He loved Imogen, so why did he feel drawn to this other person? As if in answer, Naomi bit her lip and Araz had to look away to gather his thoughts.

"Twins are forbidden," Naomi whispered. "We will both be classed as Falsebreds. This will change everything. I can't... I won't believe I am a Penta-Crypt. What does this mean?" Naomi's voice petered out as she considered everything Araz had told her. For the first time in her life she was unsure of who she was and began to worry about what else she didn't know.

"Is it so bad if you are a Penta-Crypt?" Araz reasoned.

"Bad? It means I am a total freak!"

"Well at least you're not the only one," Araz countered.

Naomi stood bolt upright, raised her arm and pushed her hand in the air, palm facing Araz. "Stop! I will not listen to another word. You could be telling me a pack of lies. I need evidence. I need to see with my own eyes."

With that she marched out of the room, leaving Araz speechless.

After a few moments her face appeared round the door. "Well, are you coming or not?"

"If we are going to find Imogen, then yes. I am coming. But we must be careful. Follow me. I know the back route to The Hub, past Karnak prison."

RESCUE

*I*mogen took the tranquilizing pen from Em, hiding it in the folds of her black councillor gown. Em gave her hand a quick squeeze in a gesture of reassurance. Imogen then she set off alone in the direction Em had described would lead her to the prison entrance.

The complex looked like a series of landscaped botanical gardens. Wide streams ran around formal meadows. Green domes, formed by thickly entwined leafy bushes, rose from the centre of each meadow. Impenetrable, arched hedges linked each dome to the next, bridging the running water as they snaked in and around the compound. They formed the corridors linking the chain of domes, each a separate prison area.

Leo should be in the far area. She pinpointed his quarters on the internal map she had memorised from the DE; grateful Shani had enlisted the help of those serving his meals to discover his whereabouts.

Imogen sucked in a lungful of cold air and projecting a sureness she did not feel, held her head high and strode along the stream edge heading for central pasture and the organic bridge leading to the way in.

A towering transparent wall on the other side of the stream shimmered on the periphery of her vision. The outer fortification. *Must be like the ice wall of The Hub.* It surrounded the entire site and was only visible when there was a break in the clouds and the light of the suns reflected on its surface. Imogen shivered. It stuck her the peaceful and picturesque setting was disturbingly incongruous, given its function.

She crossed the living bridge with a determination in her step. A Phase-Seal section of the wall melted to her touch, re-sealing once she had entered. Heart pounding, she passed through two further doors to find herself in a long, dark, foliage lined corridor. Lights in the passage came on as she advanced but no one else appeared. *They must be on sensors.*

Feigning an outward confidence, she navigated the maze of walkways and when she was only a few yards away from where Leo was being held, she slowed as she heard the loud stomping sound of booted feet heading her way.

Her stomach folded. *Repros! Stay calm! I am Naomi - I have every right to be here. Keep going!*

The sounds drew closer and four Repros turned the corner, marching straight towards her. She stopped dead in her tracks. Expecting to find Leo at the centre, it was a shock to see it was not him. Worse - this was a bodyguard for none other than Kekara, the Supreme Leader herself! Imogen nearly fainted in alarm. *No!*

Kekara raised her hand and the Repros halted. She walked from the centre of the guard towards Imogen, who was struggling to regain her composure. Close up, the face of the tall leader possessed a beauty those on Earth would describe as stunning. Her long jet-black hair was pinned up in an elaborate style with gold Flecto adornments. Her symmetrical face took on a questioning look as curiosity flamed throughout Kekara's Chroma. She stood right in front of Imogen, her deep brown eyes staring intensely down at her.

"Ah well, this is a surprise! One of our newest councillors. I have been wanting to meet you. Naomi? Is it not?"

Imogen nodded, her mind in turmoil.

"I wonder what you can be doing here in the prison quarters?" Kekara's gold-edged black authority permeated her colours, and it was all Imogen could do to stop herself shaking.

Think! Shani said Naomi was sponsored by Ubaid. Improvise!

"Your Greatness," Imogen gave a slight bow. "I am honoured to be in your presence. I was told to meet the Vizier of Vision, Ubaid, in these quarters." Imogen hoped the band of perspiration prickling at her brow was not visible.

"You were? To what purpose?" the leader's eyes bored into hers.

I can do this. Imogen forced a cloak of steely, quartz-blue honesty to engulf her swirling dark colours of fear as she responded, "Perhaps he wanted to show me the complex? I am unsure."

Kekara regarded the young councillor before her. She was unable to discern if she was lying, but the incident in the High Court, where the agent and the condemned Falsebred had paid her undue attention, had not yet been investigated.

"Tell me, Naomi, at the trial of the Falsebred, why did the prisoner and the agent look so concerned when they saw you?"

Imogen floundered. *Is this a trick question? They would have mistaken Naomi for me, but Naomi would have no reason to know either of them. Kekara thinks I am Naomi! How would she think? Stay confident!*

"I wondered about that too. I had not encountered either of them before and had only seen Tarik Zuberi on the daily broadcasts." Innocent shades of natural greens and browns accompanied Imogen's response, deterring the violet shade of lies from surfacing.

Kekara looked satisfied but her next words made Imogen's heart drop.

"Well, now you are here you can accompany me and we can ask the Falsebred how he thinks he knows you, before he is terminated. Come, this way."

Imogen wanted to scream but held onto her self-control and followed Kekara and the Repros towards Leo's cell.

Leo took a step back when he saw Kekara walk through the Repro guards into the room. It was all he could do to stop himself blurting out Imogen's name when she followed behind.

Imogen's Chroma, to his relief, flickered russet recognition and a brief warning Leo caught before Kekara pulled Imogen into the room next to her. The fading cloud of earth colours – their sign for 'hide' - was swiftly concealed under a façade of crystal detachment.

Hide? He must hide the fact he knew her. Leo stood to his full height, returning Kekara's stare, as his mother quaked on the seat behind him.

"Tarik Zuberi, please explain how you know this person?" Kekara indicated Imogen, who maintained a detached quizzical stance.

"Know her? Well, let me think? Yes, I saw her at your Kangaroo Court. Ah yes, she was the lucky recipient of my incredulity at the outrageous verdict." Leo gave Imogen an exaggerated wink, adding, "Sorry about that! Could have fixed my stare on anyone but guess you got lucky. Nudge nudge! Wink wink!"

Careful Leo! Don't wreck this. Imogen kept her cool and decided to speak to consolidate the subterfuge. *What would my clone say?*

"You appeared to recognise me?"

"Did I? Funny that, having just been found guilty of plotting to overturn the entire universe, it's near on impossible I would have looked wildly around to see who on Holis could believe those trumped up charges. Guess your smart council robes caught my eye!"

Good answer, Leo. She willed him to keep up the strategy as he continued.

"Perhaps you thought I was looking to bond? Well, sorry to disappoint, but hey, we can still get to know each other, if you fancy it? It could be a bit of a speed date. May not have much of a future, what with me being a condemned man and you being a councillor, but I say worth a shot! Always look on the bright side of life!"

Imogen feigned disdain as Kekara studied them both. Imogen prayed the cold blues infusing the Supreme Leader's Chroma, meant she was satisfied for now.

Appearing to come to a decision, Kekara indicated for Leo to go through the door. She addressed the Repros sharply. "Escort the prisoner. Sentence will be served."

Leo embraced his shaking mother and gave her a quick peck on the cheek, before leaving the room to stand in the middle of the guard, a grim expression on his face as he studiously ignored Imogen.

They set off down the passageways, Kekara beckoning for Imogen to join them.

How am I going to get out of this and help Leo?

When they reached the garden exit, the leader suddenly put her arm out to stop Imogen. She obeyed, standing still with Kekara as the Repros continued to walk through the exit. Imogen felt a rising panic as she glanced sideways at the tall figure of the leader and caught sight of an item of jewellery briefly flickering into view at the neckline of Kekara's robes. For a fraction of a second, she saw the ornament adorning the end of the gold chain. It took all her willpower not to react. *My pendant! The five symbols – it's identical to mine!* She remembered how the arrow of her locket had flashed when wet and Araz's words jumped into her mind, '*It's a key. Electro-chemical in origin. I've only ever seen one like this.*' *So, Kekara has the other key. But what does it unlock?*

"May the blessing of Ra be with you," Kekara called scornfully to Leo, as he anxiously glanced back before the door sealed him from view.

Imogen swallowed hard, tearing her eyes away from where she had seen the second locket. She held her breath. Kekara turned away from the exit and made for a nearby elevator door before opening the Phase-Seal and stepping inside. She gave Imogen a long stare and addressed her for a last time.

"So, Naomi. It was good to meet you. Enjoy your tour of the prison quarters. I will see you at the next meeting of the Supreme Council."

Imogen bobbed her head deferentially as the lift door closed. Once she was sure it would not re-open she slumped against the wall and let out a sigh of relief, nervously fingering the outline of her locket under her garments. *Worry about the lockets later. There're more important matters to sort.*

Imogen pulled herself together and summoning the internal plans of the premises to her mind, she set off down a parallel corridor to reach another exit, running as quickly as she could. *There's still time to get to Leo.*

Out by the East stream, Em, Shani and two of her underground members, Lara and Cael, lay in wait. Their Flecto outfits were switched to reflect so they were effectively camouflaged against the soft green of the surrounding forest.

"Has been gone long time," Em frowned in the direction of the far-off prison complex.

"We just have to hope it is going to plan," responded Shani.

"Shhh! – is noise! Is guard marching this way."

The group ducked down and flattened themselves against the bank of the stream as the Repros came into view.

"Now we wait," whispered Shani.

Leo glanced in every direction but could see no sign of his rescuers. Did they know his execution had been brought forward? What had happened to Imogen? She seemed back to normal but then Kekara had called her 'Naomi' and accepted her as a member of the Supreme Council. He had no idea what was going on, but as soon as he could break free he would find out. He needed to tell Imogen about her father and confess his part in his demise. He wondered if she would ever forgive him, however the immediacy of his need to escape put a stop to any further deliberations. Where is Barbara? he fretted.

Em risked a look over the bank edge. "Repro guard. Is going in wrong direction. No sign of Imogen."

Shani peered over the bank next to Em and spied two figures moving as if to intercept the Repros. "Wait – over there! It's her! Who's with her?"

Em stared hard. "Is agent creep! Not trust him. We wait here?"

"Yes, for now - perhaps Imogen has enlisted his help."

The two figures in the distance cut across in front of the Repro guard. The female shouted out an order and they came to a halt. The prisoner walked cautiously from the circle of guards and crossed to the pair who started to engage him in conversation.

Em nudged Shani. "Look – there – by tree. Is other Imogen!"

Shani saw the identical girl duck behind a tree, near to the group. "Which one is the real Imogen?"

"Is one by self," Em said with certainty. "Look – has activated Flecto robe to hide. Real one has to think fast - is clever."

Shani nodded, catching the merest reflection of light in her robes, as the hidden girl moved slowly to another tree, almost on top of Leo and the others.

"Come, let's move nearer too."

The four in camouflage crept carefully along the wooded edge of the stream, to close in behind the guard.

A heated discussion was taking place between Leo and Araz as the Repros stood just yards away, uncertain and ready to spring into action.

"What are you talking about? She's not Imogen?"

"I don't know where Imogen is, but trust me, this is not her. This is... let's just say, she is Imogen's close relative, Naomi."

"I have no idea what you are playing at, Mr. Special Agent, but you are the last person I would trust. You helped write my death sentence just a few hours ago. Imogen, what has he done to you?"

"I am not her."

"I know he has done something to you, but I will help you as soon as we can lose these gorillas."

"Where are they taking you?"

"They've messed with your mind – you knew where, just minutes ago."

"I'm not Imogen!"

"Right. Have it your way. So where am I heading? I'd love to say for a walk in the park, but my termination awaits."

"What? That's supposed to be tomorrow?"

"Yeah! Shock, horror gasp! As if anyone here is true to their word."

Araz clenched his fists and looked at Leo. "I will speak with my commanders, ask them to stay your termination until this new development has been resolved."

"Am I supposed to be grateful for this offer? You're too late, mate. Whilst you swan off to talk, I will have met my end!"

Naomi turned to Araz. "What can we do? My life may also be at risk when they find out I am not the person they thought I was."

Leo looked baffled and was about to question this statement, when another figure stepped out from behind a nearby tree, her garments suddenly switching to gold-edged black. Her face was indistinguishable from the girl who had just spoken, other than a deep, cold anger simmering behind her eyes. He stood, mouth open, as this second Imogen replied.

"I would say your life is definitely at risk. After all, you are an imposter!" Imogen glowered at Naomi who was dumbstruck to see her own face before her.

Araz rushed to Imogen's side but she put a hand up to stop him as she continued to stare at Naomi and spat out, "And you're not the only imposter!"

Araz took a step back, appalled at the ferocity of Imogen's words and the accusation in her eyes. He had completely lost her trust.

For a brief moment everyone was motionless. Naomi gawped at Imogen who glared back; Leo and Araz glanced at each girl in turn - they were exact copies of each other. The guards stared on in confusion, perturbed at seeing the two identical councillors. They began to show signs of agitation at the forced delay.

"So, you're my identical twin?" Naomi managed to stutter.

"Hardly!" Imogen retorted angrily. "Try clone!"

Naomi put her hand to her mouth as Leo and Araz gasped in horror.

The reverie broke when the Repros suddenly mobilised and started to move quickly towards their prisoner. One lunged forward to grab Leo and pulled him into an arm lock. It fumbled for its blade with the other hand. The other three Repros took up their weapons as four figures sprang out of the surrounding bushes and rushed the group from behind.

Em launched herself onto the back of the largest Repro. She clung on for dear life as it turned wildly around in circles, trying to shake her off, unable to strike her with its blade.

In the ensuing commotion, the Repros and Resistance members grappled together. Shouts and cries rang out as each tried to overpower the other.

Shani and Lara managed to knock the knife out of the flailing arms of the closest Repro, and Cael attempted to stab it with his pen. The Repro was too powerful and threw the young man up in the air. He crumpled to the ground, moaning in pain. The fourth guard quickly grabbed Shani by the neck, raising its knife towards Lara, who dodged backward and forward, trying to snatch away the weapon and prevent it from striking Shani.

Araz, temporarily immobile after recognising the unmistakeable red-haired, former Vizier, turned to witness Leo's Repro lifting its knife to strike him a fatal blow. Before he could act, Imogen launched forward and plunged her pen into its neck. It collapsed instantly. The Repro that had thrown Cael, rushed at Imogen bellowing in anger. It seized a handful of her hair and dragged her backwards, pulling her to the ground. She screamed out in protest, wriggling to try to free herself.

Araz, who had been rooted to the spot, flipped. He charged at the beast and barged into its chest, knocking it sideways into a tree, its head smacking into the wood before it slumped to the ground.

Leo jumped up to try and help Lara in her attempt to free Shani, who was turning crimson from strangulation. The Repro was wielding its knife with the other hand and managed to stab Lara in the arm. She screamed in pain and clasped her hand to the gaping wound. It bled profusely. Leo managed to kick the Repro in the legs and, as it faltered, tried to prise its fingers open to release its grip around Shani's neck. Leo was forced to leap away from the blade as the Repro recovered and slashed the air in fast movements. It increased the pressure on Shani's neck with the other hand, her lips were turning blue and she was close to passing out.

Imogen, back on her feet, raced behind the brute as it swung its blade at Leo and jabbed her pen into the back of its neck. It froze momentarily before dropping both its weapon and Shani and falling unconscious. Shani sank to her knees, wheezing as she fought for breath. Imogen rushed to her side.

Naomi had looked on in bewilderment. These people fighting the guards must be members of the Resistance. She had instantly recognised Shani as the retired Vizier of Sanctity. Why was she a part of this? Naomi also recognised the strapping woman with closely cropped hair, who had leapt onto a Repro's back. She was on Odion's suspect list. A photographic image of her face, seen in the defence base, appeared in her mind. Naomi wondered if this 'Emba' knew she was being tracked.

Her bafflement quickly turned to horror when the fighting began. Other than her recent encounter with the Repros in the depths of the Karnak Hub, she had never experienced violence of any nature in her life. She had watched some of the awful news reels from the primitive planet, but it had all seemed so distant. She was utterly unprepared for the scene playing out before her and she felt physically sick when the Repros started to wield their knives.

As Imogen responded to those in need, Naomi felt a sense of awe. Her look-a-like – was she really her clone? - was fast and seemingly fearless. She wondered how much fighting she had seen.

Her study of Imogen stopped abruptly when she saw the young female fighter cut down, her arm spurting blood. Naomi's instincts kicked in and she dashed across to assist her. Tearing a swatch from her Flecto gown, she swiftly made a tourniquet for Lara and stemmed the blood flowing from her arm, before holding the gash together until it began to heal.

A victorious cry from the final Repro filled the air, as it suddenly managed to buck Em off its back. She crashed to the ground and the Repro swept its knife into the air ready to slice down into her chest. Before the blade could impact with Em's body, Araz leapt forward and elbowed the Repro hard in the gut. It doubled over with a loud groan, as Imogen threw her pen to Leo. He then leapt upon the creature and rammed the device into its neck for the final blow as it slumped to the floor.

Reeling from the fight, everyone caught their breath and looked around at the fallen Repros. Cael got to his feet, rubbing his bruised ribs as they gradually healed. Lara's cut resealed and she flexed her arm slowly, thanking Naomi for her help. Shani massaged her neck as her crushed tissue repaired. She smiled gratefully at Imogen.

"Well, I would say that's a win for us!" grinned Leo, removing the blades from the fallen guard and throwing them into a dense patch of brambles.

"My commanders are not going to like this!"

Surprised at the lightness of his tone, Imogen turned to observe Araz's Chroma. It shone with hues of quartz-gold. He was not sorry, but proud of overwhelming these creatures. He gave her an unmistakable look of entreaty which read, 'please trust me'. Gold-flecked reds blazed in his colours. Imogen swallowed, her heart swelling in response despite her ambivalent feelings. *Can I trust him? I want to so much. After all, he saved my life on Earth and here he is, fighting alongside us. And he saved Em.*

Em walked over to Araz, hands on hips, and when he turned to look at her she glared into his eyes. He stared back, perturbed, before her face broke into a huge smile. Em clapped him on the back. "At last! Is showing true colours yes?"

Araz coughed, looking a little flustered, and merely shrugged his shoulders.

"What now?" came Naomi's voice, close to a whisper.

Leo looked from her to the other identical female. Their voices were the same, even their Chroma had the same swirling grey and quartz undertones. Could it be true they were clones? Unable to decide which one was Imogen; his question was answered when Araz crossed to the side of the silent one.

Araz first stroked, then pressed his lips to the back of the girl's right hand. As she smiled back at him, the gold flecked reds of their intense feelings glimmered briefly in both their auras. A little part of Leo died inside.

Shani broke the moment and stood, rubbing her neck. She pointed to the fallen guard. "We need to wipe their implants, so no one can replay this scene," she announced.

Cael and Lara crossed to each Repro in turn, removed their helmets and pressed a small magnetic cube to the side of each of their heads.

Araz had been aghast to see the former Vizier of Sanctity was now part of the resistance movement. He had grown up knowing her as a trustworthy and revered member of the Supreme Council. Her soft voice had spoken from the vision walls throughout his childhood. To him, she was an icon; a person to be held in the highest regard. Yet here she was with the so-called subversives, not retired or working on the dark side of Holis. If she no longer trusted their government then there must be something deeply wrong somewhere.

"Here, take one," Shani handed Leo, Imogen, Naomi and Araz their own cubes.

"Quora," he began awkwardly, not knowing how to address her. "How does it work?"

"We have been developing this since we discovered the existence of the Reproduction forces. It is not fully tested, but it should scramble the data on the implant leaving no record of what happened. It should also stop them from responding to orders and whilst this will cause untold trouble for those who control them, it could also prove dangerous to Holan citizens. These creatures are naturally violent and barbaric. They will no longer be tame and will revert to their basic nature without the control of the implants."

"So, they are not constructs?" Naomi murmured. She had suspected this from the moment she had seen the storage facility.

Before Shani could answer, a shout erupted from the distant prison walls and dozens of Repros could be seen flowing out of the area.

"Quick, we need to go! Imogen and Naomi must be separated – they cannot be seen together if this is to be any kind of advantage for us. Activate your Flecto outfits," Shani commanded. She gave Em a silent message with her eyes.

Everyone switched their clothing to camouflage as the Repros began to move in the direction of the group.

Imogen was appalled. *There are hundreds of them.*

Shani tapped Lara and Cael's arms and the three of them grouped together. "Split up! We will all have a better chance. Go!" She and her two comrades headed for the edge of the stream diving down over the bank, out of view.

Naomi instinctively dashed forward but crashed into Imogen. They both floundered, getting in each other's way as they collided, then whirled around one another before pausing, momentarily mesmerized by the mirror image of their other self.

Araz stared wildly at the two females, unsure which was Imogen.

Em stepped forward and decisively made a grab for the arm of one. Leo seized the arm of the other. Araz, with a slight hesitation, made his choice and joined Em as she turned on her heels.

"This way!" Araz indicated his route to Em and glanced back at Leo and the other female. The men nodded an unspoken exchange of forced amity, almost bordering on respect, before fleeing.

Araz, with Em and the girl he hoped was Imogen, headed over a small rooted bridge spanning the stream in the direction of the Karnak dwellings.

Leo, unsure which girl was in his charge, ran with her in the opposite direction towards the wooded copse leading to the secret passageways into The Hub.

The Repros had caught sight of the groups as they scattered, but with the camouflage of the Flecto garments added to the distance they needed to cover, the figures had all but disappeared by the time they reached the fallen guards.

Odion emerged from the centre of the new forces. He cursed when he saw the damaged Repros. On his orders, thirty of the troop set off in each direction to search for the missing prisoner and those who had helped him.

"Capture is no longer your objective," he spat. "Take them alive or dead."

ESCAPE

*A*raz raced towards the Karnak dwellings until Em steered the girl sideways into the forest. They hastily dodged between the trees, running as quickly as they could. Araz's mind was buzzing. Had anyone spotted him? If Shani had managed to wipe the Repro's implants, he might still be safe. No one would know he had assisted the underground movement. But could he be sure?

Araz evaluated the situation as he kept up the run. They must have gone half a mile or more when his mind came back to the route. It was now clear they were bypassing Karnak and aiming in the direction of a far mountain range. Baffled by the course she was taking, Araz ran alongside Em and grabbed her arm to question the direction.

"We're heading for the Tavat port?"

Em merely nodded as she hurried forward. Araz quickly caught the arm of their charge to prevent her falling over a clump of tree roots.

"Why?"

"Is necessary. You and Naomi must see for selfs."

"Naomi?" Araz made a grab for the girl's right hand as they rushed ahead. He ran his fingers over her knuckles and cursed aloud as she pulled her hand away. He stopped in his tracks.

"You knew this wasn't Imogen?"

Em's reply came in short bursts as she called over her shoulder, running on. "Of course. Not have outline of locket under robes. Imogen - is safe. This Tarik know secret routes – will protect her."

"That traitorous Falsebred!" Araz spat angrily. He felt a rising fury. He had been cheated. He should have looked for signs of the locket. He wanted to kick himself for assuming Em had chosen Imogen. It meant the person he loved was still in danger and only had an imbecilic fool to defend her. I should have checked, he thought to himself cursing his own stupidity. He had, yet again, made assumptions he should not. Punching his fist into a nearby tree trunk, Araz swore aloud and then broke into a run after Em and Naomi. He had no choice but to follow them. The Repros could be on their tails so he could not risk turning back. They needed to keep up their speed. He could only hope Imogen's wits and extraordinary intuition would keep her safe.

As Naomi ran next to Em, she analysed all the new information in the deep recesses of her mind. Something was badly amiss. Even if she barely knew this agent or these so-called subversives, her gut instinct told her everything she had taken for granted had changed irrevocably. There had been a fundamental shift in her understanding of the world and where she fitted and she needed to work out what to do. She was grateful Araz was with them, feeling the involuntary attraction she had towards him must be borne of an intuitive sense of trust. After all, he seemed to know more about her genetic makeup than she did, and his strong feelings for her identical self would possibly engender a willingness to at least work alongside her. She was, however, more than a little relieved Imogen was not with them. The anger her duplicate had directed towards her was unmistakable, although it was crystal clear from Araz's reaction and his Chroma, he was most unhappy the strangely spoken Em had chosen her and not her clone in their bid to escape.

Thankful to focus on speeding towards the base of the Tavat mountain, Naomi wondered what it was Em 'needed' Araz and her to see. She vowed she would no longer take things at face value or be swayed by others. She would find out the facts for herself and keep an open mind about everything until she had the full picture.

Imogen and Leo reached the base of the rear side of The Hub from a tortuous route along steep banks and dense thicket. The sharp branches snagged in their clothing causing tears in the Flecto, blood rising from the numerous scratches being temporarily etched into their arms and legs. Leo led the way and as Imogen watched the rips appear in their garments, she was reminded of Em's slashed clothing on their arrival on Holis. *Is this a route Em took?*

"Ouch!" squealed Leo as each injury was inflicted by the needle-sharp gorse. Imogen clenched her teeth against the sporadic pain. She barely felt it, her mind still reeling from the fight with the Repros and coming face-to-face with her clone. *Did Em mean to take Naomi?* She had no idea. *Does Leo know this is me?* They had not spoken, putting all their efforts into racing ahead, dipping and diving under the sharp bushes to stay hidden from the chasing Repros.

Imogen sensed the Repros had dropped back some minutes ago and as they made progress she was sure they were no longer following. Eventually Leo dropped his pace and, panting loudly, he indicated for her to follow him down to a shaded stream bed.

"Pity we have to feel pain, given that we heal so quickly," he remarked breathlessly, wiping the blood from a new scratch on his hand.

"It's just a flesh wound," responded Imogen as she caught up, falling into step with Leo. "You've had worse!" her eyes briefly twinkled as he glanced at her before slowing to a walking pace along the wet rocks. The giant glass mountain towered ahead of them. Imogen's breathing gradually slowed. She waited for Leo to make some quip in return, but he was strangely silent and seemed to be avoiding eye contact, his colours blazing anxiety and indecision.

Maybe his captivity has badly affected him?

As the trickle of water below started to well up to a shallow stream, Leo scooped up a few handfuls to drink, Imogen following suit. They were thirsty from the chase. He then moved up the side of the bank and walked to a set of caves, a short distance from the vast glass base.

We must be the other side to the main entrance. It looks impenetrable from here.

Leo sat down on a raised rock, just inside the first cavity. Imogen sat on an adjacent boulder and absent-mindedly rubbed at her scar as she looked around the cavern.

Leo coughed and pushed his fringe to one side. His eyes did not make contact with hers and flickered as he began to speak. Imogen noted the swirling clouds of purple-grey worry, now permeating his Chroma.

"Imogen? It's you, right?"

She gave the briefest of nods.

"You escaped the Repros in the church?"

"Only just." Imogen turned the back of her hand towards him to display her scar. When he looked baffled, she added, "Poison! They killed Father Jonathan – Tanastra. He was cut down trying to save me."

"I'm sorry."

Imogen glazed over as she tried to compose herself.

Leo furrowed his brow. "Imogen, I need to tell you about Harry - Kasmut... your dad... he's... he's..."

"I know." Tears pricked at Imogen's eyes as a lump caught in her throat.

"I'm so sorry," Leo began, but petered out.

Imogen dabbed her eyes with her sleeve and was about to say something along the lines of it not being his fault when she noted the violent spikes of deep navy in his colours. It was a shade of murky blue she had rarely seen. Her stomach folded. There was more to this than just being sorry her father had been executed. She bit her lip.

Leo tried again, "I never meant, that is, I had no idea things would go so far... I would never have... not in a million years, I would never have..."

"What? Would never have what, Leo?"

"Never have reported... reported two of the subversives had produced an unlawful child on Earth. A girl – you. I mean, I thought you had been killed in the Tractus accident. And if I had realised what would happen, I promise I would never have told them I would capture you, or where to find your dad…"

"You… you told them?" Imogen reeled.

"Imogen, I'm truly sorry…"

Imogen's hand flew up to her mouth in shock before uncurling to point a finger at him. "It was you who told the enemy about me and you agreed to take me prisoner? You then led them to my father's home?"

"I was angry. I mean, I didn't know what to do. They had my mother and I had to agree to all sorts of things. It's no excuse - I know - but I never thought they would… they would terminate him."

"My family managed to stay safely hidden on Earth for decades until you reported us."

"I know."

"My dad acted like a father to you, when you were disregarded by your own. And you betrayed him, you betrayed us all?"

Leo opened his mouth to respond.

Imogen raised her hand up to stop him. "Don't answer that," she spat. "It was a statement not a question." The disgust in her voice was clear.

Imogen, the fist of her good hand clenched, stood and walked to the opening of the cave and stared up at the two suns. She fought down the urge to vomit as she turned to stare at Leo anew. The shadowy, heavy blue hue; the filthy colour of betrayal. She could barely believe it. Leo, the traitor!

Leo sat miserably, wringing his hands. "That agent admirer of yours is right – I am a fool! I can't tell you how sorry I am. I know I can never make up for this."

"No! You can't!"

As Leo started to speak again Imogen couldn't focus on his pathetic excuses. Her mind was in turmoil. Who could she trust? Her father was dead, her mother damaged, Araz may still be wavering in his support of this corrupt regime and anyway, he had gone - gone with his own kind. She pictured Naomi looking at her in a shocked fascination. A further surge of betrayal rose to join her raging emotions.

They stole my DNA! Who the hell is she? A replica? A replacement? Her hackles rose. *And she is with Araz.*

Then Leo's confession. She had kept faith in him. She had tried to help him; risked her life for him. He was the last remaining person from Earth she had trusted implicitly. Even her father had trusted him. Leo's words, '*They had my mother*', prickled at the back of her mind but she could find no empathy and disregarded them. If the Supreme Council had not been told of her father's home, her dad would not have gone to Holis as an envoy. *He would still be alive!* As all the events replayed in her mind she also thought, with a sickening realisation, *Tanastra would still be alive. I would not be here, but safe on Earth.* She could not stop the angry tears from streaming down her cheeks or the maelstrom of rage and accusation from swamping her thoughts. *What else has he done? I will never see my dad again and it's his fault.* She suddenly flew at Leo and hammered a fist and an open hand into his chest, pounding him repeatedly, as she cried, "You... you Judas! How could you? My dad is dead because of you! I hate you!"

Leo raised his head and stiffened, allowing her blows to rain down on him until she lost all energy and slumped to the ground.

Leo hesitantly went to place a hand on her shoulder, but she recoiled from him and shook her head violently.

"Don't touch me!"

Leo blinked a tear back from his eye as he waited for Imogen to calm. He felt broken and worthless. He wished his smarting chest would not heal and continue to cause him pain - he deserved it. He was nothing but a spineless coward. He would never be able to make up for what he had done. He felt he may as well be dead. He turned away from Imogen, self-loathing racking his being, and covered his face with his hands.

Imogen's device gave a low bleep and she breathed a heavy sigh and slowly took it from the folds of her gown before answering.

"Em? Yes, I'm safe – for now."

Imogen listened to Em's voice and took in all the instructions before Em put Araz on the line. His deep voice played into her ear and she closed her eyes, visualising him next to her.

"Imogen, thank Ra you are safe! I wanted to be with you, but it all got confused." His voice then dropped to a low whisper, no doubt to stop Em or anyone else from hearing his words, "I am deeply sorry, my light." Imogen's heart lurched – she should never have doubted him. His feelings towards her had not changed and he now appeared to have resolved to stay on her side. Without her dad, she only felt safe with him. Imagining his fingers brushing her lips as he spoke in her ear, Imogen tried to concentrate on his words, "Follow Em's instructions, and we will meet you in the underground headquarters as soon as we can. Shani will also meet us there. Remember, Karnak will be on high alert. The Hub will be awash with Repros, so please be careful Imogen." His voice caught as he spoke.

Imogen managed to stammer out a hushed, "I will. Stay safe too," before disconnecting and rising to pace around the opening of the cave, forcing her anger towards Leo to subside. There were still so many unanswered questions. At least she was not completely on her own. She had Araz, Em and Shani on Holis, and the Zuberi brothers and her mother on Earth. She vowed to push her emotions to one side and think logically. Calming herself, she walked in circles for several minutes.

Imogen finally turned to Leo and stood in front of him. He looked back at her with a defeated expression, his colours dull and full of sepia shades. "I need more information about this Naomi – what do you know?"

"Nothing! It was a complete shock when I saw you both together. At the trial, I thought she was you."

Despite the quartz honesty flashing in his overcast Chroma, Imogen responded, "I don't buy that Leo. You are clearly in with the twisted people who run this government; the people who 'forced you' to betray us all. I want to know what is going on? How is it someone managed to make a clone of me? The only person who returned to Holis after my accident in the Tractus was you. Tanastra said so in the chronicles he wrote on Earth. So, what did you do? And I will not hear any more lies from you."

"I don't know. I didn't do anything, not that you'd believe me."

Imogen did not respond. She stared, the piercing yellow shades of her interrogation demanded an answer.

"I suppose they must have copied your DNA. They must have got a sample, somehow. Look, I expect you're thinking I handed one over – just like that! Well, I didn't! Unless…" Leo suddenly went silent and white as a sheet, as a flash of cobalt blue shuddered through his colours.

"Unless what?" Silver strands sprang from Imogen's Chroma and began to thread into Leo's aura, tugging the truth from below his swirls of dull hopeless greys. He stared ahead and began to answer in factual tones.

"It must have been when I returned to Holis to see my mother. When I was eleven."

"Go on."

"Eshe – she gave me something, something secret to give to Barbara. A small opal covered sphere. She didn't tell me what it was. I didn't ask – I was too excited to be returning to Holis. But I guess it must have contained a volt of your flesh, holding all your crypts. It was Ubaid – he took it from me - when I was caught visiting my mum. He threatened to kill her. I had to hand it over. I said it was only a trinket, but he wanted to know who I was giving it to. I didn't tell him. I did not let the name 'Barbara' pass my lips - or Shani, her real name. I said nothing. I did not break my oath from all those years ago. Ubaid said he would keep the object safe, like my mother, until I returned with the information he needed."

Leo's words flowed unchecked as Imogen's silver threads exposed the shining truths from below the quagmire of his miserable colours.

"They put an implant in my head before they let me go. It was not connected to a live feed – Earth was too far from Holis for that - but it would record all my movements to be examined once it was retrieved. I had to show I was willing to give information in order to keep my mother safe. When Eshe asked me if I had delivered the sphere, I lied. I couldn't tell her about Ubaid or the implant. I was too scared for my mum. It was wrong. I realise that now. I should have told the truth."

Imogen started to release the tension in her inquisitive filaments.

"When they captured me – the night you got away – I told them you were not worth chasing. I said you were an imbecile. I lied in the hope it would keep you safe, but all the time Ubaid must have known I was lying. He must have synthesised your clone from the microscopic sample. Perhaps that's why he wanted you dead – he had another Imogen – one he could manipulate and bend to his will, right here. But why go to such trouble? When he could brainwash any new-born here. It doesn't make sense."

Imogen's hypnosis strands melted away and Leo sat dumbfounded. He knew Imogen had used her intrusive cognitive powers and he didn't blame her. He was glad. He felt unburdened and at least she would know it was the truth. However, he was baffled as to why Ubaid had cloned Imogen.

"It's because there's something special about you, isn't it?" he said, almost to himself.

"So, you really don't know?" Imogen felt herself relenting slightly towards him. Leo had given up her DNA, but it was inadvertent and she had to admit he could not have known they would clone her or kill her father. Also, he had jumped back to Earth to try to warn them about the Repros before they attacked. It was obvious he was wracked with guilt. She found her animosity waning. *What's the point? Like me, he has never been in control of his life.*

"Know what? You should realise by now, no one ever tells me anything."

"And can you blame them Leo? So, why would they make a duplicate of me? Come on, figure it out – what would make me different to anyone else on Holis? No? I'll tell you - they found out I'm one of those super-freaks!"

"What do you mean?"

"This!" Imogen pulled out her locket. "I'm a Penta-Crypt!"

Leo looked from Imogen's face to the locket, his expression now one of incredulity.

"The Sanctus Cryptus!" he whispered reverentially. "Wow! Now everything makes sense!"

"Not to me, it doesn't!" Imogen glared.

"That's why they had to rescue you from the Tractus. I couldn't understand why they hadn't given up. I mean - no offence - but you'd been lost in time for forty years. We all thought you must have died long before. But they had to get you back. I mean, you're the one, the one who will lead our people in the future, the one who will challenge the corruption in the Supreme Council."

"Stop!" Imogen shouted at him. "For crying out loud, stop! It's all rubbish, this 'Sanctus Cryptus' stuff – it's a myth! No one person can sort out everything that's gone wrong here. I am just me. I am not some super powerful being, I don't have any answers, so just cut the crap!"

Leo swallowed hard and kept schtum. He was more than a little relieved to see Imogen's anger was beginning to focus elsewhere.

"I am going to find out what is going on. Why Tanastra and my parents needed to hide on Earth, why I was cloned, why the government of Holis is lying to the population and why they executed my dad. They are not going to get away with this."

Imogen swept out of the enclosure and set off for the glass mountain.

Leo jumped up and followed. He would help her, if she let him, and do his best to protect her. It was the least he could do after his deceit.

THE TAVAT PORT

*E*m steered Naomi and Araz into the cargo areas at the base of the Tavat Port mountain. She warned them Repros now guarded the pedestrian lobby in the main area. It was a relief to see there were none here.

"How do you know about these obscure entrances?" asked Naomi.

"I grew up on Tavats. This port - is like second home," Em responded. "Also know freight zone well – played here as small child."

The three adjusted their vision to the dim interior, serviced mainly by droids. Colossal containers were being silently transferred by robotic hovering platforms, taken from the vertical Velo mountain line onto the main Velo-City train. The lack of sound was eerie.

Em reconfigured her clothing and explained in hushed whispers, "Few Holans is work here. Area fully automated."

"Where are the containers going?" asked Naomi.

"Is taken across Holis – many sites. Is filled with resources and then back here. Then taken by shuttle to Tavats in space. Naomi, Araz, alter clothing – is Tavat way."

"They must be for Ankh - the Elysian Two project?" Naomi swiftly changed her Flecto gown to copy Em's newly fashioned bodysuit.

Araz also adjusted his attire to look the same. They placed a thin band of the material around their heads and activated it to reflect.

Em sneered at Naomi's question. "Is what you supposed to think. Nothing what it seem. Come, I show you – this way."

Em led them to the elevator door and tentatively pressed her hand to it, relieved when the Phase-Seal opened at her touch. "Good! Crypts still registered - for now. Leave doors for me. Your crypts maybe not good, anymore," she added darkly.

Naomi realised, too late, if Em was still being tracked this could be a real problem. Unsure if she should share this information, she merely nodded agreement with Araz and they all stepped into the tubular capsule. It shot them up to the top of the summit, to the launch pads for the Tavat shuttles.

Exiting the elevator, their clothing took on the texture of fur against the icy temperature of the open-top mountain and their warm breath formed small puffs of vapour in the cold air.

Whilst Araz had visited this area during his training, he had never been on one of the shuttles and it was all new to Naomi. She gave an involuntary shiver, not prompted by the cold, and looked on in trepidation. What did Em need to show them?

The hollowed-out summit was a hive of activity. The Tavat sector workers, all dressed in the same bodysuits with bright headbands, moved in and out of the docked shuttles. Three of these huge space vessels were parked on the ramps. The nearest one was being loaded with cargo as numerous technicians, holding a variety of tools, made external checks. The middle vessel was being unloaded as if it had just landed.

A loud klaxon rang and a transparent sheet of Phase-Seal crystallised around the furthest shuttle, sealing it off from the general area. Everyone stopped work to watch.

"Is taking off," Em said matter-of-factly.

Naomi watched, intrigued, as the shuttle ramp tilted, lifting the vehicle until it was vertically aligned, the nose pointing up to the sky. The wings folded into the central tubular body as its circular base hovered, temporarily, above the ramp which then smoothly lowered. A deep sound penetrated the air and the shuttle appeared to shudder and then move in slow motion as a mighty force pushed it upwards with a whoosh of air making everyone's ears pop. It had disappeared into the clouds above the mountain in seconds, the protective wall melting away once it had gone.

"Come – this way. Remember, on official tour. Population not yet been advised any change to status. Still think Quora Naomi is honourable new councillor."

Naomi swallowed hard, thinking this was bound to change, but she forced her mind to squash these more troubling thoughts. She resolved to concentrate on the here and now.

The three walked confidently amongst the other Holans, blending in as workers going about their business. Em took the lead and they spoke as they went.

"I hadn't seen a shuttle take off this close before! Amazing!" Naomi shook her head to clear her ears. "It's not dissimilar to the rockets they started to use on Earth, only there most of the structure was jettisoned. And they burnt such dangerous substances, fuels made from fossils - I mean, can you believe it? And it creates so many flames!"

"They do not have the power of InvertIon," murmured Araz.

"Well, actually they do, if they but knew it," Naomi added quietly. "Part of our Earth Studies research teams used space scans. They discovered large deposits of raw InvertIon under some of the inactive volcanos on the planet's fault lines."

"Is that restricted information?" asked Araz, recalling the group of agents who had been sent to Earth at the same time as him. Most of them were assigned to archaeological surveillance across the globe; the details had been kept secret at the time.

"I guess it is," Naomi said cautiously. "But I think I am done with anything labelled 'restricted', 'secret' or 'unauthorised' for now! I have been lied to about my parents and my lineage and I am not prepared to let the truth be smothered. Besides, it doesn't seem to fit with the original ethos of our race."

Araz nodded. She had a point.

"No delivery of InvertIon for centuries," Em commented. "Tavat captains, say no more on Ankh. All gone."

"Is that true or just a myth?" Naomi shook her head, seeming to pose the question to herself. She and Araz followed Em towards the nearest shuttle. Em feigned checking an under-section of the fuselage and when no one gave them a second glance, she pushed Naomi and Araz through an opening into the spacecraft.

It looked much bigger on the inside. Em put a finger to her lips and indicated for them to enter a lift capsule with her. The door sealed as they glided sideways down the length of the craft.

"Shuttle has just collected cargo from main Tavat ship in space. Now is moving to hidden containers before being offloaded."

"What cargo?"

"Shhh!" Em replied as the capsule came to a stop and the door opened. They stepped into a narrow corridor. Em put her hand to the Phase-Seal door in front of them, but it remained shut. Naomi and Araz exchanged a worried look as Em pulled out her Multi-Com from a hidden pocket in her bodysuit. She pressed the side of the device and a small arrow shaped object sprang out. She put it to a tiny indentation in the centre of the door and as the arrow began to spark, the Phase-Seal melted away.

"Is duplicate of official key," she winked mischievously.

Naomi shuddered. She knew who possessed the official key, none other than Odion. His angry eyes set into his bald head flashed across her mind. He would not be happy to see her in this restricted area.

Stepping into another corridor, they cautiously approached the end. An artificial red light lit up the storage area before them. Naomi started to ask about the light but Em put her fingers to her lips.

Em looked around the technicians sitting in front of computers near several cell doors, before decisively marching up to a short, stocky worker who swivelled round and stood up to greet her, with a slap to her open hand.

"Em! Is surprise see you!"

"Dimitri, good see you. How is it on Tavat?"

"You missing us, yes? Tavat, is same," the squat man replied, adding, "work is too much, food is terrible, is no festival break..."

"Is hard life!" Em winked at Dimitri, whose face broke into a wide smile.

"Em teases Dimitri! Tavat life always hard life. Now, who is this?" he nodded towards Naomi and Araz.

"They here, see cargo. Not worry – this new councillor - has clearance from Vizier Ubaid."

"Quora," Dimitri bowed his head to Naomi, adding, "All image capturing devices – please to put here," Dimitri pointed to a container inside the entrance. Em put her Multi-Com inside and Naomi and Araz did the same, both exchanging a look which asked the question, 'why no images?'

Em then pressed her hand onto the nearest cell door and it melted open. Dimitri nodded and didn't give them a second glance as he went back to his computer.

Em walked them into the chamber. There was an overpowering smell of uric acid. Naomi first put her hand to her nose and then swiftly cut her nasal senses. The red light was so intense, they found their Tarsus filters dropping. After blinking for a few seconds, the three looked around the large area of the cell. Araz stared in disbelief. In front of them was a number of small, ape-like creatures, chained by heavy rings of metal joining their feet together and each creature to the next. Their rubbery skin was covered in dark hair making it impossible to distinguish if there were different sexes. All stared back from the ugly, leathery folds of their facial skin, with unblinking blood red eyes. A few gave a low, pained growl setting Araz's teeth on edge.

"There must be fifty of them," Naomi exclaimed, looking at their faces intently. "No! They can't be… For the love of Ra! They're… they're Repros! But they're mammals! They're only half-grown!"

The beings huddled together and a few snarled at the onlookers. Four or five of them began to advance on Naomi, hissing, their chains rattling as they moved.

"Is Repro childrens." Em grabbed a metal stick from the wall and shook it at those moving forward. They quickly moved back, their fear of the device apparent.

"This young ones, is taken to restricted area of Hub. There, is modified – put in clothing, helmets. Trained to fight."

No one said anything for a few minutes as the full implications of Em's words sank in.

Naomi was the first to speak. "I knew they weren't constructs. Where did they come from? I mean originally? Are there more?"

"Many more. Infants and breeders - is kept on Tavats. Offspring removed when weaned."

Araz was disgusted by both the stench and what he was hearing. "So, where do they come from?"

"Is not known. Crypts held in Council of Sanctity many years. Some say these things, is original Holans, removed by ancestors in order we live here."

"I don't believe it!" Araz pressed his Flecto sleeve tight to his nose, unable to bear the overpowering smell of animal waste any longer.

"It doesn't matter where they come from." Naomi's outrage punctuated her words. "They are a subordinate species who have been enslaved by our race. This is an atrocity. Who began this barbaric project?"

Em again put her finger to her lips as Dimitri entered the cell and took the metal cattle prod from her. He touched the stick to the leg of the closest creature. It squealed in pain but reluctantly moved forward, pulling the others along with it. They filed out of the area, snarling and hissing at Em, Araz and Naomi, who pressed themselves into the wall as they passed.

Following, they watched the herd loaded into a small container. Araz quietly reached his Multi-Com and surreptitiously filmed as their chains were attached to anchors in the wall of the crate and the small beasts began to screech piteously and tug at their manacles. Dimitri closed the door and pressed his hand to the controls. Within seconds the howling screams stopped and all went quiet.

"What did he do?" gasped Naomi.

"Is gas - for sleeping. They be quiet now until reach Council of Stability."

"And what will happen there?" Naomi could not take her eyes off the crate as it slid silently into a shaft to move along to the exit.

"Shani tell us. Is surgical procedure - it bypass Repro bodily functions. Then nutriments - is input by tubes, waste output same way. Repros then taught obedience and combat. Is controlled with implant."

"So, that's how they are tamed! Their bodies are modified, then they are controlled electronically and forced to fight. I have seen the area where the fully-grown ones are stored." Naomi's horror was clear.

Araz could not help thinking she reacted just as Imogen would have done. In another part of his mind, he hoped Imogen was safe. He longed to be with her.

Dimitri flicked a switch and the full lights came on. The observers retrieved their devices and returned to the lift capsule in silence as their Tarsus filters retracted.

"Is eye opener, yes?" quipped Em, but she got no response from Araz and Naomi, who were quietly processing all this new information.

Eventually Naomi spoke, "How long has this project been in operation?"

"Fifty or sixty years. Is best kept secret. Only Viziers, Supreme Leader and those working on Tavats know truth. All swear oath - will remain secret from rest of peoples - on risk of execution."

"I still can't believe these animals lived on Holis before we colonised it. To think they were wiped out, only their crypts kept in storage," Naomi thought aloud. "Then to be, well, resurrected, only to be subjugated to the will of the government, like Zeroids. What threat was bad enough for them to do this?"

Araz scratched his head, "The Supreme Council must fear an invasion from the primitive race," he rationalised. "That can be the only reason. Come to think of it, there were no Repros until the subversives stole the Tractus technology and opened an illegal portal to Earth. If they had not created this potential threat, there would have been no need to train wild beasts for combat. Although I'm not sure what use they will be against some of the appalling weaponry there. These humans can wipe out entire cities in a flash."

Em regarded Araz with a sneer. "Logic, is twisted. Reason Tractus taken from Holis, is prevent council using space jump for bad purpose."

"I thought the purpose of the Tractus technology was to speed up the Elysian Two project?" Naomi interjected. "I mean, what else would it be used for?"

"Is good question. I am no Vatic, but can guess…"

Em was prevented from saying more as they emerged from the shuttle lift to the sound of a loud klaxon. They stopped in the shadow of the spacecraft to watch helmeted Repros flooding into the area. The Tavat workers were being rounded up and a large group cowered in the middle of the launch pad service area. Several Repros were using scanning devices to check each Holan in turn. Other Repros had started to spread out and search the area. All were armed with blades.

Naomi looked wildly at Em and Araz. "What do we do?"

"Quick, follow me!" Em crept along the side of the shuttle and round the back until they were out of view.

"Is no way out – guards on every exit. Could maybe hide, or make run for it, but not much hope…"

"Wait, I have a plan," announced Naomi. "Who are they looking for? The escaped prisoner, Tarik Zuberi, yes? And did they get a good look at those who ran with him? I think not."

Araz started to nod agreement and added, "Plus, the implants of the fallen guard were scrambled, so there will be no data from them. But how do we explain what we are doing in the Tavat Port?"

"Got it! We pursued this suspected subversive and have now taken her prisoner," Naomi declared, eagerly grabbed Em's arm.

Araz gave a broad smile and took Em's other arm.

Em pushed her elbows out, throwing their hands away. "You not touch!" she glared, backing away.

"It's just a ruse," reassured Naomi. "To get us out of here. Besides, they may be here for you. Your face is already known as a possible dissident and you are being tracked. They would have known you used the Tavat Port lift."

Em gave a deep frown, but as the footsteps of several Repros closed in on them, she gave the briefest of nods before Araz and Naomi took her by the arms again. They all stepped out from the shuttle, Em giving the pretence of trying to wriggle free.

The Repros immediately surrounded the threesome, knives raised, but hesitated when they saw Araz and Naomi.

"We have captured the alleged insurgent, Emba Lateef." Naomi announced confidently. A Repro stepped forward, saluted Naomi and scanned Em's face. It nodded confirmation to the rest of its group.

"We are taking her to the Council of Stability for questioning. Continue to search the Port for any further fugitives," ordered Araz authoritatively.

Most of the group of Repros turned and moved away to enter the shuttle, but four of their number fell in behind Araz, Naomi and Em and waited, their helmeted faces hidden.

"Looks like we have an escort," Araz murmured.

Naomi attempted to dismiss them, but they merely stood their ground and when they set off, the four Repros followed.

The large public lifts were big enough for all seven of them and as they descended to ground level, Em feigned another tussle. In the process of freeing her arms before they were re-gripped, she managed to retrieve an object from her garments and make fingertip contact with Araz.

'I take two on left, you take others,' was her cognitive message and with an almost imperceptible glance to warn Naomi, Araz secreted his pen into his closed hands, ensuring Naomi caught a glimpse of it.

"Keep still, prisoner!" Araz shouted at Em.

"You vlagging creep! You make me!" Em responded.

Araz pushed her down to her knees in a seemingly violent move. Naomi moved back against the wall of the lift as Araz raised his hand to Em as if to strike her. The Repros looked on in agitation, when Araz and Em suddenly sprang up, surprising the nearest two with a swift jab of their pens to the exposed bit of neck below their helmets. As they slumped to the floor, the other two guard jumped forward, but

Naomi tripped up the closest as Em kicked the other in the stomach. Araz found his erasure cube and pressed it under the helmet of one, next to its ear, whilst Naomi quickly did the same to the one doubled over.

The effect was immediate, the two conscious Repros groaned loudly, clutched their heads, staggered to their feet and threw off their headgear. They then sank to their knees, before making a low guttural noise and turning to crouch down on all fours. Now facing the three Holans, who had pressed themselves against the lift door, the creatures stared wildly through their red-eyes, arched their backs and began to growl and hiss. With bared sharp teeth, they were ready to pounce when the lift came to a stop, just in time.

The door opened as the three spilled out. The two snarling beasts leapt over them into the lobby area. The Repros standing guard quickly moved forward, but the deranged pair launched into those nearest, knocking them to the floor and biting any part of their body within reach. Screams of agony and angry shouts rang through the area as the Holan public came to a stop and looked on in horror.

The lobby Repros reacted by wielding their weapons and hacking at the attacking pair with ferocious force, not appearing to notice they were also cutting down both their fellow creatures and their own guards who had fallen. With the indiscriminate slaughter, there was blood splattered high and low and those watching screamed and began to scatter.

The Repros, filled with blood lust, continued to slice into the rogue pair and several other of their number, long after they were dead, smashing their bodies across the lobby floor in a frenzy of killing. It was only when the Vizier of Stability arrived and pressed the arrow on the end of his chain, the beasts abruptly stopped, freezing where they stood, heads drooped.

Araz, Em and Naomi had moved with the crowds to escape, only glancing back when they were clear of the entrance to witness Odion taking charge before the area was sealed.

Em quickly diverted them away from the main walkways, back to the edge of the surrounding forest.

"Is good work," she said to her companions.

Naomi was looking white. "All that blood! Violence such as this had not been witnessed since the reign of Anubis. It was horrific. I can't imagine the Holan people will put up with this."

"We will not have long before we are discovered," Araz added. "Our public 'arrest' of Em will have been recorded and reported to those in charge."

"You're right. When we don't turn up with Em, we will most certainly be deemed subversive too." Naomi murmured, her face ashen.

"Unless you lie. Say - I escape! In commotion," Em winked. "You return. Need people on inside. Find out what going on?"

Naomi shook her head. "I will not play spy, or double agent," she glanced meaningfully at Araz who went to protest, but instead pressed his lips together.

Em furrowed her brows and shook her head.

"But I do intend to find out the truth of what is going on. My loyalty lies with the Holan people."

Em gave a slow nod and clasped Naomi's hand. "Make sense. Is good – good you say people matter. You and Imogen, think same. So, we go separate ways. I meet Imogen and Tarik; you go find truth. Make sure, find out about Elysian Two. Araz, which side you choose?"

Araz snorted, "A typically simplistic subversive question!" However, he was pensive for a few moments before adding, in a more reasoned voice, "I have been loyal to the Supreme Council for my whole life, and I have never acted in a duplicitous way."

Naomi could see the copper indignation he directed towards her.

"I believe in the Holan people and our way of life, but that is not to say I approve of what the subversive scientists have done, or the things I have witnessed today. More importantly, I need to find Imogen."

"Go with Em," Naomi responded kindly. "I will say I was separated from you when the Repro fighting broke out. They will assume you are pursuing Em. And here – take this," Naomi handed over her erasure cube. "I'm sure I would not be able to explain why I had this in my possession!" She paused before adding, "And perhaps you would tell my..." she could not bring herself to say the word 'clone'. "My duplicate. Tell her I had no idea about her existence. I still can't quite believe it. She must know I had no part in it, I mean, who chooses how they are conceived? And... and I would like to talk to her."

The three nodded and Em held up her hand for a few seconds before Naomi took the cue and slapped her open palm as Dimitri had done.

Araz gave Naomi a gracious nod as she returned to the main pedestrian route to head towards Karnak and The Hub. As she melted into the distant crowds, he acknowledged she had an air of confidence about her that Imogen had never possessed. The difference of being raised to take high office and being raised in hiding, he reflected to himself.

Em and Araz set off for the rendezvous point at the subversive headquarters, close to The Hub. They were going in the same direction as Naomi but went deep into the forest to head along the back routes, unseen.

IMOGEN

*I*mogen marched towards the glass Hub. Leo followed a few yards behind. He did not say anything. Imogen was deep in thought and her Chroma was displaying a multitude of colours rising and falling like waves on a stormy sea as she tried to rationalise her situation and formulate a plan of action. All he could do was follow and keep a wary look out for any Repros. He hoped she would continue to relent towards him.

Imogen stopped and turned around so sharply, Leo stumbled, nearly running into her.

"Where are they holding your mother?"

"Erm… In the guarded enclosures adjacent to The Hub, I think. Why?"

"She was a member of the Supreme Council, right?"

"Yes."

"When they discovered my parents had jumped to Earth?"

"I guess so. I wasn't born then. I mean, it was before my mother had decided to do the Frankenstein thing on me."

"I need to speak to her."

"Right! Did you hear me use the word 'guarded'? That means Repros."

Imogen ignored him and continued, "Shani's people scrambled the implants of those Repros that attacked us. The other ones did not get close. No one can say they saw either me or my clone. So, it stands to reason they would still think I was her. How is anyone to know

'Quora Naomi' helped spring you free, or colluded with the Resistance?"

"And how do we know they didn't see you or Naomi? Or that Naomi hasn't reported you?"

"She's with Em and Araz."

Leo could see a bolt of deep, plum-shaded jealousy flash momentarily in Imogen's colours before she smothered her aura with ice blue shades of logic.

"And anyway, it's a chance we are just going to have to take."

"Okay, let's say everyone takes you to be Councillor Naomi and let's say she still has her privileges. What's the plan?" Leo asked, sitting on the grass bank.

"Naomi has access to practically everywhere. After all, I got into the prison as her and even Kekara didn't challenge me. So, I take you to your mother and if confronted, I say I have recaptured you and I am escorting you for one last visit before your execution. We then smuggle her out. You free your mum; I get some answers!"

"That's it? Simple!"

"Look, it was Naomi who was able to halt the Repros as they escorted you to your execution. They didn't attack until I appeared. Probably confused to see two identical councillors."

"But," argued Leo, "unlike Naomi, I am a known fugitive. Don't you think thousands of those beasts will instantly descend upon us to ensure I don't escape again? They've probably been told to kill on first sighting."

"Got a better plan?" Imogen glared.

"Well, No! And I do want to free my mother. It's just, as a plan, you have to admit it's a little vague!"

Leo was quiet for a few moments before he stood up decisively and spoke again, "High certainty of being caught or killed; small chance of success. What are we waiting for?" He was rewarded to see the first tiny glimmer of a smile on Imogen's face. His heart gave a small lurch.

"Right," Imogen indicated for him to go ahead. "Lead the way!"

Imogen and Leo watched from a rocky outcrop in the foothills by The Hub. There appeared to be only two guards outside the secure enclosures.

"We don't have much to fight with," complained Leo. "One tranquilizing pen and two erasure cubes are hardly a match for their blades."

"I am hoping we won't have to fight, but if we do we need to take them out before they can raise a knife."

"Where's a phaser gun when you need one?" Leo quipped nervously.

Imogen was about to ignore the flippant remark when a picture flashed into her mind. The cylindrical device Adam had used against the Repros in the church, on Earth. It had emitted a blast of sound able to floor the Repros. What if they could, somehow, reproduce it?

"You've given me an idea. We need to make something like those dog whistles on Earth. Something capable of producing a sound in a higher ultrasonic range - to deafen the Repros. Your dad, he invented a device to do just that. He used it in the church when they attacked. Said the Repros had ultra-sensitive hearing."

"If I had a DE, I could tinker with the recording settings," Leo thought aloud.

Imogen immediately found The Original Chronicles of Holis DE, hidden in the inner folds of her clothing and handed it to him.

"Perfect!" smiled Leo, glad to put his mind to something practical. He connected and listened to Barbara's chilling warning, realising the data must be The Original Chronicles of Holis. Concentrating on the task in hand, he coupled with the sound setting and cognitively manipulated them to the highest pitch possible. He pressed record, whistled into the device and then went to replay it.

"No!" Imogen quickly stayed his hand. "The sound will carry and we can't alert the guard."

"But I need to test it," objected Leo.

"We can't risk it. We will just have to trust it will be dependable…" Imogen stopped as her eyes bored into Leo's.

"More dependable than me, you're thinking?"

Imogen looked away, unable to answer him.

"Ouch! Okay, I deserved that!" Leo took a deep breath and, nodding reluctant agreement to leave it untested, concealed the ovoid shape in his hand.

They exchanged a brief but determined look as they set off, emerging from the rock boulders to walk towards the entrance. Imogen strode slightly behind Leo, her hand on his shoulder as if forcing him forward.

The Repros unsheathed their blades as Imogen and Leo got closer.

"Not a good sign," Leo said under his breath.

"We need to scramble their implants before they raise the alarm. Be ready with the DE," Imogen whispered.

They came to a standstill as the Repros, blades raised in the air, advanced towards them.

"Stop!" ordered Imogen. To her relief they froze but did not lower their weapons.

"I have recaptured the prisoner, Tarik Zuberi. He is allowed one last visit to his mother before his execution."

The Repros looked confused. They hovered in a flurry of wavering indecision before one suddenly rushed towards Leo, intent on cutting him down.

Leo thumped his hand onto the side of the DE. The ear-splitting sound of his whistle blasted into the air at a continuous and deafening volume. The effect was instantaneous. The Repros released their blades to put their hands to the side of their helmets and dropped to the floor, rolling around in agony.

The noise rang painfully in Imogen and Leo's ears as they also reeled against each other. Leo released the DE, the noise still ringing in his head.

Imogen winced as she grabbed her erasure cube and pressed it under the helmet, next to the ear of the nearest Repro.

Leo, also floundering from the echo of piercing noise, did the same to the other Repro before they both raced for the door.

"Ouch! I will never be able to hear again!"

"I can't hear you! I... I've gone deaf."

"Next time we need to use ear defenders," Leo shook his head over and over to try and force the white noise from his skull.

Imogen read his lips - she could not hear his words. Her head was resonating. They needed to get inside before the Repros recovered. She remembered Shani's warning, 'These creatures are naturally violent and barbaric. Without the control of the implants, they will no longer be tame and will revert to their basic nature'.

Her hand flew to the Phase-Seal door. It opened and she and Leo leapt inside, quickly closing it behind them.

"Which way?"

Leo read her lips and shrugged his shoulders.

Imogen indicated for him to follow and headed down the first corridor, opening doors either side. All the rooms were empty.

Eventually they got to a large indoor garden. They could smell the aroma of cooked food. Imogen's ears popped. She could hear people moving around from within. She turned to make eye contact with Leo and touched her finger to her ear, asking with her eyes if he could hear too? He nodded and gave a small, tense smile.

Checking there were no Repros in sight, they tentatively entered the garden area. Several residents were helping themselves to a meal from a central pot. They did not talk to each other, but took their salvers to separate enclosures to eat by themselves amongst the foliage.

The dozen or so detainees paid them no heed. Their eyes looked to be focussed on a faraway point as they ate mechanically. Imogen looked from one to another wondering why they showed no interest in her or Leo. *Perhaps they all have implants or maybe they've been erased?*

Leo spotted his mother and pulled Imogen towards an isolated mossy bench.

Sekhet did not appear to hear Leo's greeting as he sat down beside her. He put his arm around her shoulder and gave his mother a warm squeeze. She barely moved and continued to take small mouthfuls of her food.

"Mum, you need to come with us," urged Leo.

Sekhet stared ahead, glassy-eyed.

"Has she been erased?" Leo choked back a sob.

Imogen gently took one of the woman's hands in hers and lightly touched her by fingertip. Sekhet's cognitive thoughts were buried beneath a mechanical voice continually repeated instructions: 'sit, eat, sit, rest, eat'. Imogen delved under the monotony of the orders and detected an anxiety and desperation deep in the woman's psyche. *She's trapped!*

"No, I don't think so," she touched Leo's arm lightly. "And there's no sign of any silver threads to indicate hypnosis."

"It must be an implant."

Imogen sent a message via her touch, 'Sekhet, your son, Tarik, he is here. Here to help you'. A pulse of hope momentarily returned via her touch and Imogen noted the tiny surge of gold-flecked burgundy in Sekhet's Chroma, the colour of love.

She's still there! Just like Mum was still there, despite being in a coma. How do we release her?

"Leo, what if we scramble the implant? With the cube?"

"Couldn't that harm her? I mean, would it scramble her brain too?"

"Shani said the Repros would return to their basic nature once the implant was messed up. So, I guess your mum will go back to normal?"

"But we don't know for sure. It could also damage her?"

"It's your choice, but it seems to me she is calling to be freed."

Leo pushed his hand through his hair, pulling at his roots and finally nodded.

Imogen found her erasure cube and gently placed it next to Sekhet's ear and held her breath.

Sekhet lurched backward and forward and shuddered before shaking her head and turning to stare at Leo. She blinked in recognition as a smile spread across her face.

"Tarik! Is it really you?" She put her hands to his head and pulled him to her for an embrace. Leo responded by giving her a bear hug, holding her close as he muttered 'thank God'. A solitary tear ran down his face.

When he finally released her, Sekhet looked around the indoor garden at the vacant-eyed residents and back to Imogen.

"Where am I? And what's happened?"

"Mum, you've been held in these secure quarters for a long time. They subdued you with an implant. Do you remember speaking to me after my trial?"

"Yes! You… you were going to the dark side of Holis, as a punishment. That was a lie, wasn't it? They don't use such penalties anymore. Tarik, what has been going on?"

"We will explain, but first you need to come with me and Imogen. We are not safe here."

Sekhet looked warily at Imogen. "She's a member of the Supreme Council?"

"It's a disguise," Imogen explained quickly. *We need to get out of here.*

Sekhet nodded and the three rose and quietly slipped out of the garden. Sekhet began to go in the direction of the main entrance but Imogen stopped her. "Repros – wild ones," she warned. "There must be another way out?"

"This way," Sekhet motioned to Imogen, pulling Leo alongside her as they travelled down several passageways to the rear of the building. They stopped in front of an opaque wall.

"It will not open for me, or any of those detained here."

"Or me. Not now I'm public enemy number one!" added Leo.

Imogen stepped forward and tentatively touched the Phase-Seal wall. It melted away at her touch. "Well, that's good news! I still have access to everything, so that must mean Naomi is still free."

"Unless they have got wind there are two of you and you are being tracked," Leo remarked as he glanced around the open ground before them.

"Two of you?" Sekhet raised her eyebrows.

"It's complicated, but Imogen here has a double. We can explain later."

Sekhet shrugged her shoulders. In her former role she had seen enough strange phenomenon not to be surprised at anything.

"Tarik is right about the tracking. I was once in charge of security; they can track anyone they want. It used to be considered an infringement of privacy, but no doubt this is a thing of the past. They will also know my implant has been blanked. It will register with the surveillance team in The Hub."

"All the more reason to get to the Resistance headquarters," Leo added, noting the grey flurries of worry rising in Imogen's Chroma. "Plus, we need to be sheltered before it gets dark."

Imogen glanced to the sky and saw a glimpse of the corona encircling the planet Sheut as the twilight of Atma approached. Even with their Flecto clothing, they could not risk being out in the extreme temperatures of night-time.

"This way," Leo headed towards the lower levels of the glass mountain. He would lead them to Barbara along the secret passages. Then they could plan their next move.

Imogen needed to ask Sekhet a ream of questions but knew she would have to wait until they were at a place of safety. *But if I am being tracked, am I safe anywhere?*

THE COUNCIL CHAMBER

*K*ekara sat on the high throne in the grand circular council chamber. There was silence except for the noise of her fingernails as they drummed on the throne's golden arm. The vibrations of this irritated beat rose to the carved and jewel encrusted lotus flowers of the vaulted ceiling. Four of her Viziers sat nervously in the black marble tiered seating awaiting the fifth. None of them spoke.

Eventually, the bulky, bald form of Odion raced through the doorway, slowing when he saw the robed figures all staring directly at him. He looked flustered as he marched towards Kekara but appeared to change his mind and stepped back to address all those assembled.

"Apologies, Your Greatness." He bowed obsequiously. "There have been some developments following the skirmish at the Tavat Port."

"Skirmish?" Merit questioned, the note of distaste clear in her voice. "Is that what you call the bloody fight witnessed by so many of our good people? Dozens of our so-called protective guard completely out of control? Reduced to slicing each other into pieces? I think 'blood bath' would be a more appropriate word than 'skirmish'."

Odion glared at Merit and was about to respond when Ubaid stood up.

"Your Greatness, we did warn about using these creatures on Holis. The control Odion claims we have over their kind would appear to be questionable. Despite the implants they are, when all is said and done, a savage and barbarous species."

"The subversive movement is to blame!" Odion countered belligerently, looking down on Ubaid who was a good head's height shorter. "They have somehow managed to neutralise the behavioural implants. Those responsible must be found."

"We should never have used these beasts," Merit said angrily. "There have not been sufficient tests."

"It is thanks to these 'beasts' we managed to recapture members of the subversive movement on Earth," glared Odion. "We must continue to search out every last one."

"But first, we must remove the Repro forces from our cities. They are causing a rising panic in the population…"

"Which is as it should be," interrupted Kekara in a cold voice.

Merit went quiet and the Viziers all turned in surprise to face their leader.

"Do you not see? This incident will play into our hands. I want the population to be frightened. I want them to glimpse what it is like to be exposed to barbarity. A nation that has lived in peace for millennia and surrendered all weaponry is utterly oblivious and unprepared. They have no idea of what they are facing. I want them to see what it is like to be at the mercy of a primitive race. The threat must be understood."

"Ma'am, a child was almost killed in the village of Qus," Merit said with undisguised repulsion.

"Unfortunate, yes. But we are in the process of refining these reproduction life forms, are we not Odion?"

"Yes Ma'am. We are giving them an inbuilt and controlled intelligence. They will be capable of utilising their strength strategically and independently. Implants will no longer be needed so the risk of the creatures turning wild will be removed."

"How is this being achieved?" Merit dared to ask.

"That is not your concern," growled Odion. "The modifications are underway and the resultant Hypros will be a most formidable force."

"And will you be able to guarantee these 'Hypros' will not pose a danger to our people?"

Kekara banged her fist on the arm of her throne. "Your focus is misdirected. You - my most trusted Viziers - you must understand! The real danger is the existence of unregulated portals to and from the primitive world. This endangers us all! We need protection. We need to deal with the greater threat of being discovered by the humans on Earth. Come, there are more pressing matters than a few Repros losing control."

The Viziers exchanged fearful looks as Kekara indicated for them to sit, signalling to Odion to take the floor to make his report.

"Before we could carry out his termination, the Falsebred, Tarik Zuberi, escaped with the help of the subversives. We followed him for a good distance but for some unknown reason our pursuit was called off." Odion looked defiantly at Kekara who returned his look with a cold stare.

"Called off for the same reason, Odion," she responded in a frosty voice. "A fugitive from justice - at large on Holis - will cause more uncertainty and unrest. We cannot have our people becoming complacent. They believe him to have made the illegal links to Earth. He represents menace. His escape must be broadcast so the danger may be felt by all. Besides, we know he is a harmless oaf."

Odion shrugged his shoulders and picked up the report again, "He is thought to be in the vicinity of The Hub. It is only a matter of time before we find him. And I can assure you, the sentence of the High Court will then be carried out." Odion looked at his fellow Viziers as if daring them to object.

In their guarded silence, he continued, "Our surveillance team then tracked the suspected subversive, Emba Lateef, to the docking area of the Tavat Port. She had been arrested by the Earth agent, Araz Vikram and, surprisingly, the new councillor, Naomi. Unfortunately, this group were lost when the Repros went out of control. Naomi has returned and advised us the agent continues to pursue the escaped Falsebred, Tarik Zuberi. We have also just been informed, the former Councillor, Sekhet, has absconded from the quarters where she was being held. Her implant and those of the Repro guard were de-activated. Furthermore, it has been confirmed the one to open the

Phase-Seal door to aid Sekhet's escape was none other than Naomi! A strange way for a new councillor to act, do you not think? Perhaps Ubaid would like to elaborate? He is, after all, her mentor?"

Ubaid stroked his beard and looked directly at Kekara as he replied. "I can only deduce Naomi must be using Sekhet as bait to trap her son, Tarik. That must be the explanation. She is a bright youngster, Your Greatness. A specialist in Earth studies and, I believe, destined for a pivotal role in the testing times ahead."

Odion snorted dismissively.

"I have met this new councillor," Kekara responded. "There is something about her that concerns me. There are many inconsistencies. One minute she denied any knowledge of the agent who gave evidence, the next she is with him in the Tavat Port. Who gave her orders to pursue subversives or interfere with Sekhet's incarceration? Where is she now?"

"I will find her," replied Ubaid.

"Good - Sekhet must be returned to the secure unit and I will speak to this Naomi."

Odion threw a sneering look at Ubaid as he continued, "With regard to other matters, the final batches of the toxin, Expirite, are complete along with the vials of antidote. The Tavats continue to be loaded with the essential cargo for Elysian Two. The only outstanding issue is that of the Tractus technology." Odion turned to Ubaid and indicated for him to take the floor.

Ubaid looked thoughtful as he paced the council chamber in a full circle before he began, "As you are all aware, the new Elysian Two project has not yet been revealed to the population. They still hope for a return to Ankh, despite the revision of the Chronicles and the removal of all references to anything to do with its renewal. We here have known for an age, this is a false hope. Ankh is spent and beyond restoration. This, and the fact our stores of InvertIon are close to depleted - we have little more than a few hundred years supply left — has resulted in the need for the biggest change to our social policy in the history of our race. Thanks to the strength and determination of our Supreme Leader," he bowed towards Kekara. "We have the vision to lead the Holan people to new lands with ample resources of InvertIon. Our sights are set on the primitive planet. Almost the twin of Ankh, the terrain is perfect and they are unaware of the existence of InvertIon which lies beneath the surface. But we must have the technology to jump there instantaneously. We have only one operational portal and we do not have the ability to create more markers – the subversive scientists have been thorough in their coding of the essential information. The Tractus project is key to the viability of Elysian Two."

The Viziers all nodded. This was the secret they all held, one only to be discussed within the boundaries of the council chamber.

Ubaid gave a little smile. "What you may not realise is I have sent an emissary to Earth to begin negotiations with those subversives remaining there."

"Will they cooperate?" Merit asked in surprise. "After all these years of resistance?"

"Oh yes, they will cooperate. Their freedom in return for the Tractus technology."

"These subversives have broken the Sanctus Laws and put us all in danger." Odion leapt to his feet in outrage. "You had no authorisation to promise this."

"Promise. Such a strong word," replied Ubaid. "Once we have the power to replicate the Tractus device, they will face justice. The word 'promise' did not pass my lips."

Merit snorted. "You may not have promised them freedom, but you implied it. This is a dishonest way to proceed!"

Odion turned on Merit with an angry retort, "If you think we will make progress without using any form of coercion, I wonder why you hold such high office?"

"How dare you! Do you think your ruthless methods are an honourable form of conduct?"

Odion made a threatening move towards Merit and in seconds, all the Viziers were on their feet, arguing in the centre of the chamber.

Kekara put out her hand to stop the exchange. "Order! There is too much at stake here. Order!"

The Viziers went quiet, looking to their leader before sitting back in their places to listen to her.

"We must get our priorities right. We must regain the Tractus project. It is vital. Ubaid was right to offer some inducement. As to the subversive scientists being entitled to our honesty, it is they that are the law-breakers, not us. Let us leave the question of their punishment until after we have what we need. In the meantime, we will start the second phase of our public transmissions. Fear is a necessary pre-requisite for acceptance of the new Elysian project. To this end, clips of the atrocities committed by the primitives will be broadcast daily. Brutality, violence, starvation, pollution, criminal behaviour, everything we find abhorrent will be relayed to all. There must be no question of the threat to our race."

"This will greatly unsettle our people," Merit dared to comment. "And our sense of peace."

"As intended," Kekara responded dismissively. "There must be no empathy for these barbaric beings. The Holan people must feel nothing but disgust and contempt towards humans. By the end of our campaign, it will be understood they are an aberration in Ra's universe."

NAOMI

hen Ubaid returned to his quarters, Naomi was waiting for him. He glanced around the area. "Where is she?"

"Who?"

"Sekhet? You are known to have released her from the secure unit."

"I have done no such thing. But I can guess who has."

"Really? Would you like to enlighten me?"

"First, I am here to ask you some questions."

"Ah." Ubaid crossed to a crystal flask and poured two drinks into goblet shaped salvers, offering one to Naomi. When she shook her head, he sighed and sat down, placing her drink on a small table and sipping from his own glass. "Go ahead."

"I have just come from the Sanctity testing area of The Hub."

"Yes?"

"I used the Lineator."

"I see," responded Ubaid, stroking his beard and waiting for Naomi to say more.

"So, you know I hold all five lines in equal measure. That I'm a Penta-Crypt?"

Ubaid merely dipped his head sideways in agreement.

"My biological parents are Kasmut Akil and Rashida Omorose?"

Again, Ubaid nodded.

"Why was I not told? And why do I have a clone?"

"There are good reasons why no one was told you were the first 'so-called' Sanctus Cryptus. Please, sit whilst I explain."

Naomi nodded and sat rigidly on the edge of an adjacent seat.

"I did not want to draw attention to this fact. Had you or others known of your unique makeup, this may have affected how you were raised. Others would have singled you out, treated you at best with overwhelming reverence or at worst with fear and suspicion. It was better you were brought up unaware of this fact. I must also confirm you do share the same DNA as another. This was a top-secret genetic project and, I have to say, a most successful one. Naomi, I must ask, how did you find out?"

Naomi was reeling inside. The truth was confirmed. She was the result of a scientific experiment; her biological parents were members of the subversive movement. She had no time to dwell further on this. She picked up her goblet as she thought about how she should answer Ubaid. She had already decided not to mention Araz, she felt an intuitive and protective obligation towards him and still could not fathom out why she got goosebumps whenever he was near. She realised Imogen must have freed Sekhet. Ubaid was not stupid, he would put two and two together, so, despite Shani saying the hidden presence of both clones was an advantage, she rationalised she had no choice but to tell Ubaid.

"I have met my clone. Imogen. She is here on Holis. It is she who freed Sekhet. You must know Imogen was born on Earth."

"Ah," said Ubaid thoughtfully. "That would explain a lot. I think my agent, Araz, has not been altogether honest with me."

"If we are talking about dishonesty, then he is not the only one! Ubaid, you paraded me in front of my biological father under false pretences. You knew I had no idea of our connection. He thought me to be Imogen. I was unknowingly part of this subterfuge. And having used me, you terminated him." Naomi clenched a fist as she spoke.

"I have only done what was necessary, my dear. Look, I can see you are cross with me but allow me to explain. We needed crucial information. I could only gain this if the prisoner thought we held his daughter. I knew we would get what we wanted once he had seen you. Is that so very wrong?"

Naomi frowned at the elderly Vizier but held her head high. "And was this approved? Because I am sure my existence was not."

"As you are well aware, my dear, every project on Holis, big or small, is considered in meticulous detail before being approved and regulated. It is a feature of our kind – caution, care and consideration. However, this is not always conducive to progress. In fact, it can have the opposite effect; severe prudence can swamp bold new initiatives. Such was the case with the Sanctus Cryptus project."

Naomi bristled. The more her mentor spoke, the more she found herself losing what was left of any remaining faith in him. She took a gulp of the sweet honeyed liquid from her cup.

"An opportunity arose to bring you into being. The project was not subject to the usual scrutiny. Indeed, it was - if you like - carried out unlawfully. But here you are! A Penta-Crypt raised for leadership, to use your talents and your perfect balance of personality lines to assist the Holan people. To help us put the second greatest project of our race into being. To lead us to glory! Your life will have a great and magnificent purpose. You see, Naomi, some things are meant to be."

"I don't know what you're are talking about. But you have confirmed I am, by definition, a Falsebred. Worse, the use of cloning in Holan beings has been prohibited since time immemorial. I know, I looked up the records. Two completely identical Holans is a... an abomination! Once the population know, we will both be terminated, irrespective of being Penta-Crypts. You have lied to me my entire life and I no longer know where I fit in, or even if I can." Naomi felt the sting of tears at the back of her eyes as she struggled to stop herself shaking. "In creating me, you have also sentenced me to death. You had no right! I will never be accepted. My life was doomed from the start." Naomi began to sob, pulling away from Ubaid who had moved to sit next to her in an apparent attempt to console her.

"My dear, no one will know you were cloned. I will make sure of this. This Imogen does not belong here. She is the one who was falsely bred, not you. She has no knowledge of Holan life or any loyalty to the Holan people. Her one and only contribution has been to allow us to produce you. She has no further purpose and harsh as it may seem, she must be terminated."

"You expect me to agree to this?" Naomi tried to stand but found she had started to lose feelings in her legs. Her head had also started to throb. She sank back into her seat.

"Such indignation! Naomi, I fear you have no choice." Ubaid sneered. He folded his arms and slowed his speech, emphasising each word, "If you are not compliant, you will leave me no choice as to which one of you should be spared. Your double, I am sure, could be persuaded to take your place. If it meant her family would be safe. You see, my dear, it is most unfortunate, but the moral high ground is not the safest of places."

Naomi wanted to wipe the sanctimonious smile off Ubaid's face, but her vision had become blurred and she felt sick. As it dawned on her what was happening, she dropped her goblet and stared wildly from it to Ubaid's cold eyes.

"What have you d..." Naomi could say no more as she felt herself beginning to lose consciousness. Before she blacked out she heard Ubaid's final words:

"Such a shame. After showing such promise. The influence of the line of Iris is surely to blame? I may give you time to reconsider your position, but for now sleep tight, my dear."

THE RESISTANCE HEADQUARTERS

*D*eep in the adjacent mountain to The Hub, Shani greeted the two new arrivals. "Imogen - Tarik! Thank goodness you are safe. Em and Araz will be with us in the morning. It was too late to travel here, so they are staying at our smaller base hidden amongst the Karnak residences." Shani threw her arm around Leo's shoulder affectionately and nodded graciously at his mother.

Sekhet's eyes widened to see Shani. They had once sat on the Supreme Council together. "Shani! Now I know there is a worthy leader in charge of the Resistance."

Lara and Cael entered the stone space and greeted Imogen warmly. "We have a meal prepared." They led Sekhet and Leo to the dining area of the headquarters, deeper into the stone-carved room, beyond the suspension chamber holding the Tractus marker.

Shani stopped Imogen and took her to one side, dropping her voice to a whisper. "Imogen, I take it you know you are a Penta-Crypt?"

Imogen nodded silently, grey worry surging through her aura.

"From what I understand, your existence is close to miraculous! A chance occurrence. I can see why Eshe wanted to preserve your crypts - in case anything happened to you on Earth."

Imogen was relieved to see there was no condemnation, only respect and a degree of admiration in both Shani's eyes and her Chroma.

"That aside, we have been analysing the effects of travel by Tractus on your body. There may be a few causes for concern, so I need to run a couple more tests, but not on you."

"What do you mean?"

"Naomi has identical DNA. This means we can compare and quantify your results with greater accuracy."

Imogen tried to quash the annoyance she felt every time Naomi was mentioned. *She was deliberately manufactured as my double – she has no right to be here!*

"Imogen, you cannot hold this against her!"

Imogen looked away from Shani's gaze. *Can she read my thoughts?*

Shani continued, "Naomi did not ask to be created, just as you did not ask to be born on Earth. You must give her a chance. After all, she thinks just like you!"

Imogen swallowed. She knew Shani was right. *I must try to let go of these feelings of outrage. They're not helping.*

"Furthermore, Naomi has agreed to cooperate with us and has allowed Em to take a volt of her flesh. The results are being analysed by a team of scientists hidden in Qus. They should tell us the advisability of using the Tractus in the future."

"So, Naomi has not used the Tractus?"

Shani shook her head. "The direct comparison of your cells will inform us of any adverse impact. Genetically, you are even closer than identical twins. This is a unique opportunity and it's too good to waste."

Imogen bit her lip before replying. "Shani, you need to know I have not only used the Tractus to jump space, but I was also stuck inside it for forty years when I was catapulted forward in time."

Shani's mouth dropped open as she took in this new information.

"I'm actually forty years older than Naomi, but I did not age. The time vault was instantaneous for me."

"No! The Tractus is capable of leaping a person through time? Would that explain why Tarik's crypts test to be ten years younger than they should be?"

"Yes. He was shot forward ten years in a back-up plan to rescue me."

Shani blinked as she took in the information. "This is a most significant development. We must keep this information classified. I will also need to re-test Tarik's cells, and perhaps Araz will agree to take part in the trial? I take it he has only used the Tractus for space, and not time travel?"

Imogen nodded. She was desperate to see Araz again and her heart shuddered at the thought of his arms around her.

Shani took Imogen's hands and smiled. "You have deep feelings for Araz?"

Imogen blushed. "Is it that obvious?"

Shani patted Imogen's arm. "It is, if you can read Chroma."

When Imogen looked surprised, Shani explained, "Only a handful of native Holans have developed this ability. After all, there are only a few days a month when the colours are visible. I made a study of the phenomena after Tarik reported how clearly this could be seen in Earth light. I thought it could be an advantage - to detect emotions."

Imogen swallowed before asking, "And you, Shani. I saw your colours at the mention of Jabari, the former Vizier of Well-Being."

Sepia shades rippled through Shani's Chroma as she nodded confirmation. "Our relationship was secret. We could not be bonded. Viziers carry too much responsibility to be distracted by love partners. It is a sacrifice they all make. Jabari and I would discuss the troubling policies of the Supreme Council for hours every day. We grew so close." Shani blinked back a tear. "We had hoped to formulate a plan to turn Holis back to its true path. We disagreed as to the best course of action. Jabari was so strong-minded, his open challenges only won him dismissal and arrest. It was then I quietly 'retired' from office to continue our resistance undercover."

"You must miss him."

"I do. Which reminds me, our agents in the Council of Vision have reported an emissary has been sent to Earth to negotiate with the Zuberi brothers. It was done under cover of darkness. No one knows his identity, but perhaps it is him?"

"Jabari?" Imogen could see the shimmer of love and hope surge briefly in Shani's Chroma, before she stifled the rich red-golds with quartz-blue shades of reason and logic.

What would I do if anything happened to Araz?

"There's no way of knowing and it may not be him. Anyhow," Shani smiled, "we have more than enough to think about for now. Come, let us eat and sleep."

Shani took Imogen to the dining table under a cloth-clad ceiling. Everyone ate quietly. There was an overwhelming sense of tiredness amongst the diners and little will to openly discuss the events of the day. Sekhet and Leo spoke softly of his grandparents and Imogen was glad to see Leo's colours flare with warm shades as he happily conversed with his mother.

I wish I could see my mum too. A sharp stab of homesickness coursed through Imogen's body and Shani, who appeared to have sensed this, put her arm around Imogen and gave her an affectionate squeeze.

When they had finished their meal, Lara pushed the table to one side and Cael pressed a switch. A number of cushioned hammocks dropped from the ceiling area and having watched the others climb into their beds, Imogen followed suit.

Once lying within its soft folds, Imogen appreciated the privacy it afforded. Her body was completely cocooned by her hammock. She closed her eyes and used the drills her father had taught her. One by one she consigned the day's events to the recesses of her mind and focussed on calm and pleasing thoughts. Her last waking images were those of Araz's lips and embrace as she fell into an exhausted sleep.

At first light Imogen used the rudimentary bathroom facilities, braving the freezing waters of the shower. Shani had explained it was the melt water from the snow on top of the mountains. It made its way down through one of the many natural channels gouged into the stone and rock. This was far removed from the thermal bathing facilities elsewhere on Holis, and the shock of the icy flow ensured Imogen was wide awake within seconds. She rapidly rubbed herself dry with fresh Flecto, forcing some warmth back into her body. When dressed, she anxiously paced the floor of the headquarters. *Come on Araz. Where are you?*

When the Phase-Seal doorway of the lift capsule melted and Em and Araz entered the space, Imogen took one look at Araz and ran into his arms as he raced to meet her. He held her tightly and Em and Shani discreetly moved away, leaving them by themselves, Shani glimpsing the explosion of intense fervour in their soaring Chromatic colours.

"My light!" was all Araz could say as he stroked her hair and she breathed deeply of his musky aroma.

Araz bent to kiss her lips but she put her fingers to his mouth and spoke in barely a whisper, "Araz, my father. He… He's…" Imogen could not finish the sentence as her grief poured out freely. She shook beneath his comforting embrace.

"Shhh. I know." Araz pulled Imogen into a small inglenook in the side of the stone room so they could not be seen by the others. He held her tight as he consoled her. "Imogen, you must stay positive. There may yet be hope. I have resolved to believe only what I can verify to be true. I now realise Ubaid is as slippery as ice and cannot be trusted."

"I want to hope," Imogen murmured into his chest, "but every time I think about never being able to see Dad again, I feel crushed."

Araz hugged her close and kissed her wet cheeks until she lifted her chin and their lips met. Imogen was flooded with his love. As she returned his kiss, another part of her mind thought it extraordinary she could feel such extremes of emotion within the space of a few moments.

They stayed locked together in a deep embrace until Em appeared. She gave a cough and announced the others were waiting for them, muttering irritably about bonding time not being now.

Reluctantly, Araz and Imogen made their way to the living area, the hammocks now retracted into the ceiling and the table placed centrally, filled with salvers of fruits and breads. They started to eat the refreshments in companionable silence with the others.

Leo stared down at his food, which he consumed with little enjoyment. He was unable to look up at Imogen and Araz. He was no longer the relaxed person of the previous evening and his despondency was clear in both his demeanour and his gloomy colours.

Imogen deliberately sat next to Sekhet. Once low-level conversation began around the table, Em recounting the events at the Tavat Port whilst Shani talked to Araz, Imogen turned to Leo's mother to quietly question her.

"Sekhet, you were a member of the Supreme Council when my parents escaped to Earth?"

Sekhet gave a sad smile. "We had no idea they had gone. Not for years. Then I was put in charge of Nuru Zuberi, after he had been caught." Sekhet's colours flared with a sepia shaded glow of pale red-golds.

She truly loved him. She has no idea he was not Nuru, but his brother, Adam. Imogen observed Sekhet's Chroma as the older woman forced her colours to dull. *She doesn't want to dwell on these memories, they are too painful.*

Sekhet sighed and her aura settled to pale green tones of calm, underpinned with a quartz honesty. "So, Imogen, what do you want to ask me?"

"Why? Why did my mum and dad, and all those other scientists leave Holis for Earth? Why could they not develop the Tractus project here? What did they fear?"

Sekhet replied in hushed tones so only Imogen could hear. "I have been thinking on this for years. At first, I believed them to be conspirators who wished to depose Kekara. There seemed to be no good reason to jump to the primitive planet and remove such vital research from the control of our government and risk contamination from the humans. There were many rumours at the time. The line of Iris was purported to being phased out, the Chronicles of Holis were said to be undergoing a re-write to change the emphasis of our beliefs and history and there was speculation the Tractus was required for a project destined to change the course of our race. I didn't believe any of it, but then I was not privy to the meetings of the Viziers who were told more. When Jabari was removed from office and Shani suddenly retired, I decided to research my suspicions. I had been held in captivity for years - confined to my quarters - but little attention was paid as to how I occupied my time, other than when Tarik re-appeared. I looked to the work of Tanastra Thut. I realised the additions and deletions to The Chronicles of Holis would hold some clues."

Imogen eagerly added, "I have seen both the current Chronicles and the original ones. But I can't figure it out."

"They show there has been a fundamental shift in the direction the Supreme Council is taking our race. Imogen, I fear we are on the brink of a new and terrifying age. Truth is being suppressed, opposition is being smothered, we are gradually moving from a democracy to a dictatorship. I had never dreamed Kekara would become a modern-day Anubis, but I can only conclude this to be the case."

Imogen nodded slowly as she processed Sekhet's words.

"Imogen, you must know this, Kekara has secrets, even from the Viziers. As a boy, Tarik witnessed her opening a mysterious compartment in the depths of her chambers. What is concealed there is not known, but he had to run for his life. Whatever is hidden there is, I am sure, a crucial piece of the puzzle. The key for this safe, it hangs around her neck. It is with her at all times."

Imogen felt a shiver down her spine as the image of Kekara's pendant flashed across her mind. She pulled out her own locket from beneath her robes. "I have seen it – it is the same as mine."

Sekhet gasped to see the pendant symbols at the end of the chain. "You have the identical key!"

Imogen nodded and Sekhet drew her closer. "You must go there. Open the safe and recover whatever it is that evil woman is hiding there. This is your destiny!" Pressing her fingertips to Imogen's, Sekhet described the layout of the Supreme Council's living quarters and the location of Kekara's chambers.

Imogen gulped back any protest. She had read Sekhet's thoughts. This woman had lost everything because of the corruption of the government and now wanted justice and revenge.

Eshe gave me this key for a purpose. It was not just to open The Chronicles of Tanastra. I owe it to all those who have lost their lives to uncover the truth. Imogen quelled all the voices inside her head urging caution and safety. She resolved she would discover whatever it was Kekara was hiding, whatever the cost.

Sekhet, seeing the determination in Imogen's face, gave her an affectionate smile as they began to eat. She asked Imogen to tell her something about Earth and Imogen found herself describing her friends and her daily life. *It all seems so distant. Even further than twenty light years.*

The vision screen in the room suddenly burst into life, preventing any further exchange. Everyone stopped eating to watch the transmission.

Firstly, there was an announcement saying the Falsebred, Tarik Zuberi, was still at large and was considered a danger to his peers (Leo stared studiously at his image on the screen as the others glanced his way). This was followed with what was described as an 'update' on the primitive species of Earth. Clips of newsreel from Earth channels played out before them. Imogen recognised some of the footage, which had been taken from the worst moments in recent history. The aftermath of a suicide bomber – people lying dead and bleeding on the ground, violent clashes between armed police and crowds of rioters, children with horrific injuries caused by land mines, starving babies crying in the arms of their forlorn mothers in parched lands, buildings exploding and then crumbling as people ran for their lives. The unedited films played in holographic definition, showing brutal graphic detail making everyone wince. One by one, those watching put down their salvers of food, sickened by what they saw.

The transmission finished with the voice of Kekara, "This is the barbaric race of Earth. It is only by the grace of Ra, they have not yet discovered Holis. And by the power of the Supreme Council, we will prevent them doing so."

When the screen went blank, Lara and Cael turned to Imogen.

"For the love of Ra, how did you manage to live there?"

"These are selected news items from troubled parts of the world. Earth is not all like that." She looked to Araz who looked away, and then appealed to Leo who merely shrugged his shoulders. She went silent and rubbed the scar on the back of her hand. *How can I explain to them, despite their imperfections, humans are every bit as worthy as Holans?*

Shani rose to speak. "This is the first time the Supreme Council has shown our people such images. They are deliberately raising the level of threat and the sense of fear on Holis. This is no doubt intended to justify the presence of the Repro guards and increase the animosity towards those who are perceived to have made illegal contact with Earth."

Leo pushed his fingers through his hair, a deep frown cut into his forehead.

"It will not be long before the Resistance is exposed and condemned," Shani continued. "The population will be all too ready to find someone to blame after exposure to this propaganda."

Shani turned to face Araz. "Araz, your presence in our headquarters could endanger us all. I must ask - where do your loyalties lie?"

Araz frowned as Imogen looked anxiously at him, her Chroma flickering the warm reds of hope, counterbalanced with swirling clouds of grey fear.

He swallowed before answering, "I can only be honest. I am still undecided."

"Hmph!" Em's irritation was clear. "And where that leave us?"

Araz continued, aware every person in the room now had their eyes fixed on him. "I no longer feel the same loyalty to my commanders. I want to know what is going on and I am determined to uncover the truth. In the meantime, I will help neither the Supreme Council nor the Resistance. I need to be aware of all the facts before I make a final decision."

The black and gold spikes of authority permeated his Chroma and Imogen's heart sank. *Has he any idea how pompous he sounds?*

Araz stared at Leo as he continued, "What I can promise is, I will not betray any of you until I am decided."

Leo glared back at Araz and began saying, "You self-righteous pr..."

Em interrupted with a snort. "Vlagger! Call this promise?"

Araz opened his hands in a gesture of having nothing to hide. "What I mean, is - I will not betray Holis. My loyalty is with the Holan people and it is also here." He took Imogen's hand and squeezed it tight.

She looked up at him completely bemused. Whilst she appreciated his clear profession of love, she was appalled he would still consider betraying these people. She pulled her hand away and chewed her lip.

Shani asked in a cold voice, "And how will you ascertain the truth?"

Araz paused before saying, "I will resume my duties where I have access to most government areas, but it will mean leaving Imogen here. Please, you must keep her safe."

Lara and Cael went to object, "He is an agent of Ubaid. He will lead them straight to us!"

Shani held her hand up to them. "I think we have no choice but to trust this young man will make the right decision and allow him to go."

Imogen got to her feet and looked into Araz's eyes, hers simmering with irritation. "Well, my mind is made up! And I am not staying here waiting for you to make up yours. I am going to get some answers myself, so I'm coming with you!" she announced. "Besides, there is something I must do." She exchanged a look with Sekhet as she pushed her locket back inside her gown.

"This is madness," Shani began. "As soon as you are seen, the Supreme Council will realise you and Naomi are clones. You will be put on trial, or worse, terminated without a hearing."

"Shani is right…" Araz began.

As he and Shani attempted to reason with Imogen, Em started an angry exchange with Araz, whereupon all the others joined in. They did not notice the lift capsule had been activated until the door suddenly melted away. Everyone turned as Odion and several Repros burst into the space, the Repro knives glinting in the light.

Imogen let a short scream escape her mouth as she moved closer to Araz.

"So, Shani. What a surprise. This is where you've been hiding?" Odion looked at the startled Resistance members before him. "We should have known you were not on the dark side of Holis." He touched the arrow pendant around his neck as he shouted his orders. He pointed to Imogen and Araz. "Take the councillor and the agent prisoner," then added, "kill the rest!"

The Repros rushed towards those around the table, wielding their knives in the air as everyone scattered.

Lara and Cael dodged around the table, chased by the guard. Leo pushed his mother to one side as he kicked out at a swinging blade. Araz forced Imogen behind him, pressing her against the wall out of the way of their attackers and began grappling with the Repro trying to force him into a body lock. Em pushed the table over, knocking two of the Repros backwards and slowing them down.

Imogen froze in horror as one of the guards chased Shani across the room. She had made a bee line for the suspension chamber which held the marker and managed to swiftly press her hand to a hidden panel which sprang open. As the Repro caught up, she activated a concealed trigger and the marker gave a brief glow and then disintegrated, turning to dust.

The Repro was upon her. It grabbed Shani by the hair and dragged her closer to its bulk, seizing her by the neck. Imogen looked on in horror as the vile creature drew its blade and plunged it deep into Shani's chest, piercing her heart.

"No!" Imogen screamed.

Shani's eyes flickered briefly to Imogen as she gave a low groan and sank to the floor, blood streaming out of her motionless body, her colours fusing into a wisp of pure white, ascending and slowly powdering into a shimmering haze before they vanished completely.

Imogen could barely breathe. She tried to run towards the fallen leader but felt a large leathery arm close around her shoulders and neck. She was pulled away from Araz, who was now pinned to the floor unable to move. Her attacker dragged her towards the capsule door. Imogen shouted and tried to twist her body, attempting to kick the beast, but it would not let go.

Em, who had fought off a snarling Repro to witness Shani's demise, gave a bloodcurdling cry and launched herself at the Repro responsible for striking Shani. She kicked the blade out of its hand into the air, caught it and rammed it into the beast's stomach as it screamed in agony and fell to the ground. The Repros without a captive, responded by jumping on Em in a frenzy of slashing.

Imogen gurgled out a cry of alarm as she witnessed the blades slicing down in all directions, blood and gore erupting with each blow. She could not tell who was being cut, the Repros or Em.

Fear surged through Imogen's body and her heart dropped when (it almost seemed to happen in slow motion) she saw several blades raised high in the air in unison, all ready to hit their marks - Em, Lara, Cael, Sekhet and Araz. As her eyes widened, darting from one victim to the next, the space was abruptly filled with the strident noise of Leo's high-pitched and ear-piercing whistle.

The Repros dropped their blades and reeled, some collapsing to the floor. Odion pressed his hands to his ears and fell into the nearest wall. The Resistance members, Leo, Sekhet and Araz, recovered quickly and sprang free of their captors, staggering towards the capsule door trying to shake the noise from their ears.

Leo paused when he got to Odion, who was shaking his head and trying to re-gain his balance. Leo smiled and offered him a supporting hand. The Vizier hesitated, his expression perplexed. Then

Leo head-butted him square on the forehead, smacking the burly figure right back into the wall.

Imogen raced to Em's side and helped her to her feet, her face and body slashed and bleeding. She seemed unaware of both her injuries and the deafening noise as she stared down at Shani's body. Araz helped Imogen half-drag, half-pull Em to the lift, her eyes bulging with shock as she looked back to her dead friend and leader.

As the capsule door sealed and began its descent, Sekhet, Lara and Cael started to tend Em's wounds as she stood rigidly, her cut hands clenched. No one could hear her voice for the ringing in their ears, but all could read the words on her bruised and bloody lips, "Shani, I will avenge you!"

BIRMINGHAM

Once in Birmingham, the Zuberi brothers had split up. Adam and Nuru went to negotiate with the emissary whilst Sefu and Rashida returned to the site of the first marker.

Rashida and Sefu had worked non-stop for days, analysing the data of the Tractus in the Birmingham church. They had taken the spherical marker from the canopy above the altar and now worked from a safe house in the city. As far as they knew, this was the only rogue marker; the only one capable of catapulting a person forward in time.

"Why should this marker trigger the Tractus to act differently from all the others?" Rashida asked herself for the hundredth time as she manipulated a small ovoid device to mathematically test her many theories.

"Whatever changed, it happened fifty years ago," Sefu replied. "Firas was experimenting with the settings before the Repros attacked. Young Imogen ran towards the marker and was gone in a flash! It was not supposed to be possible for the marker to self-activate. I mean, Imogen should not have been able to jump, let alone vault. Her DNA was not registered in the Tractus at that point."

Rashida stood and paced the floor. She was surprisingly detached from the calamitous event which had taken her daughter and thrown her own mind into a downward spiral all those years ago. "The Tractus was unusable for forty years until we managed to rescue her, and then a further ten years whilst Tarik was vaulted forward as part of Kasmut's irrational back up plan." Rashida's eyes blazed as she rapidly examined every angle of the puzzle. "So, the wormhole remained open for fifty years, right up until several weeks ago, when Tarik returned. Tanastra disabled it and made the necessary adjustments to the marker last month. It then, finally, reverted to the original settings, becoming a means of jumping space and not vaulting time. That was tested when Tarik and the Repros jumped to this marker from Holis and back again, after they captured Kasmut."

Sefu nodded. They had gone over this endlessly. Whilst he was delighted Rashida was back on top form, using all her creative talents to troubleshoot the problem, he could not help but wish Tanastra was here to help them fathom it out. He had had one of the finest minds in the history of Holan scientists, and this was, after all, his invention.

Rashida continued, "Prior to this, this marker connected to ours on Holis – the one commandeered by the Council of Stability. But that night in 1966, the marker was freestanding. It was not connected to any other marker. Firas was testing something."

Sefu had an inkling of where this was going and eagerly added, "And on that night, it managed to open a worm hole with no fixed end. One able to traverse space at incredible speeds and return back to where it had started."

"So, if we ensure this marker is not paired to another, we could try to replicate the settings to reopen the same wormhole – it will still be held in stasis by the power of InvertIon."

"Yes, yes we could. But how would we test it? It takes ten full Earth years or more for anything to travel the unimaginable distances of the universe before it re-emerges."

"Not if we reverse the settings," exclaimed Rashida, the cobalt blues flashing like bolts of lightning in her Chroma.

"You mean – turn back time?"

"Yes."

"It's not possible."

"Yes, and no. It is not possible to reverse time but, theoretically it is possible to re-visit an earlier point in time."

"To what purpose?"

"To retrieve something, or someone."

Sefu looked at Rashida, his eyes wide. "Wait. This is too dangerous. Such an action could change history. I mean, imagine our race going back to assassinate Anubis to prevent those terrible years of tyranny."

"Now there's a thought!"

"Yes, but think about it. It might eliminate a lunatic, but it would also alter what happened since. The Holan race was only able to find peace and evolve to what it is today as a result of defeating Anubis. You cannot change the past. If the chain of events leading to this point in history were eradicated, we may no longer exist!"

"You're quite right Sefu. So, it can only be an option to retrieve something from the recent past, something having no effect on the historical timeline between then and now."

Sefu now paced the floor as Rashida started the mathematical modelling.

"Surely, there is a huge risk to employing the Tractus for such a mission? What if it goes wrong? Couldn't it interfere with the space-time continuum, causing catastrophic results?"

"You've been watching too many Earth movies, Sefu! We can test it by sending back an image capturing device. It will need to incorporate a DNA sample matching one of the three people who have already travelled in the wormhole. Either Imogen, Tarik or me. If I am correct, and I am ninety-nine-point-nine percent sure I am, the past will appear frozen to those who go back. No one in the past will be aware of the intrusion. If anything, or anyone, is removed from an earlier point in time and brought back to the present, it would simply 'disappear' from the past without trace. Those frozen in the moment would not even witness the retrieval. One second the object would be there and the next, it would be gone."

Sefu remained pensive as Rashida continued, "I will attempt to engineer the necessary changes and we will test if it is possible. It would then be a matter of trial and error to see how feasible it will be to retrieve an object. We also need to ensure we only go back to a specific time in the last few weeks. It this works, the time capability of the Tractus could be a new operational feature. We could deliberately send someone forward in time, using the reverse process."

"Rashida, this is incredible! But it also has mind-blowing implications. Imagine being able to make alterations to the past and jumping to the future. The only question is, could this be used for immoral purposes? We must contact Adam and Nuru to discuss our findings."

THE SUPREME COUNCIL QUARTERS

*T*he shock of Shani's death replayed in Imogen's head, over and over. She forced herself to detach the horrific images and push them deep into the recesses of her mind, whilst clinging to her burning rage and desire for retribution. It helped her to focus and find courage as Araz and she headed for the councillor's residential area located in the mountain beyond The Hub.

They cannot get away with it! Murdering and maiming others. So much for Holan life being sacrosanct! I will find out who is responsible and expose them. Shani, my father, they both deserve justice.

The survivors had all agreed to split up. Lara and Cael had headed to the base hidden in the village of Karnak, to update the network of Resistance members. Leo and Sekhet had gone with Em to the Tavat Port. There, they had secreted themselves on board an empty cargo crate heading for the Southern Sea.

Knowing Odion would soon be on their tails, there had been a brief and hasty discussion under the cover of the forest before they had gone their separate ways.

"Em, Shani destroyed the marker? Why?" Imogen had asked, thinking the leader may have been able to save herself had she put her energies into fighting rather than forcing the marker to self-destruct.

"Was agreed. Regime not get filthy hands on Tractus. Not use to jump to Earth and find our peoples there. Is only two Resistance markers left on Holis. Must protect."

Shani died protecting my mum and the others and preventing Odion getting his hands on the Tractus technology. How many more good people must die fighting this regime?

Imogen's thoughts had turned to those on Earth, "Someone needs to warn the Zuberi brothers about the Resistance headquarters being discovered and about my dad and Shani being... being..."

Leo, temporarily sporting a large bruise in the centre of his forehead, had answered as Imogen's words petered out. "I will jump to Earth. I will take my mum. She will not be safe here. And we can find out more about this emissary."

Imogen had pulled Leo to one side saying, "Leo, if it is Jabari, be gentle when you tell him about Shani. They were secretly bonded. And... and please send my love to my mum. Don't tell her about Dad, not yet." She had choked back a tear.

Leo had nodded and tentatively took Imogen's hand as he'd murmured, "Imogen I'm sorry, so sorry, about everything. If only I could turn back time."

This was one of her father's favourite adages and his smiling face, full of love, floated across her mind. She had squeezed Leo's hand in an unspoken acceptance of his apology.

Araz had observed them speaking together with annoyance and jealousy. When they had touched, he had stormed across to glare at Leo.

"Keep your hair on, mate," Leo had remarked, giving Imogen a quick hug. "You need to lighten up a bit." Leo had stood face-to-face with Araz as he'd added, "And good luck with finding the truth. You may not realise it, but it's singing at the top of its voice, dancing up and down and doing cartwheels right in front of you if you would only but look!"

Leo had left Araz bristling with annoyance as they had all parted company.

The forest and underground routes had taken Araz and Imogen alongside The Hub, unseen. They entered at the lowest point via a tunnel next to a stream, relieved to have got this far unchallenged. They knew Odion, once recovered, would put the city on high alert to capture them.

Inside the glass mountain, Araz had barely spoken as he and Imogen made their way along the secret passages and disguised entrance ways. His Chroma was full of flickering purples and reds, which Imogen knew to be his conflicting emotions about his divided loyalties.

They reached the route from The Hub to the adjacent mountain, going down a long narrow stone channel. They eventually came to a halt in front of a Phase-Seal doorway which led to the government residential area.

Imogen put her hand on Araz's shoulder. "Once at the upper levels, we will need to go our separate ways."

He frowned but did not interject as Imogen continued.

"You have to do whatever it is you think is necessary to help you make up your mind. And I need to find out what this unlocks." She touched the outline of her pendant under her garments.

Before he could object, she added, "Sekhet has shown me the layout of the chambers, she has even shown me the location of a secret passageway she and Leo used when he was a child. If I need to, I can find a way out, but if I am found they will all assume I am Naomi. Either way, I will probably be safer than you."

"We have been seen together in the Resistance headquarters," objected Araz. "We are both in danger." He then added, "And Naomi will also be in danger. Remember, no one else knows there are two of you. She will be accused of freeing Leo's mother and collaborating with the subversives." Araz saw a brief surge of irritation, the colour of bruising, rise in Imogen's Chroma.

"Imogen, all your life you have known you were different, even if you didn't find out why until very recently. Naomi never suspected she was anything other than a normal Holan. She only found out the truth when I told her yesterday. She had never suspected a thing, so it must have come as an even bigger shock to her."

Imogen was not sure she agreed with this. After all, in the space of a few weeks she had experienced revelation after revelation, but she knew Araz was right about Naomi's life also being turned upside down. She forced herself to quell the irrational surge of annoyance threatening to permeate her thoughts. *Why does he care if she's safe?* She tried to shake off her irritation, but it was difficult to ban the deeply uncomfortable sensation she had on hearing the softness in Araz's voice when he spoke her clone's name. Also, she could not fail but see the way his colours appeared to glint with the soft reds of fondness at the mention of this Naomi.

This is ridiculous! I'm what? Jealous because he's attracted to someone exactly like me? But she isn't me, is she?

"We need to seek her out," Araz continued. "She was going to try and uncover the truth about the Elysian Two project. She said she was going to confront Ubaid, so I will go there first."

Imogen nodded agreement, smothering any chromatic shades of envy as she replied, "Better we split up then."

Araz sighed. "If there is any sign of trouble, I will not leave you. However, if all is quiet, it will be better to go separately and then meet up later." He pulled her towards him for an embrace and realised, despite the calm shades of her colours, the stiffness in her shoulders betrayed the tension she was attempting to cloak.

"My heart is yours." Araz brushed her forehead with his lips and tilted her head upwards to kiss her mouth, murmuring, "My light."

Imogen's body responded instinctively, and she found herself returning his kiss and pressing him close, despite her misgivings. *If only I could shut the world out and stay here like this!*

Araz ran his fingers around her neck and ears, causing her to shiver, before taking a step back. "Let us arrange to meet back here in three hours. If one of us does not make it, we will meet behind the Karnak station at the time of Atma."

Atma? Oh yes, Sunset.

"If I am not there, go to Qus. Em will keep you safe. She gave me her Multi-Com, the one they had used to track her. I have disabled the tracking signal, so we can now connect in the event of an emergency. However, it will not work inside the restricted areas of The Hub. They are fitted with communication shields."

Araz took Imogen's hands in his. "Take care and please do not take any unnecessary risks."

"You too," Imogen replied, unable to ignore his overwhelming feelings of adoration for her glancing across their brief touch of fingertips. The memory of being swamped with his love when she had been close to death, after being cut with a poisoned blade, swept through her mind. This love had the power to save, to overwhelm anything standing in its way. She would hold this close to her heart no matter what lay ahead.

They both took a deep breath, Araz pressed his fingers first to his lips and then to hers and they waited for the Phase-Seal wall to melt away in front of them. They stepped out into the empty corridor and glanced around. They were now in the restricted residential area of the Supreme Council members. The wall 'repaired' instantly, the secret entrance now invisible and they both crept along the passage leading to the communal bathing area.

The internal structures of the mountain were said to have been carved from the rock to leave voids denoting a gigantic lotus flower. The lower areas consisted of the living spaces of all the regular councillors. Their rooms fanned out in petal-shaped formation from the circular hot spring pool in the middle of the enormous space. The level above held the Council Chamber and the quarters of the Supreme Leader and the five Viziers. A rock stairwell, set into the curve of the gently domed cavern wall, rose from the main pool to link to the upper level.

Upon finding the pool empty, as they had hoped would be the case, Araz and Imogen took their chance and swiftly climbed the stone steps. A wispy warm damp cloud rose from the hot spring water and dappled light reflected on the low curved ceiling. Their footsteps echoed around the cavern. They both breathed a little easier when they had reached the top.

Imogen checked Sekhet's maps inside her head. She knew the Council Chamber, the central ovoid-shaped flower blossom, occupied the core space above the pool. *It must be behind this stone wall,* she touched the rock in front of her. The private rooms radiated out from this chamber as the six upper petals of the lotus flower. Curved corridors separated each area, affording complete privacy for each head of state.

Imogen looked at Araz and they nodded silently to each other. It was time to part. Araz turned determinedly in the direction of Ubaid's quarters; Imogen faced the opposite way, towards Kekara's rooms. Glancing back only once, with a reassuring nod, they went their separate ways both hoping the thump of their hearts was not audible to anyone else.

Imogen forced herself to walk confidently down the labyrinth of winding corridors, the lights turning on as she advanced, reassuring her there was no one ahead. She soon passed the upper entrance to the elite area, the one taking the leaders directly to The Hub. She hurried past the sealed doorway. *The guards, if there are any, will be on the other side.* If anyone entered now, she would be found. To her relief, the door remained closed and the passageways empty as she plotted her route from the map she had memorised.

The opening of the Council Chamber was around the corner and as Imogen neared she slowed to listen for voices. When she heard none, she walked through an elaborate archway to look inside, surprised it was not sealed by a door. *I suppose only Supreme Council members have access to this area.*

The beautiful, domed stone cavern, which brought to her mind the shape of the Pantheon in Rome, took her breath away. Clad in sparkling black marble, tiered seating encircled the space, a gold throne placed centrally in the upper tier. The walls were decorated with jewel encrusted lotus flowers and the individual symbols of her pendant; one for each of the five sub-councils. She turned full circle to take it all in.

So, this is the seat of power where they decide the fate of people like my parents. Imogen pursed her lips and turned her back on the chamber, refusing to be intimidated by its opulence.

Silently, she made her way to the furthest 'petal' quarters, passing the doorways to three other areas. Each entrance had the symbol of the sub-council carved into the stone. She named each as she passed, attempting to calm her nerves.

Solid circle, that's Ra and the Council of Enlightenment. Who's the Vizier? Merit! Now the solid star – Nut. The Council of Sanctity. Shani was once the Vizier. Oh, poor Shani. Imogen quelled the rush of emotion as she moved to the next doorway. *Concentrate! Clear Star, Hathor, Council of Well-Being, once Jabari's council They were next to each other.* Not allowing her focus to stray, she marched on to the next rooms. There they were, all five interlinking symbols carved above the door, identical to her pendant. She had arrived at the chambers of Her Greatness.

Imogen took a deep breath before putting her hand to the Phase-Seal entrance to Kekara's rooms. Nothing happened. Imogen's heart sank. *I should have realised the door would not open for me.* She floundered, unsure what to do, when a tiny mark in the material of the door appeared to glisten. With trembling hands, Imogen pulled her locket from her robes and held it close to the mark. The arrow of her pendant started to glow with sparks of gold and silver. She tentatively placed the point of the arrow against the shining spot. For a split second the pendant fused to the Phase-Seal before it released. The door melted away in front of her.

Imogen, heart pounding, pushed her locket back under her outfit and entered the brightly lit room, relieved the door sealed behind her the moment she was inside.

She stood completely still, closed her eyes to heighten her hearing and listened for any noise to indicate she was not alone.

When she was sure there was no one else there, she opened her eyes and looked around in amazement, blinking to reassure herself she was still inside. For every section of the floor, walls and ceilings were covered in what must be a continuous vision screen. This was set to show the peaceful valley of Karnak. Grass meadows covered the floor, clouds skittered across the roof space and birds flew around the walls. Waterfalls poured down from a few points around the room, giving the illusion you would only have to put your hand out and you would be able to touch the liquid as it flowed down the mountainsides. It was incredible. Imogen felt she was standing outside in the fresh, clean air. The only giveaway it was not real, but holographically engineered, was the lack of sound.

Imogen bent to touch the floor. It felt and even smelt like spongy grass. She sank down to her knees to gaze around. Her tension gave way to a sense of peace as she beheld the magnificent scenery. This was the exact angle from which she had painted her picture. She knew this landscape intimately. It felt part of her being and connected to her in some deep and inexplicable way. She closed her eyes and without the distraction of the surroundings, forced her mind to do one of the many drills her father had taught her. *Stay on task! Find the secret compartment; this sense of peace is a deception.*

Imogen opened her eyes and blurred them, to look beyond the screens. She knew she must deactivate them in order to search for the hidden safe. She remembered Araz had merely flicked his fingers to mute the sound, back in Qus, so she began to experiment. A click of a finger and thumb brightened or muted the light, a wave changed the scene to night-time. *What will make it stop?* She pressed her fingers together as she thought, but quickly separated them when the recurring vision started to encroach. She rapidly clapped her hands together to dismiss the horror of being chased into a dead end by Repros. The screens instantly responded and reverted to glistening stone walls, filled from floor to ceiling with hieroglyphic cyphers.

The shock of the rock appearing so suddenly, above and below, made Imogen gasp. It was like being flung from a mountain top into an enclosed stone tomb, albeit a large one, and she felt slightly dizzy as she got to her feet. A feeling of foreboding rose within the pit of her stomach. She felt trapped.

No wonder Kekara prefers the outside setting. This is like being buried with the Pharaohs.

Fully alert, Imogen started to trace her hands around the encryptions on the walls, looking for some kind of clue as to the whereabouts of the compartment. After half an hour or more she was ready to give up.

I need to get out of here before Kekara returns.

She stood back and looked at the carved walls with frustration. *Think!* Her eyes picked out the symbols of her pendant. They featured in five different segments of the walls and appeared to describe the various attributes of each personality line. The ancient marks seemed to burn the back of her eyes and were beginning to make her head swim when she suddenly noticed something out of place. The segment about Iris had many clear circles, but one of them, half way up the wall, had been altered. The circle had been carved over to look like a loop on top of two crossed lines. Imogen recognised the emblem from her school lessons on Earth. This was the 'Ankh', the symbol of eternity. She recalled the ancient Egyptians were frequently depicted as holding the Ankh as they entered the underworld, in the hope of salvation.

That must be it!

Imogen put her hand to the mark. Unlike the others, this was rough to the touch. She closed her eyes and traced the outline. *There! Where the loop meets the cross. A tiny indentation.* Imogen's eyes sprang open and she grabbed her pendant and repeated what she had done to open Kekara's door.

Upon touching the arrow point to the indentation, the Ankh appeared to dislodge and came free of the surrounding wall. Imogen carefully pulled it away from the rock and investigated the safe beyond. A small egg-shaped stone, the Ankh symbol carved into its surface, was the only item in there. Imogen hesitantly picked it up. It was surprisingly light and looked like an ancient Data Encounter. However, there were no indentations on the object and no apparent way to 'open' it. *A DE? It must be encrypted, like the one Tanastra left me.*

Knowing she had been there for too long, Imogen fashioned an inner pocket from a pull of her Flecto garment and pushed the oval shape inside. She hurriedly replaced the Ankh into the wall and clapping her hands to reactivate the screens, she ran for the door.

Out in the corridor she tingled with both fear and excitement. *I did it! I have Kekara's secret – whatever it is! Now I need to get out of here.*

Allowing herself a small smile of self-satisfaction, Imogen re-traced her steps to the lower level. She rushed around the pool edge towards the exit but slipped in a puddle of water. Regaining her balance, she heard a sound, too late, and came face-to-face with a small robed man sporting a pointed beard.

No! It was none other than Ubaid who had stepped out by the water's edge, looking equally surprised to see her.

Imogen looked wildly around. *Where's Araz? He had gone to confront this man. Did he do something to him?*

Her first instinct was to turn and run, but Ubaid thrust a hand out to grab her arm. With surprising strength for such a small man, he pushed her down to the wet stone floor and knelt beside her.

"Well, this is interesting." Ubaid's face was so close to hers she recoiled from his spittle, which sprayed over his beard and caught her cheek. She hurriedly wiped herself clean with the back of her hand.

He instantly caught her arm and turned her hand over, examining the scar. "A scar? Goodness! What could have caused this? Perhaps a poisoned blade? How extraordinary, to have survived such an injury."

The gleeful note in his voice set Imogen's teeth on edge as fury rose within.

"But I must apologise, we haven't been introduced."

"I know who you are," Imogen shouted angrily, pulling her hand away.

"And I know who you are! Imogen, daughter of Kasmut Akil and Rashida Omorose. At last we meet." He put out his hand as if to shake hers.

Imogen pushed herself across the floor, away from him. She was repulsed by the Vizier who was now staring intently at her every feature. *He is disgusting. How the hell can I get away?*

"I believe you have met your counterpart? My Naomi?"

Imogen merely stared back wishing she could laser him with her eyes.

Ubaid stood and took a step backward as he observed Imogen's reactions. "Yes, **my** Naomi! You see, she has been rather like a daughter to me. I have known her since her inception."

Imogen gave a snort of disgust.

"And, I have to add, she has a much gentler demeanour..." The words: 'than you', were left unsaid as Ubaid fingered his pointed beard. "But then she was not raised amongst barbarians."

As Imogen glowered, Ubaid took a few steps backwards and forwards, regarding her with a supercilious smile.

"Well, Imogen, I must say your timing is close to perfect. You see, your twin has recently become incapacitated."

Imogen did not react outwardly, but a feeling - close to regret for Naomi - surged within. *What has he done to her? Has he done something to Araz too?* Her heart lurched.

"And it is just as well," Ubaid continued. "You see, herein lies the problem, there cannot be two of you. Dear me, no! You must know you will both be terminated if the other is discovered? Cloning is completely forbidden on Holis. And so, I am faced with a problem. Which one of you should live and which one should die? You may want to reconsider your attitude?"

Imogen seethed but knew she had to do something to escape. The plan came to her in a flash. She looked away and summoning every Chromatic cloaking technique she had ever used, she burst into tears and started to shake.

Ubaid, disconcerted, remained standing as Imogen sobbed.

"Please, give me a chance. I have never belonged anywhere. I want to find my true home. I am not ready to die."

"What are you doing here, in the restricted areas of the Supreme Council?"

"I came to seek you out and resolve this problem."

Ubaid put out a hand to help her up. "Come, we should speak further in my quarters, where we cannot be seen."

It took every ounce of self-control for Imogen to graciously take his hand as he helped her up, and to quash the need to recoil when he put an arm around her shoulders. She gave the impression she had relaxed her muscles and even leaned into the odious little man, as a sign of compliance. He led her back to the stone steps at the edge of the pool.

"Please," Imogen stopped and gave Ubaid a shy smile as she dabbed her eyes. "I never fitted in on Earth. All my life I knew I had a higher calling. Tell me what it means to be a Penta-Crypt. I want to know my destiny, even if you decide I am not as worthy as my double."

Ubaid glanced around the pool area. They were still alone.

"You are playing a game with me?"

"No, I would not dare. And why would I risk coming here to find you? I know you are the only person who can help; the only one who knows Naomi and I are clones. I have weighed everything up and I realise there is only one outcome. You are right. It is either me, or her."

Ubaid scratched his head. Even though it was not unexpected, he was taken aback at how alike this Imogen's tone of phrase and mannerisms were to those of Naomi. She was an exact replica. He had not made a study of reading Chroma, but this version was emanating the colours of truth and trust. Perhaps, he thought to himself, she would be easier to train than Naomi, who had started to become rebellious.

"Well, what can I tell you? The one holding all five lines, the Sanctus Cryptus, such an idealistic concept," he began, launching into a history of the years spent trying to create one and the reasons the project was discontinued.

Imogen feigned a fascinated interest and waited until the wariness in his colours had started to subside, gradually being replaced with the gold and black spikes of self-righteous authority. When she was sure he had dropped his guard sufficiently, she began her questions.

"So, how did you discover I was a Penta-Crypt?" Silver filaments stirred within her Chroma and began to cross and infiltrate into Ubaid's aura, unseen.

"Pure chance, but look, we should not talk here," he indicated the stairway, putting a foot on the first step. However, he then turned back, slightly confused as his eyes began to glaze over.

"Was it the sample Eshe sent from Earth?" Imogen persisted, her filaments firmly weaving into his, pushing down the onset of suspicion in Ubaid's colours before they could rise. "The one you found in Tarik's possession?"

"Yes, such a surprise. I had been hoping the sphere contained information about the Tractus, not a volt of flesh. But then I tested it and… well, to be given such an opportunity. To produce a Penta-Crypt, loyal to the Supreme Council. The Resistance had played right into my hands and better still they would not know it. I had that Falsebred cornered. He would never talk."

Leo, he is talking about Leo. Imogen resisted the temptation to slap this arrogant man across the face and put all her energies into teasing out the truth with her hypnosis strands.

"Who else knows about Naomi?"

Ubaid began to answer mechanically, the truth spilling from his mouth unbidden, as the silver threads twitched at the sapphire facts buried below layers of falsehood.

"No one. The geneticist who helped me to create her met with a nasty accident. Got in the way of the early experiments with the Repros. Messy, but no one suspected anything and the knowledge died with her."

"And Naomi's mother?"

"Naomi's birth mother was duped into thinking she was producing a descendant to the famous Tanastra Thut. Who wouldn't volunteer to be a surrogate to bring such a revered person back?"

"And Naomi, what have you done to Naomi?"

Ubaid, now in a trance, continued to answer, unaware he was speaking the truth aloud for probably the first time in his life.

"She was becoming difficult. I placed her in a suspended form of animation. I think it is called a coma on Earth."

"And where is she now?"

"She is in my chambers."

"Where is Araz?"

"I don't know. He will have to be eliminated. He can no longer be trusted. He lied to me – told me the Earth clone was dead. I will find him and punish him."

Imogen breathed a sigh of relief. If Araz had reached Ubaid's chambers, he would have found Naomi. Ubaid began to shake his head and Imogen tightened the hold on her threads, hurriedly re-focussing her concentration.

"Why did you want the Earth clone dead?" Imogen could see Ubaid's eyes had gone glassy. He was not consciously aware he was talking to the same 'Earth clone'.

"One of them must die. There cannot be two Sanctus Crypti! The Supreme Council must not find out I used illegal cloning techniques. My problem is, which one to eliminate?"

Imogen was appalled at his cold, calculating rationale and felt her blood run cold. "So, which one should be eliminated?"

Ubaid, detached from the damning truth he was speaking, replied, "This is my dilemma. The Earth version would not have had the vigorous training of being brought up on Holis. However, she may hold qualities Naomi does not. After all, the Earth girl was raised amongst primitives and could therefore have greater resilience and fortitude. Also, her Earth experiences could be turned to our advantage in the future. That's why I had to meet her. Araz was instructed to capture her and bring her to me, so I could decide which clone would live and which would die."

"Did Araz know this?" Imogen held her breath to hear the reply.

"Of course not. He would not have agreed to capture the clone for possible termination without reference to the Sanctus High Court. Araz is not a rule breaker. Such noble aspirations for a young agent. He was told the girl was a Falsebred and held invaluable information on the Tractus project. He did not need to know anything else."

"And why do you need the Tractus technology?"

"For Elysian Two. We must be able to cross space instantaneously."

"To clean up Ankh?"

"No, there is no hope of that. Ankh is spent. This is for the new Elysian Two project."

"Explain?"

"Elysian Two. It has a new focus. This… this is restricted information…" Ubaid hesitated and began to fight Imogen's threads. She could feel herself losing control as he abruptly put up his hand and shouted out loud, "Stop!"

Imogen reeled as Ubaid, now free of her manipulation, looked thunderously at her, a snarl starting on his lips. He looked as if he could murder her and she cowered away as he raised his fist in the air.

"You… you sorceress!"

Before he could strike her, he suddenly appeared to lose balance and with a cry, toppled over, falling into the pool with a loud splash. Imogen looked up. Araz was in front of her, hands forward. He had pushed Ubaid into the water.

Imogen glanced past him and saw Naomi, unconscious and slumped against the wall at the top of the stairway.

"Quick, we don't have long."

Araz ran back up the steps, threw Naomi over his shoulder and half-stumbled, half-ran back down. Imogen saw Ubaid reach the edge of the pool, staring angrily at the three of them before activating the clear circular pendant around his neck.

The unmistakeable sound of the stomping of heavy booted feet began. A strident klaxon filled the air and the lights started to flash on and off.

Imogen grabbed Araz's arm and led him towards Sekhet's former chambers, hurrying to turn the corners ahead.

Araz was straining under the dead weight of Naomi and when she fell from his shoulders, Imogen managed to catch and steady her so they could pull her forward between them. *We won't get far with her like this.*

Imogen's mind was racing as she followed Sekhet's floor plans and they finally reached the entrance to her former rooms. Thankfully, the Phase-Seal responded to her touch and when it quickly re-sealed, muting the noise of the klaxon, she turned to Araz, "Quick - Hide! With Naomi - now!" she pointed to the bathroom leading off the main area. "I will lead them away."

Araz went to object but Imogen's eyes bored into his and he closed his mouth. The jagged black spikes of authority in her Chroma would brook no argument.

"As soon as they follow me, get out! Go for the other secret exit." She glanced his fingertips, communicating the precise location of a second Resistance doorway. The jolt of Araz's acute fear of them all being caught slammed back into her head like an electric shock and did nothing to help her own terror. But there was no time to think.

Araz lifted Naomi and stumbled into the bathroom. Imogen raced towards what Sekhet had said was a shutter opening in the wall, praying it would still be there. Finding both the aperture and the hidden switch, mentally blessing Sekhet for describing the location in such detail, the cover split and retracted.

As Imogen ducked down to dive through the opening, the Phase-Seal entrance to the room melted away. The noise of the klaxon and the Repros burst into the space and ran towards her.

Springing to her feet within the narrow stone passageway, she started to run for her life.

It was all too hauntingly familiar. Her terrifying vision did not need to replay. It was here, happening now. And she knew she was careering towards a dead end and that plummeting waterfall.

LEO

The journey to Qus had been hot and uncomfortable in the empty crate. Sekhet and Leo had made the most of their reunion and had talked non-stop, partly to put aside the horror of the Repro attack.

They recalled Leo's happy childhood before he had been discovered, and Leo described what it was like to live on Earth. He tried to reassure his mother most humans were nothing like those shown on the government transmissions. He also began to teach her a few words of English to pass the time. Em listened in a distracted way, her thoughts constantly returning to Shani's death.

When they neared their destination, the conversation lulled and Sekhet turned to Em. "Who will lead the Resistance now?"

"Is problem. Only few in Resistance know 'Barbara' is Shani. Now she gone, need new Barbara. Need strong leader."

"Is there anyone in Karnak?" Leo asked.

"All follow Shani. Only others capable, is far away, on Earth."

"You mean my father? Or his brothers – I mean, brother?"

"Yes. Was Kasmut but now only Zuberi brothers left." Em rubbed at her spikey hair and then sprang to her feet, her face no longer sombre. "You! You have Zuberi blood! You bring brothers back here. Need come home. Lead Resistance. If Supreme Council find last markers, may be no way back from Earth. Must fetch them, bring them here. Is good plan, yes?"

Leo saw the sense in Em's words but could not bring himself to tell her he had barely spoken to his father. Also, what would their reaction be when they discovered it was he, Leo, who had betrayed them? That it was his fault Kasmut was dead? He gave a non-committal nod of his head. "I can try. I will do my best," before falling silent for the last section of the trip.

At the Qus Velo-City station, Em led Leo and Sekhet to the surface via several ventilation shafts to avoid the Repros guarding the entrance. They took a circuitous route to the seaside town where Em met a fellow Resistance member, Hanh. He gave them access to his rooms and brought them salvers of food. The strapping young man, his skin a deep chocolate hue, sported the same style of tattoos as Em. Once inside, they had both activated the symbols on their hands and faces in an air of defiance. The symbol of Iris shone high above one of Hanh's cheekbones. It had been decorated with multi-dimensional dyes to look like an open eye, matching the deep brown colour of his own eyes. This gave the disquieting and somewhat menacing illusion of Hanh having three eyes. Leo suppressed the need to make a quip about monsters and tried to look at Hanh's mouth instead.

"You will not be safe here for long." Hanh stood firmly against the Phase-Seal entrance listening for any approaching steps. "The Repros do regular searches. The residents of Qus now live in constant fear. Guards check everyone going to and from their daily tasks. If any citizen does not have full clearance they are held in a form of prison, unable to contact their friends or family."

Em shook her head as the three quickly ate.

"I mean, it is more than just rumours these Repros can turn wild. They inflicted severe injuries on a four-year-old boy who got too close to them. Vlaggers! Poor lad has been mentally maimed. He is undergoing untested therapies to try and bring him back to normality. Children are now accompanied everywhere; no one feels safe. What will you do, Em?"

"Will take escaped prisoners to marker. This Tarik and Sekhet, they jump to Earth. Will return with reinforcements. New leaders for Resistance."

Hanh's face broke into a wide smile and he slapped Leo on the back. "Ideal!"

Leo, nearly choking on his food, gave a weak smile in return. He had no idea if anyone on Earth would listen to him. Why should they? His thoughts turned to Imogen and he hoped she was unharmed. He hated the idea she was with Araz but at least, he thought grudgingly, Araz would protect her.

Sekhet placed her empty salver down and started to question Leo about the Tractus. He attempted to sound relaxed, but his forehead beaded with sweat as he described the sensation of being transported across the folds of space. He felt intrinsically worried every time the travel device was mentioned. However, he promised his mother she would be safe, inwardly praying this would be the case.

Hanh listened to Leo with interest. "Must be a strange experience. Actually, I am working on the test results with Imogen and Naomi's DNA. Shani briefed our team. I mean, the opportunity is unique. With them being clones! The comparison will tell us what impact, if any, the Tractus jumps have on our basic genetic makeup. Shani certainly had concerns."

Leo glared at Hanh. This would not help his mother's nerves. He turned his back on Hanh. "We will jump together," he smiled, squeezing Sekhet's hand.

"It will be good to see your father again," Sekhet murmured, the hope and longing in her chromatic colours evident to Leo.

"Yes," he answered half-heartedly before turning to Em. "Which Earth marker will we jump to?"

"Can set to one of many now on Earth," Em replied. "You decide. Is just names to me. Information hidden in marker cave."

"Come," said Hanh. "It's time to go."

It had begun to rain outside. They joined a large group of Qus residents who were about to go out fishing. They adjusted their clothing to match the others by moulding pieces of their Flecto clothing into wide waterproof hats. Em, Leo and Sekhet then slipped into the centre of the crowd where they managed to stay concealed. The Repros on guard did not bother checking those who boarded the flotilla of ships. Battered by the rain which was now a downpour, they knew the fishing trip would not be leaving the vicinity and assumed they were merely going out to sea. The fishermen and women had, after all, always returned after a few hours.

Em had selected a small rowing boat for the three of them and once a good distance from the shore, they broke away from those fishing, hidden by the low rain cloud. They took the vessel further down the coast and once out of sight, beached it before crossing into the rainforest.

They arrived at the marker cave just before Atma. Leo and Em shook off the rainwater inside the cave. Sekhet lagged, clearly worried about her imminent departure to Earth. Leo noticed how pale she had become and gave her a hug. It did little to reduce the swirling clouds of grey in her colours. Leo cursed his ever-improving ability to read Chroma which gave him even more to worry about. It was obvious his mother was not just bothered by the Tractus, but the prospect of meeting his father again.

Leo and Sekhet hurriedly changed into black bodysuits at Em's behest. She said something about it being the code of practice, how they must be careful no Flecto samples could be found on earth in case they were discovered by the authorities there.

Leo checked the destinations from the information on the communication DE and made his choice. "London! We'll head there. And I know how to avoid the enemy portal," he smiled confidently at his mum.

Em set the marker and gave Leo and Sekhet a final nod.

"Come back with leaders! Soon!"

Leo barely had time to bow his head in response. He had his mother's hand squeezed tightly in his own as the marker glowed and the airless blackness hit them.

IMOGEN

The steps down the narrow stone passageway were steep and slippery. Imogen nearly lost her footing several times, but the sound of the Repros at her heels spurred her on. The deeper she went the louder the noise of rushing water became. Soon it was all she could hear and her terror increased with the deafening sound.

The passage ended abruptly as she leapt into a small cavern. The reality was even more frightening than the premonition which had intermittently burst into her consciousness over the last week. Water poured into stone funnels above her head, roaring thunderously around the spray-filled space before crashing down into a waterfall beyond a low, natural rock wall. Imogen looked wildly around. *There must be another way out. Perhaps I could climb up the water chase to a higher level?* But she realised it was too late. The Repros were here.

The first one rushed into the chamber lunging towards her and she stumbled backward feeling for the wall. The snarling beast moved quickly and was almost upon her. Heart in her mouth, Imogen rolled over the wall and plunged down into the moving water as the freezing temperature took her scream and her breath away.

Imogen was sucked under the surface. Her heart hammered in her chest. The stab of the bitterly cold rush of water prompted a rising panic. She twisted and turned, trying to right herself, but found she was at the mercy of the plummeting icy torrents. Her waking nightmare was now a terrifying reality.

Imogen was tossed around helplessly. Her foot struck the edge of a jagged stone and she was catapulted down a helter-skelter of rapids. Her lungs were screaming in pain.

I'm going to die.

Images of her mother and father flickered into her mind as her strength began to ebb away into the icy waters... and then Araz's face before her. He was mouthing something. The thunderous waters took every sound. She was losing feeling and focussed on his lips.

Fight! Imogen don't give up - Brrr... Br... Breathe!

The currents temporarily slowed as the water cascaded over a shallower incline. Imogen grasped the opportunity and pushed her back into position to slide against the smooth stone channel, her head finally breaking the surface. Gasping a lungful of air, she forced her body to stop thrashing and straightened out. She intuitively crossed her arms over her chest, letting the gushing waters carry her. Now able to keep her face above the glacial cascade, she was carried relentlessly down endless chutes. She could barely feel her arms and legs in the bitter cold.

I have to get out of here or I will freeze to death.

The melt water river ran into others and started to get deeper. Imogen's legs dropped and pulled behind her as she tried to swim to keep afloat, her arms feeling like lead. Swirling around a larger cavern, Imogen spotted the rising steam from what must be a thermal pool. She could see a protrusion of rock next to the watercourse. As she rounded the bend, she threw out her arm. With a supreme effort, she managed to hook her elbow over the stone outcrop and lift her chest out of the water. Suspended above the racing course and unable to feel her hands she used every ounce of strength to haul herself firstly to her waist, and then her whole body right out of the icy flow. Exhausted, she pulled herself along the rock bank with her elbows and flopped into the still warm waters of the higher pool.

Imogen shrieked as the blood rushed to the nerve endings at every point of her skin, causing excruciating stinging burns and taking her breath away. The agony finally subsided as her tingling body began to warm and regain circulation in the hot bath. She ducked her head under the surface, braving the shock of heat to her face, and gradually started to thaw out.

She began to think straight. Torn between the exhilaration of escape and fear for her predicament, her thoughts turned to Araz and Naomi. *I hope he managed to get her out of there.*

Weary, Imogen clambered out of the pool and winced. She could not put her weight down on one foot. Pulling off her sopping Flecto footwear, she checked the damage. Her big toe was badly dislocated, pointing across the others at a gruesome angle. She gritted her teeth and with one strong move, lifted the toe and popped it back into place, panting against the sharp pain with short shallow breaths.

The smarting began to subside. *Thank goodness!* As she waited for the toe to begin to heal, she summoned her maps of the area to mind and looked all around. Sekhet had not described this pool so she had no idea where she was, but a dim glimpse of light seemed to indicate a route through hollow channels in the rock.

Imogen's teeth began to chatter as she started to shiver again, her dripping body and clothing evaporating her newly found heat. Tentatively standing to test her toe, she hobbled forward to the edge of a sink hole. Greeted with an upward blast of hot air, just like those in the Qus bathing areas, she gave a smile and stripped off her soaking Flecto robes. She turned slowly round letting the heated jets massage her aching body. Once completely dry, she retrieved the Multi-Com and the DE she had taken from Kekara's safe, hoping the icy waters had not damaged them beyond repair. She then held the Flecto material in the airstream, watching it rise sail-like until it had dried.

Fashioning a close-fitting, belted bodysuit, complete with hidden pockets for her devices, Imogen used some of the warm water to wet and soothe her suddenly unruly hair into place. She set off along the narrow rock catacombs until she finally saw the brighter red glow of the Holan light at the end of the passage. She emerged outside, on a bank above a sparkling stream.

Now, to find Araz and Naomi.

Imogen switched her Flecto outfit to reflect, hoping it would keep her camouflaged. She decided to follow the river upstream, reasoning it should lead to the mountain range of The Hub. From there she could find her way to the Velo-City station. She prayed Araz had made it there safely with Naomi.

She had only gone a short distance when a small voice called out, "Who are you?"

Imogen swung round to find the voice came from a low shrub. Peering into the foliage, she saw a small mischievous looking girl smiling back at her. *She can only be seven or eight years old.*

"Erm – hi. I'm Imogen. Are you here by yourself?" Imogen scanned the bank for others but could see no one.

The child stood up and stepped out of the bushes. She held a rush basket filled with twigs and leaves. Her eyes fixed on Imogen's mirror clothing and she walked around her, dodging this way and that, laughing at her distorted reflection in the folds of Imogen's bodysuit.

"Yes. I'm Leyla. I'm collecting samples from river plants. Did you know, the leaves encase themselves in an armoured layer at night time? They go rock-hard to keep out the freezing cold. Nothing can penetrate the night shell. If we can mimic the enzymes causing the change, we could invent a new type of Flecto, one able to harden." The girl touched Imogen's sleeve absentmindedly and then stood back in alarm. "I'm not supposed to tell you that," she put her hand to her mouth.

"It's okay – I know about the leaves." Imogen recalled the botany information from the library Data Encounters.

"But you don't know why we need to turn Flecto into body armour..." Leyla stopped abruptly and stamped her foot in frustration. "I've done it again!"

Imogen could see from the girl's rising grey chromatic shades of worry, she was trying to quash her quartz reasoning. She bent down to reassure her. "It's ok, Leyla. I can guess." Thoughts of the armed Repros sprang into her mind. "Knives will not be able to penetrate reinforced Flecto. In medieval times, I mean ancient days, they used chain mail. It's a great idea."

"I wasn't supposed to say. Neith told me not to tell anyone."

"Who's Neith?"

"My mentor. She's a Vatic and she's also my biological grandmother."

Imogen recalled Shani saying Eshe was said to have been a Vatic, or type of prophet.

"Wait!" Leyla's eyes widened. "I know your face – you're that new councillor, Naomi. Why did you say your name was Imogen?" Leyla looked horrified and took a step backwards, giving a quick shrill whistle.

Before Imogen could respond, she heard a whistled reply.

Time to go! Imogen gave the girl a brief, apologetic look and started to run along the riverbank.

Ahead, a wiry woman, her hair a cloud of tight curls, her eyes a piercing hazel, had jumped out from a line of trees and stood in her path. Imogen debated changing course, but something about the woman's challenging stare and folded arms made her slow until she came to a stop in front of her.

The woman had the physique of a teenager but the lined face of a much older person. Her Chroma shone with the most extraordinary crystal blue shades.

Those eyes. She looks as if she could see into a person's soul.

A breathless Leyla caught them up and in between gasps, she spoke first. "She says she's Imogen. But she's... she's that new councillor, Naomi, and she knows about body armour and something called chain mail. What does medieval mean?" The girl was silenced by the woman's stare. "I'm sorry Neith, I didn't mean to tell."

Neith put her hand on Leyla's shoulder and waited for Imogen to speak.

"My name is Imogen. I look like Councillor Naomi - I am a close relative to her," she began.

"Not true," the woman snapped.

Imogen quickly started to cloak her Chroma.

"Do not attempt to conceal your true colours. I am Neith and I am a Vatic." She made a sweeping movement with her hand, catching Imogen's sleeve and returning Imogen's clothing to their plain stone shades, reiterating camouflage was unacceptable.

"Imogen, Naomi, whoever you are, I know your face – it is written in the minds of all Vatics – we have seen."

Imogen floundered. She knew instinctively she would be unable to deceive Neith. She had no choice but to be open with her. *After all, her granddaughter was helping her to devise protective clothing against the Repro weapons.*

Imogen started to stammer out an explanation. Neith put a finger to her lip then took both of Imogen's hands and turned them palm upwards. Imogen's words died on her lips. She felt helpless to resist as the mystical lady pressed each of her small hands over her trembling ones until their fingertips touched.

"Be still," soothed Neith as the connection was made.

Imogen gasped as her mind flooded with Neith's thoughts and premonitions. In bursts of light she saw the peace and harmony of Holis shattered, Repros maiming and killing, children weeping and hiding. Then came armies of...? Holans? Humans? They were headed for Karnak in armoured tanks and aircraft. Missiles were launched and hit The Hub which shattered into millions of gigantic shards as it was razed to the ground. The images became more gruesome with bodies piled high on the ground and bloated remains floating in the once peaceful alpine streams. Imogen, horrified at the scenes, tried to release her hands but Neith's eyes bored into hers and maintained the bond. The appalling images suddenly froze and shrank. Instead, Karnak was back to normal. The Hub sparkled above crowds of celebrating Holans. Peace was restored; humans and Repros banished. A figure was raised on the shoulders of those in the middle of the multitudes. Victorious cries filled the air. The image homed in on the one they held high. Her face was unmistakeable.

"No!" Imogen prised her fingers away and looked defiantly at Neith.

"You are the Sanctus Cryptus. The one we have been waiting for."

"Stop!"

"You cannot deny the vision of what will come, but I have seen your mind. You are not ready. Your beliefs are undisciplined and confused."

Realising the woman shared her gift of cognitively reading hidden thoughts, Imogen gave a deep sigh. There was no point denying anything. Neith had seen everything and knew she was scared and lacked confidence. She now knew about Naomi, Araz, her father, Leo, the scientists left on Earth and the DE she had stolen from Kekara's safe.

"No, I am not ready. I don't even understand what's going on."

"So, who will save our people?" Neith asked. "You, perhaps? Or your other self?"

Imogen shrugged her shoulders. She felt close to bursting into tears. It was too much responsibility, too much to expect of her. She barely knew these people and did not know where to turn.

Neith, sensing her distress, sat Imogen on the grass and produced salvers which she filled with clear water from the stream. She, Leyla and Imogen drank deeply of the fresh water.

"You are not safe here. You must return to your first home and seek guidance," Neith declared. "But know this, your destiny is to lead our people to a new age. Deny this, and you deny our race."

Imogen looked intensely at the blades of grass, wishing she was anywhere but there, until Leyla broke the awkward silence.

"What is chain mail?"

"Show her," Neith waved her fingertips.

Leyla opened her hand and looked eagerly at Imogen.

With a sigh, Imogen connected with the girl, and put her focus on the illustrations of a long-forgotten history project, cognitively transmitting pictures of chain mail across the link.

"Perfect!" Leyla's eyes shone. "We can connect rigid Flecto in links to make it flexible for those wearing it."

Imogen looked at the little girl in admiration. She had seen into Leyla's mind's eye where she was mathematically modelling and designing the modified Flecto. Her science was the equivalent of

University level and her nature was pure, intuitive and trusting. Imogen could not stop herself murmuring, "Clever girl."

Neith stood and pulled Leyla to her feet as she turned to Imogen. "You must go. But be warned, the Velo-City station is under close guard. Whether or not you meet up with your bonded one, you should travel to Qus – to the portal. I must tell you, the destiny of this Araz is unclear. I have also seen his face and know he plays a part in the troubles to come. However, I cannot predict which direction he will take."

Neith touched Imogen's fingertips one more time to communicate the route she should take to reach the station. With it came a last warning, 'Ubaid spoke one truth. You will not both be allowed to live. I have seen it. Either you or Naomi will die."

ARAZ

Once the Repros had ducked into the passage to chase Imogen, Araz had summoned up a super-human strength to carry Naomi and run from the Supreme Council quarters. He got her to the secret resistance exit and, once the Phase-Seal had closed, had gently placed her on the floor. Gasping for breath, he took out his Multi-Com. There was no signal from Imogen. He could only hope she was safe. He was also unable to raise Em, but she was no doubt deep underground on the Velo-City heading for Qus.

Irritably snapping the device back into his pocket, Araz regarded the sleeping Naomi. She was every bit as beautiful as Imogen and right now she looked just as vulnerable. What had Ubaid given her to knock her out? He noticed a small stain on her outfit and sniffed it. He knew that smell. He trawled his memories of his early training as an agent. They had been given a liquid, disguised with honey, to subdue opponents. He ran through the formulae of this and the antidote in his head. He realised the nearest place to get the remedy was the agent training grounds in The Hub. It would be risky, but it was probably the last place Ubaid would expect him to go.

He moved Naomi down the corridor and placed her in the recovery position on the floor near the exit into The Hub. He had no choice but to leave her there whilst he went in search of the cure. They would get nowhere until Naomi was awake.

The training areas were empty. Araz figured all the agents had been called on active duty to hunt down the subversives which, he thought wryly, would now include him. He crept around the storerooms and sleeping quarters but there was no sign of any of the immobilisation tools usually stockpiled on the shelves. He realised, with a heavy heart, he would have to go into the bowels of The Hub to the Council of Stability surveillance suites and the restricted areas of defence. There was a Resistance entrance down there. Em had described the one they had used to intercept Imogen when she was lost in those corridors. Araz swiftly plotted his route and found his way to the subterranean area and the sealed doorway of the research facility. It stayed locked to his touch.

Thinking on his feet, he remembered the arrow key Em had concealed in her Multi-Com at the Tavat Port and pulled the device from his garments. He was relieved to find the arrow still there. Having been appalled Em had a duplicate of Vizier Odion's key, he was now the one to be using it illegally. He suppressed a guilty shudder. The Phase-Seal melted before him. Needs be as needs must, he thought to himself.

The research laboratory was a hive of activity and Araz pushed himself against a side wall, holding his breath as he observed a dozen or more staff going about their business. It was not long before he realised the masked workers were all Zeroids, acting on rote. They went to and from the test beds in a mechanical manner and did not even look up when he stepped forward, grabbed a mask and walked amongst them.

About to enter the storage area on the far side of the lab, Araz noticed the large boxes of Expirite being loaded into cargo crates and a few small accompanying cases, labelled 'antidote'. He deduced this Expirite was a poison but had no idea why so much of it had been stockpiled, however his curiosity was piqued. If this was anything like the poison used on Earth which had nearly killed Imogen, it was lethal. He suddenly felt compelled to take a quantity of the remedy. Feigning slow deliberate movements, akin to the Holan shells performing mundane tasks around him, Araz retrieved a box of the antidote, prised it open and removed a handful of the phials before closing it and returning it to the crate. He then ambled across the floor space and slipped unseen into the storage area.

It did not take him long to find the containers of honeyed sleep inducement liquor and the reversal tonic. Pocketing a couple of each, to add to the Expirite cure, Araz slipped out of the laboratories.

He was about to retrace his steps to the exit when sounds of activity drew him to a far glass wall. Approaching quietly, he realised it was a viewing area, set high above a well-lit space reminiscent of the operating theatres in Earth hospitals.

Araz peered down on the moving machinery below and gasped. Several Repros lay prone on slowly moving beds. Automated probes were performing surgery. They appeared to be implanting tissue into the Repro heads and altering their facial features.

Araz looked closer as the full horror of what he was witnessing was revealed. Mechanical hands sealed head wounds on the sleeping Repros. As the probes moved away, the Repro faces came into view. Araz broke into a cold sweat. Their heavy rubbery features had now transformed to the sleeping visages of what could only be former Holan citizens. Araz steadied himself against the glass, suppressing a surge of nausea. Unable to look away, he watched with revulsion as the modified figures glided into a further space. He only caught a glimpse, but there appeared to be hundreds of them.

Swallowing bile, he filmed a short clip of the scene on his device before turning away. With a heavy heart and clenched fists, he left the facility and headed back to wake Naomi.

"So, you seem to be making a habit of rendering me unconscious?" Naomi asked groggily, a smile playing on her lips as she began to revive. She ached everywhere and her head was banging.

"Save your breath and wait for your head to clear," Araz ordered in a mock severe way as he handed her a cube of Baladi.

Watching her nibble at the cube, Araz added, "Your memory should confirm it was in fact Ubaid who drugged you."

An image of the goblet hovered in Naomi's mind and she shivered, nodding for Araz to continue.

"I'm not sure you should consider him to be your mentor anymore!"

"I think I had reached that conclusion myself!"

"You should know, he tried to overpower Imogen. I overheard him telling her he would kill one of you to cover up his illegal cloning. So, you see, we are both in trouble. You, by just being you, and me for evading the guard and stealing the antidote to your sleeping draught."

"I will vouch for you," the words burst from Naomi's lips before she could contain them, and the blush of her face matched those in her rippling burgundy Chroma.

"Yes, but my crimes continue." Araz seemed unaware of her fluster. "You see, I have witnessed things I should not..."

"What things?"

"They are modifying Repros – some form of head surgery," Araz could not bring himself to tell her the full extent of what he had seen. "I dread to think how this will change their capabilities."

Naomi frowned. "It's not a crime to witness something."

"No? And I have also stolen these." He held out the phials of Expirite antidote.

Naomi recognised the symbols on the outside. She had seen the poison and the cures being made when she and Horus had been guided around the restricted areas.

"I know what they are for," Naomi whispered, her colours fogging over. She took one of the containers from Araz's hands and held it up to the light. "This is the protection against the new poison, Expirite. It must be administered before or immediately after exposure to the poison. Did you know the antidote will only work on Holans? It stimulates our self-healing cells. Any creature without our modified immune system would be wiped out by the Expirite."

"I suppose we need some form of self-defence," argued Araz. "Should humans ever attack Holis. They have all manner of lethal weapons." Araz fell silent before adding, "Although even on Earth, the use of nerve agents and poisons are internationally condemned."

"What if it is not for self-defence?" Naomi asked in a hushed voice. "A microscopic amount will kill. The quantity of Expirite produced is vast. Enough to wipe out…" Naomi trailed off as the full realisation hit her.

"… wipe out an entire planet?" Araz's voice had dropped to a whisper.

"What if the Elysian Two project is no longer to clear up Ankh, but to colonise another world?" Naomi's eyes were wide.

"A world with ample stocks of InvertIon?"

"A world with a troublesome native population. A species many would term to be barbaric…"

Araz and Naomi stared at each other, suddenly realising the enormous repercussions of their theories.

"Can this be true?" Naomi had paled to a deathly colour.

"If it is, it's no wonder the Tractus technology is so crucial. This could not be accomplished from a distance of twenty or more light years. Instantaneous travel would need to be a pre-requisite for the colonisation to work."

"The scientists who jumped to Earth, do you think they knew?"

"They certainly wanted to keep the Tractus from the leaders of the Supreme Council." Araz shook his head in disbelief before saying, "This is just supposition. We do not know this for sure. The effects of Tractus travel haven't been properly tested. It is still not known if it is reliable; if it can cause long term damage."

"Araz, we need to get to the bottom of this. I feel our race is on the brink of disaster and one false move could send us hurtling towards a terrifying future. Will you stand with me and find out what is going on?"

Araz hesitated. "I also want to discover the truth, but I have to tell you, my first priority is to ensure Imogen is safe."

"Okay, let's find her." Naomi suppressed a somewhat grudging thought of how lucky Imogen was to hold the heart of this fierce protector. "Perhaps it would be better to send her back to Earth. Only Ubaid from the Supreme Council knows there are two of us. And whilst it would not serve him well if his use of cloning was discovered, it would be the end of us. Imogen and I cannot be seen together. Will she be protected there?"

Araz nodded before adding, "Unless they use the Expirite."

"Well, give her the antidote. At least she will be able to inoculate the Holans on Earth, if what we fear to be the plan is indeed true."

Araz nodded and as she tried to hand him back her phial, he closed her hand over it. "I have another. You keep this, just in case. Now, we must make haste and try to find Imogen. That is, if she has manag... managed to escape the Repros." Araz stuttered out the last few words and Naomi touched his arm before secreting the phial into her gowns.

Araz tried his Multi-Com again and then Em's. "Her communication device still isn't working," his hands flexed into fists.

"We will keep trying as we go. If there is one thing I have learnt about Imogen in the brief time I have known her," soothed Naomi, "she is strong and determined. If anyone can escape the clutches of those beasts, she can."

Araz, deep worry etched on his brow and unable to take comfort from her words, helped Naomi to her feet and they moved towards the exit. Araz only hoped Imogen would be there at the rendezvous point behind the Velo-City station in Karnak.

IMOGEN

*I*mogen got to the Velo-City station just before Atma. The entrance was heavily guarded and Repros were stopping and searching every Holan going in and out. Imogen kept to the shadows at the rear of the station, glancing out every few seconds. Her worries grew with each passing minute and no sign of Araz or Naomi.

Her Flecto bristled against the growingly cooler air and her mind began to revisit Neith's visions and warnings. *Is it possible humans will attack Holis? A war of worlds? That would be unthinkable, wouldn't it? What did Neith mean by my destiny being to lead Holis into a new age? And why the hell did she say either me or Naomi must die? That's just ridiculous!* As she chewed it all over, she started to feel overwhelmed.

Imogen's device buzzed and she hurriedly pulled it from her hidden pocket. Thankful and a little amazed it was finally working again, she almost cried with relief when she heard Araz's voice.

"Thank heavens you're safe!"

"You too. I have been so worried. Are you at the station?"

"Yes."

"Imogen, I should be with you soon but if there is any trouble, go to Qus. You cannot stay in Karnak, it is too dangerous. You must get back to Earth. You... you will be safe there."

They exchanged a few more words and then finished. Imogen put the Multi-Com away. She was troubled by the tone of his voice. He seemed unsure she would be safe and said nothing about going with her. She wished he were in front of her, so she could read his Chroma. *I can't go back without him, or is that what he wants?*

Several minutes later, and full of trepidation, her heart leapt when she spotted Araz in the distant shadows of the river walk. She could see he was not alone, his companion disguised under a hooded cloak. Even swathed in these coverings, Imogen could not fail to recognise the familiar gait. *It could be me! It's Naomi! So, he managed to revive her. Why didn't he mention her when he called?*

Araz wended his way in and out of queuing groups of passengers towards her. It took all her self-control to stay concealed and not to run to meet him.

As they got closer, Imogen started to raise her hand in the air but quickly stopped when a loud shout sounded from the entrance and Araz came to a sudden halt.

"There!" a familiar voice boomed.

Odion! Imogen's heart thumped in her chest.

Araz began to retreat, wildly scanning the area with his eyes, when the troop of Repros guarding the station broke rank and raced towards them pushing several groups of people aside. Araz and Naomi were quickly surrounded.

No!

The Repros all brandished their knives high in the air as the bald Vizier, Odion, stepped into the circle and marched up to Araz, grabbing him by the throat. The Holan crowd gasped and took several steps backwards as they watched in horror. Odion looked around and, seeing the shocked faces watching his every move, appeared to recover himself and released Araz. Words were exchanged and Naomi threw off her cloak and addressed the people standing outside the ring of Repros. Imogen crept forward to hear what she said.

"Citizens of Holis, you know me to be Naomi, one of the new members of the Supreme Council. And this agent you know to be Araz Vikram. He gave evidence in the Sanctus High Court at the hearing of Tarik Zuberi. Be assured, we are not subversives. We have both loyally served the Supreme Council and the people of Holis."

Odion counteracted, "These so-called loyal servants are responsible for releasing the Falsebred and other members of the Resistance, exposing us all to danger."

Naomi raised her voice even louder, "We seek to find the truth in these dark times."

Odion advanced on Naomi and looked as if he would strike her with his fist, but Araz caught his hand as the Holan audience cried out 'No!', 'leave her' and 'let her speak'. A Repro got Araz into a body lock and Odion snarled. He again looked at the onlookers and Imogen could see traces of fear flare in his colours.

He doesn't want to start a disturbance or anyone to witness a Vizier behaving in a brutal manner.

Odion gave a nervous twitch and lifted his hands to the crowd in a placatory gesture. He loudly directed the guard to sheath their blades and escort the pair to Karnak Prison for further questioning. The public murmured approval and Odion politely advised them to disperse.

Grappling with two Repros who attempted to push her away from the station, Naomi shouted. "True citizens, I trust in you all to ensure we have justice. Let the Sanctus High Court hear our case. Let the Sanctus Laws prevail…"

A large hand clamped over her mouth and Araz and Naomi were jostled away from the entrance.

Imogen looked on in dismay. Her heart pounded. *What do I do now?*

The Holan onlookers gathered in small groups discussing what they had seen. Conscious if anyone spotted her, they would know she and Naomi were identical, Imogen quickly took off her Flecto belt. She stretched it into a scarf which she threw round her head to cover her hair and the lower part of her face. She dived into the entrance of the station, no longer guarded, and with other passengers made her way down to the platforms.

I have to get help. Em will know what to do and if she doesn't I will jump back to Earth. Adam and his brothers will have to do something. I just hope Leo and Sekhet made it back.

Cloaking her colours and keeping her head down, the other Holans paid her no heed as she boarded the shuttle and then the main train back to Qus.

Scheduled to arrive early the next morning, she managed to find a quiet carriage in which to sit and brood on the day's events. Wringing her hands in worry and frustration, she had never felt more miserable and alone.

She must have fallen asleep at some point, as Imogen woke with a crick in her neck when the passengers started to disembark onto the Qus shuttle. She re-made her loose 'hijab-styled' scarf and filed onto the linking platform full of anxiety.

What if I can't find Em or the others?

The stairs up to the exit of the station were lined with Repros at every twenty or so steps. Imogen hesitated. *What other route can I take?*

As she looked around, she noticed a person in the shadows, close to the shuttle track. He peered back at her and she risked lowering the covering from her face. He instantly waved for her to come over to him.

Cautiously approaching the figure, she was relieved to see him briefly activate the tattoo of an eye, high on his deep brown cheekbone. *Like Em's – he's one of us!*

He pulled her into a recessed area by the track, and through a doorway into a space not dissimilar to the ventilation shafts of the London underground. *At least we are not being chased by Repros on this occasion. Let's hope I am not speaking too soon.*

"Hanh!" the figure called over his shoulder as he raced ahead of her. "Em sent me to get you. I see you are alone. So, erm, which one are you? Imogen or Naomi?"

"Imogen."

"What happened to Naomi and Araz?"

"They were arrested at the Karnak station."

"Em was worried this would happen. At least you got away."

Ascending a ladder structure in the middle of the shaft, they stopped speaking using all their breath for the climb.

At the top, Hanh helped her through the opening and gave her a beaming smile. "Wow! I mean, sorry, I didn't mean to stare. It's just I've never seen twins let alone clones. We just don't have them... er, well you know what I mean!"

Imogen looked away, her frustration all too clear.

Hanh mumbled an awkward apology and changed the subject to the route they would take to the rainforest cave.

Keeping to the dense jungle-style walks, Hanh started to tell Imogen about the tests he was running.

"Your DNA should be identical to your clon... I mean Naomi, but there are some key, if subtle differences. We can only put these down to your use of the Tractus."

"What differences?" Imogen felt a deep knot in her stomach.

"Well, I had intended to run the results past Shani. I need an experienced geneticist to confirm my theories. In her wake, I think there could be someone in the Council of Sanctity who might assist. Someone who could be favourable to the Resistance, but I'm waiting for Lara and Cael to make an approach."

Imogen said nothing, unsure she wanted to hear more.

Hanh continued, "The thing is, travel by Tractus involves the spatial compression of all your cells. This enables you to cross instantaneously through the 'voids' of space. Repeated travel - repeated compression - appears to have an adverse effect at the micro-biological level."

What adverse effects? I can't imagine this will be good news for me. "So, can you give me any idea what that means?" *Do I really want to hear?*

"It wouldn't be appropriate. I mean, apart from it not being ethical - to give out results before the tests are complete (we still have to look at Tarik's results) - they have not been corroborated by someone of a higher proficiency than me."

Imogen stopped and leant against a tree. *I'm not sure I can take any more.* She felt sick.

Hanh turned to gaze at her. "Sorry. Look, don't get too worried. The changes are infinitesimally small, but it would probably be advisable not to use the Tractus again unless absolutely necessary. Not until we can analyse the effect accurately."

"I have to go back to Earth!"

"That may not be prudent."

Imogen began to despair but then felt a rising anger. She was fed up of having no control over her life. Her DNA had been used to make a clone, she was in the Tractus contraption for forty years through no fault of her own, and she had no idea how this might impact on her future. She found herself almost shouting her response to a perplexed Hanh, "I don't care. I am going back to Earth and no one is going to stop me."

Hanh nodded and gave Imogen a weak smile. "Sure, come on, we must hurry. Em is waiting for us."

Imogen instantly felt sorry for being so irritated with him. Following in his steps, she quietly asked him about the others.

"Tarik and Sekhet have safely jumped to Earth. Em is keeping guard on the marker. There are only two of our markers left. I mean, if anything happens to them, there will be no way to or from Earth. The only other markers are under the control of the Supreme Council."

Imogen shuddered. The thought of being trapped on Holis, never to return to Earth or see her mother again, was as painful as the thought of leaving Araz here and not knowing his fate. She tried to banish the stream of incessant worries now slamming into her mind, longing to find someone who would take charge of the situation. *Hopefully one, if not all the Zuberi brothers will take the helm.*

Hanh delivered Imogen to the marker cave before heading back to Qus. He promised Imogen he would let her know the test results as soon as they had been completed and checked. His last words to her were, "remember, only use the Tractus if there is no other option."

Lit by dim torchlight, Em gave Imogen an enormous bear hug when she reached the inner cave. "Is good see you. You find what you looking for?"

Imogen nodded and felt her robes for the outline of the ovoid stone she had taken from Kekara's safe. "I think so, but I'm not sure if it's damaged."

"And others? Naomi? Araz?"

"They were caught at Karnak station. They've been taken to the prison, but Naomi appealed to all the witnesses there to hear their case at the Sanctus High Court. What chance will they have?"

Em shook her head. "Not sure. Without leader, we have no plan. Need strong persons."

Imogen nodded her head in agreement, then realised Em was looking intently at her. She shrugged her shoulders. "It's no good looking at me, Em. I wish I was strong, or a born leader, but I don't know what to do. If only my father... If only Adam were here."

"Who is this Adam?" Em looked askance.

"I meant one of the Zuberi brothers," Imogen quickly covered up her error.

Em did not seem to notice and added eagerly, "Or mother! Your mother, Rashida, she strong scientist. Shani tell me."

"Yes, but Mum has been ill."

"You must go Earth. Need new leaders, quickly. Not trust this Tarik, he act bad before. Think better, you go! You tell situation properly. Bring back help."

Imogen could see the sense in the plan and, if it were not for leaving Araz, she longed to go home. But Hanh had told her she was only supposed to use the Tractus as a last resort. She trembled. *What will happen to me if I use it again, or is it already too late?*

Em suddenly leapt to her feet. "Shhh – is noise."

Imogen strained her ears and could hear a distant and muffled sound of movement.

Em's Multi-Com flashed. She put it to her ear, listening intently for a few seconds. Her eyes widened, and she looked at Imogen in alarm before hissing, "Was Hanh. Have been tracked. Repros – here! Have surrounded entrance. Is no way out."

We're trapped! Imogen's heart pounded, and the image of Shani being stabbed through the heart flashed across her mind.

Em hurriedly lunged for the glowing marker and placed it on the floor, grabbing a cylindrical device and pointing it at the globe.

"No!" hissed Imogen, pushing the cylinder upwards and racing for the device. She picked it up, holding it protectively against her chest. "We can't destroy it. It's our only way out!"

The stomp of boots started in the rock corridors leading into the cave.

"We have to jump!" Imogen swiftly examined the marker, noted the destination, realising Leo and his mother had gone to this location. She activated it and clutched it to her heart with her good hand.

Em was frozen to the spot, staring at Imogen as if mesmerised. The thumping sound got louder.

Seconds counted down and Imogen made a desperate grab for Em's arm but her scarred hand would not close sufficiently onto Em's sleeve, and it slipped.

Two Repros burst into the space, the beams from their torches crisscrossing in the air. The ingrained horror of her childhood nightmare almost poleaxed Imogen. She fought back a scream and forced her open hand to reach out again to Em, pleading with her eyes for her to grasp it.

A Repro launched itself at Em who at the last moment seemed to revive and turned to slam her shoulder into its chest, sending it flying. The second charged towards her. Em pointed the cylindrical device and fired it. The Repro seemed to instantly shrink and fold in on itself before disintegrating. Em looked on in revulsion, dropped her devices to the floor and took a swift step towards Imogen where she seized her open palm with both of her hands.

The first Repro was back on its feet and gave a loud screech filling the air. A split second before it hurled itself towards the linked figures, the dim cave switched to utter blackness as Em and Imogen were sucked into the Tractus and disappeared.

THE HOLAN INQUISITION

*A*raz and Naomi had been separated on their arrival at the Karnak prison. They spent the night in confined quarters contemplating their situations. Both slept fitfully.

At the break of day, a young, nervous-looking man wearing council robes opened the Phase-Seal to Araz's room. In clipped and formal tones, he instructed Araz to follow as he set off down the corridors.

The councillor silently led Araz to a dining area, a small indoor garden where only one person was seated. Naomi was slowly eating from a full salver of sweet-smelling porridge. As soon as she saw Araz she sprang to her feet and gave him a pinched smile.

"Araz! It's good to see you. Come, sit down and eat. I hadn't realised how hungry I was." She turned to the councillor. "Horus, do you know how long they are going to hold us here?"

Araz glanced back at his escort as he sat and began to eat. He gave Naomi a questioning look.

"Horus became a councillor at the same time as me," she explained as she indicated for Horus to sit and join them. Horus remained standing and shook his head.

"So, do you know?"

Horus looked around cautiously before replying, "You're in big trouble Naomi."

"Yes, being placed in Karnak prison was a bit of a clue."

"What were you thinking? Freeing a long-term prisoner! Sekhet was the mother of that Falsebred and he is still on the loose. It is rumoured you have joined the subversives; your fascination with the primitive planet having clouded your judgement."

"Rumours and facts are two different things!" Naomi replied, her irritation clear.

"I have been sent to tell you, you have both been summoned before the Holan Inquisition."

Naomi and Araz exchanged worried looks as they continued eating.

"Also, you are to have a private meeting with the Vizier of Vision. He is here." Horus snapped his heels together and stood to attention as Ubaid entered the garden area. Two Repros guarded the doorway.

"Leave us!" Ubaid ordered Horus waving his hand to the door.

Horus hesitated. "I was... I was supposed to escort them."

Ubaid marched up to Horus and pushed his face right up to Horus's chin. "Do I have to tell you twice? Go!"

Horus recoiled and quickly fled the room.

The small Vizier sat across the table from Naomi and Araz, twiddling with his pointed beard and fixing them both in his gaze.

Naomi and Araz slowly pushed their salvers of food away and glowered back at their adversary.

"Oh dear, I detect a degree of animosity. But I should warn you, your future - your very lives - depend upon your full understanding of the situation. So, I suggest you listen and listen well."

Araz glared and Naomi folded her arms. They said nothing.

"Please, continue eating whilst I speak."

"My appetite has gone," Naomi responded frostily.

Araz just stared at his former commander who addressed his next comments to Naomi.

"I am glad to see you are well. You have to know my actions were entirely to protect you."

"Hmph," Naomi snorted, pursing her lips together.

"We do not have much time. You need to be aware of two key facts. Firstly, I am the only councillor who knows you have a clone, or that she was here on Holis."

Araz inwardly noted the past tense and hoped this meant Imogen had managed to escape.

"This must remain a secret. Whilst I can always deny any part in your evolution, you cannot deny you are a genetic aberration." Naomi winced as Araz opened his mouth to object.

Ubaid swiftly put his hand in the air to halt Araz's words without looking at him. "Your life would be over before you managed to do anything useful for your people."

Naomi swallowed hard. She knew what he said was true. Whilst he could squirm out of any charges, she would be facing termination.

Ubaid stood and paced the floor before turning to them both. "Secondly, there is much more at stake here than merely your lives. The future of Holis is on a knife edge. Unless action is taken, our race is facing certain annihilation."

Naomi and Araz looked sceptical.

"Are you going to explain?" Araz asked, unable to keep the sneer from his voice.

"I can see your contact with the subversives has infected you with a deep cynicism. There are however, undeniable facts to do with our sustainability on Holis. The truth will be revealed to the populace once a solution has been established, but you will only be allowed to hear it if you persuade the Inquisition you are worthy citizens."

"And how do we do that?"

"You have to show you are willing to protect the Holan people. At any cost. After all, that is why you, Araz, became a special agent and why you, Naomi, became a councillor and public servant."

Naomi looked at Araz then spoke to Ubaid in a conciliatory tone, "Can we have a few moments alone?"

Ubaid stroked his beard thoughtfully. "You will be escorted to the hearing in five minutes." He gave a short bow and left the room. The Repros remained at the door.

"We cannot trust him," Naomi began as they both turned their backs to the guard and spoke in hushed tones.

"But we need to get to the truth. We cannot do that if we are terminated."

"What are you saying?"

"We cooperate or appear to cooperate. The only subversive acts the council knows about for sure, is that you freed Sekhet and we were in the Resistance Headquarters when Odion attacked."

Naomi looked confused. "But that wasn't me."

"They do not know it was Imogen, so we must say it was you, to preserve both of your lives."

Naomi looked incredulous. "So, we just have to come up with a reasonable explanation of why I freed the mother of a Falsebred and what we were doing in the heart of the resistance? You are suggesting we lie? Well, perhaps you can make something up; it's probably second nature to you. However, any form of dishonesty is a stranger to me." Naomi's colours flared gold-black spikes.

"Have you any idea how self-righteous you sound?" Araz growled with irritation before stopping short as he remembered these were the very words used against him.

Naomi flushed, bit her lip and muttered a sorry.

"Look," Araz continued in a more placatory manner. "Let's convince the Inquisition we are not subversive, but loyal. If that means glancing over the details, so be it. We'll worry about the ethics later. If we are allowed to survive until later."

"So, what do we say?"

"I have an idea." Araz lowered his voice further and quietly outlined his proposal to Naomi.

When their five minutes were up, the Repro guard ushered Naomi and Araz from the prison towards the Supreme Council quarters in the adjoining mountain to The Hub. They entered on the upper level and were asked to sit in two seats in the centre of the empty council chamber.

They looked around nervously. The jewel encrusted lotus flowers and the five symbols of the sub-councils decorating the circular walls, glistened in the light.

After just a few moments, the five Viziers filed in and sat on the lower tiered seats of black marble. Ubaid appeared to be studiously ignoring them.

When Merit entered, Naomi gave her a weak smile, but Merit's face remained stony.

The Viziers rose when Kekara arrived. Araz and Naomi quickly got to their feet. Once she was seated on her high golden throne, they all took their seats and the proceedings began.

Odion spoke first. "Your Greatness, members of the Inquisition, I bring before you the new councillor, Naomi and the agent, Araz Vikram. They are called to account for their actions. Namely that they appeared to have arrested the subversive, Emba Lateef, at the Tavat Port. This was without any authorisation from the Council of Stability. They did not bring this fugitive to the prison, saying they had 'lost' her. Secondly, it is known Councillor Naomi illegally freed the prisoner, Sekhet, with no reference to anyone on the Supreme Council. Thirdly, both Araz and Naomi were there when we raided the Resistance Headquarters. They were with this same Emba Lateef and other members of the subversive movement including the Falsebred, Tarik Zuberi and his mother, Sekhet. At those headquarters, despite the assault on the guard and my person," Odion rubbed his hand over his forehead as if remembering an old wound. "They did not assist. Indeed, they left hastily with the other subversives. We finally caught and detained them at Karnak station yesterday when they were attempting to flee the capital."

Araz stood. "We were not attempting to flee."

Kekara put her hand out to Odion, who was about to silence Araz.

"So, Araz Vikram, what were you doing?"

"Your Greatness, we had followed a group of subversives to the Velo-City station. We intended to discover the whereabouts of the other subversive bases.

"Explain," Kekara asked in an icy voice.

"I persuaded Councillor Naomi to help me with an undercover mission."

"Undercover?" Kekara glared at Araz.

Naomi stood and spoke before Araz could reply. "Your Greatness, I had the idea from my Earth studies. Where primitive nations are at war, they use double agents. It is termed 'undercover' when, disguised as loyal members of one country, they secretly gather information for another."

Araz quickly joined in, "It is the basis on which I was sent to Earth. To act as one of the primitives whilst working for the Supreme Council. This is what I was trained for."

"When an opportunity arose to gain the trust of key members of the Resistance, Araz allowed Emba Lateef to go free and I agreed to release the Falsebred's mother," Naomi explained in a matter-of-fact manner.

Araz was intrigued to see Naomi's Chroma showed no hint of a lie. She must be able to cloak her colours like Imogen, he thought. He quickly realised his admiration for her must be apparent to anyone who could discern his aura and hurriedly masked his own.

"And it worked," Naomi continued. "They led us to their mountain base."

Araz took over the explanation, focussing his inner thoughts on the Velo-City mathematics to disguise his deceit, "Before we could report this, Vizier Odion launched a surprise attack on the base. We had no choice but to look as if we were still loyal to their movement. The advantage we gained would otherwise have been lost and then what chance would we have of discovering their plans and other bases?"

The Viziers all listened intently, and Naomi was gratified to see Merit giving her a trace of a smile.

There were several moments of silence before Kekara stood and went down to the lower circle where Araz and Naomi waited nervously. She walked the full perimeter around them.

Naomi held her head high, although she had to exercise a great deal of control to stop herself shaking.

Kekara then stepped in front of Araz and speared him with her eyes. "Tell me, Araz Vikram. Do you know the colour of lies?"

The formulae Araz was endlessly repeating in the back of his mind evaporated, and he felt his blood run cold. He tried to look beyond her piercing stare and force his thoughts to centre on logic and reason, but he could not hold down the swell of anxiety and worry which flooded his Chroma. Kekara seemed to look right into his core.

"No answer?"

"Sorry Ma'am, I am unsure what you are asking me." Araz stared ahead, desperately trying to regain his internal composure.

Naomi, seeing Araz was floundering, blurted aloud, "Violet!"

Kekara's head snapped round to Naomi, who shrugged her shoulders and added in a calm voice, "The colour of lies. It was advantageous that I could detect if our opponents were telling the truth and it will be an advantage in the future if we can continue infiltrating their movement."

"She can read Chroma?" Odion asked incredulously.

"It would appear so," Kekara responded, not taking her eyes off Naomi. "And how did you find your tour of Karnak prison, Councillor Naomi? The one you had just prior to the escape of the Falsebred?"

Naomi blinked and maintained a calm exterior as she hurriedly formulated a suitable response. She knew this was a test. Had Imogen encountered Kekara in the prison? It was possible. Naomi's mind raced. The Supreme Leader could no doubt read Chroma, so she would have to be careful to speak only the truth. The ability to cloak her own colours was a new phenomenon to her; she had never before lied or disguised her emotions. However, since her encounter with Araz and discovering her very life was based on deception, she had rapidly gained a degree of proficiency in concealing her real feelings. "Your Greatness, the events of the last few days have overtaken my every thought." This was true, and she knew her crystal colours spoke this. "Karnak prison is impregnable. No one should be able to escape." The statement was incontrovertible and it neither confirmed or denied she had been in the prison area.

Merit spoke quietly from her seat, in response. "The Falsebred did not escape from the prison, but outside on his way to his execution."

Naomi was relieved to turn away from Kekara's stare as she nodded towards Merit, feigning surprise as if this was news to her. "I wondered how he managed to escape," she commented innocently.

"And I wonder how you two managed to team up to work 'undercover' together? You said you had never met this special agent when we spoke," Kekara's eyes bored into Naomi's.

"I have always had an interest in the primitive planet. At the trial, Araz spoke of having visited Earth and I decided to seek him out as soon as I could, as I wished to learn more." Naomi maintained a conviction in her voice to match the sincerity of her shining blue-white chromatic shades.

Araz, his emotions back in control, spoke next, "Your Greatness, we ask you and your esteemed Viziers to look at our histories. I have trained for years as a government agent and travelled to the primitive planet, risking my life for the Holan people. Naomi has achieved the highest accolade in being admitted to the Supreme Council on her coming of age." Araz's colours shone quartz blue truth, tinged with an edge of a true copper indignation.

Kekara studied the two in silence. Minutes passed. The tension was palpable. She then suddenly clicked her fingers and Horus appeared at the arched entrance.

"Take these two to the waiting area. The Inquisition will discuss their futures."

Araz and Naomi were about to follow Horus out of the chamber when Kekara suddenly grasped Naomi's right hand. Naomi resisted the urge to pull it away, allowing Kekara to hold it in her own. She scanned Naomi's hand as she turned it over, palm down, and then released it.

Naomi gave an involuntary shudder, unsure why the leader had done this.

Araz paled. He felt sick to the pit of his stomach.

Horus led them out and for the next hour, they paced the corridors until they were summoned back.

The only two people left in the chamber were Ubaid and Kekara. Horus was dismissed as Ubaid indicated for Araz and Naomi to sit back on the central seats.

Ubaid spoke first. "The verdict of this assembly has been divided. On the one hand you have both loyally served the Holan people, on the other there are inconsistencies with your actions."

Naomi and Araz sat motionless and after a pause Ubaid continued. "We have decided to give you a second chance, but this is tempered with our need for assurances."

Naomi exchanged a brief glance with Araz before looking up to Kekara, seated above them in her high throne. Her expression was impenetrable.

"You will be entrusted with a mission, Araz."

Araz looked at Ubaid in surprise.

"You will return to Earth and bring back the Tractus technology intact, with or without the emissary. The future of the Holan race depends upon it."

Naomi and Araz did not risk looking at each other or asking Ubaid to explain. They knew if they voiced their suspicions, they would be sealing their own fates.

"You will not have long to complete this task and if you do not…"

"If I do not?" Araz asked, dread filling his heart.

"Councillor Naomi will be deemed a traitor and erased."

"What?" Naomi jumped to her feet.

Ubaid rudely pushed her back into her chair. Araz stepped angrily towards Ubaid as if to retaliate on Naomi's behalf, but he was stopped as Kekara's voice spoke directly in his ear. He had not noticed she had descended upon them.

"You will bring back the Tractus design data and you will also bring back the item stolen from my quarters."

"What?" Araz attempted to feign surprise.

"You know what I mean," Kekara hissed, adding, "If you do not, Naomi will be eliminated. Not just Naomi, but your parents and anyone who supported Araz Vikram. Furthermore, you will be publicly decried as the person who colluded with the enemy and betrayed his entire race."

Araz baulked at her meaning.

Naomi, rendered speechless, looked aghast.

"You have until the next Lotus Festival before we use other means to retrieve what we need." Kekara turned and left the chamber.

Several Repros stomped into the area and two pulled Araz to the door. He tried to resist and turned to speak to Naomi, now firmly held in an arm-lock by Ubaid.

"I will return," he promised.

Naomi gave a slight nod as she stared wildly at Araz. Her eyes and her Chroma pleaded with him to help her, as he was hauled out of the room. A solitary tear rolled down her cheek.

EARTH

"Vlag! Vlag! Vlag!" Em repeated over and over as she shook her head and rubbed her eyes.

"Shhh," Imogen entreated. Her Multi-Com was switched to torch and she was retrieving items of clothing and money from the hidden safe in the wall. "The enemy marker is very close. It will be guarded and we must not be heard."

Em gave a low moan from her crouched position on the platform of the disused underground station. Imogen tried to give Em a carton of juice. "Here, drink this."

"Is problem. Can't vlagging see!" Em hissed, ignoring the drink and rapidly opening and closing her eyes.

Imogen shone the torch at Em's face. "Your Tarsus filters have dropped. You don't need them in Earth light. Just relax – they should retract in a minute." Imogen inwardly prayed she was right.

"Here, drink." Imogen gently placed the container in Em's hand.

Em took a deep breath and closed her eyes as she drank deeply from the carton. When she re-opened them, her inner lids lifted. She focussed on Imogen's face before breaking into a smile and sighed with relief. "Thank Ra! Mmm! Drink, is good." She got up and peered around at the grimy, tile covered surroundings.

"It's orange juice," Imogen said, quickly changing her Flecto clothing for a t-shirt, jeans and trainers, and mentally thanking Adam for having placed her attire and spare sets in the safe, in readiness for her. He had also left her a cell phone. There was only one number in the contact list. She sent a brief message, hoping she would get a response telling her where to go.

"O-ran-ge," repeated Em, looking at the picture on the carton and nodding approval. "Is strange salver," Em muttered and then gestured around the dark tunnel. "Is primitive planet, yes?" Without waiting for an answer, Em tentatively raised her limbs in turn and began to jump up and down, slowly at first, then faster. "Body – it feel strange. Is lighter, stronger."

Imogen flapped her hand to stop Em making any more noise as she whispered, "Gravity – it's not as strong as on Holis. You'll be able to run faster here."

"Em not run!" was her indignant response as she added, "This Earth, it very dark."

Imogen smiled. "We're underground. This is a kind of rudimentary Velo-City line."

Em's face dropped. "Must get back Holis. Enemy will take Tractus marker from Qus. Is not encrypted."

"It's ok," Imogen replied, opening her hand and showing Em the marker. "I brought it with me."

Em regarded the marker and then looked at Imogen's face.

Imogen had never seen Em look scared, but her wide eyes and chromatic flurries confirmed she was suddenly filled with fear.

"This mean only one marker left on Holis. Is on dark side. Is only way back," Em gulped.

Imogen gave a shudder. *She's right. There may be lots of markers on Earth, but now there's only three left on Holis, and two are under the control of the Supreme Council.* Araz's face jumped into her thoughts and she felt a stab to her heart. *Will I ever see him again?* Forcing herself to quell a rising panic at the idea of being permanently separated from him, Imogen threw her devices, the oval stone she had stolen from Kekara's chamber and a quantity of money into a small rucksack. She then handed Em a set of clothing and helped her to change, grateful for the distraction.

The dark trousers were too short, ending half way up Em's calves and she had ripped both these and the black shirt when she had tried to force her legs and then an arm into the material, expecting it to stretch like Flecto. As Em grumbled at the inferior garments, Imogen realised Em's tattoos were visible in Earth light. She smiled to herself at the overall effect of Em's strapping figure dressed in the ripped clothes. The closely cropped hair and bold tattoos made Em look every bit an on-trend, if formidable, resident of Earth.

The rumble of a distant tube train caused Em to glance nervously at Imogen. Imogen heard her cell phone buzz, and she retrieved it to glance at the message on the screen, exhaling with relief before returning it to the bag.

"This way." Imogen recalled the plans to this section of the London underground, committed to memory on her last visit. She quietly led Em up the abandoned run of escalators and service shafts, thankful there was no sign of the enemy forces.

When they reached the ground level and stepped into the bright daylight of London's rush hour, Imogen had to steer Em in the direction of Euston station. Em kept stopping, her mouth wide open, as she stared incredulously at the busy streets filled with shoppers, commuters and traffic. "Vlag!"

Leo and Sekhet sat nervously at a small table in the Plough and Harrow pub in Birmingham. They had stayed overnight in a London hotel, giving time for Sekhet to acclimatise to life on Earth, and furnish themselves with clothing and stores. Leo had managed to reconfigure his Multi-Com and send a message to his father.

Leo looked at his mother as she sporadically swallowed down some food and realised she was more apprehensive than he was. He also knew this was not connected with it being her first time on an alien planet.

When Adam arrived he saw Leo first, Sekhet having her back to him. He gave his son a wide smile and stepped forward to shake his hand. "Tarik, it's good to see…" his voice petered out as Sekhet turned and gave him a long stare.

"Nuru. It's been a long time."

Momentarily stunned, it took him a few seconds to collect himself. "Adam! I am known as Adam now. Sekhet, I can't believe you're here." Adam sank into a chair, unable to take his eyes off her.

"She was imprisoned by the Supreme Council. They used implants to subdue her. Imogen and I freed her."

Adam kept his eyes fixed on Sekhet as he asked Leo, "Where is Imogen?"

"Still on Holis. She went back to The Hub, she insisted. I have no idea if she's safe. But Araz was with her."

Adam took one of Sekhet's hands and stroked her palm in a gentle caress. "I am sorry Sekhet. Sorry for my dishonesty, sorry for leaving you."

Sekhet's eyes brimmed with tears. "I am sorry too," she looked at Adam as an unspoken exchange passed between them.

Leo coughed and Sekhet glanced at him, adding, "but I will never be sorry for bringing our son into being."

"We are, then, in accord on this." Adam grinned at Leo, keeping Sekhet's hand firmly in his own.

"Erm, can we move on," Leo's eyes flitted about the room, his cheeks flushed with embarrassment. "Anyway," Leo added. "I am not sure you will be so pleased when you realise I led the Repros to Kasmut." Leo cast his eyes downward. "It was me and I know I can never make up for it."

Adam put a finger to his mouth to hush Leo. "We know."

"What? How?"

"The emissary from Holis has given us the full background."

"But you don't understand. They terminated Kasmut, he... he's dead." Leo choked back a tear.

"We know you were being blackmailed and we know you were forced to act in this way. You were only a child, and anyway, you were not to blame for the despicable actions of a corrupt government."

"Please don't make this easy for me. At least Imogen recognised my treachery. She was heartbroken. I know what I did, and I am ashamed."

Adam felt his mobile buzz and quickly looked at the screen before sending a text reply, his eyes glistening with emotion.

Leo pushed his hands roughly through his hair as he shook his head from side to side. To his amazement, his father put both arms lovingly around his shoulders and gave him his first ever embrace.

Rashida and Sefu were back inside the Oratory church, across the road from the Plough and Harrow, with their latest set of test results. They had had little contact with Nuru and Adam who had spent days in discussion with the emissary from Holis. It could not be revealed there was a third Zuberi brother, or Rashida was back in full health. Aside from keeping a low profile, they were fully occupied with their investigations.

They had re-fitted the Tractus marker to the canopy over the altar a few days before. They had then devised several control tests to painstakingly catalogue and double-check the new experimental settings.

"So, we have managed to return a DNA impregnated device to a specific moment in time in the recent past." Rashida was flushed with excitement as she summarised their progress and recalled their earlier successes. Their first experiment had returned a snapshot of their faces just a few moments before the globe was sent back. They had not been aware the device had appeared or taken a picture, and when it reappeared in the present, discovered it had captured a frozen instant in time.

"We have done it!" Sefu had shouted with glee.

They then sent the device back to slightly earlier times over the last day, delighted to find time-lapse images of a cleaner at work and different stages of a mass which had taken place in the morning.

"But we have only gone back to a maximum of twenty-four hours and have been unable to either leave or retrieve anything from the past," Sefu countered.

"However," Rashida argued, "we now know it is theoretically possible. I suspect we would succeed if we sent back a living being, not a device."

"It's out of the question." Sefu held his hands up, palms out. "It would be far too dangerous to attempt such a leap. Look at the catastrophic results for you and Imogen, after being vaulted forward in time."

Rashida gave an involuntary shudder. She had nearly died and she had nearly lost her daughter. Before any remembered anxiety could surface, Rashida employed Sefu's new drills to quash all memory of the terrible events, and she returned to setting up the next test.

"We must decide what limit to set on how far back the Tractus should be allowed to travel," she mused. "Perhaps we should remove the restrictions completely? See how far back in time the device would go? Would it go back to when it was first commissioned? Some seventy years? Or would it go back further? Two hundred years? Two thousand or more?"

Sefu shook his head. "Let us think on it. We have done enough for today. The church will be in use again in a few hours and we have been called to meet the emissary."

"I thought we had to steer clear of this negotiator from Holis. Our existence to be kept secret?"

"Something has been decided. We have been summoned."

"That sounds ominous!" Rashida smiled, unable to cloud the exhilaration of their achievements. "Where do we go?"

"Over the road. Adam has got us a meeting room above the pub."

Rashida closed down the marker and gathered her equipment.

"Rashida, you need to know something before we go."

"Yes?"

Sefu replied in a low voice and when he had finished, Rashida stared at him in surprise. She dropped all her things and ran out of the church, Sefu gathering the items into his arms as he followed her.

With more than a little feeling of Deja-vu, Imogen and Em got out of the taxi outside of the Oratory church. It evoked such feelings of terror and pain, Imogen was glad to turn her back on it and steer Em towards the pub opposite.

At last! Adam and his brothers will know what to do. Will Mum be there?

Her heart gave a little leap as they entered the Plough and Harrow and climbed the stairs to the upper room, the staff of the genteel pub looking more than a little horrified at Em's appearance.

Imogen could hear familiar voices when she got to the landing. Sighing with relief, she pushed the door open. She had barely gone two steps when several voices cried out, "Imogen!" She was swept off her feet by Adam who swung her two full circles. When he placed her down, she was then enveloped in a bear hug by Leo, closely followed by Sekhet.

Everyone seemed to speak at once, 'You escaped!', 'Clever girl!', 'What did you think of Holis?' 'Who's your friend?', and as she nodded and smiled, Imogen saw all three Zuberi brothers grinning back at her.

All three in the same place! Wow! They are the spitting image of each other. Like Naomi is of me... Before her thoughts of her duplicate crowded into her mind, an inner door opened, and to her delight, her mother came running towards her.

Catching her breath, Imogen rushed to meet her. They laughed and cried and hugged, as the others in the group moved to the door to greet Em, giving mother and daughter some privacy. Imogen could see her mother was no longer under the control of her fragile nerves, but confident and assured. *Sefu has worked wonders.*

Eventually the group sat in the comfortable sofas as Imogen, arm linked to her mother's, started to give them an account of her journey. "I hardly know where to begin. I've only been gone for a week... It seems like a lifetime."

Finally, back with her mum, Imogen's internal spring - holding back all her tightly coiled anxieties - snapped. Thoughts began to crash into her consciousness, Araz's anger when he discovered she was a Penta-Crypt, his kiss and touch as he spoke the words 'my light', her encounter with Kekara at Karnak prison, Leo's unfair trial, her clone – she still could not believe it, she had a clone – and Naomi's bewilderment when she had seen Imogen for the first time, the Ankh symbol in Kekara's chambers and the flat oval stone she had stolen. Echoes of words bounded in every layer of her mind, Em: 'Must know, Holans not have scars', The Chronicles of Holis: 'One day a Penta-Crypt will be born and will lead our people to a new maturity'. Ubaid: 'One of you must die. There cannot be two Sanctus Crypti', Hanh: 'Repeated travel by Tractus appears to have an adverse effect', Neith: 'I have seen it: either you or Naomi will die'. The faces and words filled her psyche and her thoughts started to spin in turmoil. She was unaware she was in a room with friends. In her head, Repros chased her, klaxons sounded, freezing water crashed down as she was pulled below the surface unable to breathe, and her heart raced.

The onlookers watched Imogen with alarm. She had turned as white as a sheet and her eyes had glazed over, perspiration beading on her brow.

Rashida gently shook Imogen who blinked and looked into her mother's worried face. *Dad!* The image of her father slammed into the forefront of her mind and overtook every other thought. She put her hand to her mouth and gave a strangled cry.

Rashida looked alarmed as Imogen tried to stammer out the words she had been dreading to speak, "Dad, Mum… he… he's…" she couldn't finish the sentence as her body was convulsed with sobs.

Leo rushed to Imogen's side. "Imogen, the emissary from Holis…"

Imogen looked blankly at Leo, tears streaming down her cheeks.

'It is not Jabari. He… he was terminated. It's as well poor Shani never knew."

"I don't know what you're trying to tell me," Imogen wept openly, only one thought going around her head - *I have to tell Mum about Dad.*

Rashida, also in tears, seized Imogen's hands and gently placed her fingertips against her own.

Imogen received the cognitive message, blinked back her tears and looked at her mother in disbelief. Realisation began to sink in. *The emissary – could it be?*

Then she heard it, that all too familiar voice.

"Imogen, my dear Imogen."

Imogen turned to the door and there he was. Her father, the man she had called grandfather for most of her life, looking back at her, filled with pride and love.

"Grand... Dad!" the words emerged as barely a whisper. She rose and crossed the room as if she were flying, and fell into his strong arms, relief and overwhelming love flooding her every cell.

"My darling girl!"

Imogen buried her face in his chest.

At last, she felt utterly and completely safe. She had come home.

Appendix

Chroma

The aura of colours we all unknowingly exude which show our deepest fears, emotions and thoughts. The aura can only be seen in visible 'white' light and then only by those who possess 'tetra-chromatic' sight, like Imogen. Those with tetra-chromatic sight (having a fourth light receptor in the eye) are able to see not just seven, but twenty-one distinct colours. Imogen has learnt to read Chroma as a form of extra sensory perception. She can distinguish the varying shades of each colour and is able to understand what each means. For example, the red of anger is a shade different to the red of excitement or the deeper shade of love, or the red of fear.

The Chromatic range of emotions and feelings:

White & Quartz: Honesty / Logic / Reason / Truth / Clarity

Reds – Hot colours: Passion / Fear / Love / Attraction / Anger

      Red flickering white: Hope

      Red flickering white gold: Intense Love / Devotion

Oranges: Humour / Laughter / Calm

Yellows: Enquiry / Prying / Questioning / Searching

Blues – Cold colours: Logic / Reason / Aptitude

      Cobalt Blue: Inspiration

      Sapphire: Genuine

      Navy Blue: Hurt

      Murky Blue: Betrayal

Purples – Dark colours: Worry / Suspicion

Plum: Jealousy

Violet: Lies / Untruths / Injury

Greens & browns – Calm earth colours: Relaxation / Trustworthiness / Loyalty

Russet: Recognition

Sepia: Sadness / Grief

Deep Greens: Pride / Adoration / Sacrifice

Sage Green: Admiration

Grey: Worry / Confusion / Anxiety

Black: Authority / Power

Copper: Indignation

Bronze: Frustration

Silver: Hypnosis threads / Control

Gold: Power / Intrigue / Seduction

Characters on Earth:

Imogen Reiner. (The name Imogen means innocent and Reiner means warrior from the Gods.)

Araz Vikram – Agent for the Supreme Council. (Araz is taken from Arash, meaning 'bright arrow' and Vikram means brave or valiant.)

Leonard Newall (Leo) aka Tarik Sekhet or Zuberi. (Tarik means warrior or 'morning star' and Zuberi means strong.)

Harold Reiner, Imogen's father aka Kasmut Akil. Scientist and inventor. (Kasmut means 'high priest'.)

Elizabeth Reiner, Imogen's mother aka Rashida Omorose. Scientist and artist. (Rashida means wise or righteous.)

Sefu, Nuru and Adam (Amsu) Zuberi (triplets). Experts in bio-chemical communications.

Imogen's friends at Forrester College:

Chrissie / Danny / Richard / Katie / Leanne

Deceased:

Father Jonathan aka Tanastra Thut. Author of the chronicles and inventor of the Tractus. (His name is unique.)

Eshe Serq aka Margaret. Distinguished geneticist. (Eshe means life.)

Firas Lateef. Scientist who developed the Tractus, originally conceived by Tanastra. (Firas means perceptive.)

Characters on Holis:

Em aka Emba Lateef (Emba means loyal or reliable.)

Shani - former Vizier of Sanctity (Shani means wonderful.)

Jabari – former Vizier of Well-Being (Jabari means brave.)

Lara / Cael / Hanh – members of the resistance on Holis.

Neith – a Vatic.

The named members of The Supreme Council:

Kekara – Supreme Leader (Kekara from Keira meaning black-haired.)

Odion - Vizier of Stability (Odion from Odin meaning fury.)

Ubaid - Vizier of Vision (Ubaid means servant.)

Merit – Vizier of Enlightenment (Merit from Mert meaning courageous.)

Sekhet Kemet – former member of the Supreme Council and Leo's mother (Sekhet means 'she who is powerful'.)

Naomi - new member of the Supreme Council (Naomi means congenial or pleasant.)

Horus – new member of the Supreme Council (Horus means 'distant one'.)

Repros: Reproduction life forms used as a fighting force by the Supreme Council.

Hypro: new and lethal hybrid of a Repro.

The Five Lines and personality types of Holis:

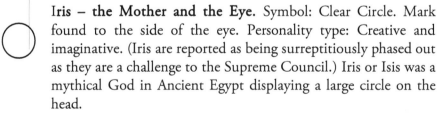

Ra – the Creator and Head. Symbol: Solid Circle. Mark found at the back of the head below the ear. Personality type: Strong minded, decisive and energetic. Ra was the God of the Sun in Ancient Egypt.

Iris – the Mother and the Eye. Symbol: Clear Circle. Mark found to the side of the eye. Personality type: Creative and imaginative. (Iris are reported as being surreptitiously phased out as they are a challenge to the Supreme Council.) Iris or Isis was a mythical God in Ancient Egypt displaying a large circle on the head.

Nut – the One of Rebirth and the Hand. Symbol: Solid Star. Mark found on the hand between the thumb and first finger. Personality type: Practical and calm. Nut was the God of the Sky in Ancient Egypt.

Hathor – the Fertile One and the Heart. Symbol: Clear Star. Mark found on the centre of the chest. Personality type: Compassionate and caring. Hathor was the God of Destruction in Ancient Egypt.

 Amon – the Hidden One and the Feet. Symbol: Arrow. Mark found at on the sole of the foot below the big toe. Personality type: Disciplined and persistent. Amon was the God of Magic or Mystery in Ancient Egypt.

Dominant Personality Lines:

Uni-Crypt: most common – one line is more dominant than all the others so only one body mark is visible.

Bi-Crypt: Two of the five lines are held in equal measure.

Tri-Crypt: Three of the five lines are held in equal measure.

Tetra-Crypt: Four of the five lines are held in equal measure.

Penta-Crypt: All five lines held in equal measure (known as the Sanctus Cryptus or sacred crypts and not considered possible after many failed attempts to genetically engineer a Penta-Crypt).

The Five Councils of Holis:

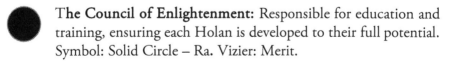 **The Council of Enlightenment:** Responsible for education and training, ensuring each Holan is developed to their full potential. Symbol: Solid Circle – Ra. Vizier: Merit.

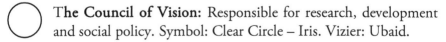 **The Council of Vision:** Responsible for research, development and social policy. Symbol: Clear Circle – Iris. Vizier: Ubaid.

The Council of Sanctity: Responsible for Genetics, storage of the DNA of all life forms and identifying personality types and health. Symbol: Solid Star – Nut. Vizier: was Shani.

 The Council of Well-Being: Responsible for food, transport and internal affairs. Symbol: Clear Star – Hathor. Vizier: was Jabari.

 The Council of Stability: Responsible for defence and communication. Symbol: Arrow – Amon. Vizier: Odion.

Holan Terms:

Ankh: The original home of the Holan people and a satellite or moon of Sheut. It orbits on the exact and opposite side of Sheut to the moon of Holis. Ankh turns on its axis. Its motion is parallel to the motion of Earth as it orbits our Sun. Its terrain was like that of Earth.

Anubis: (The Reign of Anubis) The dictator who reigned on Holis thousands of years ago. His reign was the worst in Holan history and included the slaughter of innocents, persecution and ruthless control of every aspect of Holan life.

Atma: Sunset or the darkening of the sky.

Baladi: Edible cubes full of nutriments.

Crypts: Holan term for DNA.

Data Encounter (DE): Device connecting cognitively (via fingertips) to provide information. Similar to having a multi-dimension, instant internet at the fingertips of the user.

De-Atma: Sunrise – opposite of Atma (sunset)

Flecto: The organic material used for clothing and footwear. It can be activated to reflect the surroundings or display plain colours. It responds to temperature, keeping the wearer cool or warm, and can be fashioned into any garment.

Holis: Home to the Holan race and a satellite or moon of Sheut. It has a dark side and a light side.

The Hub: The glass mountain of central government. The sub-councils are based here and all crypts are logged and stored in the Council of Sanctity areas.

Ib: A dying star (red dwarf) outside the Ka solar system. Ib gives off a red light flooding the sky of Holis in a cyclical pattern, strong or weak depending on the time of the month.

InvertIon: A super-conducting element mined on Ankh. The key to clean, organic power on Holis and an essential component of the Tractus device.

Ka: The central white star of the solar system in which Sheut is the fifth planet. It provides life-giving white light to Ankh and Holis.

Karnak: The capital of Holis located in the north.

Kushari: Holan dish of vegetables and pulses.

Lineator: The mercurial orb identifying personality lines and family background.

Lotus Festival: A three-monthly short break from work with festivities.

Multi-Com: Communicator Device.

Phase-Seal: The doorways or entrances activated by touch (providing the DNA is registered at The Hub.

Qus: A small town on the Southern Sea.

Salvers: Organically grown containers for food and drink (released only to those whose crypts are registered).

Sanctus High Court: The central decision-making body of Holis where all those who have 'come of age' (seventeen years) have a vote.

Sanctus Laws: The governing laws of Holis.

Sheut: The large dead planetary mass and fifth planet from the sun of Ka. Ankh and Holis are satellites or moons of Sheut.

Tarsus Filter: The inner eye lid of Holans. It drops when the red light of Ib is at its strongest enabling the eye to filter out the red. (Chroma is not visible in this red light or when the Tarsus filters cover the eye.)

Tavats: Large spaceships or arks, capable of transporting vast amounts of cargo to and from Holis and Ankh.

Tractus: A device capable of folding of space, enabling a person to 'jump' vast distances. Markers open each 'end' of the wormhole created by the Tractus. When opened by only one marker, unlinked to another, the worm hole forms a loop which essentially turns the Tractus into a Tempus, capable of catapulting a person forward in time. (It is said that it is not possible to travel backwards in time with this device.)

Vatic: A type of mystic with the gift of prophecy. Vatics are said to be able to see into the future (only a few Holans have this gift, including the late Eshe).

Velo-City: The underground transport system linking all the areas of Holis.

Volt of Flesh: The microscopic sample of DNA required to register the crypts of Holans at birth.

CHROMA: BOOK 3

Coming soon...

Imogen's Destiny

The third and final part of the Chroma trilogy.

Imogen has returned to Earth with Leo.

Araz and Naomi remain in captivity on Holis.

The Supreme Council, determined to get their hands on the Tractus technology whatever it takes, have only just learnt the device has a time travel capability.

Imogen's clone, Naomi and Araz have uncovered the production of a lethal poison and a new hybrid version of the brutal Repros.

What is the new focus for the Elysian Two project? Does the Earth face an unforeseen danger?

Imogen holds the key to Kekara's secret, but can she uncover the truth and fulfil the prophecies to realise her true destiny?

THANK YOU

Thank you to all my Beta readers, my launch team, my ace family and friends, and Julian, my wonderfully supportive hubby. I couldn't have done it without you!

Massive thank you to Jonathan Moseley (grandson of Barbara Baggaley) for the cover.

Thank you for reading Imogen's Journey. If you could find time to leave a review (long or short) on Amazon I would be most grateful. Written reviews are the life-blood of authors and can make all the difference between the novel languishing on a virtual shelf or being widely read.

More information about the Chroma Trilogy, and about me, can be found on my webpage: www.bfleetwood.com

The Oratory Church, Birmingham

The Plough and Harrow Hotel

(JRR Tolkien worshipped at The Oratory Church & frequented the Plough & Harrow Hotel)

11473824R00170

Printed in Great Britain
by Amazon